The
SPANISH BOW

The
SPANISH BOW

~

ANDROMEDA ROMANO-LAX

Harcourt, Inc.

ORLANDO   AUSTIN   NEW YORK   SAN DIEGO   LONDON

Requests for permission to make copies of any part of the work
should be submitted online at www.harcourt.com/contact or mailed
to the following address: Permissions Department, Harcourt, Inc.,
6277 Sea Harbor Drive, Orlando, Florida 32887-6777.

www.HarcourtBooks.com

Lyrics from Mahler's Second Symphony are translated
from the German by Steven Ledbetter. Used by permission.

Library of Congress Cataloging-in-Publication Data
Romano-Lax, Andromeda, 1970–
The Spanish bow/Andromeda Romano-Lax.—1st ed.
p.   cm.
1. Musicians—Fiction.   2. Madrid (Spain)—Fiction.   I. Title.
PS3618.O59S68   2007
813'.6—dc22   2006100937
ISBN 978-0-15-101542-9

Text set in Fournier MT Tall Caps
Designed by Liz Demeter

Printed in the United States of America
First edition
A C E G I K J H F D B

A Brian Lax y Elizabeth Sheinkman,
con respeto y gratitud.

PART I

~

Campo Seco, Spain
1892

CHAPTER

~ I ~

I was almost born Happy.

Literally, Feliz was the Spanish name my mother wanted for me. Not a family name, not a local name, just a hope, stated in the farthest-reaching language she knew—a language that once reached around the world, to the Netherlands, Africa, the Americas, the Philippines. Only music has reached farther and penetrated more deeply.

I say "almost born Feliz," because the name that attached itself to me instead, thanks to a sloppy bureaucrat's bias toward Catalan saints' names, was Feliu. Just one letter changed on my death—yes, death—certificate.

My father was overseas that year, working as a customs officer in colonial Cuba. The afternoon my mother's labor pains started, my father's elder sister changed into a better dress, for church. Mamá bent over a chair near the kitchen doorway, legs splayed, ankles turned inward, as the weight of my dropping body pulled her pelvis to the floor. While she begged Tía not to go, Mamá's knuckles whitened against the chair's straw-plaited back.

"I will light candles for you," Tía said.

"I don't need prayers. I need—" My mother moaned, angling her hips from side to side, trying to find a position where the pain eased. Cool water? A chamber pot? "...help," was all she could say.

"I'll send Enrique to get the midwife." Tía pushed the ebony combs into her thick masses of gray-streaked hair. "No, I'll go myself, on the way. Where's Percival?"

My oldest brother had slipped outside minutes earlier, bound for the bridge and the dry wash beneath it, along which the local shepherds drove their flocks. He and his friends hid there frequently, playing cards amid orange peels and broken barrel staves that reeked of vinegar.

Percival was old enough to remember the previous disasters in sharp detail, and he didn't want to witness another. Mamá's last baby had died within minutes of birth. The one before had survived only a few days, while my mother herself hovered near death, racked with infection-induced fever. In Campo Seco, she was not the only unlucky one.

My mother blamed the midwife who had moved to the village four years earlier, accompanied by her husband, a butcher.

"They don't wash their hands," Mamá panted. "Last time, I saw the forceps she used. Broken at the hinge. Flakes"—she squirmed and jammed the heel of her palm into her back—"flakes of rust."

"Ridiculous!" Tía drew the lace mantilla over her head. "You are worrying for nothing. You should pray, instead."

My two other siblings, Enrique and Luisa, remained stoic in the face of my mother's barnyard moans, the slick of straw-colored amniotic fluid on the floor, which five-year-old Luisa wiped away; the bloody smears on the wet towels, which seven-year-old Enrique wrung and dipped in a wide porcelain bowl. By the third dip, the blue flowers on the bowl's painted bottom disappeared, obscured beneath a smoky layer of pink water.

Thirty minutes after Tía departed, the midwife arrived. Mamá panted and strained from her marriage bed, pushing with all her strength while she struggled to keep her eyes open. She scrutinized the dirt crescents beneath the midwife's fingernails. She twisted her neck to follow every step the midwife took, to catch fleeting glimpses of the tools displayed on a square of calico covering the bedside table, and the coil of gray cotton string that brought to mind the butcher's leaky, net-covered roasts. When the midwife's hands came near, Mamá tried to close her knees, to shield me from ill fortune. But the urge to push could not be stopped. I was coming.

And then—just as suddenly—I stopped coming. What had once moved too quickly stopped moving at all. Mamá's belly rippled and bulged a final time, then hardened into one long, unceasing contraction. Her jaw went slack. A blue vein bulged at her temple. Enrique, lingering in the open doorway, tried not to look between her legs, where the combination of taut, pearly flesh and wet hair made him think of washed-up jellyfish, collapsed against the weedy shore. The midwife caught him looking and snapped the sheet back into place, over Mamá's legs and high, round abdomen. That gesture hid one disturbing view, but it only drew more attention to what remained visible: my mother's red face, beaded with sweat and contorted with pain.

"Here," Mamá would say later, in recounting the story of my birth, "is where you decided to rebel. Whenever someone pushes you too hard, you do the opposite."

Actually, I was stuck: feet twisted up toward my neck, rear facing the only exit. A living *churro* tied into a bow.

The midwife grunted as her hands pushed, prodded, and massaged beneath the loosely tented sheet, a question darkening her face. Forgetting Enrique, she tore away the sheet and whimpered at the sight of a small purple scrotum appearing at the spot where a crowning head should have been. She watched that spot for ten minutes, twisting the cloth of her apron with red fingers. Then she panicked. Ignoring Enrique's incredulous, upturned face and Luisa's round eyes, she pushed past them both and down the stairs, missing the bottom step entirely.

The midwife had left to fetch her husband, who was two blocks away, wiping his own stained hands. She could have sent my brother or called from the balcony to one of our neighbor's fleet-footed children. But she wasn't a bright woman. And she knew that a third infant death in one family would invite costly gossip. Already, she could envision the sea of dark shawls that would greet her from this day forward— the back of every neighbor woman's averted head and rounded shoulders, snubbing her if I died, and my mother with me.

Left unassisted, my mother summoned her resolve and tried to breathe more deeply. She felt safer with the midwife gone, ready to accept whatever happened. She asked Luisa to retrieve a bottle from the cellar and to hold it to her lips, though nausea allowed her to drink only a little. She called Enrique to come and take the forceps, to dip and scrub them in a bowl of the hottest water, to be ready.

"They don't open very well," he said, struggling with the oval-shaped handles. They were fashioned from twisted iron and padded with small pieces of stitched dark leather that reminded Enrique of a sweat-stained horse saddle. "Are the pieces supposed to come apart?"

"Forget it. Put them down. Use your hands."

He blanched.

Mamá heard Luisa start to cry, and ordered her to sing—anything, a folk song, or "*Vamos a la Mar,*" a happy round they'd all chanted on picnic trips to the Mediterranean coast.

"…to eat fish in a wooden dish…" Luisa sang, again and again, and then: "I see something! It's a foot!"

Another push. A narrow back. With Enrique's help, a shoulder. My mother lost consciousness. I've been told I hung there for a while, the picture of blind indecision, with my head refusing to follow my pasty body. Until Enrique, decisive enough for us both, stepped forward and pushed a small hand into the dark, hooking a finger around my chin.

Following my final, slippery emergence, he laid me on my mother's belly, still attached by the cord to the afterbirth inside her. There was no spank; no bawling cries. Mamá briefly surfaced into consciousness once again with instructions for Enrique on how to tie the cord with the gray string in two places, and how to cut the flattened purple cable in between.

He moved me onto my mother's chest, but I didn't root. One of my legs hung more limply than the other, the hip joint disturbingly flaccid. No one cleared the white residue plugging my tiny nostrils. Mamá's arms lay at her sides, too tired to embrace me. There was little point. My eyelids did not twitch. My rib cage did not swell.

"It's cold," Luisa said. "We should wrap it."

"*He's* cold," Enrique corrected.

"A boy." My mother sounded both pleased and resigned, her cheeks wet as she relived what had happened before and would happen again: the increasing pain as her adrenaline ebbed, the incapacitating fever, the deep plunge into confused sleep from which she might not return. "Tell the midwife it was not her fault. The notary will come to the door. There is a blank card with an envelope in the drawer, with the money. Write the name down for him, so there is no mistake: *Feliz Aníbal Delargo Domenech.*"

She gritted her teeth, waited for a spasm to subside. "Is it cold in here, Luisa?"

"It's hot, Mamá."

"The notary will inform the priest"—she sucked in a mouthful of air, then bit down on her lower lip—"and the engraver."

"The engraver?" Luisa asked, but Mamá did not explain.

"Enrique—you know how to spell Aníbal, like your great-uncle." Enrique shook his head.

"Like the conqueror from Carthage, the man with the elephants."

"I *don't* know how," my brother protested, more alarmed by the request to write my name than he'd been by the drama of pulling a reluctant baby from the womb.

But the long list and the imagined tasks ahead—a letter to Papá, a visitation, a burial—had exhausted the last of Mamá's stamina. She closed her eyes and swung her head from side to side, trying to catch an elusive breeze. She began, "A-N-I-B..." and then lost consciousness again.

Luisa and Enrique did not understand that Mamá considered me already dead. They wrapped me and took me down to the cool, earthen-floored cellar—a cellar that Papá excavated and enlarged on every visit home. He'd always dreamed of starting a fine liqueur-making and exporting business in the cavernous room beneath our three-level stone house. Other local families had succeeded at the same dream. At one time, fourteen different sweet liqueurs—colored grassy-green to honey-yellow, with aromas of herb and hazelnut—were made and shipped from Campo Seco and a cluster of neighboring villages. We had the grapes, we had the train, and we had the confidence: Catalans, like Basques and other ancient seafarers, had traded and prospered long before there was a unified nation called Spain.

In the meanwhile, the cellar was simply an empty space, save for one rustic bench and one rough-hewn table, joined without screws or nails, suitably pitted and gouged, so that it looked like a place where Don Quixote might have dined three centuries earlier. On this table Luisa had placed a pot of cooling water dipped from the larger pot the midwife had prepared, and a hot chocolate serving set with delicate tulip-shaped cups, which she arranged while jostling me importantly over the shoulder. She'd already pushed one of her doll's bonnets over my sticky head. Now she worked a cocoa-soaked finger between my pale lips.

Enrique had changed out of his stained shirt and slipped into the too-small military uniform he wore for costumed play, a gift from my father which gave him comfort. He picked up his homemade flute. Because the rustic instrument always set Mamá's teeth on edge, Enrique had grown used to playing here, below street level and away from open windows. Between the warm shaking, the bitter taste of Luisa's fingers and the shrill ancient music, I opened my ears, eyes and mouth for the first time. I prepared myself to live.

Upstairs, the midwife had returned at last. Finding the baby gone and Mamá barely conscious, she sent her husband to notify the priest and began to massage my mother's distended belly, trying to stimulate contractions that would expel the afterbirth and stem the flow of blood. In the midwife's refocused mind, there was no time for gratitude—not to my siblings, for having removed the stark evidence of the day's tragedy, nor to God, for having spared one life when He easily could have taken two.

From the cellar, Enrique heard Mamá scream with renewed vigor, and at the same time, a knock on the door. He climbed the ladder to the foyer and pulled the heavy front door open to find the notary waiting there, just as our mother had predicted.

"The midwife, please," he said, just as Mamá howled again.

"She's occupied. Wait, please."

"The baby is with them?"

"No. We already brought it to the cellar."

The notary winced. "It can't stay there, you know. It will…" he paused.

"Smell?" Enrique guessed.

"Well, yes. But not for a little while."

"No—it already does!"

The notary shook his head.

"A fait accompli," he said. "So, there is no blame."

"Not the midwife's fault. That's what Mamá said. Wait—the envelope!"

"And your Tía?" he inquired as my brother hurried away, to retrieve the money.

"She's at the church," Enrique called over his shoulder. "Lighting candles."

"I see."

As the notary waited, he hunched his shoulders, looked back at the street, and then took a few steps forward, into the protection of the foyer. The men of the town paid him little mind, but the women had poured buckets of water on him from their balconies, to protest the food taxes levied on any item unloaded by train. At least it wasn't boiling water they poured or—God help him—oil. One particularly feisty grandmother had been fined for scalding his predecessor. It was a difficult freelance existence, checking stamps here, imposing duties there, notarizing official papers on the side, writing important letters for the more than half of the village population that was illiterate. And notice how they sought him out during land deals, or when someone needed to protest a notice of military conscription. No buckets of water then!

Anyway, here came the boy—my brother, Enrique, out of breath from climbing and descending the two flights of wooden stairs to my mother's bedroom.

Together they filled out the papers, stumbling over the questions my mother hadn't anticipated and my brother wasn't sure how to answer: maternal grandmother's last name? Paternal grandmother's? Parents' birthplaces? All the while Enrique worried distractedly about the four names he had managed to write in a shaky, left-leaning scrawl: my first name, quickly, my second name—the one that troubled him— less so.

"A-n-í-b-a-l—can you read it?" he fretted.

"Yes, that's fine."

But neither noticed how the notary had botched my first name, misreading the z at the end as a long-tailed, sloppy u.

"The money." Enrique presented his clenched fist.

The notary tugged open my brother's fingers and counted the treasure inside. "It's not enough. I'll be writing two certificates."

At that moment, my Tía rounded the doorway, her black skirt flapping at her ankles, stirring dust motes into the bright shaft of light penetrating the foyer.

"What's this?" she said, pushing past the notary, who touched his hat in greeting. She moved Enrique aside and peered at the certificates in the notary's ink-stained hand. Reading the words, she crossed herself.

"The boy paid me for the first one, but I need money also for the second."

"Why two, if the infant was born dead?"

"You can't have a death certificate without a birth certificate."

"But why can't you put 'born dead' on the birth certificate, and leave it at that?"

Out of habit, the notary retracted his head into his stiff, high collar.

Tía barked, "Shame on you, arriving even before the priest."

"I do a service, Señora. I am a—"

"Vulture."

"—a legitimate representative," he continued, "of the provincial authority."

"I doubt you collected two certificates when Señor Petrillo's infant died. You know a shoemaker has little money, but you think we have more than our share. Bureaucracy—"

The notary interrupted, gesturing toward the stairs. "Once these have been stamped, the service is fulfilled. Payment must be made."

"—before spirituality, I was saying. That's where this country is going."

"The boy's mother understands. Without these certificates, funerary benefits can't be paid to the father. The shoemaker does not work for the colonial government administration. He has no right to such benefits."

As they argued, no one noticed Enrique hopping side to side, trying to interrupt. Tía stirred her fingers around the bottom of her leather pouch, still mumbling about the decline of piety and the problems of empire, while the notary wagged his head. Finally, after more coins and handwritten copies of both certificates had changed hands, Tía turned to my brother.

"Out back," she ordered, irritated by his hopping. "Before you have an accident."

"I don't have to go."

"Well, what then?"

"Feliz isn't dead."

"Who?"

"The baby, Feliz."

"The boy is confused," the notary said. "The baby's name was Fel*iu*," he said, stabbing a finger at the certificates in Tía's hands.

She squinted as she read. "I'd be very upset to find out you copied the name wrong."

"Like the saint. It means 'prosperous,' I believe."

Tía muttered, "Not very prosperous to be born dead."

Enrique tried again. "But the baby—he's in the cellar. You can see."

"It's the midwife I need. Here and here—she will need to put her mark," the notary said, accenting the last word acidly just as the woman's heavy descent sounded on the staircase.

The midwife acknowledged the adults with a weary nod, made an X just above the notary's ink-stained fingertip, then turned to Tía. "She seems comfortable now. Make sure she doesn't use the stairs for a week. Even then, if the bleeding increases…" She paused, hoping the notary would excuse himself so she could deliver more intimate instructions. When he made no effort to leave, she changed the subject. "I can speak to the carpenter for you, about a coffin. But he'll want measurements, so as not to waste wood. If you'll bring me the body, I have a piece of string left, to measure it."

Tía stood erect with indignation. "You mean to say you didn't get a good enough look when it came out?"

"I ran to get help. I didn't see it at all. It isn't in the bedroom."

"It's in the cellar," Enrique said, and then louder, fists curled with frustration, "Feliz is in the cellar!"

"Stop this nonsense!" Tía scowled. "Felix, maybe, or Feliciano, or Feliu—but what is this Feliz?"

"I imagine," she continued, facing the midwife, "that you expect full payment, even though you managed to miss the birth."

No one noticed my mother descending the stairs, one painful step at a time, pale hand gripping the banister. She sat down on the bottom step. Her nightdress billowed around her bare feet. Her damp, dark hair flowed over her pale shoulders.

"I just wanted my baby to be happy," she said. And then louder, so that the notary, the midwife, Tía and Enrique all turned, "Not prosperous, not successful. Just happy."

"See?" Enrique said.

The midwife opened her mouth to reprimand my mother for getting out of bed, the notary pursed his lips in preparation for defending the spelling on his certificates, and Tía ground her jaw, gathering the residue of her complaints. But before any of them could speak again, a piercing squall came from the cellar's open trapdoor, in the far corner of the foyer. Luisa's head followed it, then her shoulders, over which I was still crudely positioned.

"Happy?" Luisa called out, over the sound of my furious mewling. "He can't be, with this black, tarry stuff coming out. He started crying when I tried to wipe it, and now he's turning purple."

The adults gasped as they saw her head and shoulders sway unsteadily, one hand over my furiously shuddering body, the other gripping the ladder rungs. Tía, the midwife, and the notary remained frozen. My mother lifted her arms, but she was too dizzy to rise. Only Enrique bolted into action, pulling me away from my sister's unsteady shoulder so that she could haul herself the rest of the way out of the cellar. In the ensuing confusion, no one mentioned the certificates again.

My mother laughed through her exhausted tears as Enrique brought me to her: "Call him anything, I don't care." And from that moment, she didn't. She had traded her initial, plain hope for an even more basic one: that I would simply survive.

Tía and the midwife broke free from their paralysis and gathered around my mother. They grasped her elbows in order to coax her back up the stairs, and reached forward to take me out of her arms, muttering cooing sounds to stop my crying.

"Leave us be, and let him cry," Mamá said, refusing to let go as she unbuttoned the top of her nightdress, preparing to nurse me on the stairs. *"Es la música más linda del mundo."*

It's the most beautiful music in the world.

Now, all of this story I'm telling you so far, I wrote down quickly, one night in October 1940. I began it at another man's request, but did not deliver it to him.

You're not asking me why. I'd like to attribute your reticence to shyness. But your trade requires the opposite; requires, perhaps, the impatience I see when I look in your eyes, where I'd like to find—what? Forgiveness?

Perhaps simply: Understanding.

Writing these memories pained me. Less so the earliest childhood parts, which is why I started with them; certainly the later parts, as I was forced to review the course of my life, the development of my ideas and stances, which were to prove inadequate to the complexity of those times. But the discomfort of recollection was only a shadow of what was to come, when I would lose nearly all that was dear to me.

For the last year, the curators of the new museum of music in Spain have been hounding me with letters and telegrams, asking for my bow. The museum people have no idea that I wrote my memoirs thirty-odd years ago, and that I have them in my possession still. I bring you here not to discuss the bow—which I shall donate as promised—or to thrust into your more capable hands all my papers, which I can share only in my own way, in my own time. To understand and appreciate what they contain, you must go slowly with me; you must indulge my interpretation. You must be a better man than I was—more sympathetic, at the very least.

I realize the later parts of my story are the ones you most want to hear. You would have me begin with Aviva, all the better to have a living picture of her in your mind. Or at least with Al-Cerraz. You have asked already about the final 1940 concert, and I throw up my hands— I can no more start with that than I can play the Bach suites backward, from the last note to the first. I have never been that sort of a trick-performing prodigy. I have always been methodical, essentially conservative, by which—I see your smile—I don't mean politics. You will forgive me for being a classicist always, insistent on symmetry and proportion. You will allow me, at my advanced age, this last kindness— truly an indulgence, considering my lack of cooperation with your past journalistic efforts. In return, I will be honest.

Wilhelm, I have done a terrible thing.

Yes, please—a glass of water.

But I have left you with the impression of a baby, barely alive and mistakenly named. Please, if you will let me introduce you to the boy, just beginning to understand the beauty and difficulty of life in that time, in that place.

CHAPTER

~ 2 ~

"I'm going to the train station," my mother announced on a cold morning, nearly six years after my birth. "Your father has arrived."

I'd had a nightmare and woken from it breathing hard, just as the women in the house were stirring and whispering. Now, as I struggled to lace my boots, Tía mumbled over my shoulder, "Go back to bed with your brothers and sister. You'll only delay your mother."

Ignoring my aunt's reproachful expression, I stepped out into the dark street with Mamá.

"Your nightmare wasn't about a box, was it?" she asked as we hurried along.

No, I told her. It was about a wintry, unfamiliar beach of cold, dark, wet sand, and what lived in the holes.

"Good. Never mind."

We continued in silence, holding hands; past connected, multistory stone houses like ours, and shuttered stores. As we zigzagged down the oddly angled streets I struggled to keep up, a jerking tail behind Mamá's purposeful kite. The sidewalk was barely wide enough for one person, made of a smooth and slippery stone so burnished by decades of passing feet that it glinted silver. I skidded along its surface while my mother stumbled over the cobblestone road, yanking me each time her ankle turned, both of us struggling downhill toward the station in the dark. When I slipped and fell, skinning one knee, Mamá said nothing, only pulled me up by one arm and kept going.

A barnlike oak door creaked open, and a woman's craggy face emerged, illuminated by a candle lantern.

"*Buenos días, Doña.* Meeting the train?"

"Meeting my husband," Mamá answered.

"*Madre de Dios,*" the crone grunted, crossing herself before she withdrew into the shadows. The door's ring-shaped knocker clapped hard as the door slammed shut.

Black sky lightened to deep navy as we cut across the town plaza. At the church, I ran one hand along the old building's pockmarked walls, remembering my brother Enrique's words (*Yes, they're bullet holes; even the priest says so. He has a jar full of the slugs...*) until my mother glanced over her shoulder and jerked me out of my reverie.

"Filth!" she yelled. "Look at your hand!"

"What? I can't see it."

"I don't have time for this, Feliu!"

We veered into the alley behind the fish market, hopping the channel of wastewater spilling from the market's open back door. In the golden, lamplit interior, I could see men heaving crates and shoveling chipped ice. Fish scales sparkled between the alley's wet cobblestones like trapped stars.

Deep navy yielded to peach-tinged blue by the time we reached the station, where the train waited, warm and rumbling, still dribbling steam. Mamá freed herself from my sweating hand and marched onto the platform, where several men gathered around her. Within moments she was seated at a bench against the station wall, pulling coarse twine from the lid of a large box the men had placed at her feet. It was about as wide as my mother's outstretched arms, made of an unfamiliar reddish-brown wood. There was a single small clasp on the fitted lid. Instead of a lock, there was only a twist of heavy wire attached to a yellow card bearing official-looking stamps and our address.

"Perhaps you should wait," the stationmaster was saying. "Who knows what's in it? Take it to the church. I'll have a wagon brought around for you."

But my mother blotted her face dry. "I've waited months," she said, and glared until the stationmaster patted his vest pocket and strode away.

As Mamá untwisted the wire, she whispered, "You've seen bones, haven't you, Feliu? It is probably mostly ashes, but there may be bones." She worked her fingertips under the lid. "Don't be afraid."

I held my breath and stared. But when my mother pried the lid free with a dull pop, *she* was the one who gasped. Inside, there were no bodily remains.

"Presents!" I cried out. "From Papá!"

Mamá studied the straw-padded contents, fingering each object in turn: a compass, a blue bottle, a glossy brown stick, a jungle cat carved from dark wood, a cigar box with a small blank diary inside. At the bottom of the box lay an old suit jacket, neatly folded, which she took out and held to her face, inhaling. Reluctantly, she lifted out two notes—one printed on a card, a few sentences surrounded by blank space; the other larger and rough-edged and handwritten. She read the first quickly and let it drop onto the sticky station floor, shaking her head when I leaned over to retrieve it. A breeze flipped the card over twice, then sent it toward the tracks. The second note she read slowly, silently, smoothing it against her lap. When she finished, she folded it carefully, tucked it away in a pocket, and sighed.

"They've broken their promise. Whatever remains they retrieved after the rebellion were buried in Cuba. The American victory changed their priorities. Now they're too busy getting out the living to worry about the dead."

The details meant little to me. Two months earlier, my mother had perched my siblings and me in a row of five dining-room chairs—even Carlito, who kept squirming off his seat—to tell us what had happened. Rebels fighting for independence from Spain had triggered an explosion in the harbor. The building where my father worked had caught fire, killing Papá and nine other men. Now America—a place that meant nothing to me, beyond the fact that Spanish ships had discovered it—appeared ready to enter the fray.

Mamá cupped my chin in her hand. "Your Papá should have lived three centuries ago, when the world was getting bigger. Now it's getting only smaller and more loud."

As if to prove her point, the train departed at that moment, wheezing and clanging, south toward Tarragona.

When it was out of view, she said, "Papá meant to deliver these gifts with his own hands. They're from his travels. He had his own intentions, but I'll leave the choice to you."

I picked up the compass first, watching the little copper-colored needle spin and bounce. Then the blue bottle. Then the jungle cat. They were enticing, but I did not choose them. Maybe I felt contrary on this rare morning alone with Mamá, away from the superior airs of my elder siblings; maybe I felt the need to reject the gifts that had the most clearly childish appeal. I picked up the one object that made no immediate sense: the glossy brown stick. At one end it had a rectangular black handle dotted with one small circle of mother-of-pearl. At the other end it had a fancy little curve, like the upswept prow of an ancient ship.

I lifted it out of the box. It was longer than my arm, a bit thicker than my finger, and polished smooth. I held it out in front me, like a sword. Then upright, like a baton.

"It's pernambuco—a very good South American wood," Mamá said, her eyebrows raised.

The anticipation on her face made my throat tighten. I returned the stick hastily to the box.

"Tell me," I said. "I don't want to choose wrong."

I expected her to reassure me. Instead she said, "You *will* be wrong sometimes, Feliu."

Her lecturing tone reminded me of the times she had helped tie my shoes, tugging the laces hard enough to upset my balance. I couldn't know that those days of playful rough-handling were numbered, to be replaced by a grief-filled overprotectiveness.

When I still hadn't chosen, Mamá asked, "Do you remember your Papá?"

"Yes," I answered automatically.

"You can still see him in your mind? As clearly as you can see me?"

This time, when I didn't answer, she said, "Always tell me the truth. Maybe other people need to invent drama. Not us. Not here."

I'd heard her say this earlier that year, as the survivors of the *Desastre* of '98 had straggled into town, living ghosts from failed faraway colonial battles. The Americans had invaded Cuba, Puerto Rico, and the Philippines, Spanish colonies already struggling for independence. The last vestiges of the Spanish Empire were collapsing around us while another empire rose to take its place. Now the soldiers and bureaucrats and merchants were returning—limbs missing, heads and torsos wrapped in stained bandages. Many who passed through Campo Seco seemed lost—they weren't our missing men, we had nothing for them, so why had they stepped off the train here? We rented our cellar to one of them, moving all the casks and wax-sealed bottles aside, furnishing the dark, cool room with a cot, one chair, and an old cracked mirror. The man paid in advance for a week's stay but left after three days, without explanation, prompting Tía to castigate Mamá, "I told you not to put the mirror down there. A man like that doesn't want to see his face."

I closed my own eyes and tried to see Papá. He was a blur, except for his dark mustache, thick under his nose, curled and twisted at the tips; and the wide bottom cuff of his pin-striped suit pants. I had clung to those pants while he directed the secular village choir. And I had perched high on his shoulders, smelling his hair tonic while we watched local processions. Papá had little interest in the Catholic festivals that clogged our village streets. But he had loved when the traveling musicians came, with their gourds and broomsticks strung as homemade mandolins, guitars, and violins. I'd begged my father to buy me instruments like those. That had been close to two years ago, when Papá had last visited home.

"The stick!" I called out suddenly. "Is that what he wanted for me to have?"

"*Bow*, Feliu. It's an unfinished bow, without the hair."

"I knew it!" I retrieved the stick from the box and began to saw at an imaginary instrument across my chest.

After a moment I stopped to ask, "What kind of bow?"

The question gave her pause. "It doesn't matter," she said, and part of me knew that she wasn't telling the truth. "One bow is the same as any other."

I danced in circles as my mother spoke with the wagoner and watched his assistant load the box onto the wagon bed. Then I remembered my unanswered question: "Is that what Papá wanted me to have?"

The wagon jerked forward, steered by an impatient driver and eager horses.

"Up, Feliu," she gestured, her arms beckoning me toward the seat. "Your brothers and sister are waiting for us. Father Basilio is expecting a coffin. You made your choice. Now come."

Back home, Enrique stole glances at my strange wooden stick, which made me hold it closer, working it under one armpit and finally down into one leg of my pants. But any incipient jealousy was dampened when he realized it was a musical object. "A bow?" he snorted, slapping my back. "I thought it was a musket plunger."

Enrique, age thirteen, was our little soldier; he claimed the compass, a handy instrument for making sorties beyond the olive- and grapevine-covered hills. Percival—at sixteen, an adult in our eyes—stayed above the fray, accepting the blank diary. In the years to come, he'd never write a word in it, only numbers: gambling odds, winnings, and debts. Luisa, age eleven, wrapped her chubby fingers around the jungle cat, refusing to let go until Mamá offered to fill the blue glass bottle with perfume, if Luisa would give the cat to two-year-old Carlito. When the divisions were made and all brows smoothed, Mamá exhaled deeply, saying nothing more about my father's undisclosed intentions.

Many years later, it would become an insomniac's preoccupation for me: What if Enrique had taken the bow? He'd been in Papá's choir, and had demonstrated greater musical aptitude than any of us, even if guns amused him more. If he'd walked with Mamá to the train and back, with more time to consider, would he still be alive? Would the compass have helped Percival or Luisa to better find their ways? And Carlito: Well, there was no saving him. He would die of diphtheria seven years later, to be buried alongside our two siblings who had perished as infants. At the funeral, Percival would lean into me, whispering, "We beat the odds—that's all it is."

There's a saying in our corner of northeastern Spain: "Pinch a Spaniard—if he sings out, he's a Catalan." We considered ourselves a musical region, and yet even here, among troubadours, my father had stood out. In his spare time, he had been the director for our local men's choir, a group that took its cue from the workingmen's choirs of Barcelona—proud men, singing our native regional language at a time when Catalan poetry and song were briefly blossoming.

In 1898, the year my father and several other prominent local men died abroad, the group disbanded, replaced by a choir led by Father Basilio, who had come to us from Rome. This later choir was never as popular. Following the priest's lead, it sang in Italian—a disappointment to nearly everyone, even my Cuban-raised mother, who had never felt entirely comfortable with the Catalan language. The secular Italian choir folded a few years later, leaving only a few hard-core devotees, the poorest singers of the lot, to sing in Latin during Masses. Our town, once a multilingual bastion of song, had grown unexpectedly silent and dour.

My mother had met my father at an arts festival in Barcelona, where they discovered that they shared similar backgrounds, as well as a love of music. Both of them had been born in Spain and had spent their childhoods in colonial Cuba, returning with their optimistic parents to Spain in time for the short-lived First Republic, in 1873. My mother had been renowned for her voice, though she claimed later she'd never had any professional ambitions. By 1898, she didn't sing at all—not even the simple rounds and folk songs she had once sung for her children.

Lying together in the bed we shared, Enrique would sometimes sing to me a remembered line or two, very quietly in the dark, as if it were a secret no one should hear. When I asked him to sing more, he would tease me: "You know that song. Come on...." I had a good memory for most things, so the complete unfamiliarity of what he sang drove me to distraction. I'd beg him again, and he'd tease me more, until I felt panicky. Only when I was on the verge of tears would Enrique relent and finish the song, sedating me with belated satisfaction. It occurs to me now that Enrique was old enough to be embarrassed by those lullabies, but he didn't want to forget them, either. He wasn't trying to torture me so much as give himself permission to remember.

In the years before he accepted his post overseas, Papá had been our town's music teacher, keeping a piano for that purpose in a room between the church and the school. Following his death, my father's best piano student, Eduardo Rivera, approached Mamá to offer condolences. A month later, he came to ask her to sing to his piano accompaniment. We didn't own a piano anymore, she told him. She had given Papá's piano to the priest, Father Basilio, to compensate him for the memorial service—or at least, that's what we were told.

Eduardo reassured Mamá that he had his own piano, of course. She could come to his house and sing. Mamá changed the subject immediately, pretending not even to hear the request. But to make up for the rudeness, she did let him stay for lunch. He came uninvited a second time, and a third, and perhaps because he was my father's student—or perhaps because my mother was still stunned with grief—she didn't turn him away. Finally, he figured out the surest way to win her favor was through an intermediary. Eduardo stopped petitioning for my mother's accompaniment and offered to give me music lessons, instead.

For as long as I could remember, local children had called my new teacher "Señor Riera." The nickname was our local word for the town dry wash that flooded seasonally, just like Eduardo's own drooping, allergy-prone eyes and nose. Eduardo had a thin version of my father's mustache, but his was always damp. Because of his clogged sinuses, he'd developed the habit of leaving his lips slightly parted. His upper lip was hidden, but his fleshy lower lip protruded clearly, like some exotic pouch-shaped orchid hanging from the scruffy bark of a jungle tree.

Señor Rivera, as I learned to call him more carefully now, owned a piano and a violin. I chose to learn the violin because I wanted to use the bow that my mother had sent away to Barcelona to have finished for me, with horsehair and new silver wire. She used government money to pay for it, saying it was better that my father's final pay be used for something we could keep and cherish, not just coal or bread.

Each day, Percival and Enrique stayed after school to earn a few coins doing the schoolmaster's chores. My mother and Tía were busy tending Carlito and Luisa, and happy to have me out of the house each afternoon. Señor Rivera kept the violin at his home, where I practiced, but I carried my bow with me to lessons and back, in a leather-covered tube from my father's custom files that had once held harbor maps from North Africa and the Caribbean. Every time I held it to my face, I inhaled a dizzying smell of sea salt and ink and sweat—the smell of foreign shores, and also of my father's arms, which were harder to recall with every passing day.

I loved carrying that indestructible tube and hitting rocks with it as I walked. Once, when I'd made the mistake of dallying too long in the dry wash under the bridge, I attracted the attention of two older boys the same age as Enrique. They teased me, calling me *Cerillito*, or "Little Matchstick"; the dislocated hip had never healed properly following my birth, leaving my left leg thinner and slightly shorter than my right. The nickname didn't bother me. I'd heard the same and worse already from my own brothers. But when they started insulting my father, I hit one of them with the tube end, splitting the boy's lip before I managed to run away, incredulous at my small victory.

When Mamá found out about the fight, she punished me for it, but she did not take the tube away. I think she sensed I needed some protection. My teacher thought the tube was ridiculous, though, and the bow itself strange—"too thick, too heavy, probably not made for a violin. Anyway, it's too big for you."

"So is the violin," I retorted. Señor Rivera pinched my arm hard enough to leave a mark, but I didn't care. He'd cuffed me several times when I talked back or disobeyed him. At the time, I assumed he wanted my prize objects for himself. Now I realize he considered the bow an irritating reminder of my father.

Señor Rivera was half my mother's age. It seemed ridiculous that he kept coming to our house every Sunday afternoon, bringing Mamá and Tía stale cookies that were never sweet enough for two women who had been raised on plentiful Caribbean sugar. My mother was beautiful, with shining chestnut hair and a strong jawline that might have appeared masculine were it not tempered by full lips. Many men sought her, even while an equal number criticized her for what they perceived as haughtiness and disrespect. In a town where many women were merely "Señora," she was "Doña," in deference to her noble bearing and education. Even in the loose-waisted, soot black dresses she'd worn since my father's death, she could not fade into safe obscurity, though she tried.

It didn't surprise my mother that playing the violin came easily to me. Everyone in our family was musically inclined. "Don't be vain about your gifts," she said. "Music is everywhere, and there is no one alive who can't appreciate it. To love music is easy. To play it well is no different from knowing how to make shoes or build bridges."

She did not teach me, did not directly encourage me, but she couldn't help asking questions that reflected her own musical past. When I returned from lessons, she would say, "Were you relaxed? Did you play naturally?" They were unusual questions for such corseted, high-collared times; they were the same questions I would ask myself ten and fifteen years later, as I strove to develop my own relaxed bowing style.

I learned scales and études and easy salon pieces. I liked the violin, but I wasn't passionate about its shape or sound, which in my unskilled hands came out as a tinny screech. The adult-sized violin that Señor Rivera let me use was so heavy that I could barely manage to hold it upright, my left wrist throbbing so fiercely I barely noticed what my right hand was doing. Besides, I hated standing to play. My matchstick leg didn't hurt in those days, but because the knob of the thighbone didn't fit the socket properly, I had trouble mimicking Señor Rivera's stance. Occasionally the entire leg would start to tremble, and I'd have to shake out the spasm to regain my balance.

"Feliu, pay attention," Señor Rivera said one afternoon, assuming I was falling asleep on my feet. "This is what you may someday hope to do." He tossed his head, drawing attention to his fashionable shoulder-length hair and the glistening Cupid's bow visible through his thin, damp mustache. Then he launched into a piece by Pablo Sarasate—our Spanish Paganini. He winced when he missed a note, but he recovered quickly, fingers slamming like pistons up and down the black fingerboard, the dynamics as dismayingly even as the tempo was not. I hated his theatrics. Quick fingers did not impress me. Long hair did not impress me.

Please, God, I thought, don't let Señor Rivera move into our house.

"Someday, Feliu," he said, and I gulped before I realized he was referring only to my own future chances with the Sarasate theme. "Now, hold that violin straight—straighter!"

Redemption came, as all things great and sorrowful did, by train.

The train meant everything to our village, which modern times might have forgotten if not for those parallel steel bars pointed south toward Tarragona, the town of Roman ruins and busy plazas, and north toward Barcelona, the city of commerce, art, and anarchy. Our narrow, twisting streets were lined with three-story stone and plaster buildings that cast the streets in shadow for all but a few midday hours. When the rains came, they resculpted the sinuous, gravel-lined gully that ran through the center of town. But the train tracks ran straight and hard through gusting winds and bright sun, exposed to anything the future might bring. The station itself was an oracle, bearing posters and flyers about upcoming events. I read my first words not in school, but on tiptoe outside the brick-walled station, puzzling out a three-colored flyer headlined "Los Gatos," The Cats. A musical quartet, Enrique explained.

"Will they be playing here?"

He squinted at a dense block of smaller type. "Barcelona—Sitges—Lleida. No, they're not stopping here."

"Where is Sitges?" I asked him. When he didn't answer, I tried again: "Where is Lleida?"

"Mamá is waiting at the footbridge. We're already late."

"You don't know where Lleida is?" I asked, dismayed by his ignorance.

I kept pestering and he kept changing the subject, our voices rising. By the time we reached the bridge where my mother stood with Carlito on one hip and Luisa collapsed at her feet, I was crying, my skinny arm blazed with a red mark left by Enrique's final twist, and Enrique himself was stuttering a dozen excuses. My mother only sighed.

For the next couple of years, I read those flyers as The Cats—as well as many Donkeys, Bulls, and Bandits—bypassed our village. But the sting of those anonymous rejections resolved into a sense of destiny the day I spotted a flyer headlined in big, blocky type, "El Nene—The Spanish Mozart." By now I could decode the small print without help: "And His Classical Trio." No animals this time; no gourds or broomstick mandolins. And yes, they were stopping at Campo Seco, as well as a dozen other small towns up and down the coast.

El Nene was our country's best-known pianist, a prodigy who had toured the world since the age of three. His nickname hinted at his dual reputation. *El nene* means "baby boy," but it can also mean "villain." The pianist wasn't a true *traidor* or *malvado*—not yet, anyway—but he did have a reputation for mischief. At this point, he was a precocious adolescent in a hefty man's body, constrained by a toddler's nickname, and performing with men many years his senior.

Dust hung in the hot air that day, obscuring the view of yellow-leafed vineyards on the hills beyond town. The town leaders had planned a parade, and the town ladies spent all morning pouring buckets of water on the main road, just to keep down the dust. We were a little embarrassed not to have wide boulevards to show off, or intricately tiled, fountain-filled plazas.

Señor Rivera was smitten. "I may ask him to hear me play, after the crowds have gone," he bragged during our midday meal, to which he had sweet-talked yet another invitation. "Do you think that would be unbecoming?"

Mamá, who dealt increasingly with annoyances by simply enduring them, shrugged.

He persevered, "I've heard he asks ladies to sign his touring book. Would you like me to ask him on your behalf?"

"Carlito!" Mamá wailed, as my little brother tipped his soup bowl into his lap.

"I could ask El Nene to listen to Feliu play the violin," Señor Rivera continued more loudly, competing with Carlito's shrieks of pain as the hot soup drained into his best sailor suit. "I'm sure he must suffer excited parents in every village, but I did help to arrange the concert venue."

I stared into my soup and felt my face getting hotter. So this was how Señor Rivera hoped to profit from the trio's visit—by showing me off and increasing my mother's sense of obligation.

With Carlito wriggling and wailing under her arm, my mother raised her voice above the squall. "I am not so impressed by this Nene—this performing monkey—forced to tour the world before he was old enough to stop sucking his thumb. His parents should be ashamed."

Luisa, who'd shown no interest in El Nene's visit, perked up. "He's a monkey?"

Mamá exited with her thrashing wet bundle. Señor Rivera's eyes darted around the room, his hopes and expectations unspent. He looked like a swimmer desperate for air, but still three hard strokes short of the surface.

"You," he said, fixing on me, as if my elderly aunt and three other siblings weren't there at all. "You will play for El Nene and his trio. You will demonstrate how much I have done for you."

"Yes, sir."

"And I warn you, *enanito*..."

"Feliu is a dwarf?" Luisa cried out gleefully.

"Dwarves make great entertainers," Percival said. "The royal family keeps them around for fun."

"He *is* a dwarf," Enrique said, without lifting his gaze from his soup bowl. "But he's *our* dwarf."

"I warn you," Rivera continued, oblivious to the interruptions, staring me into submission. "Do not humiliate me."

Everyone came, wearing their finest. Matronly ladies decorated their upswept hair with large combs and lace mantillas unearthed from ancient trunks. Younger women wore fashionable gowns with puffed sleeves that tapered at the elbows into tight cuffs. Boys squirmed in black suits with short breeches. Veterans tottered under the weight of brass buttons. Our three Civil Guard members strutted between the church and the train station, their shiny black finned hats flashing in the sun.

And yet none of us could compare with El Nene.

"Look at his hands," Percival whispered to me when we lined up alongside the train that afternoon, watching the performer disembark. "Each finger is wider than a piano key. He's too fat to play."

I started to object, but Percival didn't wait to hear. He pushed his hands into his pockets, looking for the little diary in which he recorded every wager. "Do you want to bet?"

The concert was held in the school, a low stone building attached to the larger and more ornate church. An overflow crowd filled the plaza in front of the buildings, and the school doors were propped open so that everyone would have a chance to hear. Apartment dwellers opposite had decorated the railings of their balconies with satin bows and dragged chairs outside, to listen from their high, private perches like royalty at an opera house.

Mamá gave up on restraining Luisa and Carlos, and set them loose to gallop and charm their way among neighbors, accepting sugared orange peels and fingerfuls of quince. I skipped the treats and the preconcert parade in favor of getting a front-row seat inside the school itself, well before the concert started. My older brothers came with me. Percival didn't care much about the music, but he couldn't wait to settle our bet about El Nene. Enrique came simply because he was Enrique; the first to punish or tease, but also the first to guide and protect.

Inside, the crowds were flushed, buzzing with questions about this famous man we'd seen only in black-and-white newspaper photographs.

"No one knows where you were born," a man called to the impromptu stage. "What are you, El Nene?"

When the pianist smiled, the long waxed tips of his mustache rubbed against the red apples of his cheeks. "Spanish, *ciento por ciento,*" he said. One hundred percent. "But surely the ladies here won't fault me for having a little Moorish and gypsy blood."

Satisfied titters ran through the crowd.

A woman yelled, "How old are you?"

"How old are *you?*" he shot back.

"*Olé!*" someone shouted.

An unseen voice: "Is it true you stowed away to Brazil when you were seven years old?"

He stroked his beard. "My music has allowed me to travel far and wide."

And another, from a sultry-voiced woman in the rear: "When are you going to stop being called Baby? You look like a big boy to me."

El Nene made a show of lifting a piece of sheet music and fanning himself with it. "Dear lady, if your impure thoughts have become too much to bear, there's a confessional right next door."

El Nene nodded across the room to the partners he'd failed to introduce, flipped his coattails out of the way, slid onto the piano bench and launched solo into an opening chord struck so ferociously that a girl in the audience cried out. Embarrassed laughter followed, but the pianist only smiled slightly and kept playing, as if the girl's reaction and anything else our unsophisticated audience might produce—whispers, gasps, applause at inappropriate moments—were to be both expected and forgiven.

As the audience settled and quieted, El Nene began traversing the keyboard—octave by octave, at high speed, in showy hand-over-hand displays. He spread his arms wide and brought them together again, and I half-expected the keys to hop off the keyboard and pile with a clatter between his hands, like dominoes gathered at the end of a game.

Some of the assembled farmers and vintners, fishermen and bakers had been dragged to the concert by their wives; they had taken their chairs wearily and had endured El Nene's preconcert banter with haughty expressions. But as he played, their faces softened and grew attentive. They leaned forward in their seats, hands on their knees or their chins, recognizing the athleticism of his attack and marveling at sounds and feelings they could not name.

As for dynamics, they were limited: loud, louder, and loudest. But to this crowd, it didn't matter. Later, I would recognize this as El Nene's trademark: his chameleonlike ability to judge a crowd, and to play to it. Among kings and queens, he played with lighter strokes and more *ritardes*. In Britain, he tried to sound more southern; in Italy, more northern. The crowds adored him, but the critics abroad sniped too frequently: *not Spanish enough*. It infuriated him, how little they knew about Spain, and how even though he knew so much more, he couldn't please them all.

Except on an evening like this, in a small town, without music critics. Perhaps that's why he'd come. For the duration of the piece, the audience remained silent. The only stray noise I heard, in the quiet interval before applause erupted, was a quiet, disappointed groan from Percival, who had lost his latest bet.

If the concert had ended there, it would have stayed in my memory forever. But something more astounding happened when the violinist and the cellist joined the pianist. I looked to the violin first, because it was familiar; I knew I'd learn something by watching, and was hoping to see El Nene's violinist put my own teacher to shame. The cello, played by a man named Emil Duarte, didn't interest me because it seemed like nothing more than an oversized violin. But then Duarte pulled his bow against the larger instrument's strings, and my face turned to follow the sound. I was thankful that El Nene had played solo first, because once the cello started up, I never looked at the violin or piano again.

Duarte's cello was a glossy caramel color, and the sound it produced was as warm and rich as the instrument looked. It sounded like a human voice. Not the high warble of an opera singer or anyone else singing for the stage, but rather the soothing voice of a fisherman singing as he mended his nets, or of a mother singing lullabies to her sleepy children.

When the cellist reached a crescendo on one of the lower strings, I felt a strange sensation, both pleasurable and disturbing. It reminded me of holding a cat, feeling its purrs resonate with me. Listening, I felt the sensation strengthen, as if the cello's quivering vibrato were actually boring into me, opening a small hole in my chest, creating a physical pain as real as any wound. I was afraid of what might fall out of that hole, and yet I didn't want it to close, either.

As Duarte climbed to higher notes, I followed him. I watched the way he bent over his instrument to reach the most precarious pitches, like a seated potter wrapping his arms around unshaped clay, stripping away its first layers, revealing rather than creating. El Nene had seemed like an actor, a showman—and a talented one at that, able to accept a role and play to his audience's expectations. But Duarte seemed like a craftsman—the kind of craftsman I had been raised to respect.

As I listened, my nose began to itch, a warning sign that tears were imminent. Horrified that Enrique would see me cry, I blinked hard, without luck. I wrapped my fingers around the edge of my chair's wooden seat, hoping to inflict myself with splinters that would require sudden, pained attention. When that didn't work, I played a mental game, trying to taste Duarte's strings as he played them. The lowest and fattest string, C: bitter chocolate. The G, next to it: something animal. Warm goat cheese. The D: ripe tomato. The high, thin A: tart lemon, to be handled with care. The highest notes, played near the bridge, could sting, but Duarte tempered that sting with a sweet vibrato.

The cello contained everything I knew—a natural world of tastes and sensations—and much more that I did not. After watching El Nene, I wanted to see him play again. But after watching Duarte, I wanted to *be* him.

When the trio had finished, my mother sent my brothers and sisters outside and guided me backstage, where I treaded for an eternity in a sea of wide-legged trousers and puffy skirt flounces. While I waited, I mentally replayed the cello parts I had heard, desperately trying to commit them to memory. I felt ill and giddy—drunk, just like the time my brothers had dared me to sip from one of Papá's cellared bottles of liqueur.

My mother's hand pushed from behind me, willing me forward with the crowd. Finally, the autograph seekers and civic well-wishers parted, I inhaled fresh air, and I heard Señor Rivera introduce me to El Nene, Emil Duarte, and their French violinist, Julien Trudeau. They stood just feet from where they had played, gods transformed back into men. There was the black piano bench and El Nene standing next to it, with a cigar in his mouth and a glass in his hand. There was Duarte's glossy cello, recovering from its amazing performance—and looking for all the world like a curvaceous woman reclining on the beach, one arm flung over her head, trim waist and wide hips accentuated.

Señor Rivera was still talking—I saw his lips moving, and heard the rumble of the three musicians chuckling politely in response. I heard my mother's higher, strained voice behind me. Someone pushed a violin into my left hand, where it hung, lifeless and unforgiving. My mother handed me my bow. More hands pushed me forward. Waves crashed in my ears.

I walked forward three steps and half-collapsed into the nearest chair.

"Feliu?" I heard my mother say. "Feliu?"

I started playing, in a daze. First slowly, then with gusto. Yes: It was easier this way. I could even wiggle my left fingers a little, to bring out that honeyed vibrato. My body swayed slightly as I played. All that longing I had felt during the concert was propelling my bowing hand, helping it flow expertly across the strings.

But the men were laughing again—uncontrollable bellows, instead of the polite chuckles of a moment earlier. Out of the corner of my eye I saw El Nene's head tip back, so that his open mouth was facing the ceiling and his drink spilled onto the floor. Still I didn't stop until I felt the sting of a hard slap against my face. My eyes followed the invading hand up a dark sleeve and into the face of Señor Eduardo Rivera. My cheek flamed. My stupor dissolved. It came to my attention, with the same sticky realization that one has upon waking just as one is wetting the bed, that I had been playing the violin as a cello. I had perched it on the seat between my legs. Duarte's playing had affected me that much—I could imagine no other way to play a stringed instrument! Perhaps, in my dream state, I was only seeing the future.

The musicians were laughing too loudly for me to gauge whether they'd heard much of my minuet. Even played in the wrong position, it hadn't sounded half bad to me. But perhaps because I did not look contrite, only groggy, Rivera lifted his hand again, to deliver a second slap.

In those days, when schoolteachers swatted students and shopkeepers chased away delinquents with brooms, Rivera would have been forgiven for the first slap. But not—in our family—for the second. My mother had been holding my leather bow tube for the duration of my

short recital, and now she raised it to one shoulder. El Nene and his trio
stopped laughing. My mother squeezed her eyes shut, cocked her right
elbow and swung. With a muffled crack, the leather tube made contact
with Eduardo's infamous beak, and the flood-prone "Riera" flowed
once more, this time in red.

That night we hurried home and packed our bags for an impromptu
holiday on the coast, at a family friend's summer cottage.

"But when are we coming back, Mamá?" Luisa asked as we tossed
clothes into our bags.

"About three weeks, I think. By then, Señor Rivera's nose will have
healed."

"Are the violin lessons done?" I asked. "Will he come to our house
anymore?"

"Yes, *querido*. And no," she said. Then she laughed as she hadn't
laughed in years—an explosive laugh, unexpected, brief and wild. It
reminded me of a rising flock of startled birds, sending hope scattering
in directions too varied for my mind to follow.

We had just gathered with our suitcases in the foyer when a knock
came at the door. My siblings and I all looked to Mamá, who stiffened,
and then to the line of dancing light under the heavy wooden door's
warped bottom, where we could see the shadows cast by an impatient
set of small, shifting feet. A messenger boy's grubby fingers pushed an
envelope through the wide crack.

Evidently, El Nene had sympathy for my inauspicious debut. He'd
taken the time to pen a handwritten letter of introduction recommending me for an audition with a *real* cello teacher, in Barcelona. It was
signed with the pianist's full name, Justo Al-Cerraz (I hadn't realized
he was called anything except El Nene) and decorated with a *peseta*-
sized, humorous self-portrait.

My mother smiled at the letter but frowned at the caricature. Then she folded the letter and instructed us to wait as she went to put it away in the family Bible, with the last letter from my father. "Barcelona," she said, "is far away."

Despite the sober silence that followed, I could still feel the warm glow of my mother's earlier laughter. The future was uncertain, but at least it was exposed and alive. No matter where my father's unreturned bones lay, turning to dust in a land Spain no longer possessed, the rest of us could be flesh again.

CHAPTER

~ 3 ~

After we returned home from our vacation of discretion, I was delighted not to be making music with Señor Rivera anymore. But the feeling faded by Christmas, when I longed to hold an instrument in my hand again.

"When can I learn to play?" I badgered my mother.

"There are no cellos here, Feliu."

"Even a violin."

"And who would teach you?"

"Mamá, I'm getting old!" I was nine years old when I first said this, and Mamá laughed. But as the months passed, and I kept repeating it, she stopped tousling my hair or smiling in response to my plea.

The new century pulsed with a mania for novelty and precocity. Young performers from England, Austria, and Russia visited Spain. A girl from America, younger than me, was performing virtuosic works on the cello—*my cello*, I couldn't help thinking. None of these performers came to our village. I read about them in the newspapers and at the train station, where the posters announced *Madrid—Sevilla— Granada—Córdoba—Valencia—Barcelona*. Never Campo Seco.

Whenever I passed Eduardo Rivera, he crossed to the other side of the street or lifted his chin away from me. I recognized the terrible loneliness in his droopy expression. I wanted to shout, "I feel it, too!"

"Barcelona is far?" I'd pester my mother.

"Too far."

She said the same thing about the beach that we no longer visited to-gether. "I can't carry you if you get tired on the way back," she told me. "You're too big for that now."

"I won't get tired. I promise." I tried not to notice her eyes drop-ping to my left leg.

"Don't make promises you can't keep."

"But I *do* promise." Frustration burned in my stomach. I knew my older brothers and sister would get to go. I wanted to run with them, even fall or tire, without consequence, and without worrying that I had gravely inconvenienced or saddened my mother.

"Here's a better idea," she said. "Let's rest at home today. When Carlito naps, I'll read to you from *Don Quixote*."

And maybe because that book's adventures came to seem like a pale substitute for the physical adventures I wanted to have, I never cared for Cervantes. She read me those stories, I began to suspect, not as an inspiration to dream, but as a caution against dreaming. "How silly—and how terrible," she'd say about the deranged protagonist, whose self-delusion earned him every kind of sadistic torment, reminding me that beneath a veneer of humor, the world was actually cruel.

I asked Mamá one day, "My bow—it really is a cello bow, isn't it?"

She was seated at the dining table sewing a dress for Luisa, her hands struggling to align two pieces of cloth, her mouth clamped over a threaded needle. Tía, a more expert seamstress, watched from a cor-ner, shaking her head at Mamá's mistakes.

"How did Papá know I'd like the cello more than the violin?"

My mother mumbled something, her mouth still full of thread, but I couldn't make it out. I tried again, and this time she didn't answer at all.

But Tía had no stomach for a child's insolent questions. She lashed out, saying what my mother had never considered, or never wanted to admit: "Your father knew about your lame leg, *entiendes?* He figured you could sit and play for your dinner, at the very least. Even a beggar needs a gimmick."

My mother separated the pieces of cloth in her hands and removed the needle from her mouth. She seemed to be choosing her words carefully, but I was faster: "I don't care. Even if I had good legs—"

She interrupted me. "You'll never be a beggar—don't worry about that. We'll find you something to do for work."

"I don't care about a job," I started to say, but my mother's soft look hardened, stopping me.

"No person can have dignity without work. I've told you before. Music is fine, but it's not work."

"You said it was no different than making shoes or building bridges. So it is work."

"Things change, Feliu. Everything changes. When things are good, there is time and money for music. When things are not good—*hostia!*" She threw down the dress she had been sewing, wagging the finger she had pricked, and continued to swear, using words I'd never heard come from her mouth. Her face reddened as she held her breath, desperately trying to restrain herself, but a few more words leaked out. "Damn you" were two of them. The third wasn't so easy to hear.

As Mamá rested in her dark bedroom with a headache, I'd thought about what she'd cursed—from the Communion wafer to a dozen other holy objects we weren't supposed to mention in anger. But of people, she had named only one: Reynaldo. It was Papá's name, seldom uttered. She was cursing him not only for failing to return, not only for leaving her with five children and a difficult sister-in-law, but for delivering into my hands a hope that she couldn't fulfill.

———

Around this time, Father Basilio decided that I might have the makings of a priest—a solution to one of my problems, if not both. It had started with the chocolate. From the time I was old enough to attend school, Percival, Enrique and I had set out together from home with our breakfast in our pockets: hard, dark, dusty chocolate squares, speckled with bits of dried fruit and nuts. We were forbidden to eat them on the way to the Mass we were made to attend before school, because Communion required a pure, empty stomach. After Mass ended, we and our young neighbors filed out of the church to the plaza, where—with Father Basilio's words about kindness and brotherly love still fresh in our ears—we raced and taunted and pushed each other in hopes of grabbing a seat on the nearest outdoor benches. There we could sit and eat the treats in our pockets. Ten minutes later, a bell rang to call us into school next door.

Percival, who was in his last year of school, invariably ate his chocolate square on the way to Mass, daring us to tell on him—which we never did. Enrique respected the prohibition and adhered to it. But he wanted the chocolate so badly that his fingers crept into his pockets and nestled there, melting the treat into a lumpy puddle. Once, just before placing the Communion wafer on his tongue, Father Basilio paused and asked Enrique to hold out his hands. When my brother presented his sticky brown, trembling fingers, the priest assumed he'd been nibbling in the back of the church all through the service. Enrique was sent away without the wafer and given a paddling later that day at school. But the very next day, his fingers wandered into his pockets again.

I, too, loved chocolate and I, too, felt tempted. But I did not let my fingers touch the chocolate, or even the edges of my pockets. As I experimented with delaying gratification, I found a savory quality to self-denial that was even more powerful than the satisfaction of sugar. At some point my mother discovered my secret and had a meeting with the priest. He was the one to ask me, on a Monday afternoon after school, why I had accumulated twenty-seven squares of untouched chocolate in a box under my bed.

He did not bother to ask if I'd stolen them from other boys, which must have seemed unlikely, given my unimpressive physique. Nor did he ask if I disliked chocolate, since Mamá had assured him it was my favorite treat. Finally he tilted his head and tried, "Are you saving it for the poor?"

I'd never given the poor a thought. I'd been too busy over the last five and a half weeks enjoying the sparkly lightness in my head, the way hunger extended the church bells' dull metal echo, the feeling of defiant strength in my heart—as compared to the weakness in my hip and leg—when I walked into school unfed, feeling proud of myself for doing without.

"Yes, Father—for the poor," I lied.

"Remarkable," he said, and let me go home.

The next Sunday after Mass, Father Basilio invited me to his private study, a dark, airless room with heavy wine-colored drapes. He asked, "Have you thought of the priesthood, Feliu?"

"Is being a priest work?"

"The hardest work."

Thinking of my mother, I asked, "Is it *dignified* work?"

He laughed. "Dignified—of course it is! There is nothing more dignified."

Father Basilio directed me to various Bible readings, which I promised to contemplate and sometimes did. He helped me with my introductory Latin and taught me a few words of modern Italian, explaining they would come in helpful if I visited Rome someday. These same Italian words, he added, were used by musicians and composers across Europe. At this, I sat up and paid attention, learning how to pronounce and spell *adagio, allegro, andante, presto, maestoso*.

Father Basilio's hopes for my clerical future lasted about six months. By this point, I hadn't played the violin for over two years, but I knew that in preparation for a future cello, I should stay physically ready to play. Alarmed that the calluses I'd developed on my left hand had faded, I discovered a way not only to renew but to increase them—by rubbing my fingertips against stone, at least twenty minutes a day. I always walked on the left-hand side of the street so I could drag my fingers against the rough stone as I walked. In bed at night, in the dark, I rubbed one finger at a time against the wall next to my bed. With time, my fingertips became stiff and waxy, capped with impressively thick, light-yellow pads, the fingerprint lines nearly invisible.

One day at church, as we were leaving Mass, Father Basilio wished me well and took my left hand in his—a spontaneous, collegial gesture. I watched as he squeezed harder, flattening his fingers against my own, feeling them. His face fell.

In confession the following Sunday, he asked, "How old are you now, my son?"

"Eleven years old, Father."

I heard him sigh. "And already committing the sins of adulthood."

I waited, confused.

"Feliu, you must resist your desire."

The desire to play cello?

"Our Lord knows what you have been doing."

I swallowed hard. "I'm not doing anything, Father."

He sighed again. I heard the wood settling under his bench as he shifted.

"Have you been helping your brothers with any olive trimming?"

"Only once last year. I fell off the ladder. Sometimes I visit Percival and he tells me to lie on my back on the ground and look up, to tell him where I can't see blue sky, so he knows where to trim more."

The priest grunted. After a while, he asked, "What hand do you write with, Feliu?"

"My right hand."

He paused again.

"I believe you have promise; I hope to help you find a meaningful vocation. But first, you must stop what you are doing."

"What am I doing?"

"*God* knows."

"But *I* don't know, Father."

"The thing you keep doing every day, over and over. The thing that is making those hard spots on your fingers."

"Oh," I said, relieved—but only for a moment, until I realized where his request was leading. I said more quietly, "But I need to do it. And I like to do it. I can't stop now."

Father Basilio's normally melodic voice lowered into a growl. "Of *course* you like doing it—that is the problem. I understand your father is dead, but hasn't your mother taught you anything?"

I leaped to her defense. "She has, Father."

I recalled what I knew about Father Basilio: that he had dissolved the Catalan-language community choir in favor of an Italian one. Perhaps he wasn't in favor of Catalan music—or musicians—at all. Why else would he discourage me?

Father Basilio gave me the cold shoulder for several weeks. Then he approached me one day and again clasped my hand. It was as calloused as ever. Feeling its hard patches and raised ridges, he released it and spat, "Considering the defilement this hand has suffered, I shouldn't even touch it!"

When I told Mamá that Father Basilio had decided to stop touching me, she turned to me, her eyes wide. "Touching you? Feliu—don't be alone with that man. Don't spend any more time in that church than you have to."

Sorry that I had alarmed her, I said, "All right, Mamá." I knew, though, that I'd miss the singing at Mass, however halting and off-key; and the church's inviting coolness; and the feeling, brief as it was, that one adult seemed to believe I had some kind of calling.

———

Eduardo Rivera continued to avoid our family, but he had an older and more powerful brother—*Don* Miguel Rivera, as my Tía reminded us to call him—who was not so easily rebuffed. Instead of being repelled by my mother's unladylike show of force the day of El Nene's concert, Don Miguel was intrigued by it. At any public gathering, he made sure to approach and greet my mother, and to ask after Tía's health—though he could have asked Tía herself just as easily, since he saw my aunt every week in church.

Don Miguel had inherited his father's job of managing the vineyards and olive groves owned by his patron, the Duke of Oviedo. As Don Miguel gained power and prestige, we saw him more around town. Even in scorching summer, he wore a vest and double-breasted suit jacket, bunched over his paunchy middle. Wandering away from Campo Seco's twisting streets toward its cracking, yellow-soiled fields, he looked like a crow, black coattails flapping in the heat.

Despite his increasing wealth, Don Miguel was struck by the same tragedy that befell so many of the villagers, when his thin, meek wife, Doña Clara, died giving birth to their long-awaited first child. He grieved intensely for one month, and then let it be known, with the frankness of a man shopping for a particular breed of horse, that he intended to marry again, as soon as possible. This time, he would seek out a stronger, sturdier woman. Women of unproven fertility need not apply.

If many widows expressed interest in Don Miguel's matrimonial quest, our family didn't hear about it. We had our own death to mourn. One month shy of his ninth birthday, my brother Carlito contracted diphtheria. What seemed at first like little more than a sore throat advanced to swollen lymph nodes and painful breathing. The inside of Carlito's throat darkened from inflamed red to a leathery gray. Within a few days, several more local children had caught the disease, and there was talk of quarantining Carlito and the others. A doctor from Barcelona was hailed, but before the man arrived, Carlito passed away.

Don Miguel was among the first to visit our house that week in 1905, when others were still deterred by the worry that fatal spores lurked in our hallways. He arrived flanked by two quieter men, who removed their hats while Don Miguel kept his own head covered. Tía brought them all glasses of sherry. Despite what they had in common—not least, the recent death of loved ones—my mother couldn't seem to find any words to share with her guest. She paced silently the entire time he sat drinking, his eyes hidden under the shadow of his hat brim as Tía refilled his glass again and again.

Finally Don Miguel explained why he'd come: not only to pay respects, but to offer to help carry Carlito's coffin. Mamá insisted that the task was well within the abilities of our two neighbors, Percival, and a visiting uncle. Then she resumed pacing between the table and the doorway, willing her guest and his silent cohorts to leave.

But Don Miguel wasn't to be so easily dismissed. He returned with a freshly plucked chicken and said that he hadn't had a good meal since his wife had died. Mamá had no choice but to invite him to stay and dine with us. Once again, the hat and jacket stayed on. The chicken was stringy and tough. It was the quickest midday meal we ever ate; ten minutes after she'd set the plates in front of us, Mamá swept them away, impervious to Don Miguel's quizzical expression and Tía's disapproving stare.

A few weeks later, Don Miguel delivered a letter informing us that Enrique had been accepted at the military academy in Toledo, near Madrid. Enrique had sat for the examinations several months earlier, and had been waiting in anguish to hear. We couldn't understand how Don Miguel had received the news first. "Perhaps it helped that I put in a good word when I visited the capital," he told my mother, but later, she took pains to tell Luisa and me that she was certain Enrique had passed the exams all by himself.

Don Miguel remained eager to impress, and a couple of months later he returned to our house with another scheme. He'd heard I was still pining to play music. Why not let me use my father's old teaching piano, which remained in the room between the church and the school?

"I understand it's a little far for the boy to walk each day," Don Miguel said, lowering his eyes to me with exaggerated sympathy. "But move it to the house and your problem is solved."

My mother reminded him, "It's Father Basilio's piano now, not ours. I gave it to him to settle a debt."

Don Miguel shrugged. "The priest doesn't mind. He has his own debts to settle. Tell him I asked, and he'll assure you—he doesn't mind at all."

Mamá said, "Besides, Feliu wants to play cello. He has no interest in piano."

"You played once yourself," he said to my mother. "You could teach the boy."

"*No tengo ganas,*" she said, and I knew it was true. She no longer had the desire to have anything to do with the piano.

"It's true you don't want to play piano?"

I was staring at Don Miguel's hat, wondering why he wouldn't remove it. I didn't think he was bald. I could see oily tendrils curling in front of his ears and along his neck. If anything, he seemed unusually hairy.

My mother touched my arm. "Feliu, he's talking to you."

I startled out of my daze. "Piano? Yes—any instrument, at this point." My mother's eyes widened. She twitched her head to one side, as if she were shaking a fly away from her ear. But I had already missed the cue.

"Good. It's settled," he said, scraping the chair legs against the floor. My mother pushed herself up slowly. He took her hand and mashed his lips and nose into it. After the front door closed, she collapsed into a chair and whispered, "We'll never be rid of him now."

The next evening, as Campo Seco awoke from its late-afternoon slumber, curious onlookers flocked to our street. Men headed downhill toward the church in twos and threes, dabbing their necks with white handkerchiefs, as if just the thought of moving a piano was sufficient to make a man sweat. At the threshold of the church's side door, volunteers had coiled ropes and heaped up pulleys, creating such a profusion of snakelike piles that one might have thought our church was engaged in an exorcism.

A dozen men had rolled up their sleeves in eager sympathy, but only four men would do the bulk of the work: Don Miguel, two of his taciturn associates, and the sniffling, sensitive, thin-armed Eduardo. I'd already begun to feel compassion for my former teacher, but today, seeing Eduardo's bullied expression, I felt doubly sorry for him. He removed his dress collar, unfastened the shirt's top button, stretched his arms out, rebuttoned his shirt, and would have repeated the process again if his two fellow movers hadn't yanked him into the church.

A half hour later, just as observers were getting restless, the brown lid of the piano appeared in the doorway, then withdrew. We onlookers could hear the sound of muffled voices and a dull thud. The piano top appeared again, protruding a few inches farther this time, before a second retreat. The piano was stuck, unable to move around a tight corner. We heard a curse and a clank. Then a shiny object sailed through the doorway, landing at our feet. It was one of the silver candelabras, now bent, that had been screwed to the piano's face, above the keyboard. The men hadn't thought to remove it first.

Eduardo squeezed through the doorway, past the stuck piano. He crouched into midwife position on a lower step with his hands and one cheek pressed hard against the piano, waddling backward, trying to maintain his footing and resist the brunt of the piano's weight, while inside, Don Miguel pushed and pulled and turned, trying every angle. A leather strap around the piano's top alternately slackened and tightened, reining the piano upright when it leaned too far down the outside stairs.

For several minutes, progress continued. The counterbalance worked. Then, just at the most delicate stage in the birthing process, as the piano passed more than halfway through the church door, its lidded top began to tip earthward. Eduardo squatted more deeply, his knees turning out in a *grand plié*. But the tipping continued; the piano seemed determined to end up in his lap. At the last moment, just as three hundred kilos of wood, wire, and ivory seemed poised to pin him to the ground, he leaped sideways, sending the piano, honking like a strangled goose, down the steps and into the street.

My mother buried her eyes in her hands while Luisa patted her hip consolingly, whispering, "It only fell a little bit, Mamá." The men in the crowd looked down at the ground or up at the sky, embarrassed to have been caught witnessing such a botched moving job.

Without meeting any of our glances, Eduardo reshouldered his load and the second half of the piano slipped out effortlessly. The instrument was set down, and we all leaned forward to get the first glimpse of Don Miguel's face as he turned toward his brother, red cheeks quivering between labored puffs.

"It's just..." Eduardo stammered. "If we had...but here, if I..."

Don Miguel resettled his skewed hat and pulled the brim forward, obscuring his eyes. Then he spit into his hands, rubbed them, and grunted, "Grab the ropes."

Now that the piano had cleared the narrow doorway, the four men strapped it to a wide stretcherlike board. They counted to three before lifting, and in that long second before the piano defied gravity, I saw Eduardo Rivera's eyes survey the course ahead of them: the long and painful trek down the cobblestoned street, potholed and steep, to be followed by the even more perilous lifting of the piano, via block and tackle, over our second-story balcony. He was not the right man for the task; even the youngest boys gathered knew it. And there were a dozen heartier men eager to take his place—men who had spent countless festivals practicing for just this sort of processionary task, carrying plaster Virgins and enormous papier-mâché heads through slippery, candle-wax–spattered streets. Why couldn't Eduardo simply refuse?

As if in response to my silent thoughts, Don Miguel cleared his throat and announced, "At some point, we must all make amends. By the time this job is done, the Delargos and Riveras will be one family." I'm not sure who looked more ill at this comment: Eduardo or my mother.

During the hours ahead, the piano would be dropped several more times. It would crush two toes, dig a deep gouge into a neighbor's arched wooden door and, while rising to our balcony, chip several century-old stones off our house's street-facing wall. When it was finally in place, a man came to tune it, thanks again to Don Miguel's charitable assistance.

My mother had no interest in teaching me, so I taught myself, tackling easier pieces by Bach and Schubert and Brahms. Don Miguel invited himself over every few months, and each time I was trotted out in front of him and made to play. Everyone marveled at how quickly I had learned, how well I played. But it was like the violin—far better than nothing, but not quite right. Playing the piano was like filling up on bread and water while the smell of a neighbor's roast wafted in through the windows. It helped me to know that somewhere a cello was waiting for me; the bow, my father's gift, was proof. I took it out once each month, wiped the wooden stick with an oiled cloth, twisted the pearl-dotted adjuster that tightened the bow's horsehairs, and loosened them again before replacing the bow in its sturdy leather tube.

Over the next two years, Don Miguel attempted to court my mother. With his younger brother, Mamá had maintained a stance of polite indifference. With Don Miguel, she expressed her disdain openly. It made little difference to him. Their tepid courtship proceeded slowly, interrupted by Don Miguel's journeys to manage distant olive groves and to conduct business in Madrid. My mother breathed more freely every time he went away. "Another city, another farm—he'll turn some girl's eye," she said once.

"You're wrong," responded Tía. "He likes a challenge. You've made it clear you think you're better than him—that was your mistake."

One morning Don Miguel stopped by to let us know he was back from Madrid and to invite himself to dinner. Enrique had just begun his second year at the academy, and Percival now lived with his employer, at the olive press where he was apprenticing. For Luisa, who was nineteen, Don Miguel brought a hand mirror, its silver handle patterned with bas-relief roses.

For me, Don Miguel brought a magazine called *ABC*. The issue celebrated the anniversary of King Alfonso's marriage to Queen Victoria Eugenia, informally known as Ena. Though our King, now twenty-one years old, had wed Queen Ena a year earlier, the Spanish public was taking some time to accept Alfonso's blond bride. The granddaughter of Britain's Queen Victoria, Queen Ena had converted from her Protestant faith to Catholicism two days before the royal wedding, but that renunciation hadn't changed her reputation as a rather frosty, distinctly non-Iberian foreigner.

Luisa, Mamá, and Tía took turns passing around the magazine. Even my mother couldn't resist poring over the glossy pictures and gossipy captions, but when she flipped past them, she saw why Don Miguel had brought me the magazine and handed it back. The next piece was a profile of El Nene, who had finally shed that nickname and was now called Justo Al-Cerraz. The pianist insisted on the hyphenated version of his last name, drawing conspicuous attention to the Islamic prefix, which was part of his new mystique. His mother was said to be Moorish. Or gypsy. Or both: a distant descendant of some Moor pretending to be a gypsy following the seventeenth-century expulsion of the Moors from Spain. Though Christian, Al-Cerraz claimed he could orient himself toward Mecca even blindfolded, unless there was a piano nearby. (Wasn't there always some piano nearby?) Any stringed instrument, he said, disturbed his "magnetic energies."

In the six years since I'd heard him play, Al-Cerraz had toured briefly with a *zarzuela* company, spent a few months in the royal court of Madrid, then rededicated himself to his own musical education by briefly joining the composer Richard Strauss in Germany. The last episode had not gone well, as evidenced by Al-Cerraz's willingness to poke fun at his short-lived mentor. At the time of Al-Cerraz's visit, Strauss was still basking in the success of his *Don Quixote: Fantastic Variations on a Theme of Knightly Character*—a dissonant production full of bleating trumpets meant to sound like sheep, wind machines, and other noisy post-Wagnerian inventions. When the *ABC* reporter asked what Al-Cerraz thought of Strauss's "variations," the pianist sniped, "They are certainly fantastic. I had no idea that any musical production could have quite so many sheep. I thought I was right back in the Spanish countryside. I forgot I was listening to music at all."

Undoubtedly he was still bristling at Strauss's claim that "A Spaniard will not be the one to write great works about Spain. You are a nation of bullfighters, not composers." For as the article made clear, playing music—even playing for royalty—was no longer enough for Al-Cerraz. He wanted to compose, too.

Reading the article, I didn't sympathize with Al-Cerraz. I had my own miseries to contemplate. I was young, yes, but not so young in a country where the King himself was still learning to shave. At twenty-five, Al-Cerraz was older than our monarch, but look how much he had done! Here he was, embarking on a second career. I hadn't even started my first.

This notion of a profession was no small thing, as my mother's repeated comments had made clear. My leg was as weak as ever. I'd never be able to follow Enrique's footsteps into the army, or Percival's path into the laborious agricultural trades. Recently, setting her sights lower, Mamá had tried apprenticing me to a shoemaker, but even he had deemed me unworthy. My fingers were too clumsy, the shoemaker said, adding, "A good thing you have taught him numbers and history so well, Doña. Perhaps he will serve as his father did, as an inspector or diplomat. But as for a real trade, he is hopeless."

At my age, Al-Cerraz had been in demand all over the world. I was not in demand anywhere, except perhaps at home, where I was expected to empty chamber-pots and help pull my aunt out of bed when her joints stiffened.

Lost in melancholy, I continued to stare at Al-Cerraz's photograph. I didn't notice Luisa sneaking up behind my chair until she pawed the magazine out of my hands. I grabbed at it, and the pages tore. A shredded slip of paper—showing Al-Cerraz's wide fingers clutching a cigar—fluttered down upon the ripped face of Queen Ena, her pale, sorrowful eyes separated from her thin and colorless Victorian lips. Furious, I jumped up and retrieved Luisa's new silver mirror from the dining-room table. I held it over my head, tossing it lightly from hand to hand.

"Give it back!" my sister howled, as I made the mirror sail in widening daredevil arcs.

"Look at you," she laughed, changing tactics. "You're such a child. You're probably afraid to look into that mirror. You know you'd break it."

I tilted my face toward the ceiling, closed my eyes, and kept tossing.

"Really, Feliu. Just look. You look like Papá." She feigned tenderness.

I sneaked a glance at her through slitted eyes, and saw her own eyes narrowing, while her lips curled into a smirk. "Except that you're shorter. And skinnier. And by the time he'd lost his hair, he had a mustache."

I stopped, mirror gripped in one fist. Luisa had found my sore spot. I'd been born with a high forehead and a receding hairline; when I was worried, or concentrating, with my eyes slitted and lips pursed, my mother said my face looked like the bottom of an orange.

I heard Mamá and Tía on the stairs, ushering Don Miguel up the narrow staircase from the street. Frantic to pick up the shredded magazine before Don Miguel saw it, I rushed to the table and slammed the mirror down, cracking it. Luisa burst into tears just as Don Miguel appeared, cradling a white box in his arms.

Mamá didn't even notice the mirror. She was arguing with Don Miguel about the box. "Just open it," he said, and Tía echoed him, pushing it in front of Mamá's face. Mamá relented and unfolded a pale yellow dress, which she lifted halfheartedly to her shoulders.

"*Qué guapa!*" Tía crooned.

"Put it on," Don Miguel said. My mother hadn't worn anything but black since the day at the train station—the day my father's remains did not arrive, the day of the bow. Now she hung her head as Don Miguel persisted, his voice rising. When Mamá looked up, finally, I could see her dark brown eyes swimming behind barely contained tears.

Tía, uncharacteristically animated, took control of the room. She hobbled between Don Miguel, my mother and me, in a triangular trajectory that was both determined and unsteady, like that of a ship captain crossing a deck in a storm. While Luisa settled to sulk in a corner of the room, Tía poured a grass-colored liqueur for Don Miguel and pressed it into his hands. She flapped her arms toward the staircase, gesturing to the bedrooms above, where my mother was again commanded to change into the new dress. Ignoring the broken mirror, she pushed me toward the piano. "Play! Play!" she croaked, and then more softly, "It will bring peace." My mother disappeared up the steps, each footfall slower than the last. All of us strained to hear her reach the landing and close the bedroom door behind her.

Don Miguel gulped the liqueur with one swift tilt of his head. Tía, who had reentered the room with a tray of salt-encrusted sardines and bread, wheeled back toward the kitchen and returned with the liqueur bottle to refill his glass. He tossed back the second glass. Tía looked relieved when he reached out and took the whole bottle, saving her from the task of anticipating his desires. He drained his third glass of liqueur, and set both glass and bottle down. Then he reached to remove his hat.

Performed by any other man, it would have been an empty gesture. But for Don Miguel, it was a ritual. He fingered the hat brim, all the way around. With the other hand, he batted at the small table next to his chair, whisking away any invisible dust. Then he lifted his hat off and set it aside. That was it—no surprises beneath it after all, just thick dark hair, slightly flattened—and yet the gesture and what it might herald made my stomach knot.

Swinging around, I started to play. But above my leaden fingerings, I could hear Don Miguel shift restlessly.

"Is she coming?" he called out to Tía.

"*Cierto, cierto*," she called back from the kitchen.

I reached the end of the piece and started the repeat.

"Why isn't she down here?" he called again, louder.

Tía reentered the room. "She must be doing her hair." She managed a dry laugh that sounded like a cough. "It's never good to rush a lady, you know."

I played a second minuet—"Such happy music! Don Miguel, doesn't Feliu play wonderfully now?"—and a third, and still Mamá had not returned to join us in her new yellow dress. Her new yellow *betrothal* dress, I thought, my mind fixing on the word that had appeared a dozen times in the gossipy captions of *ABC Magazine*.

At least I had an excuse to turn away. Luisa watched the bottle gradually empty, and Don Miguel's face redden, his voice slurring with increasing fury. "Why isn't she coming?"

Tía flattered and cajoled, pressing more food into his hands to counter the alcohol's effects.

"That day with my brother, she showed her true colors," Don Miguel said. "She has no respect for this community."

"She's had difficulties," Tía countered.

"She shouldn't have hit a man in public. Do you know how that looks? Six years, and my brother still hasn't married. What woman would respect him now?"

"It's a shame, *sí, sí,*" Tía said. But her airy ramblings didn't soothe him.

"Someone should teach her a lesson."

I had been playing softly, all the better to eavesdrop, but now I pounded on the keys. I did not want to hear more. I wanted to vanish inside the music, to lose myself the way I'd lost myself listening to El Nene's cellist. But the piano was not my instrument. Playing it, I could hide, but I could not disappear.

The song ended; as I racked my mind for another, I heard Don Miguel's chair move. I exhaled with relief, thinking he was rising to leave. He headed toward the staircase, and I waited to hear his footsteps descend. Instead, he climbed—toward the third floor, toward my mother.

"Don Miguel, I'll go with you," Tía said.

He grunted one word: "Stay."

Luisa whispered, "Feliu, what is he doing?"

Outside of marriage, men and women didn't visit in bedrooms or within sight of any bed. For this reason, we wouldn't have professional nurses in Spain for another decade, not counting a few poorly trained nuns. Death, it seemed, was preferable to dishonor.

I heard Don Miguel rap three times on the door over our heads, echoed by Tía's distressed hobble. I heard my mother shout through the door: "I don't want to see you!"

"This door is locked," Don Miguel called down to us. "Someone bring the key."

No one moved. Don Miguel repeated his demand. I started to stand, pushing myself up from the piano bench.

"Good, Feliu," Tía whispered hoarsely. "You bring him the key. It's the black one in the top drawer, in the kitchen."

"I'm not bringing him the key," I whispered back.

But I had stood up. Why? I bit my lip and said, "I'm going to help her."

Don Miguel was pounding on the bedroom door.

"Yes," Luisa said. "Please, Feliu. Hurry."

"You can't help her," Tía whispered.

"We can throw him out," I said.

"He's an important man in town...."

"We'll leave," Luisa said. "We'll move to another town!"

"Every town is like this town," Tía said, no longer caustic, suddenly and unnervingly calm. "This was meant to happen. You'll see. It's better this way."

She limped toward the kitchen and returned with the black skeleton key clutched in her bony fist. Luisa called out to her a final time but she continued slowly up the steps. I hadn't given up—I was thinking hard, trying to sort things out, wishing that Enrique were home. But I did not come to any decision. I did not act. I did not follow my heart. Perhaps I lost a piece of it then and there.

We heard Mamá shout through the closed door above us, *"No pasará!"* Which meant, in that economical way that has no English equivalent, both *He won't come in,* and *It won't happen.* Again and again she shouted the phrase, imprinting it in my mind. Decades later, I'd hear nearly the same words, said to a slightly different purpose: *No pasarán—They will not pass.* They were futile words, on both occasions. Don Miguel did enter, and they did pass, the fascist Nationalists who would end up ruling Spain. The worst part for Mamá, I imagine, was that her own loved ones were accomplices.

We heard the door swing open, and once more my mother shouted *"No pasará!"* Then all was quiet.

Tía reappeared, dug her fingers into my shoulder, and said, "Play now and play loud. For your sister."

For a moment I did not understand, until the sounds started above us, worse sounds than the shouting. Then I did understand, and I began to play, hating the fact that music couldn't stop what was happening upstairs, only drown it out.

I couldn't sleep that night. My mother hadn't come out of the room since Don Miguel had left; only Tía had seen her. Every time the wind blew against the house or the floor creaked, I thought it was Don Miguel coming back. I kept thinking of the sounds I'd heard from upstairs and the songs I'd pounded out on the piano, to cover the other sounds.

An hour before dawn, I sneaked into the bedroom Mamá and Tía shared, slid the Bible out of my mother's nightstand drawer, pulled out the letters inside, and tiptoed downstairs to the kitchen, to examine them by candlelight. The letters were both dog-eared and smudged, which surprised me. I could imagine my mother reading and rereading the first one from my father, which bore the stamp of the customs service, and the 1898 date. But I was surprised to see she had equally worn the second. Dark stains tattooed its yellowed, softened surface. Opening it, I nearly ripped the letter in three parts at the crease lines, where it had been folded and unfolded countless times. Wax had dripped onto the paper near Al-Cerraz's self-caricature.

How could it be that my mother had worn this letter to its present state, without ever letting me know that she had taken its brief message and its grand possibilities into serious consideration? Evidently she had deliberated for years, paralyzed by anxiety and pessimism. Worse than disregarding the letter, she had worried it nearly to shreds, unable to make any decision at all. We were not so different, she and I.

I heard a whisper at my shoulder: "Careful, Feliu. Don't tear it. We're going to need that letter now."

I jumped, nearly knocking over the candlestick. Turning, I saw her face, half-illuminated, half in shadow. I was afraid to look, but when I did, I found with great relief that there were no bruises or physical marks. It helped me to pretend that everything was going to be better, that we weren't simply running away from Campo Seco, but running toward a future that had awaited me all along.

PART II

~

Barcelona

1907

CHAPTER

~ 4 ~

"And how many years has he played?" Don José asked my mother after we had presented Al-Cerraz's letter at the Barcelona Conservatory.

"Violin, two years—a fast learner, even without a good teacher. Piano, about the same. His father—"

The professor interrupted. "No, Señora, how long has he played the violoncello?"

"He has not, sir, but he has great desire to learn."

Don José muttered under his breath.

"It's a rare instrument," my mother said. "He hasn't had the opportunity...."

"Rare? If only," he said, glancing toward the half-circle of students assembled before him. One boy, about my age, tapped his bow against his knee. A girl yawned.

"I don't accept beginners," Don José said. Then, noting my mother's crestfallen expression, "But you've come a long way. I can provide the name of a tutor who can give your son private lessons."

He took a pencil from the music stand nearest him and withdrew a slip of paper from his jacket pocket.

"But where would Feliu live? We have no family here in the city. We were looking for a full-time school, perhaps a stipend—"

"Your son has demonstrated no ability. If I may be frank, he is too old to begin a new instrument."

"Too old? He's only fourteen."

"I have more skilled student cellists than the entire world can employ. Perhaps you can find some trade for him before he is a burden to you and your husband."

"My husband is deceased."

"My condolences," Don José said, pausing to write quickly on the slip of paper and hand it my mother. "Students await me."

My mother shuffled despondently along the Ramblas, Barcelona's broad main boulevard. I should have been dejected, too. But the city radiated energy and promise. More was happening here between two divided lanes of traffic than in our entire village. A policeman haggled with two wide-hipped women who gripped their burgundy-colored skirts in defiance, baring their ankles as they sashayed toward the waterfront. Knots of people clogged the walkways—here, a group of older men spilling out of a narrow bar, enveloped in cigarette smoke; there, a flock of younger men competing for a pretty flower-seller's attention. A boy plucked an orange from the bottom of a fruit pyramid and ran shrieking from the avalanche. In Campo Seco, the vendor would have known the boy's name, perhaps would have chased him down the street. But here, with a half dozen customers waiting, the vendor simply gestured for his younger assistant to chase the rolling oranges while he reached out a hand to steady the swinging scale.

Light filtered through the plane trees overhead, and beneath the green canopy, stacks of golden cages lined the walkway, forming a sun-dappled tunnel that blocked the views of carriage traffic left and right. Within those cages, a hundred yellow birds sang.

"They love music here, I know it!" I shouted to my mother, but my words were swallowed by the raucous birdsong.

Past the cages, we found ourselves funneled between rows of finished paintings. Mamá apologized every few steps, as if trespassing through someone's private studio; but there was no other way to pass. We threaded our way through mazes of café tables, and I ducked just in time to avoid colliding with a tray billowing with garlic-scented steam. Rubbery pink tentacles overflowed the sides of diners' plates. I tugged on my mother's arm. "*Calamar!*" she explained over her shoulder, barely sidestepping a second waiter approaching from the side. She started to apologize, then stopped at the sight of him. From the waist up, he was dashing: white ruffled shirt, black bow tie, tray balanced on one upturned hand. From the waist down, he was dressed as a horse, a costume complete with head and bushy tail swinging loosely from threadbare suspenders.

"*Paella?*" he droned, citing the day's specials. "*Gambas al ajillo? Biftec?*"

I thought his appearance was spectacular, but Mamá recoiled, saying "No, no," as she quickened her step.

We were carrying everything we'd packed hastily that morning in Campo Seco. The air under the plane trees smelled sweet and green, but the humid press of bodies all around us was harder to bear than Campo Seco's dry heat. The Ramblas was like a river, its current at midday in full force. Newspaper stands and café tables were like boulders in the stream, serving only to quicken the flow of people trying to get past them. Mamá's bag crashed into a pram, provoking a litany of insults. I paused to set down the suitcases, and a man bumped into me from behind. I was still muttering apologies when a woman's swinging arm clipped my shoulder. Leaning over to reshoulder a bag, my mother tripped over her own dragging skirt hem. Tearing it, she cried out, "Is there nowhere to sit?"

"Of course there is," a man said from behind us, and shoveled my mother into a chair mere steps away from the pedestrian flow. He set before her a goblet as big as a fishbowl, filled with ruby-colored liquid and bobbing fruit peels of yellow, orange, and green.

Mamá glanced around, pulling her bags closer to her feet as I slipped into the chair next to her. "We don't want to eat," she said.

"No menu?" the man said. "That's fine. I'll be back."

"Muy amable," she whispered as he walked away, setting her lips into an approximation of confidence.

"What is that?" I asked, pointing to the goblet.

"I'm not sure. Don't touch it."

Mamá had just opened her fan when the man appeared again, slid a slip of paper under the goblet's stem, and disappeared. Mamá pulled it out and studied it. "But I didn't ask for this!" A second waiter appeared, his hand extended. To her explanation of the misunderstanding and her protest that she hadn't taken a single sip, he merely retied his apron strings and stared into the distance, signaling over his head with one finger. From across the Ramblas, the same policeman we'd seen earlier nodded briskly and stepped toward the street, pausing for a horse-drawn cab to pass.

My mother slammed down her fan, upsetting the glass, and sending a spray of red liquid across her torn dress. We both jumped up. "Fine—take it!" Mamá yelled and fumbled in her handbag for three coins that she pushed into the bored waiter's hand.

We were a block east, swept by the Ramblas's ceaseless current, before she turned to me. "Two days' grocery money—gone. And you know the worst of it, Feliu? I'm even thirstier than before." Under her breath she added, "It's the thing I hate most about cities."

"What?"

"The way they make you want what you didn't even know you should want. The way they make you crave what you can't have."

But I haven't explained about our abrupt departure that morning from Campo Seco, or how it came to be that our world was split in two, with Mamá and me on one side, Luisa and Tía on the other. Tía had expected the previous day's nightmare to yield an honor-salvaging wedding to Don Miguel. Even as we'd kissed her dry cheeks and promised to write soon, she'd refused to acknowledge that we were leaving. Luisa understood that someone had to stay with Tía, and the big city was no place for a girl—especially when we had no idea where we'd sleep. But she seemed to believe Mamá when she said she'd be back soon, even as Mamá packed up her silver candlesticks, two lace-edged tablecloths, and a rolled tapestry inherited from her parents.

In our town, Mamá had seemed eminently worldly, but here in Barcelona, no one would call Mamá "Doña." Though she had visited this city in her youth, and traveled to other places besides—Cuba, Cádiz, Madrid—the passage of years had diminished her confidence. In Barcelona, Mamá did not know where to rest, how to demand good service, or how to interpret the directions given us by lethargic cigarette-sellers and apathetic street-sweepers. As we wandered the boulevards and alleys looking for the address of the tutor Don José had recommended, strangers jostled her and cast disparaging glances at her country clothes. Every time she paused at an intersection, lost and weary, she seemed a little smaller, her head no higher than the spoked wooden wheels of the endless wagons and carriages groaning along the narrow, traffic-choked streets.

We finally found the home of the tutor along a side street that reeked of rotting shrimp, urine, and other alley smells against which Mamá and I stiffened our faces, each hoping to disguise our repulsion from the other. The ground-floor tenant, an old woman with rounded shoulders and a crooked spine, heard us slapping our hands against the locked wrought-iron gate.

"Alberto Mendizábal?" she mumbled, indicating the stairs. "He doesn't get many visitors."

The marble steps leading up the cool, unlit stairs hinted at elegance, but each slippery step had been rounded by the passage of countless feet, and unswept dirt and debris darkened the corners of the landings.

In response to several uncertain bouts of knocking, Mendizábal opened his own door, wearing a baggy cardigan so loosely woven I could make out his grayish white shirt between the gaping holes. He was unshaven, the silver stubble at his jaw a shade lighter than his close-cropped gray hair. Below his eyes sagged pillows of yellow-speckled skin. When he smiled, his heavily lidded eyes closed entirely.

"Call me Alberto," he said, neglecting to take my offered hand. "I have no use for titles."

Alberto listened to our story about visiting the conservatory and squinted at Al-Cerraz's introductory letter. "You think this city should welcome you just because of your name?"

I stared at him blankly. By now I knew the story of my birth and misnaming, but I couldn't see what it had to do with my present circumstance.

"Aníbal," said the tutor emphatically. "The great man who led his army of elephants against the Romans. His father was Hamilcar Barca, the founder of Barcelona. Doesn't anyone read history anymore?"

I summoned my confidence and said, "I don't know about conquering, but I know that with a bow in my hand, I don't fear anything."

"A fighter—good. In this town, an artist has to fight, just to be heard above the explosions."

Noticing my raised eyebrows, he added, "City of Bombs—you know that's what they call Barcelona? At least once a year the Ramblas is filled with smoke. Between that and church burnings, the city is re-born. It isn't a bad thing, necessarily. There are some nice public plazas where cathedrals once stood."

Mamá lifted her chin and let her eyes sweep around the apartment in a studied display of unconcern.

"If city life frightens you, turn right back around," Alberto said. "Get on the train, while the tracks are still there."

Alberto rocked back on his heels, considering us. Then, with a sigh, he relented. "Oh, it's not bad. Too quiet, actually. Come in; sit down. We have much to discuss."

That afternoon, Alberto invited me to become his student. His wife had passed away some years before, and his daughter had married and moved to Valencia, so he offered to rent a room to us as well, the first payment deferred until Mamá found local employment. In bed that night, Mamá whispered, "He is an intellectual and an anarchist. But he is harmless enough. At least he is cheap."

The next morning, Mamá and I woke early. We ate some rolls left from the previous day's train trip, and drank some stale water from our wicker-wrapped jug. My eyes flitted to the kettle, but Mamá said, "Wait until it's offered." Alberto was nowhere to be seen.

We proceeded to the main parlor to wait for him. Several heavy, leather-upholstered armchairs lined one wall, but they were filled with books and clothes. Mamá's eyes lit up when she spotted missing buttons on two wadded shirts. She went to fetch her sewing bag, grateful for something to do, and a reason to move the shirts off the chair so she could sit. I, meanwhile, perused the titles on the bookshelves—Pío Baroja, Unamuno, the ubiquitous Cervantes, and many names I didn't recognize at all. Finally, I lifted the lid on the grand piano and pressed down on one of the white keys. To my astonishment, there was no sound. I tried a few more keys and then banged out a chord: nothing.

"Broken," Alberto said as he entered the room, coughing. "And scavenged for parts. But for dinner parties, it seats six or more—with the lid closed, of course."

He wore the same shirt and cardigan sweater as the day before, over baggy pajama bottoms that Mamá took pains not to notice.

"This bow of yours, let me see it." I expected him to marvel at the fine wood, puzzle over the bow's origins, ask me more about my father.

Instead he said simply, "It's picked up oil and dirt, as if it's been toyed with too often."

Mamá looked at me. I looked down at my feet.

"That's our first subject: respect for the tools of our trade," Alberto continued. "I know carpenters who take better care of their hammers than you've taken care of this bow. When do you plan to rehair it?"

Mamá consulted with him about the bow as best she could while keeping her face tipped up, away from his improperly attired lower half. Then she slipped out the door with the bow, looking relieved to have an errand to do.

I expected our lesson to start in earnest now, but it did not. Alberto went back to his bedroom. I was left with a mute piano and a wall full of Spanish literature. I read awhile, then penned a long and lonely letter to Enrique, the only person I trusted to interpret in a positive light everything that had happened so far.

The second day, Alberto talked about proper left-hand position. He demonstrated how to place the fingers on a cello's neck, using a broomstick and corks wedged between my fingers. If a cork slipped as I moved my stiff hand up and down the stick, then I was not maintaining the proper finger intervals. But Alberto had not demonstrated anything on a real instrument. I hoped his cello hadn't suffered the same indignities as his piano.

Later that morning, as my mother was slipping out the front door with her bag of silver and linen, en route to a pawnshop, he asked her, "When are you going to purchase an instrument for the boy?"

"He can't share yours? At least in the beginning?"

"Oh, no. Mine's in a sorry state."

That night, as I lay on the floor next to my mother's narrow bed, I whispered, "Are we certain Alberto knows how to play the cello?"

"Don José wouldn't have recommended him otherwise."

"But what kind of musician doesn't play his instrument anymore?"

My mother didn't answer, but I sensed her body go rigid beneath the stiff sheets.

"If I don't hear or play a cello soon, I might as well be home in Campo Seco. At least there, I played the piano every day. Here I play only a broomstick."

"Do you want to go back?"

"Of course not," I said. "Do you?"

"Maybe," she said quietly.

"Even though it's not safe?"

"It's my home." She started to sigh, then caught herself and modulated the exhalation into an exaggerated yawn. "We'll make the best of things, for now. Tomorrow I will talk to the man who rehaired your bow. He knows all the music shops nearby. Perhaps he can help us." She rolled away from me then, but I could still sense her alert wakefulness, even in the dark.

The third day, Alberto went to the kitchen and returned with a grease-spotted corner of butcher's paper. On the back he scrawled a list and handed it to my mother. She hesitated before taking it, and I could see her making fretful mental calculations.

"Pedagogical supplies," he explained to me after she left. Noting my blank expression, he added, "Beginners' music, scales and études— that sort of thing."

Still wearing his pajama bottoms, he spent the morning lecturing me. After explaining how limited the cello repertoire was, compared to the piano or violin, he traced the incremental advances of the instrument from the baroque chamber sonata through eighteenth-century Italy, France, and Germany, pacing the room slowly. At Bach he stopped, his back to me. "Too much to say. We'll come back to him when you are ready."

Beethoven came next, and here his step quickened. Then Brahms—did I know he'd played cello as a child? Lalo, Saint-Saëns,

Chopin: "His final sonata, dedicated to a cellist! Let me hum it for you, if I can."

And then, he said, consider Rachmaninov, who just six years ago had introduced a new sonata in which the cello really carried the melodies—"You haven't heard the scherzo? You haven't heard of *Rachmaninov?*" I couldn't tell him I hadn't heard of more than half the composers he'd named. Much as I feared that Alberto would turn out to be a fraud, I was even more afraid he'd discover *my* fraudulence. I knew nothing about the cello repertoire.

But self-doubt didn't stifle my appetite. As Alberto talked and whistled and finally sang, my stomach grumbled with mounting insistence, until my new tutor finally paused to say absentmindedly, "Yes— we should eat something," as if he'd been waiting days for someone to help him reach that conclusion.

Since we'd moved in, Mamá had tackled the mess in Alberto's kitchen, clearing away stacks of dirty plates and black-bottomed cups. That morning, Señora Pacheco, the old lady from downstairs, had dropped off some meat and produce, which she purchased for him twice weekly, saving him the trouble of going out. Instead of cooking, though, Alberto shaved and changed into a fresh, collarless shirt and shapeless jacket, and stood by the door, his hand on the knob. He cleared his throat a few times, then finally said, "Well? Are you coming?"

I did not know this was a momentous occasion for him. It seemed a momentous enough occasion for me. I hadn't left Alberto's building in three days. As it turned out, he hadn't left it in three weeks. He wasn't truly phobic of the outside world, only melancholic, we would have called it then.

Alberto took me around the corner to a café. At a crowded table in the rear, surrounded by mirrors, five men in wool watch-caps and berets hailed my tutor and slapped me on the back and ordered me a shot of anisette in a frosted shot-glass that burned my fingers. Talk quickly turned to politics—"It usually does," Alberto said with a puffy-eyed wink. But when the conversation lagged, a burly, dark-skinned man named Cesar said, "We thought your maestro was rotting in a hospital room somewhere, or in some jail. It looks like you've resurrected him."

I shrugged and smiled.

"So you want to be like your teacher? Play where he played, that sort of thing?"

I shrugged again. "I don't know where he played."

"Doesn't know where he played!" howled a thin man named Ramón, whose too-short jacket exposed bony wrists and hands covered with shiny ribbonlike scars.

"The perfect match," laughed Cesar. "A student who doesn't ask too many questions and a maestro who doesn't like to answer them."

It hadn't occurred to me to ask any questions. A boy didn't ask a grown man for his credentials. I tried to look away, to avoid all the laughing men's stares, but with the mirrors all around us, I couldn't evade anyone's stare, even my own. Three versions of my own boyish face—round cheeks, high forehead—taunted me from all directions.

"You were born when?" Ramón asked.

"December 29."

Ramón found this hilarious. Still laughing, he shoveled a handful of almonds into his mouth. When he chewed, I could see the bones moving at his temple and in the shadowy depression between his jaw and ear.

"The year, boy," he said as he scooped another handful of nuts. "Ninety-four? Ninety-five?"

"Eighteen ninety-two," I said.

"He's not young, we're just old," Cesar said, in a voice that was friendlier than the others'. "We're still arguing about things that happened before he could walk."

I looked to Alberto, but his face was placidly unrevealing, his eyes twinkling above their pouchy bags.

We ordered *bocadillos* filled with potato omelet. Ramón bought me a second anisette. The thick sweet liquid went down easily, but within minutes my head was spinning. The mirrored reflections all around us—on the ceiling, behind our table and behind the bar—amplified my dizziness.

Alberto must have noticed my expression. "Time to get this one home. Lessons in the morning," he said—though it was scarcely midday now.

We'd all been wedged around the back table, so our exit was cause for a deep chorus of shuffling, chair dragging and table bumping as we worked our way free. Ramón knocked his ebony-handled cane onto the floor, and when I bent to retrieve it, his face met mine.

"If it's lessons you want, you should visit the wax museum three blocks from here. Plenty to learn about the world, there."

Cesar laughed and added with a sneer, "The whole neighborhood will teach you a thing or two."

On the way home I asked Alberto about Ramón's hands.

"He was an oboist, before his hands were burned. They're so tight now, he can't flex the fingers properly."

"That's terrible."

Alberto stiffened at the note of sympathy in my voice. "Never mind—it's nothing he didn't deserve. It's nothing *most* of us don't deserve."

I could tell from his tone that I shouldn't ask anything more. A block later, he patted me on the back once and spoke as if there'd been no interruption. "We all get inflexible with age. Not just our fingers, but our attitudes. Music is the easy part, Feliu. It's everything else that's hard."

I didn't see much of my mother that first week. When she wasn't spending the last of our money on musical necessities, she was looking for work. Returning from either kind of task, her face was knit with worry. Everything cost so much here, and her original plan—to find some piecemeal commission, sewing at home—had yet to produce any income. Even on our first Sunday, when nearly everything was closed, she left the apartment early, directing me to go to church with Alberto while she vanished in the opposite direction.

Alberto laughed when I suggested we go to Mass together. He said he was not a churchgoer, but he directed me toward the nearest house of worship and I walked there alone, obeying my mother almost without thinking. Still, I had no desire to go inside. I loitered around the edges, watching other unescorted children my age from the corner of my eye. One boy sang near the church entrance. I watched for an hour as his upturned cap filled with a dozen coins. After he left, I hurried to the same spot. I'd never sung at home, but a new city seemed to make new expressions of self possible, and now I began to belt out one of the Italian songs favored by Father Basilio's defunct choir. I had no cap, so I removed my shoes and set them in front of me. Mass ended, families flowed outward, and a few coins landed in one shoe. The thrill of my success ignited me, and I sang louder, calling up any of the fragments I could remember from Enrique's nighttime singing. With a satisfying tinkle, more coins landed on top of the first few.

A number of younger children—some with ragged clothes and bare feet—loitered around the plaza, watching me. Feeling proud of my own rapidly developing street savvy, I emptied the filling shoe into my pocket, so that the layer of silver wouldn't attract too much attention. Then I placed the empty shoe back on the ground and began to sing again, thinking of how I'd spend my money. Perhaps I would go to the wax museum, as Alberto's friend had suggested. Perhaps I could take my mother out for an elegant lunch. Or better yet—to the opera. The sprawling Gran Teatro del Liceo was only blocks from Alberto's house, its glittering chandeliers and green-and-gold columns a beacon along one of the Ramblas's busiest intersections.

Just as I was envisioning Mamá and me dressed for an evening out, strolling the boulevard arm in arm, a blur of motion caught my eye. One of the young waifs had darted forward, snagged both my shoes, and disappeared around the corner. I stood, dumbfounded, jangling the silver in my pocket as I realized he'd never wanted the coins after all.

When I got to the apartment, Alberto greeted me at the door. Behind him I could see Mamá, still wearing her coat and head scarf.

Alberto hurried me inside. "Come see what your mother brought you."

But Mamá's face fell when she saw my shoeless feet.

"You lost them?"

"They were stolen!"

"Off your feet?"

"Next to my feet."

"But why weren't you wearing them?"

"I was singing. For coins."

"Begging?" It came out as a shriek.

Alberto touched my mother's arm, but she pulled away sharply.

"I earned a little money—"

"Not enough to buy shoes, I'm sure. Feliu—we can't afford to buy you new shoes."

"It's all right," Alberto tried to intervene.

"I just spent the last of what I had," my mother wailed. Burying her forehead in her hands, she dislodged the scarf. It slid onto her shoulders, revealing a ragged bob that had been cut just below her ears.

"Mamá, your hair!"

"We shouldn't have come to Barcelona," she said under her breath.

Alberto stepped between us expertly, mumbling into his chest, "If it's not the fashion yet, it will soon be." Then he turned and, with hands on my shoulders, guided me away. I heard my mother's feet on the stairs, the sound of fading sobs.

Alberto marched me into the living room, where I expected him to lecture me. Instead, he spun me around three times playfully, and pointed. There, in the opposite corner, sat a cello. It was not caramel-colored like Emil Duarte's. This one had an olive cast, a few scratches near the bridge, a chip in the scroll-shaped head, and some dark putty near the retractable endpin, to keep it from falling out. It was beautiful.

"This is what she spent her last money on?"

"What did you think?"

"I thought she spent it on that hairstyle."

"No, *hijo,* she sold her hair to a wigmaker. And that was only for the first rental payment. She starts a new job tomorrow to pay for the rest." He pushed me toward the cello. "Go. Pick it up."

"She looks terrible." My voice was unsteady.

"Hair grows."

"How fast?"

"Your first cello!"

"Tell me—when will her hair be long again?"

"I don't know. A centimeter a month. Two years, maybe, and it will be well past her shoulders."

"Then that's how long I'm studying with you."

"You're in no position—"

"After that, I will audition for Don José, and I will be accepted into his school. Mamá will look decent enough to be seen again."

"She can be seen now."

"By people who matter," I spat out the words, and then wiped my nose on my sleeve. "By family, I mean. By friends."

"So you're just as eager to send her back home, whether or not it's a good idea."

It bothered me that my mother already felt close enough to Alberto to confide our personal problems, including, evidently, the real reason we'd fled Campo Seco.

"Two years," I repeated, hoping for my sake I'd have at least that much time.

"*Está bien*," Alberto replied. "Then we have no time to waste."

CHAPTER

~ 5 ~

After the cello came, my world both shrank and brightened, like a piece of wood burning down into red-hot coal. I woke, for the first time in my entire life, knowing exactly what I needed to do. Never mind the unexplored city all around me. Home became that circle of space around my chair, its radius defined by the movement of my bowing arm. By midday, the nerves in my tailbone tingled. After five to seven hours of sitting at the edge of the chair, it hurt to stand up, but the electric jolts down my spine told me I had done my best and could forgive myself for not being able to do more.

Once, on the Ramblas, in a vendor's trunk, I saw a sepia-toned picture showing three men smoking opium, each of them lost in his own dreamy cloud. That's how I must have looked during my first days with the cello. I was no more eager to leave Alberto's parlor than those smokers were to leave their Chinese den. No one needed to urge me to practice, then or at any later point in my life.

Alberto seemed equally enlivened to find himself teaching again. The music seemed to draw him from wherever he was in the apartment. He would enter the living room to shower me with directions, then exit the room backward, watching me until the last possible moment. Minutes later, he'd reappear with bread crumbs on his unshaved jaw and a knife in one hand, talking with his mouth full, delivering the correction that could not wait. He would stand to one side, retracting from my view, before pouncing on me again, his outstretched hands so close to the cello's neck that I thought he was going to pull it away and begin playing it himself. But he never did. Nodding and clapping and waving his arms, he orbited around me. Was it my fault that I began to feel like the center of the universe?

It was a good thing for both of us that my energy always outlasted his. Near the end of each morning session, when the sun's rays illumined our slot-canyon street for a precious hour or so, I would spot him lounging on the balcony at the parlor's far end, a book on his chest, stubbled cheeks glinting. He left the double doors open, so that the sounds of people and horses passing, bottles clanking, and wagon tailgates slamming blended with my études. Once I was immersed in a challenging piece of music, I didn't hear them at all.

I couldn't have played well in the beginning. I'm equally sure that it didn't matter. Every virginal sensation was sublime: the friction of the minutely ridged strings against my fingers, the silkiness of the black fingerboard beneath, the first catch of the well-rosined bow against the string, the vibration of the instrument between my knees. My senses were so overloaded that I couldn't objectively hear myself play. I just knew how it felt every time a well-pitched note resonated through the cello's body and into mine: like an itch being scratched. Except the itch never went away. Every day, in fact, it grew stronger. Sometimes, I couldn't get to sleep at night because I couldn't silence the music in my head. Lavender bruises stippled my inner knees, where I'd clenched the cello too tightly. My right shoulder throbbed and the fingers on my left hand twitched. But I invited these insomniac spells. I knew my mind and body were making up for lost time.

Señor Rivera, my violin teacher, had emphasized mastery of the first position, each finger corresponding to a single note, with slight shifts forward and back for sharps and flats. Once I had my own cello,

Alberto dispensed with the corks and had me playing all over the fingerboard. It was his feeling that young players became fearful of the cello's highest notes and advanced positions, closer to the bridge, only because they typically learn those perilous notes last. The same note could be played with any finger, depending on where the hand was positioned; the same note could also be played on many places all over the cello, always with a slightly different tone. "It's a problem to solve," he'd say. "Your problem. Doesn't that feel wonderful? Isn't it amazing how simple wood and wire and hair can produce better riddles than an Egyptian sphinx?"

I had my own less-philosophical questions. I tried asking him, "Am I any good?"

He wouldn't answer me directly, even when I baited him with self-deprecating remarks: "Maybe I'm terrible, Alberto. Maybe I can't play at all."

He'd reply, "Does it sound terrible? Do you feel terrible when you play? No audience is going to answer that question for you, past the novice stage."

I heard his remark as a tentative compliment—evidently, I was no longer a novice. What I did not hear was what Alberto truly meant: that I had to trust myself, had to know myself. An artist was destined to judge himself the most harshly. An artist could easily end up alone.

If my shoulders or left hand tightened up, he ordered me to stop playing, drape my arms over the fingerboard down the face of the cello, toward the bridge, and simply cradle the instrument. "See? You can reach every part. These distances that feel so vast when we're nervous aren't large distances at all. Don't look—just feel your way and listen. It's easier to play the cello than to scratch your own back. If it doesn't feel easy, you're doing something wrong."

He encouraged me to use loose fingers, to reach forward or back with a relaxed left hand. But his unorthodoxy had its limits. Mixed into

his liberated style were traces of the stiffer nineteenth-century tech-
niques he himself had been taught. "Get that elbow down," he said
whenever my bowing arm floated too far away from my side. "Stop
stabbing at the air."

I listened to him as best I could, not because I feared him, but just
the opposite—because I trusted him. Unlike Señor Rivera, he wanted
nothing from me and did not goad me with any kind of future visions,
glorious or doomed. But it was difficult. Sometimes, I slipped away and
did not hear him until his soft voice had escalated to a grumble. Out of
the corner of one eye, I would see his hand go up, gesturing me to stop
playing mid-measure; but I could not stop, not until I'd finished the musical phrase. And even then, I would have preferred to finish the entire
piece. As the months wore on, I grew accustomed to ignoring him, to
indulging my own desire to enter that tunnel of light that appeared
when the music was going well. I could fall into that light and block out
everything.

Once I looked around mid-lesson and could not find Alberto at all.
I remembered that he had been waving at me, calling out to me about
dynamics, but now I could not find him. The balcony was empty. I
hadn't heard the front door close. Yet it had—with a slam, he told me
later. In a pique, he had left for the café.

Years later, critics would underestimate the influence of my
Barcelona years. They would refer to me as essentially "self-taught,"
and I would not correct them. I prided myself on having learned so
much under Alberto's light hand, forgetting that his leniency was a lib-
erating gift that lesser men, like the Rivera brothers, did not know how
to give. Alberto was not without opinions or methodology; he spent
hours guiding me through scales and positions and teaching me how to
hear. But when my eyes glazed over, when I started to withdraw into a
dazed cloud of sound, he recognized the signs and understood the limits, both his and mine. In my lifetime, I would meet priests who had

never learned to turn the other cheek, communists who had no interest in sharing so much as a cigarette, fascists who extolled order but couldn't walk a straight line. Alberto believed and lived a single idea. He was his own man. He struggled to let me become mine.

My mother usually woke three hours before I did, in order to make the long commute into the industrial neighborhood called the Eixample, where she had found work at a calico-weaving factory. She stood for fourteen-hour days in front of a loom, alongside hundreds of other women, in a giant industrial shed that was hot in summer, freezing cold in winter, and painfully noisy year-round.

Alberto's and my mother's schedules were so different, I assumed my tutor and mother rarely saw each other. But one morning when it was still dark I woke and went to use the bathroom down the hall. Passing the unlit hall that led to the kitchen, I heard voices, hers soft and high, his gentle and low, both of them surprisingly relaxed and informal—like old friends who had grown used to having coffee together. No wonder Alberto had trouble waking up in time for our morning sessions lately, I thought, and felt my chest grow heavy with the weight of an unfamiliar emotion.

Alberto spent less time worrying aloud about my future career than about my mother's immediate employment. "It's a bad time all around," he told me later that autumn, over our bachelors' dinner of sardines and bread. "The cost of food, the strikes. They've talked about closing your mother's factory. With no colonies to export to, it's hard to sell calico now. Still, it's hard work for a woman her age. She's lost weight since coming here."

Lost weight? How closely was he scrutinizing her shape? Yet even I had noticed how small she looked beneath the grayish white sheet, without the crinoline and corset and heavy skirts.

"You make it sound like it's my fault," I said.

"You could help her—earn some money, so she can work less. There is a café nearby looking to hire musicians."

"You asked my mother about it?"

"I did. She doesn't like the idea."

"She doesn't believe I can make money playing. She doesn't believe playing music is real work."

"Oh, I don't know."

"She doesn't believe in *me*, Alberto."

His heavy-lidded eyes met mine; his lips formed a patiently condescending half-smile.

"Maybe *you* aren't the thing she doubts."

I didn't understand.

"Music isn't everything, Feliu."

So it was not only my ability and fortitude that were suspect, but music itself? But of course, I'd always known it.

My irritation made me less shy. "Why don't you play the cello anymore, Alberto?"

"I have not played my own instrument for years. Teaching doesn't require it."

"Don't you miss it?"

"A little, yes."

He'd said this before, and I'd never pursued the question any further. But I wasn't going to let it go this time. Something in my expression must have told him so.

"I was employed by an opera company and later, by a symphony. I toured all of Europe, of course—"

"Europe!"

Alberto shook his head, cautioning me not to interrupt again. "And at least I had the sense to save some of those earnings. But I missed many years in my daughter's life. Now she has moved away. She doesn't write. I played through my wife's illness, and she died. And I played through my own illness, wishing to die."

I looked down at my hands, folded in my lap.

"But that wish was not granted," he continued. "I got better. I dedicated myself to one instrument for two-thirds of my life, but I never found an answer to one question: *Why?*"

"Why play?"

"Yes—what point does it serve? What is music *for?*"

"Why does it have to be for anything?"

"I played for powerful men and saw them, a day after crying to my cello, govern without mercy. I played for workers and saw them no better able to feed their families. I asked myself—"

"You must not have loved it then," I interrupted. "If you loved it, you would play music for its own sake."

"What in this world exists for its own sake? Food nourishes. Water quenches. Women bear children."

"Beauty—" I started to say.

"A flower is beautiful, Feliu. But a flower's beauty and scent have one purpose: to attract a bee. To allow pollination to take place. To allow life to continue."

"Art exists for its own sake."

Alberto shook his head vigorously. "No, that's not true. Anyway, I loved it *too* much. Too much for it to be mere entertainment, for me or anyone else."

I did not like this side of Alberto. I did not understand how he could speak ill of something so obviously wonderful and pure. But I felt even more displeased by what he said next.

"Your mother understands this. I know she gave up her own music career. I know that after your father's death, she had to give up many things. Maybe that's why we understand each other." He sighed, "It's good to have a friend in times like these."

To hear either of them talk, the world wasn't nearing its end, it had already ended. Didn't they see how unfair it was to make a young man feel that he'd been born too late, that he was lucky to have survived at all, that there was no point in believing in anything anymore?

One night at the café, Ramón, the scarred oboist, asked what concerts I had attended.

"None," I told him.

"Not even the Liceo?"

"He doesn't belong there," Alberto said quickly. I took this to mean I was too young, too low-class, ill-mannered and ill-attired. I wouldn't have denied any of it. Just passing the brightly lit, block-long building made my heart pound in my chest.

Ramón persevered. "How can a boy learn classical music without hearing it?"

I'd heard many musicians on the streets, I told him—Andalucían guitarists, strolling violinists, comical performers playing reedy Moorish flutes, even an African drummer.

Ramón cocked an eyebrow at Alberto. "Is that what you're preparing him for—to busk on the Ramblas?"

When Alberto didn't answer, Ramón continued, "Would you have been content with that kind of life? Do you think he should play it safe just because of your mistakes?"

Alberto had been staring at his own crossed forearms, propped on the table. Now he peered up through his gray eyebrows. "*Our* mistakes, you mean."

The next day, Ramón showed up at our apartment door cradling a large box. "Your maestro loaned this to me three years ago. I am returning it."

It was the first phonograph I'd seen up close, a portable hand-cranked model set in a burgundy box, with a cone-shaped amplifier made of cardboard. I found it difficult to believe Alberto's explanation that he had given it away when his neighbors complained about the noise, since the sound of my cello playing was much louder. But I had to honor the restrictions he imposed as a condition of my keeping it.

"You can play it between five and seven in the evening, and no more," Alberto said. That, conveniently, was the time he went to the café, during his more energetic weeks. Other weeks, he had resumed his habit of not leaving at all.

"And only on the days you finish the schoolwork your mother sets out for you," he continued. Mamá had threatened to take away the cello if I didn't start spending at least part of each day reading the school-books and filling the math ledgers that had once belonged to Enrique, which she had brought all the way from Campo Seco. I hadn't believed her about the cello, but I believed Alberto about the phonograph.

"And if it breaks, I can't afford to fix it," Alberto said as I jumped up and down within a handbreadth of the cardboard cone.

Ramón also had brought a stack of thick shellac records. As we studied the labels, I tried to imitate the way he held them, the white patches of his scarred palms pressed gingerly against each disk's shiny black edges. He held up one, indicating the label with his chin. "Principal cellist—A. Mendizábal," it read, in tiny, curling script.

"I'll take that one," Alberto said. I never saw it again.

Enrique's letter came just in time, during a week when Alberto's moods were sliding downhill. I thought it was my fault, given our many argu-ments about my bowing arm. Alberto advised me to keep it pressed more closely to my body, while I was interested in experimenting with more varied positions, letting it move away from my body as I bowed. Exasperated, he tucked a thick book between my right elbow and rib cage, and ordered me to hold it there as I played. The result produced tension in my forearm, my shoulder and my wrist—I knew it couldn't be right, and I knew it contradicted everything he'd taught me in a more cheerful time. To spite him, I complied, but let the bow skate over the strings, filling the parlor with alley-cat screechings and yowlings that punished us both.

After the midday meal, Alberto retreated to his bedroom. I dragged a chair to the balcony, to read Enrique's letter.

Toledo, April 12, 1908

Dear Cerillito,

We wake every day to music here, or bugles at least. Do you think you could march with a cello? That would be a trick. If not, I guess you'll have to stay in Barcelona, eating pastries and watching girls.

How are your legs doing? I hope you don't sit the entire day playing your instrument, without exercising. Here, they make us march to the point of collapse. You would think all the men would be fit, but that isn't the case. I thought of you the other day when I entered the mess tent and heard three men harassing a new cadet. I couldn't see his face at first, but I could hear his voice. It was high and whistly like a parakeet. Anyway, he is very thin and the men keep calling him Matchstick and it makes me think of you. Also he is your age and height almost exactly, unless you have grown a lot since I saw you last. I inquired about him and he was sent to Toledo by his mother, who probably doesn't realize her Paquito will become the butt of jokes here. The men hide his clothes and his books and torment him, but I can't say he complains. He keeps to himself mostly and does not seem to want or need a friend. But I will try to keep an eye out for him and I hope you have someone there who will keep an eye out for you.

They are recruiting many new cadets all the time. All talk is of Morocco.

Send my love to Mamá and I hope you have news of Luisa, Perci-
val, and Tía, since I haven't heard much from them. Do you send them
money, now that you are a famous musician? Or does that come later?
Con cariño,
Enrique

Alberto's moods continued to wax and wane. On the upswings, he brought out new pieces of music and lectured me about various composers and their styles and strategies, the particular problems they'd had to solve, and the times that had shaped them. On the downswings, he slept late and retired early, leaving me to practice old pieces to death, fussing with the bowings and trying to correct the tinny quality of my open strings or the woof of my high F. The more I played, the less happy I felt with my playing. My ear was improving faster than my hands, my expectations rising ahead of my abilities. It was not pleasant to spend so many hours alone.

In December of that year, I turned sixteen. I was no taller than I'd been at fifteen, but deeper voiced, and certainly more prone to dark moods of my own. The novelty of playing all day and doing little else was wearing thin. I listened to the phonograph more and more, but the recordings, primitively made as they were, only made me more morose. Symphonic music in particular brought me to tears—all those instruments playing together, so much richer and more complex than the simple études and salon pieces I played without accompaniment. Still, I cranked on, starting before five and continuing longer and longer past seven each evening. One night, at a quarter to nine, Alberto flung open his door, stomped into the parlor, and snatched the Beethoven record that had been playing. His hands shook as he turned left and right, looking for a place to crack it in two. Then his shoulders slumped. He turned away and set the record on a chair.

"Get out," he growled, pointing to the door. "I need quiet. Here." He thrust his hand into his pocket, then extended his fist to me. "A boy shouldn't be inside all these hours. Go find something to do. Go." He released the coins into my palm, and I saw that his hand was still shaking. "To the waterfront. To the wax museum. Waste some money. Waste some time! Get out of this building and act your age."

That was how I found the book. If the phonograph had wedged open a gap in my confidence, suggesting that perhaps my own music-making was nothing special, then the book split my confidence in two, exposing me as unexceptional, untalented, and—despite my own best efforts—woefully untrained.

I had walked toward the waterfront, as Alberto had suggested. Past the glittering lights of the Liceo opera house, past the vendors and cafés, toward the lower, seedier streets where prostitutes milled about, flaunting their cleavage beneath the city's gaslights. Two blocks short of the waterfront, where the statue of Columbus stands on a high pedestal with his back to the city, I turned left. A half-block more, and I arrived at the Museo de Cera.

Waiting behind a line of couples at the ticket window, I studied the museum posters under dirty glass. The main attraction seemed to be wax effigies of local criminals who had been put to death by the museum's founder, who was also Barcelona's executioner. Without a girl on my shoulder, feigning distress, I wasn't terribly interested, even though other people—first Ramón, later Alberto—seemed to think I should be.

Instead of buying a ticket, I wandered away and down the curb, where vendors offered eclectic wares. A postcard vendor displayed lurid images in a velvet-lined trunk: belly dancers whose bare breasts were plainly visible beneath sheer scarves, acrobats whose pear-shaped bottoms rested on trapeze bars. They were of a different caliber than the images sold higher up the Ramblas, better matched to the wax museum clientele, eager for lurid mementos.

"Look through here," the vendor said, holding up a black box, and when I peeked inside, I was confronted with the tableau of a naked woman recoiling dramatically as an ax fell toward her neck. I shrank back, then looked again.

"I have more, but it costs," he said. "Already you see two times for free." I shook my head and started to walk away.

My mother wouldn't want me to be here, I thought. But then I remembered Alberto's words: "Waste some money. Waste some time. Act your age."

"You like oddities?" the vendor tried, and pulled out an entire box stuffed with postcards, photos, pamphlets, and books. I glanced at the spines: *Slaves to Love. Oriental Secrets. The Marquis de Sade.* A sixteen-year-old boy should have been drawn to those books. But it was a thin gray volume with silver type that caught my eye, instead—*Tortured Genius: Two Centuries of Musical Prodigy.*

"You don't want that one," the vendor said. "Not many pictures. Only little girls and boys." Then his eyes lit up. "Unless you *like* little girls and boys. In that case, I have better—no words, all pictures. Wait and see, I will get. Separate box."

But I was already digging in my pocket. He shrugged and took what I had. As he passed the book to me, the loose title page shifted and fell free from its broken binding. Our eyes locked; he could see I still wanted the volume, but he conceded the damage and left one coin in my palm, pitying my lack of perversity. He pointed me back toward the Ramblas. "You have enough left for an ice cream. Go."

And so it was that I read about the misery of genius, and other truths that had been withheld from me. I read about Franz Joseph Haydn being torn from his home, neglected, and caned after misbehaving at school; about Mozart being exhibited relentlessly by his domineering father; about the violinist Paganini being starved and locked in his room for endless practice sessions.

These names I knew. Others were unfamiliar, and they bothered me even more, because they made musical suffering and sadism seem banal and—here, the possibility that bothered me—perhaps essential. The father of a motherless German girl named Gertrude Mara tied her to a chair whenever he left for his work; yet she went on to become a skilled violinist, and later, singer. Crippled, yes, but skilled.

Across Europe, children were beaten, pushed off piano benches, deprived of food, stripped of their playthings, even the dolls or marbles brought to them by musical admirers. And the torture seemed to work. Children—at least the ones who were the focus of this slim gray volume—excelled and became famous. The bruises faded. The music lasted.

An entire chapter in the prodigy book was devoted to Justo Al-Cerraz and the many ways his father goaded him into early performance, following abandonment by his unnamed gypsy mother. When an early patron presented him with a large stuffed hobbyhorse, Al-Cerraz's father sawed off the horse's head and scooted its body closer to the piano, so the boy prodigy could keep playing as he rode. The text claimed the young pianist had burst into tears at seeing the patron's gift mutilated, but in the accompanying photograph he looked radiant atop the oddly beheaded horse. Perhaps that inner light came from the music itself. Or perhaps—my envy soared here at the thought—it came from the absolute knowledge of one's future path, and the sense that a parent, kind or cruel, wise or misguided, believed without a doubt that one was destined for artistic greatness.

Punishment aside, the book highlighted all the subjects these brilliant young musicians were learning before they outgrew their sailor suits and banana curls: music theory, composition, solfège. I'd assumed that learning to play an instrument was enough. What if it wasn't? And what was this French thing, solfège?

I had bought myself an ice cream, as the vendor had advised, and ate half of it in the brightly lit parlor, the book in my lap, the ice cream thick in my throat. Finally, I gave up, leaving a melted puddle of cream in the bowl.

"Not good enough for you?" the barman said as he watched me ease myself off the high stool, face pinched with nausea. And then, under his breath: "Spoiled kids."

It was true. I *was* spoiled. But was it my fault? I'd wanted to play the cello for years, but my mother had held me back. I would rather she had tied me to a practice chair than lured me back into bed on a Sunday afternoon with promises of *Don Quixote* and an extra chocolate square, if I lay particularly still. Most recently, my mother had brought me a manual for the repair of phonographs. Alberto's wasn't broken, but Mamá seemed intent on interpreting my love of the phonograph as a boyish fascination with machines, rather than a young man's dedication to serious art. She'd even hinted I might find a future career in a repair shop, if I took up mechanical tinkering. (And yet, she did not push this idea, either. Even her discouragement of my dreams had a passive, ambivalent quality.) As for Alberto, just when I wanted to study more and harder he slept half the day, unwashed shirts again collecting on armchairs and the sink filling with towers of dirty dishes—proof indeed of my spoiling, since no one demanded I wash them; proof of Mamá's overworked distractedness, since she did not even see them; and proof of Alberto's low expectations, since he seemed to think it normal for an apartment to reek of old rice and beans.

I craved rigor and order, and instead I spent the day surrounded by entropy, while the streets outside offered more of the same: graffiti, peeling posters, slogans and mottoes protesting the government, denouncing the King, defying military conscription. How could someone learn amidst such chaos? Only by turning further inward, learning to block out everything but the clean and orderly perfection of music itself.

I hid the book in a drawer under my socks, like a pornographic postcard, and I didn't mention it. But I continued to look for every indication that Mamá and Alberto had never taken me seriously or, worse yet, that I was truly soft inside. I received a letter from Enrique describing a three-day field exercise he'd suffered through, during which several men had fainted from heat exhaustion. Enrique had soldiered on, of course. Even the skinny-legged Matchstick had made it, Enrique troubled himself to write. I did not appreciate being constantly compared to that friendless waif. Was it Enrique's way of saying that if I were a real man, I would have joined the military, too?

That week, I began practicing harder and longer. Instead of resting after lunch, I repeated my entire five-hour morning drill. For days, Alberto said nothing. Finally, on Friday evening, when he saw me struggling to stand up from my cello chair, he said, "There's no need to injure yourself."

I lashed out, cheeks flushed: "Paganini practiced ten hours a day!"

Alberto shrank back, pantomiming shock at my outburst. "Until he was twenty years old—then he never practiced again. Besides, he was sick all the time."

"You haven't taught me solfège," I grumbled through gritted teeth.

Alberto made a quizzical sound, then nodded with understanding. He began to sing an ascending scale: "*Do re mi fa so...*" He paused. "You know that, don't you? It's just sight-reading those tones. I've heard you do it on your own."

"That's solfège?"

"That's solfège."

I rubbed the small of my back with one hand, reached forward to set my bow on the music stand, but a sudden pain shooting down my left leg made me drop it. I swore under my breath and bent to pick up the bow, hot tears pooling. Rising, I kicked over the music stand.

"You don't seem happy, Feliu." There was no humor in his voice now.

I shouted back, "I'm not supposed to be happy! If you knew anything about teaching, you would know that."

"I see," he tried to say lightly, but there was a catch in his voice. "It's cruelty you want."

I didn't have the words to explain the frustration in the pit of my stomach. I sputtered and looked around. The music stand that I'd knocked down belonged to Alberto. It was one of the few musical objects he displayed with pride, fashioned from thick mahogany, shaped like a lyre with scrolled edges. I kicked it again and heard the wood splinter. Before I had time to exhale, Alberto was pulling me by the wrist into the kitchen, around the table, and toward the pantry closet. He nudged me inside and slammed the door. Suddenly, I was immersed in darkness, surrounded by the musty smell of mold and mouse droppings.

I waited a minute, unsure if Alberto was still on the other side.

"You're supposed to lock me in here with my cello!" I called out.

I heard the groan of wood—Alberto leaning against the door. His muffled voice answered, "That closet's too small. If you wanted to be locked away with an instrument, you should have stuck with the violin."

Silence again.

"I'm not afraid of you," I shouted.

"Of course not. You want a tyrant for a teacher. I refuse to be a tyrant. And I'm not starving you properly, either. If you feel around, you'll find plenty to eat."

"Then why I am in here?" I yelled, my eyes bulging, trying to see past the darkness.

I barely made out his soft reply: "You tell me."

The darkness made five minutes feel like fifty. Groping above my head, I managed to knock over a bag of something soft. I felt a film of powder settle on my face, smeared a finger against my cheek, and tasted it. Flour. Reaching around, I knocked over another bag. Something grainy spilled out. I plunged a finger and then brought it to my lips. Sugar.

The door opened. Alberto was silent, but his shoulders were heaving. For a second, I thought he was sobbing. Then I saw he was laughing silently, tears streaming down his cheeks.

"You're white as a ghost," he said when he'd caught his breath. "You look more like Paganini already."

I didn't laugh.

"The other day, when I asked you to go to the wax museum, did you go?"

I wondered if he'd found my book. "I walked there, but I didn't go inside."

"I gave you the money. You should have gone inside. Do you see? Even when I try to guide you, you don't listen."

When I didn't respond, he added, in a lower voice, "I never asked you to come to me. If your mother hadn't been so desperate—and so kind—I would have turned you both away. I did *try* to turn you away. You should know more about the people you trust to teach you."

He ran his hand through his short gray hair and nodded three times, like a railroad worker practice-swinging his mallet before raising it high, for the heavy blow. "If you'd gone to the wax museum, you'd understand something important about me. But never mind that. Today I learned something about you. For the time being, I am resigning as your teacher. If it's cruelty you want, you'll find it in the streets."

Then Alberto told me the new rules: I was expected to contribute to room and board, which my mother had fallen behind in paying. I was expected to vacate the apartment every day after lunch and not return until dinner, honoring his new need for privacy. He didn't want to hear the phonograph anymore. He didn't want to hear my incessant cello playing. He didn't even want to see the cello—I was to take it with me each day when I left.

"We don't need to tell your mother," he added. "It would only upset her."

The small spark of fury I had been fanning leaped suddenly into a roaring flame. Heat smoldered in my chest; my tongue felt dry. I couldn't speak. He was kicking me out—like Haydn! He was expecting me to earn my own money—like Mozart!

I'd never felt such righteous anger in my life.

I'd never felt so grateful.

CHAPTER

~ 6 ~

My mother hadn't wanted me to perform publicly. Perhaps she was worried that I would fail. Or perhaps she was worried that some small taste of success would give me false hope and lead to some larger failure in the future. If she feared only that a busking or café career might inflate my vanity, it was a needless concern. Curious stares aside, I received little attention over the winter months that followed, regardless of how and where I played.

Barcelona itself was a spectacle. The young Picasso had shown his work at the Quatre Gats and then sailed off toward Paris on the winds of his rising fame. Gaudí, the architect, had designed an entire fairy-tale suburb of abstract pavilions and serpentine, mosaic-covered benches. Even the local fish market was a splashy affair, its main gate decorated with green, amber and deep blue circles of glass cut from bottle bottoms, no two of them identical. The thickness of the glass, the presence of waves or bubbles or cracks, the direction of the sunlight all added variety and texture, an infinite number of hues.

Whenever I walked past the gate, I thought of the way Alberto had explained the cello's tone colors to me, the individuality and interpretive possibility inherent in a single note. The cellist's left hand was a technician—to find a quarter note of B on the A string, it headed to the first fingering, in first position. The right hand, on the other hand, was an artist, whose palette included the weight of the bow, the speed of the bow, the proximity of the bow to the bridge, all of which colored and shaded that note an infinite number of ways. From the simplest materials, so much was possible in Barcelona—or felt possible, anyway, which was the first step toward innovation, as well as the first step toward disillusionment and rebellion.

Visitors came to see Barcelona's color and strangeness. Residents took pride in its booming modernity. Street revelers shot off guns when they were joyful and dynamite when they were not. A distant explosion might be a religious festival; every third day, some saint was being heralded in some corner of the sprawling city. Or it might be a revolution. At the center of such a visual and auditory kaleidoscope, it was easy to go unseen and unheard.

While there was little glory or attention for a young unknown musician, there was ample opportunity. On my first attempt, I procured a job at the back of a café, replacing a violinist who had been jailed for punching a tax collector. The violinist returned after one week. But the next job came just as easily, when I wandered into a movie house. Barcelona had eighty of them at least, most of them small and shoddy and subject to frequent changes in ownership. Noticing my cello case, the theater owner pulled me aside and immediately offered me a position. His daytime pianist had disappeared, and the first round of replacements hadn't been quick enough to master the scores that accompanied each new film. Meanwhile, the audience was getting restless. They had come to see silent films, but they didn't expect *silence*. Nothing was more awkward than a "flicker" absent the musical cues that told the viewer when to laugh, cry, or close his eyes in fright.

I quickly extracted my cello from its case and played a sliding high note that sounded like a woman's shriek. Then I played a rapid trill on the lowest string, to suggest the tremor of suspense. I asked to see the piano music. The manager handed me a sheet upside down; I don't think he could read the alphabet, much less notes. Within minutes I had translated the first measures of a rather contrived piano score for two hands into a simpler one-line bass-clef melody, dressed up with the occasional double-stop chord.

"You're hired," the manager said, sweating as he watched the audience file toward their seats. "This one's a train picture. There's lots of ladies with their mouths open, fainting all over the place. Just do that screech and add the rest when you get it figured out."

I lasted five weeks at that job, twelve-minute reel after twelve-minute reel, until the theater closed. "It wasn't your fault," the manager said kindly, surveying the empty theater with an unlit cigar in his mouth. "You play that big violin pretty good."

The café was four blocks from Alberto's building; the theater, five—all close enough, but not an easy trek with a cello case bumping against my bruised hip. The instrument that had been the easier choice when I played only at home was the least convenient now that I needed to pursue employment. Just descending the stairs from Alberto's apartment, I'd strained my hip repeatedly and added a few scratches to the cello's face besides. I considered a map of the tram routes, wondering how much farther I was willing to travel with an instrument both taller and wider than I was.

Of course, the perfect place to play was just around the corner. But the world-famous Ramblas intimidated me. Most of the audience at my first café job had been drunk; at my second job, in the theater, essentially blind, their eyes focused on a screen instead of on me. On the Ramblas, I would be under clear and sober scrutiny. To play in an open-air setting, on the boulevard that had bewitched me on my very first day in Barcelona, seemed a kind of graduation—a necessary one.

At least the season made it easier. In late winter, half the seasoned street entertainers headed to indoor jobs or warmer climes, reducing the competition among musicians. Fortunately, many of the tourists remained. Afternoons, when local residents had already returned home from their market shopping, Englishmen loitered around the news

kiosks, a mob of white suits, straw boaters and two-tone shoes demanding their copies of the London papers. Pale ladies whispered and turned,
tickling passing waiters with the wayward plumes of their enormous
feather-decorated hats. Eastern European aristocrats inhabited the cab-
stands—a motley crowd of dark suits and drooping cravats, exchang-
ing pleasantries in incomprehensible accents.

But there was another language on the Ramblas, and this one I
could fully understand: the music of the boulevard itself. By mid-
afternoon, commerce in all the adjacent markets and side alleys slowed,
leaving only the main walkways faintly pulsing. Flower sellers swept
up fallen petals and clipped stems. On the boulevard's far side, where a
perpendicular street opened into the Saint Joseph market, produce vendors piled up boxes of blemished, unsold fruit. For the rest of my life,
whenever I would hear the first uncertain sounds of an orchestra tuning, it would remind me of the sleepy Ramblas on a winter afternoon:
the tap of crates, the squeal of departing carts and creak of closing
awnings—discordant, and yet full of promise.

This pause, which seemed a quiet lull to the tourists sipping their
cooling coffees and their warming *manzanillos,* was electrifying to me.
I knew what came next. Once the vendors had departed, the street entertainers could take up their stations, spaced more or less evenly along
the Ramblas's kilometer-plus length.

The day I found my courage was brisk and overcast, with mattress-
thick clouds. I hadn't brought a chair, but under a tree I spotted an
overturned box made of thin wooden slats that sufficed as a low seat. I
hadn't brought a music stand either, and I struggled to arrange some
sheet music around my feet, the papers' edges held down by my open
cello case. I'd just picked up my bow and was tightening the hairs when
one of the sheets blew free. It fluttered toward a cabstand, where it
stayed wrapped around a horse's leg long enough for me to retrieve it,
risking the cabdriver's wrath and the fate of my unguarded cello. I was
just loping back to my makeshift seat when I saw a second page of

music flutter free, and then a third. I grabbed at the pages that remained, and was just tallying my losses—the second page of a Popper étude, the first and second pages of a Bach minuet—when a voice from behind my shoulder said, "You're doing it all wrong."

I twisted around, relieved to see a boy instead of a policeman. He was a year or two older, and taller, with a forelock of black hair that lay flat against a pimply forehead. A battered violin hung from the long, thin fingers of his left hand. A dark, oversized coat draped his bony shoulders.

"This isn't a concert hall," he drawled. "If you need sheet music, you shouldn't play here."

"I'll decide that for myself," I said, swallowing hard.

The young violinist smirked and raked one hand against his forehead, pushing his hair from his eyes. "I was trying to be"—he searched for the word—"charitable. This is my spot. That is my box you're sitting on."

He was French Basque, he said; his hometown was to the northwest, across the border. The wooden purfling along his violin's edges was nearly worn away. One of his coat pockets was torn, attached at the bottom seam by just a few stitches. It flapped uneasily, like a piece of torn skin.

"You know how long it took me to get this spot? How much it cost me?" When I didn't answer, he proceeded to tell me the story of his mentor, a stiltwalker and juggler who had demanded that the violinist hand over half of his earnings to share the right to play under this tree.

"Until the day," he crowed, "that his stilt fell into that hole, just there." He pointed at a saucer-sized drainhole in the Ramblas paving. "His ankle turned 'round as easily as a balloon on a string. It looked like his foot had been put on backward. And the sound he made!"

"Didn't anyone help him?"

The violinist studied the back of his free hand, pretended to buff his black-edged nails. "He made it to the cabstand. Eventually." Seeing my disturbed expression, he added, "This was a man who could walk on his hands! He had lost only the use of one foot!

"Anyway," he continued, his voice a notch lower, "do you want to see something?" He propped his case on the ground, opened it, and pulled out a round object wrapped in a white handkerchief. He unwrapped it to show me the cast-iron drainhole cover. "Do you have any idea how much work it was to pry this loose without anyone noticing?"

He was a survivor, and I liked him. It had been months since I'd talked with anyone my age. I told him my name. He told me his—Rolland—and a dozen other things, perhaps half of them true. Even as he explained that I couldn't possibly share this spot, that I didn't deserve it and wasn't ready for it, I knew it was already partly mine. He needed company too badly to turn me away. He wanted a confessor and a protégé, someone to guard his cheap wooden box when he went to relieve himself or scrounge for restaurant leftovers. I wasn't going to have these honors for free; I'd have to pay a generous share to him, just as he'd paid a share to the stiltwalker. "But that won't amount to much," he said. "Don't expect to get rich. And with that—what is it?"

"Cello," I said. "Short for violoncello."

"Of course," he said. "I couldn't remember the word. You can stroll with it sometimes?"

"No. I have to sit."

He made a sucking sound, his tongue pressed against his front teeth. "A disadvantage. You are an orphan?"

"No."

"You have a place to sleep?'

"Yes."

His eyebrows went up. "Is it a good place?"

I checked myself from answering, remembering all the warnings I'd ever heard about feeding stray cats.

"It's crowded. I'm already sharing a small bed." I added quickly, "With a woman."

"With a woman?" He grinned and looked me over again, from top to bottom. "Perhaps you're not so helpless as you look. We make partners?"

For every twenty minutes he allowed me to play, Rolland would allow himself an hour. If four or five people started to gather around my cello, he ended my turn immediately and began to play himself, hoping for the coins to fall into his propped-open violin case. After all, I had a place to sleep.

But usually, crowds did not gather. Women pulled their shawls over their heads and men flipped up their collars, intent on continuing briskly to more sheltered destinations. The cafés had pulled in most of their tables, leaving only a few here and there for the hardiest outdoor patrons. An appreciative passing nod or a coin flipped from afar was the most reward we generally received.

As the winter wore on, stiff winds blew up the boulevard, rattling the sword-shaped palm leaves on the trees at the Ramblas's farthest seaward end and carrying the salty smell of the Mediterranean and the storms building offshore. Rain came suddenly, in driving sheets. We packed our instruments quickly and cowered in any storefront we could find; easy for Rolland to do but hard for me, with my bulky instrument earning the scowls of inconvenienced strollers as we all competed for the same cramped shelter. When the downpour stopped, we'd make our way back across rain-glazed cobbles to the wet box, and stand around rubbing our stiff fingers and waiting for our sleeves to stop dripping cold rain onto our wrists.

On our slowest days, we closed our cases and talked. Rolland told me fantastic stories about crossing the mountains, hiding in farm outbuildings, evading the angry fathers of the pretty maids he had kissed, stealing a sheep that he butchered with a dull knife. "But you know all about that kind of adventure," he said. "Here in Spain, every man is an El Cid, or a Don Quixote. True?"

It was just like a foreigner to mention Quixote. People who couldn't or didn't read seemed to think Quixote was an honorable, happy-go-lucky dreamer. They didn't realize how savage the tale was—full of violence, ridicule, and humiliation. Quixote's story didn't encourage romance or chivalry; it convinced the reader that Spain's chivalric age was over.

I couldn't explain all that, and I didn't want to offend Rolland. So I simply said, "I'm not sure a musician can be that kind of hero."

At this, Rolland looked more affronted than ever. He held up his violin and bowed a series of lightning-fast, off-pitch arpeggios. "*I* am a hero," he said. "What are you waiting for—some queen to knight you?"

When I didn't answer, he said, "There will be no royalty at all, someday. We got rid of ours, and you'll be rid of yours soon, too. But there will always be Don Quixote. You are placing your bet on the wrong side."

I murmured assent, but it wasn't emphatic enough for Rolland.

"You want to be a hero, too," he continued. "Even beneath the blank face—beneath the mask of *humilité*—I can tell."

I laughed involuntarily. That only egged Rolland on.

"No? Well how is it that you don't play with an orchestra, or at least with a quartet? Nearly every music job in this city is an ensemble job. There are flyers advertising for musicians to play in the pit at the Palau de la Música Catalana." That was the elaborate new musical palace being built for workers and their liberal patrons, a palace that might someday rival the bourgeois Liceo.

"I haven't seen any flyers."

"Solo jobs are one in a hundred," Rolland continued. "You found two already, and now you're on your third."

His points rattled me; I couldn't deny them.

"You pretend to be shy, but you're a soloist, a principal." He laughed out loud, overjoyed at his own bull's-eye. "You are not Feliu Delargo. You are Feliu *del Arco*."

He spun to face the hunched-over Ramblas walkers, shouting it into the wind at the top of his lungs: "*El Rey del Arco*—The King of the Bow!"

The worst of the winter storms had passed, and the weather had mellowed to a disagreeable coolness, when my busking partner informed me of the favor he'd been doing me all along. To play in this spot on the popular boulevard, Rolland had the informal permission of the local musicians' associations, which regulated every possible aspect of public performances. He rattled off the acronyms of the various organizations, which all sounded as confusing and mind-numbing as the political factions Alberto so often talked about at the café with his *tertulia* friends. In Alberto's leftist world, there were the anarchists, the radicals, the syndicalists. In Rolland's world—and now, my own—there were the West Side Wind Regiment, the Juvenile Songsters of Our Lady, the Mechanics' Union Percussionists. Every group had its own arcane membership and performance rules. "It is like Barcelona—all very confusing. Don't even try to understand," Rolland laughed.

Within our own group of string classicalists, there were strict requirements about what music could be played at what spot along the Ramblas's length, to avoid repetition and competition, he said. "It only makes sense, or everyone would be playing the same minuet and none of us would make any money. The associations were not enforcing before, because Ramblas traffic was so light, but with winter ending soon, they must be strict again."

I nodded my understanding.

"It's divided by nationality," he said. "Unfortunately, I missed the last meeting, so German, Spanish, and French were already taken."

"So, we...?"

"Norwegian."

I still felt self-conscious about my limited musical knowledge. "Such as...Grieg?"

Rolland rubbed his tongue against his front teeth. "Yes."

"Who else?"

"Any Norwegian."

"What Norwegian composers are there besides Grieg?"

"I am not sure. We stick with Grieg."

That afternoon, I headed to the Casa Beethoven, a tunnel of a music shop—two shoulder-widths wide and at least two rooms long, with racks of sheet music lining both sides and a dark curtain at the back. There I pawed through the scores, performing the most rapid memorization I could manage. The next day, I played a melody by Grieg. On Rolland's turn, he played something I didn't recognize—he claimed it was Grieg, too—and I learned to copy it, so that by day's end I had at least two acceptable tunes in my repertoire.

Hardly a week had gone by when Rolland mentioned that the assignments had changed again. Now we were to play Czech music, he said wearily.

"But that's great," I said.

"It is?"

"That's Antonín Dvořák—he wrote a famous concerto for cello."

"You know it?"

"I should."

That afternoon, I made a second trip to Casa Beethoven. The shop owner watched me curiously but his wife, straddling the threshold to the curtained back room, where she was sorting sheet music, called out, "This isn't a library!"

After Rolland had taken his cut, most of my money was going to Alberto; I couldn't afford the Dvořák score. I kept looking at it, scanning as fast as I could, until the shop owner's wife came toward me and ripped the score from my hands. "This is stealing," she yelled. "Forget what you were reading or I will call the police!"

"I'm going," I said, my chin tucked into my chest.

She held me by the sleeve. "Start humming."

"What do you mean?"

"Hum something—other than Dvořák."

I tried to pull away from her. Her grip tightened.

"Something Spanish," she insisted.

I glanced around wildly. "I can't think of anything."

"*Carmen*—the 'Toreador Song!'" she demanded.

"That's Bizet. It's French."

She lifted a thick music book in her other hand, preparing to swat me.

"If you insist," I said, and started humming, feeling the Dvořák score slip painfully from my mind.

When I told Rolland the story, he listened intently, then burst out laughing.

"You win," he said.

"Win what?"

"The truth, for entertaining me so well." He stifled his mirth by rubbing his tongue against his front teeth. "There are no assignments."

"The street organizations don't care?"

"There are no street organizations."

We were sharing the box, crowded onto its narrow, pinching slats. I turned away from him.

After a minute, he nudged my shoulder with his. I nudged back.

"Why did you lie to me?" I asked.

"It was a gift. I am teaching you not to be so easy a fool."

I muttered under my breath.

"When you are famous—when you are a hero cellist—you will say I was one of your teachers." He added, "And you *will* be famous, Feliu. You are a quick learner, that is for sure."

"*Hmmph.*"

"But you need to be stronger—not to believe so much in everyone and everything." He added, "Fool that you are, I am surprised you have not yet lost this woman you are sleeping with. Another man will steal her, if you are not more careful."

And so it was with skepticism that I listened, some weeks later, as Rolland told me another story. It was a dreary afternoon of few tourists and fewer coins, and we were preparing to quit for the day and go our separate ways. I confessed my great desire to see inside the Liceo. Rolland said it was no problem to sneak in, but I'd better dress well, to fool the doormen and the ushers. If I looked bohemian, they might do more than just toss me out.

"Fifteen years have passed," he said with a dramatic nod as we sat on the wooden box. "But they still remember."

"Remember what?"

"You don't know? It was the Ramblas's bloodiest day. That's saying a lot."

I steeled myself for another tall tale, listening with an impassive face.

It happened in November 1893, Rolland said. The opera was Rossini's *William Tell*—

"I know how it starts," I interrupted. "It's played by the cellos. A beautiful passage. I read that Rossini studied the cello, in Bologna. I tried playing that passage once and Alberto went all white and didn't speak the rest of the day."

Rolland leaned forward to close his violin case. This story had nothing—but nothing—to do with cellos. If I planned to interrupt again, he needn't tell it to me at all.

This thing happened, he continued—trying to conjure again the gloomy aura that I had deflated—in the second act, when Arnold and Mathilde meet in a valley by a lake, to pledge their love. Whispers quieted as the audience turned their opera glasses from each other toward the stage. A mining developer from Bilboa wrinkled his nose and twitched his walrus mustache, trying to conceal the emotion threatening to take control of his face. A lady named Doña Clementina reached for her décolletage and found herself twiddling the glistening, apricot-sized pearl that rested in the soft hollow at her throat. And up in the gallery, a man named Santiago Salvador attempted to extract two heavy metal objects from his jacket pockets.

The objects were precisely the size of oranges, except that they had spikes, and gleamed silver under the house lights that were always on, so that the wealthy could see and be seen—which was one reason everyone went to the Liceo, and the same reason that Santiago Salvador hated the bourgeois palace, which represented everything that must die in order for Barcelona to be reborn. However, no one was looking at Salvador. The flashing of the orange-sized objects could not compete with the winking of the chandeliers overhead, or the gleam of gilt that framed the murals on the walls. He decided to wait a little while, to savor the moment that might be his last, enjoying the feel of the spiky little orbs, which had the satisfying heft of bocce balls.

As it turned out, the first bomb was a dud. But the second one sailed into the air like one of Galileo's apocryphal cannonballs falling from the Tower of Pisa. It landed in the orchestra pit, where it exploded with a flash. There were screams and a little smoke; away from the mayhem, some of the private box–holders' first thoughts were what a shame it was, that this four-thousand-seat theater, gutted by fire just a generation earlier and rebuilt at extravagant cost, would go down in flames again. They couldn't see the human wreckage below, how much blood was obscured by the theater's trademark red velvet seats. Rossini's opera was cut short. Men and women fled, tripping over the women's long trains and grabbing, in their desperation, the flowing black tails of strangers' coats.

The final toll: twenty-two dead, fifty wounded—among them, many of the musicians, who did not earn in an entire year what Doña Clementina had paid for her apricot-sized pearl.

"Apricot-sized—that's certainly a large pearl," I said when Rolland's story was finished.

He looked incredulous. "That's all you have to say?"

"Well, it's a terrible story."

"If you don't believe me, go to the Liceo yourself."

"Why? Do they have a plaque there explaining everything you just told me?"

"No." He screwed up his face. "They'd rather pretend it never happened."

I pursed my lips, a little smug. "No record of this infamous disaster? No effigy of the criminal?"

Rolland frowned. "Effigy? Yes, come to think of it. Not at the Liceo. It's at the wax museum. That's where they display all the anarchists who lost their heads to the guillotine. And I think, on the wall, there are framed drawings from the trial."

At the mention of the wax museum, my smile faded.

"The trial?"

"There was a rumor that the musicians, including some of the worst injured, had been part of the plot. They helped Salvador sneak into the Liceo early. They showed him where to aim if he wanted to hit the fanciest private box, the one next to the stage. I guess he was not a very good shot."

I felt my chest tighten, a creeping acidity in my throat. "The musicians? They went to the guillotine, too?"

"Not a one. Their injuries saved them, I think—burned hands in bandages and that sort of thing. No one believed they would make themselves a target. Why would a musician risk losing his hands?"

The shock lasted several hours past Rolland's telling; it helped me sneak into the Liceo that evening. I didn't look nervous or shifty, only vaguely nauseous. That discomfited look was a badge of the privileged; I saw it flash across many of the theater patrons' faces as they pushed through the crowd in the foyer or signaled for attention from the cloakroom attendant.

The opera had working-class seats, too, I later discovered. These were in the "chicken roost," as it was called—fifth-tier seats above the top of the stage curtain, from which one couldn't see the opera at all, only hear it. To reach these seats as well as the poor ones on the fourth floor, one used a separate, less opulent entrance, on the side street. If I'd known, that's where I would have entered. But I didn't know. I didn't have any plan at all.

I still had my cello with me. I had worn my best pants that day, but the pants were tight, and my thick knee socks itched. I looked like an uncomfortable boy. Pushing through the foyer with my cello against my hip, I attracted the attention of a stage manager, a thin man with a pince-nez.

"Is Don Verdaguer waiting for that?" He gestured frantically at my cello before I could answer. "Curtain is in twenty minutes!"

He led me down a curving hallway, leaning as he pumped his long legs, like a racehorse on a track. Carrying the cello, I could barely keep up. I was out of breath by the time we found ourselves on the wings of the darkened stage, near the stairs leading down to the rapidly filling orchestra pit. He ordered me to leave the cello to one side, against a wall. Then he vanished. I stood there a minute, breathing heavily. I pushed the cello a little farther into the shadows, reasoning with myself that no one had asked for this cello, so no one would notice it. And then, with guilt pinging in my chest, I left my instrument there, bringing my bow—as always—with me.

I was well inside the theater now, but still without a ticket. I made my way up and down the second-floor hallways just outside the auditorium, crowded with gowned women and stiff-suited gentlemen, all heading for their seats. I went with the traffic as far as I could, then turned and walked against it.

A woman in a pale green gown was watching me. Her blond hair was coiled in a half-dozen ropes, pinned to her head and strung with thin ribbons and gems as small as seeds. When she tilted her head up to whisper into a man's ear, I turned away, but a second later I felt a lady's gloved hand on my shoulder.

"Are you looking for your parents?" she asked.

"Yes," I answered without thinking, and my eyes must have glistened authentically.

"Where did you see them last?"

Praying to have the skill of Rolland's quick tongue, I blurted that they'd gone to meet some friends elsewhere in the theater, and we'd become separated. Her face lit up. "I know just where to look."

Turning a corner, she gestured me toward a vast and rapidly emptying room.

"The Hall of Mirrors," she explained, as I tipped my head back and gaped. "This is a place friends often meet. Do you see them anywhere?"

Straining to appear sincere, I studied the room until my eyes fixed upon a long line of words stenciled around the high ceiling's edge. *Music is the only sensual pleasure upon which vice can not impose.* I thought about that and read the phrase twice, three times more, willing it into memory as I had willed the music scores at the Casa Beethoven.

Then I read the second—shorter, simpler: *Art does not have a fatherland.*

The green-gowned lady followed my gaze. "They're beautiful sentiments, aren't they?"

I nodded, and kept looking.

"You're sure you don't see your parents?"

I kept staring, not out toward the mirrors and the dwindling reflections of the last exiting patrons, but up, up, to the inspiring statements that had guided years of Alberto's life. For this, I now knew, was where he had played, as well as where he had stopped playing. He had been one of the collaborators who helped Salvador. That bloody day had ended his music career.

"Perhaps your father is in the gentleman's club?" the lady fretted.

I was tempted to tell her I didn't have a father, didn't have much of anyone, even a tutor I could entirely trust, and that was why it mattered to be here, to contemplate these words that might give me a sense of direction and purpose.

"...but I can't go there," she was saying. "We're out of time. You poor boy."

She pulled me away back toward the auditorium. Ushers chimed the final warnings. Closing doors huffed their final rebukes. She left me standing against a wall as she talked with a uniformed man; then she blew me a kiss and disappeared.

The usher took me up yet another marble staircase and found me an empty seat on the third floor. He warned me sternly that I'd better stay put until intermission and turned to go. It didn't seem to occur to anyone that a boy would have sneaked into an opera house; if anything, they all seemed worried that I'd sneak out.

The opera was about to begin. I did not even know what the day's production would be. "Wait," I called, and I was surprised when he turned lightly on his heel, his face suddenly placid. He thought I wanted to give him a tip.

"I'm just a little scared," I whispered as I fumbled in my pocket. "Being without my parents, I mean. Is it true someone threw a bomb here once, and killed a lot of people?"

The usher smirked. "Of course it's true. Nasty business. But that was years before you were born."

Not so many years, I thought to myself. But of course he probably took me for a child. I pushed a coin into his hand.

"You're not going to die here today." He winked. "You'll only wish you had." Then at my puzzled expression, he gestured toward the stage, where the curtain was rising. "It's all in German."

I never did go to the wax museum. There was no more I wished—or needed—to know. Besides, I had a natural dislike for the dissonance of complicated truths. I preferred to hold in my mind's eye the words I had read at the Liceo, in that vast, light-filled Hall of Mirrors: *Art has no fatherland*. Art could, I felt sure, rise above everything.

CHAPTER

~ 7 ~

My partnership with Rolland ended as quickly as it had begun. It was the first truly beautiful day of spring, sun shining down through the Ramblas's greening trees, waiters strutting importantly as their tables filled, vendors complaining—ah, to complain!—that an unexpected deluge of customers had bought the last good cigar, the last newspaper-wrapped cone of almonds, the last untorn gossip magazine from Madrid.

Rolland had taken a break from playing and was removing his jacket; it was hot now, even in the dappled shade. I wiped my palms against my brow and dried them on my pants, then started tightening my bow, preparing to begin. Two men in berets approached to watch; two ladies behind them strolled arm in arm.

Rolland turned to me and said, "It's easy to be friends in winter, but not so easy in spring."

"Is that a Basque proverb?"

"No. It's my way of explaining"—and here he paused, tapping his fingers against his fingerboard—"It was nice having company when the crowds were thin, but now I've got to earn a living." I stood for a while, dumbfounded. Finally I loosened my bowhairs and packed up.

I supposed I could have wandered a block in either direction, struck up a conversation with a contortionist or a silhouette artist and offered to pay them a share of my earnings if they would move over just a bit. The contortionist, especially, didn't need much room to earn her coin. But my heart wasn't in it. I had lost my place on the boulevard. I had lost my first real friend.

Wandering up the Ramblas toward home, I saw the Casa Beethoven owner running toward me. I stopped in my tracks and cowered, squinting to see if he was followed by his wife. But he was alone. When he reached me, he grabbed me by one elbow.

"There you are! I have been waiting for you to come back to my shop."

"Come back?"

He rubbed his chin. "I was worried I wouldn't find you again." He handed me a thin brown-wrapped parcel. "Go ahead, open it." Inside was a German edition. The green-bordered cover said *Bach Solo-Suiten*. "Six suites," he said. "All for solo cello."

"I haven't played this. I haven't even heard it played," I said.

"Nor have I. But I was impressed by your desire, that day in my shop. Bach can be a little cold. Maybe your passion will warm it up."

He wouldn't take any money. It was rude of me to start reading the score before I had thanked him, but I couldn't help it. Each of the suites was divided into a half-dozen or so dance-inspired movements—allemandes and courantes and gigues and sarabandes.

"Incredible," I said. "It looks like a lot of work."

"A lifetime's work," he said. "Don't let my wife know I gave it away."

We parted before it occurred to me to ask his name.

In my first Barcelona months, my world had been compact and circumscribed—no bigger than the space of my cello, my chair, a radius defined by my bowing arm. Now it was large, larger even than the Ramblas itself, that flow of people and sounds, colors and ideals. Music, once my intense and solitary child's game, had become a world. There was room in it for more things, good and bad.

I took my time walking home. I knew where I would find Alberto: on his balcony, soaking up the ephemeral midday sun. He asked me if I had found what I needed and was ready to be his student again. I said I had, and I was.

The calico factory laid Mamá off that spring. She was upset by the news; we were relieved. Alberto and I admitted that I had earned money from months of busking without her knowledge. It meant her debt to Alberto was a fraction of what she'd assumed, but she did not look pleased to hear it. I expected her to ask me more about what I'd experienced—or to lecture me about how I had overtaxed myself, dragging a cello up and down staircases and across cobblestone streets. But Mamá's anxiety faced forward, never back. She had other worries to occupy her, including the need to pay for military exemptions. Percival would make an unlikely and uncooperative soldier; I was underage and physically unfit for conscription, but as Mamá reminded me, standards often changed as a war progressed.

Everyone seemed to be talking about exemptions, with glances east to the waterfront, where every day new soldiers boarded ships bound across the Mediterranean, to Morocco. In the cafés, old men hunched low to the tables, muttering about Rif tribes, iron-mining interests, protecting Spanish capital, sacrificing sons—and refusing to. I kept my ears closed as best I could, feeling even then, in 1909, that this was an old and broken record, this talk of colonies and bloodshed.

While Mamá recuperated from her long spell of overwork, Alberto entered one of his more energetic stages. Perhaps it was the season, the burst of red flowers on the balcony and the sounds of spring parades in the streets. Perhaps it was Mamá's presence, or the long break he'd had from me. He was less reclusive and more eager to play the active tutor again. He left the apartment more frequently, and invited me to go with him. I accepted his lessons, but I declined his company. Not only did I wish to avoid his pontifications on current political troubles, but I feared overhearing any references to the past that would force me to evaluate my feelings about him.

Alberto had his secrets, and so did I. The prodigy book had been one. The Bach suites became the other. All spring and early summer I chose not to mention the gift given me by the music shopkeeper. The Six Unaccompanied Suites for Cello were deceptively easy to begin playing. The cover of my edition said they were simple studies that any intermediate cello student might attempt. But that was and was not true. Any cellist could play the basic notes, rigorously and mathematically sequenced on the page. It took a master, however, to make those long trains of ascending and descending notes sound like music, to find the dynamics and articulations and phrasings that turned a scalelike passage into a melody—uplifting, heartbreaking, human. I played them only when Alberto was out of the apartment, struggling with them, savoring them.

Exposure was inevitable. As the days grew hotter and the air inside the apartment stuffier, I drew my chair closer and closer to the French doors that opened onto Alberto's balcony. By June I was playing on the balcony itself, sweat running down my temples and into the neck of my shirt.

One day I had just finished the climactic, double-stop ending of the first suite when I heard a voice, three stories below.

"*Eso es!*" Alberto shouted up from the street. "That's it! But three measures back, if you will start on an upbow…" He turned at the sound of a horse-drawn cart advancing on him. "Just wait—I'll be right there!" And he bounded out of the way, through our building's black gate, and up the stairs.

As I listened to his advancing steps—his boyish eagerness to reach me, the measured footfalls as the first burst of energy waned, the slowing pace as he neared the top, winded, doubled over, becoming old again—I nearly felt sympathy for him. But I fought it. I thought of the Liceo, the gleaming Hall of Mirrors, the words high on the wall that were like a hand on my shoulder, pushing me toward perfection and success. I steeled myself to be silent, undemonstrative. And yet Alberto was barely through the front door when I found my feet and my voice. I stood in the center of the room, shouting: "Why didn't you tell me?"

Alberto lifted his head to me, laboring to form a puzzled smile as he caught his breath, hands on his knees. Then he stepped sideways and collapsed into a chair, still grinning.

"The Bach suites," he panted. "You've discovered them."

He gestured toward another chair. I stared at it for a few seconds; and then, relenting, backed into it, my arms crossed.

"You're angry with me for not teaching them to you? Well—you weren't ready, that's all. And now you are!"

He flapped a hand toward the kitchen, gesturing for a glass of water. I did not rise. He accepted my rudeness—too easily, it occurred to me, even then. He dropped his hand into his lap. "There's nothing wrong with waiting."

I asked again, "Why didn't you tell me?"

"A novice can't see the patterns. It's like a child who doesn't understand life—who thinks everything is black and white. With Bach, you have to see between the notes. Some people call them études, and without insight, it's true—they're not much more than that. But you're ready." Alberto sat up straighter now, taking a full breath. At last, he met my eyes. His smile faded. "You have something to say to me. Not about Bach, am I right?"

I inhaled deeply. *"Art has no fatherland."*

He waited.

I tried again. *"Music is the only sensual pleasure—"*

He completed the phrase: *"—upon which vice cannot impose.* Yes, I remember those words, too. But vice *did* impose, did it not?"

"Ramón's hands..."

"And many other scars. Not all so visible. So you finally did go to the Liceo. And you know the whole story."

"Not the whole story."

Alberto gestured firmly for me to stay where I was, sitting in the main parlor. Then he disappeared into the kitchen. I heard a cupboard opening, a glass knocking against wood, a long silence as he drank and finished catching his breath—while I also caught my own, calming myself down, as was his plan.

He returned and took his seat. I waited for his nod before asking, "Did you help that man?"

"I never helped Salvador directly."

"But you knew of his plan?"

"I'd heard whispers of it."

He saw my scowl and countered it with his own raised voice. "Do you think it's easy going to work thinking someone might bomb the place where you're performing? It wasn't the first time we'd heard something might happen. If we stayed home every time, or told every audience, there'd be no concerts or plays in Barcelona. Do you think that's a better solution? There are threats every day here—it's been that way as long as I can remember."

I hadn't thought of it that way. But I didn't want to be convinced of his innocence.

Alberto continued, "If I'd told the Liceo's management, they would have canceled that concert—and many others. At the time, I believed that fear was not a way to live, that life itself should go on." A less charitable expression crept across his face. "I thought music was everything. Does that sound familiar?"

"You were a collaborator," I tried again.

"You will find," he said calmly, "that *collaboration* is an imprecise word. The longer you live, the more you know people from all walks of life—and sometimes their paths intersect yours in unexpected ways. Listen," he added, "I would never hurt anyone on purpose."

"But you *do* feel guilt. You stopped playing."

"I didn't stop because of the bombing, but because of what followed. The main tragedy of my life was personal, not political. All real sorrows are personal sorrows."

He went on to explain how the trial had shamed his daughter, who was nineteen at the time, and ruined her chances of marrying her true love: a young man from an illustrious family of Catalan bankers who could trace their professional heritage back to medieval times. The boy bowed to family pressure and withdrew his marriage offer. In the end, Alberto's daughter settled for a marriage of convenience arranged by second cousins, to an apothecary from Granada.

"She has not forgiven me." Alberto shook his head. "I don't believe that music can actually do bad, but neither am I sure that it can do any good. It didn't prevent the horror of what happened that day. I haven't seen it prevent any injustice since. I did not help Salvador. But I did begin to ask myself—what is the point? And without a point, I have not let myself play."

"But maybe you will find a way to do good with it, Feliu; just as you will find your own way to interpret Bach. Don't you see? Maybe you'll find a way not just to *be* good—the best—but to *do* good."

That night, I had trouble sleeping, thinking of what Alberto had told me, and feeling the residual smolder of some dark emotion. Was I angry because he would not accept blame for his involvement? Did I dare admit to myself that his situation reminded me of my mother and Don Miguel; that even if he hadn't helped Salvador, he hadn't stopped him, either, and that was enough to make me feel sick inside?

Or did I feel resentment that he expected me to do what he could not—to not only be good, but to do good? Perhaps I simply felt fear:

the fear that I might not be able to live up to his final wish for me, much as I wanted to.

I left the bedroom to use the bathroom at the end of the hall, and heard voices in the kitchen.

"A general strike—yes, all right," Alberto was saying. "But it will be more than that. The radicals want one thing, the anarchists another, the Republicans a third. Even my old colleagues are angry with me, because I refuse to join them in taking advantage of the chaos."

The conversation paused, and I started to creep back to the bedroom, trying to avoid the squeakiest floorboards, but then I heard Alberto say, *"Alma."* I stopped. I'd never heard Alberto use my mother's first name.

"You will have to leave," he said, so softly I had to strain to listen. "Go home, now that you have that option."

"Gracias a Dios," she mumbled.

"There will be problems in the villages, too. But at least there, you'll be among familiar faces."

"Feliu won't want to leave Barcelona."

"But he'll have to," Alberto said. "It's a good time for the audition. Regardless of the outcome, he will understand that we are done. If he passes, it will mean a different teacher, somewhere else. If he fails, he goes home—but at least he'll be safe."

"That's all I've ever wanted for him." Her voice dropped to a whisper.

"I know," he said, and the chair scraped, as if he'd moved closer, to comfort her. "But what about you?"

"Me?"

"What will you be looking for, when this is over?"

I covered my ears, not wanting to hear my mother's breathy voice and Alberto's reassuring masculine grumble. But near my bedroom door, just as I put my hand on the knob, I uncovered them again.

"It's just not the right time," my mother said.

"Will it ever be the right time?"

"Maybe not."

The next day, when we started our lesson, Alberto explained that he was thinking of contacting Don José.

"The sooner the better," I said.

Alberto lifted an eyebrow but said nothing. Then he reached for my stack of scores and tablets, which now stood knee-high.

"You should prepare something. Perhaps a Sibelius theme? And he will want a sonata. I leave the choice to you, but what about Chopin's Sonata in G Minor? The scherzo would demonstrate your bowing."

"Not Chopin."

"Lalo?"

"No."

"Then what do you want to do?"

Finally I said, "Bach's first cello suite. C Major."

"What movement?"

"I'll start at the beginning and play until he stops me."

"You're making this sound like a bullfight. The goal isn't to last until he tosses you out of the ring. It's to play well. Besides, the first suite is the simplest. It doesn't sound like a performance piece."

"It will when I play it."

"Don José might be more impressed with something modern."

"Then he should listen to jazz on a Victrola."

Alberto raised his palms, indicating surrender.

I continued to sit with my cello between my legs, tapping restlessly at the fingerboard with my left hand, baiting him to rebuke me. But he simply waited, and then said, "It's your choice, Feliu."

His pacifism only raised my ire. "Would you like to remind me that your reputation depends on this as well?"

"No, I would not," he said. "And it does not. My reputation depends on my own actions."

"So you have no expectations for me." My lower lip trembled.

"I have tremendous expectations. More than a man should have for a boy who is not his son. But only a few of them have to do with music."

My head felt impossibly heavy, my fingers fat and dull. A moment earlier, I had been testy, but now I felt only depressed. I was too upset to play, and I could not even understand the source of my sudden balefulness.

It was almost a relief when Mamá burst into the room, panting, "The music-shop man has sent his brother to come and take Feliu's cello! We were only a few days late, but he says he doesn't want the weekly payment now, only the balance— or the instrument."

Alberto stepped outside and returned a few minutes later, weary and resigned. "He's closing his shop and leaving the city, because of the rumors. He's collecting on debts and selling his instruments. Perhaps you could trade your bow, Feliu. It's worth more than the cello."

"Not my bow."

"*Está bien.*" Alberto placidly removed the cello from between my legs and put it in its case. The dropping lid reminded me of a coffin. I was seeing my first cello for the last time.

At the school, we waited outside Don José's classroom door, the three of us pressed together on a narrow bench. "They're ending the term early this year," Alberto whispered to my mother. "Vacations, they call it, but it's a week early."

To me he said, "Another few days, and you wouldn't have gotten to play for Don José at all."

Mamá was distracted. According to the newspapers, young men from across our region, men like Percival, might receive military notices any day. In addition, Mamá had received word that Luisa's boyfriend had already sailed for Morocco. My sister was distraught.

A secretary appeared. She ushered us into the room next door where Don José sat, once again surrounded by a half-circle of cello students. Alberto and José embraced, and I heard a murmur of *Mendizábal* go around the room as the students recognized this name, which had meant nothing to me two years earlier.

"Don Mendizábal, honor us." Don José held out his own bow.

Alberto clasped his hands together, studied his feet, and launched into an eloquent refusal. But Don José persevered. "I am doing you a favor today, is it not true? So first do *us* a favor. Play something. It has been too long."

I did not expect my tutor to relent. I'd badgered him the entire time I had known him, yet he'd never played more than a few instructive measures at a time for me. But now he nodded deeply, pulled up an empty chair, accepted Don José's cello, and sat down to play. No introduction, no apologies, not even the name of the composition. He simply pulled the bow across the strings, and we all leaned forward to listen.

Alberto's playing mirrored his personality: It started slowly but built as he played, gained shape and discipline and volume, sounded noble and certain even when a note fell ever so slightly sharp, until the very end, when it became a whisper: a *pianissimo* ending that spoke of surrender. Mamá's head bobbed along the entire time he played, as if to say, *Yes, this explains everything.* If I had not already recognized that she was in love, that day I could no longer have denied it.

The only technical surprise was Alberto's pronounced breathing. He inhaled and exhaled audibly, filling his lungs at the more demanding moments, and I thought, Breathing, I've never even considered my breathing, and all the hubris of the last months drained out of me. I had underestimated him. I had thought he was a nobody, which made the mild praise and gentle direction he gave me worthless, and so I had underestimated myself. My egotism and insecurity and undeveloped sense of self were inseparable. I don't castigate myself for it. I was young. I had done nothing and been nowhere. I was no prodigy—not a Mozart, not even an El Nene.

The moment the last note faded, Alberto stood and handed back the cello, without glancing at his audience. He had no interest in applause, only duty.

"And now, the student," Don José announced. He gestured toward a lanky boy, who pushed his cello toward me with a dutiful nod. I was relieved the maestro had not asked me to explain my own lack of a cello.

"I did bring my own bow." As I struggled to extract it, the students all stared at the velvet-lined tube with interest, though one boy snickered.

I sat down and began to play the first few notes of Bach's first suite, as planned. But my right arm shook, and I could barely keep the bow perpendicular to the string.

"He needs rosin," I heard Mamá say, and a flurry of student hands passed up their amber-colored chunks, which I applied to the bow hair with quivering fingers. I set the bow upon the string again, but anyone could see it was a hopeless gesture.

"The book," Alberto stage-whispered—referring to the pedagogical restraint he had inflicted on me long ago. He meant it as a joke, but there was a commotion to one side of the room, and before I knew what was happening, a student had brought forth a hefty tome and wedged it under my right armpit.

"Do you see?" Don José replied. "I'm not the only teacher to inflict *el libro* on you." He nodded at me. "Go ahead now. That will stop the trembling and keep your elbow where it belongs, too." Across the room, Alberto flashed me an apologetic grin.

Clamping my arm to my side, I began to play again. Bach's baroque braid of sixteenth notes climbed and fell, gently, evenly, rhythmically. Changing strings, I felt the book slip slightly, and I clamped my right arm more tightly. The spasms subsided; I began to feel my muscles warming and cooperating. I even dared to glance up: Don José was watching dutifully, the students' faces were regarding me with mild approval, and my mother...was twirling a loose strand of shoulder-length hair.

A hearty shout echoed outside the classroom window—a rally down the street—and I cursed the cheerful disorder in the man's voice. A bird flew by, nearly strafing the top of a clothesline where some protest banners had been hung, oddly placed between an assortment of chemises and socks. Several pairs of eyes followed the bird; a student noticed the undergarments for the first time and giggled.

I stumbled on my shift to the A string. Don José sighed deeply. Still I kept my composure, until my eye fell on my mother's hand. I watched as it wandered from her neck, to her lap, to the head scarf sitting beside her. I had played for less than a minute; I was only one-quarter of the way through the first movement; the melody was only beginning to build. But already, the audition was over. She knew I had not played well. She was fingering the knot of the head scarf. She was preparing to leave.

I closed my eyes. I loosened my right hand, which had been wrapped, clawlike, around my bow frog. I pictured the water flowing alongside the seawall, glittering golden in the sunset, and the pillarlike statue of Columbus above it, seeing more than just an endless train of waves; seeing possibility; seeing beyond the curve of the earth.

I relaxed and divided the sixteenth notes slightly less mathematically, extending them subtly as the melody arced. I relaxed my right arm. The book fell to the floor with a resounding boom. I heard gasps, but I did not open my eyes. I kept playing, and my right elbow began to lift away from my body, feeling lighter with every measure now that the infernal book was out of the way, and my wrist could flex naturally as the bow traveled across the string. The bow changes were much easier now— like sewing deftly through felt with a thick needle.

Now the suite reached its tensest moment, when the notes cascade in a downward spiral. It would have been so easy to storm down them, to throw my head around like Eduardo Rivera, or even like Rolland. It would have been easy to make the vibrato tremble and sob. Instead I kept my eyes closed and the notes terse and quick, subtle pressure changes against the strings infusing them with color and variation. I was not playing for coins, or for fainting girls, or for anyone but myself—and the hope that I could transcend the frustrations and limitations of this particular place, this particular time.

After that: I do not recall. I know I made it through the dramatic broken chords that resolve and close the piece, played on all four strings. I did not so much play them as hear them played. Then I opened my eyes and set aside the cello. Returned my bow to its case. And left the room.

Alberto was laughing as we walked the seven blocks home. "He was furious with your mother—*furioso!* He said she should have brought you to Barcelona years earlier, when you first showed talent on the violin. He said she had almost—*almost*—obstructed God's will!"

Mamá did not speak. She was not tickled about being rebuked by the same man who had refused her nearly two years earlier.

"It doesn't matter, Alma," Alberto continued. "He was angry at me, too. He said I was hiding talent. He said I should have spoken to him after Feliu had played for a few months. Not that he thought our boy's playing was perfect, mind you. Would you like to know what he said about the Bach, Feliu?"

I toyed with the idea of not responding, but my curiosity was too great.

"He said it demonstrated excellent potential, but that it was 'Too beautiful, too heroic.' He said, 'One should approach Bach more...objectively.' He was particularly dubious of the bariolage at the end. He said it sounded as if you were playing two cellos, instead of one. Ha!"

Alberto ran forward a few steps and raised a fist to the sky, then turned and noticed my wounded pride. "You made him think! He didn't even mention the book dropping, or the way your elbow kept stabbing at the air. I'm sure he would have loved to tie your bowing arm to the chair, but he was too busy hearing a new interpretation—hearing music. Music, Feliu!"

I took a deep breath. "I'm not sure I want to study with him."

"I agree," Mamá said quietly, astounding me.

"You're both being irrational," said Alberto. *"No importa.* Don José doesn't want to teach Feliu, either."

Now it was Mamá's turn to be surprised.

"Feliu is already more skilled than his other students," Alberto explained. "Don José will get no credit for having discovered him because I tutored him for two years."

"But that isn't fair!" Mamá cried.

"It's for the best. It's better than the best! Don José doesn't want Feliu to study in Barcelona, where there will be too many comparisons to his own students. He is recommending that Feliu study with Count Guzmán. At the Palace. In Madrid. It is a giant leap forward."

"Madrid?" I echoed, my voice cracking.

"Count Guzmán is the court composer. He taught Justo Al-Cerraz for a season, until Al-Cerraz's father insisted the boy return to touring. Feliu, you will be walking in El Nene's footsteps!"

"No," my mother said firmly. "Those are the last footsteps I'd have him follow."

"And he will be away from Catalonia. At least for a while." Alberto paused, letting the idea sink in before he added with a smile, "Madrid is a safe place, Alma. It's a place of royal balls, not rebellion—tedious as that sounds."

That settled it.

———

I took the train, alone, to Madrid. It was nearly empty, though at every stop the platforms were crowded with families tearfully embracing their conscripted sons, who were boarding trains headed the opposite direction, toward Barcelona, for transport across the Mediterranean. Internal battles already raged. Workers called a general strike. In the days to come, martial law would interrupt train transport. Radical groups would dynamite several rail lines, and roads to and from Barcelona would be barricaded. What Alberto had predicted, what he and my mother had wanted to save me from, was happening: chaos and insurrection. People I met on the train heard I was from Catalonia and assaulted me with questions: "Is it just an antiwar movement? Or is it a Republican uprising? Have they really burned a hundred churches? Is it true the women are fighting next to the men, that even the prostitutes are armed?" I couldn't answer their questions, except to say, "I think it was about Morocco, mainly."

I hadn't paid attention in the week before I left town. I didn't even recognize the names of the various faction leaders. I had no opinion about the men who faced execution once the fighting ceased. *Semana Trágica*—The Tragic Week, it would be called later, a prelude to violence in the decades to come. I had been immersed in my own world, the world of the cello. I can't say I regretted my ignorance—if anything, I took pride in it, the luxurious and self-deluding pride that only youth can afford.

PART III

Madrid

1909

CHAPTER

~ 8 ~

"Do not mention Barcelona," I was warned by a lady dressed in bumblebee stripes of yellow satin and black lace as we stood in the palace antechamber.

"Don't mention Catalonia at all," an older woman added. She had red satin flowers pinned on top of her head and held a matching fan to the bodice of her red ruffled dress.

"Nor even the train ride here," the bumblebee lady said. "It upsets her terribly to think about the rails being blown up. She's ridden on those same rails—in her own private car, yes, but on the very same rails!"

Not Barcelona, not Catalonia, not the train, I thought.

The count parted the throng of women with an outstretched hand, steering his way with surprising skill for a man who was nearly blind. "Music, Master Feliu, that is all you need to discuss."

The count nodded in the direction of the halberdiers as we passed into the official chamber. It was as elaborately furnished as all the rooms we'd passed through so far. Cherubim floated between puffy clouds on the painted ceilings; chandeliers hung from bunched satin ropes.

Another man introduced the count. The count introduced me. The ladies took their seats against the wall. The Queen Mother, Maria

Cristina, gestured toward an overstuffed, tapestry-covered chair. I had to jump up a little to sit on it, and my heels hung slightly above the floor. Two small dogs with bulging, black-olive eyes circled my feet warily before returning to recline at their mistress's feet.

"You had a good trip here, I hope?" the Queen Mother said, enunciating each word slowly. She had a pinched nose, thin lips, and ashen eyebrows. Her hair was silver and tightly curled. It seemed as if every ounce of color and life had been drained from her—cut off at the wasp waist molded by her tight ivory bodice.

I didn't know how to answer her without mentioning the train. I tensed my shoulders slightly—an unintentional, exhausted twitch— which she accepted as my answer.

"I look forward to hearing you perform soon with our Conde Guzmán's dear daughter. Until then," she continued, expelling the words with what seemed to be a great effort, "let us set aside the topic. Talking about music without hearing it is nearly as dull as talking about food without eating it, don't you think? Tell me about yourself."

My mind sifted and discarded numerous possibilities. I glanced back quickly, searched the room for clues, and tried to send a meaningful and beseeching glance the count's way, but that was a wasted effort. I looked up and nearly lost myself in the mural high overhead—muscular arms and babies' bottoms and tunics billowing everywhere. How could anyone stand being stared at so relentlessly? Perhaps it was easier to be blind in a room such as this one.

The count's cough brought me back to the present moment. The Queen Mother gazed into the middle distance, her eyes avoiding mine.

"One man has suggested I offer you an allowance," she said finally. "This man believes you have something to contribute to your country."

I did not know how to respond without mentioning music, a subject she had already dismissed.

Finally she snapped: "Tell me dear, where are you from?"

Not Barcelona, not Catalonia. I stammered, "From near the sea, Your Majesty."

She pressed her lips together, which made the skin of her soft jawline quiver. "And which sea would that be?"

"The Mediterranean."

I heard the shuffling in the back of the room, the stiff rubbing of the ladies' gowns as they stifled giggles.

"Your father, what does he do?"

"A customs inspector," I blurted, eager to have stumbled into safe territory. But the relief didn't last. "Except he died. In Cuba. *El Desastre.*"

"I am certain he served Spain well." But she looked unsettled. "And your mother? Was she also in Cuba?"

"No, in Catalonia." I winced at the mention of it, and kept going. "But yes, she was raised in the colonies, and moved here only later."

"Marvelous. And how did she compare the two places?"

I paused again, but the Queen Mother's hard dark eyes seemed to caution against obfuscation. I rambled, "Mamá's uncle was hanged. Plus, there were the diseases. She never wanted to go back, even before Papá died. So I guess she thought Spain was better."

The count rushed up behind me, guided at his elbow by the bumblebee lady. Now he was the one stammering. "Feliu, why don't you say something about your musical training?"

The Queen Mother waved him away. Her two dogs launched into orbit around her legs, their little black paws beating at the floor in excitement. "No, it's quite all right. I'm more interested in knowing what this boy is like, even when his cello is in another room."

"Actually," I mumbled, "I don't have my own cello."

"What's that?"

The count put his hands on my shoulders to silence me, but the Queen Mother had heard. "We do have a royal luthier, if you need a cello made. A gift to welcome you to Madrid. Unless you insist on something German or Italian."

"Spanish is fine. I would be grateful."

"Very good," she said, pleased to have ended our interview on an efficacious note.

Count Guzmán made me recount the whole episode for the condesa to hear. I had joined my new teacher and his wife at their royal apartment for the midday meal, as I would join them often for the next several years, before I returned to the small room in the servants' quarters, one floor above, that I shared with an architecture apprentice from a small town outside Lisbon.

"Well, at least we'll always know what this boy is thinking," the condesa laughed. "A far cry from some of the students that Maestro Guzmán has had."

I wanted to hear about these other students and their illustrious careers. But just then, the count's daughter entered the room.

She was wearing a simple white sheath that bunched just under her breasts, and an open neckline that revealed perfect rosy skin. Her auburn hair was swept away from her forehead and dropped to the sides in long sausage curls.

"Don't you stand when a lady enters the room?" she asked. I stumbled to my feet and waited for some acknowledgment. She prolonged my discomfort by studying me from head to foot.

"You looked much taller sitting down," she said.

"Isabel," her mother chided, and nodded at me to return to my seat. "Come hear this funny story." And I had to repeat it all over again: my insipid conversation with royalty, and my tactless mention of family sorrows, which had ended miraculously with the offer of a cello.

Count Guzmán's daughter feigned huffiness. "We've had family tragedies, haven't we? If I'd known it was so easy to get a royal instrument, I would have cried to the Queen Mother myself."

The count humored his daughter with a smile, the dark skin around his sunken eyes crinkling. Except for his impairment, he was a handsome man, clean-shaven, with a sharp jaw and a fine wardrobe that his wife and daughter fussed over, just as they took turns satisfying all his needs.

"I've played for the royal family at least two hundred times. Haven't I, Papá? I mean, really..."

The count wiped his mouth with his napkin and then set it aside, raising his palm, commanding full attention before he spoke. Isabel stopped talking. The condesa set down her fork. I had just loaded a too-large bite into my mouth and it took me a while to finish chewing, which evidently he could hear. Giving up, I swallowed hard, and winced at the knot of food caught in my throat.

"Now seriously, Feliu," he said. "About the Queen Mother. You were lucky today. But be careful. In this palace, she is the one to impress. She loves music, and she loves her musicians, and she loves her private chamber-music parties. But don't make any mistakes."

I nodded and swallowed again, my throat still aching slightly.

"If she asks you your favorite cellist, the answer is Boccherini. He was court composer a century ago, but she acts as if it were yesterday. If she asks you what foreign language you are learning, the answer is French."

"That's true," I started to say, my mouth empty at last. "French and English, and a little German—"

"The answer is French," he repeated. "Now, what else?" He tilted his face towards the condesa's. She didn't answer, but he nodded tersely as if she had.

"If she asks you about the weather outside, fine," he continued. "But if she asks you about the temperature inside, play dumb. Every winter, there is some disagreement about whether the palace is too cold."

"Every winter for the last three years," Isabel interjected.

"What happened three years ago?" I asked. The count, the condesa, and their daughter all stared at me.

Of course. The royal wedding.

"All the members of the royal family have their own apartments, obviously," the count continued, and I nodded again, because I had heard it was so, and I had puzzled over the idea of a young man sleeping in a bedroom far from his young wife.

"And likewise," he said, "each has his own friends. And the friends of one are not necessarily the friends of the others, if you understand me. So be careful what you say, and to whom; or better yet, say nothing at all."

The condesa smiled heartily and lifted her glass for a toast. "Here's to the luck of being a musician—someone who does not need to speak, and so may live a long and happy life!"

Isabel lifted her goblet in front of her nose, so that her face was mostly hidden. But from the side, I saw her clowning, her lips puckered and her nostrils flared. She noticed me noticing, and made a show of becoming sober again, as if she'd only been fighting a sneeze.

Setting my glass back down I asked, "But why do I need to impress the Queen Mother most? Doesn't the King care about music?"

At this, Isabel guffawed, a spray of wine leaked from the condesa's mouth, and even the count chuckled tenderly, reaching out with fumbling hands to offer his own napkin.

"The King cares about polo," Isabel said.

"He doesn't go to the opera?"

"He goes, but not for the music. The problem is that he doesn't always come back."

The count's fond smile faded again. "You see why my not-so-young daughter hasn't married yet? She always takes things just one step too far."

Isabel looked down at her lap. I persevered: "And the Queen?"

This time, Isabel knew better than to speak. Finally the condesa, her chin wiped and her calm restored, answered me. "She *does* love music, actually. She hosted her own private concerts before Alfonsito, Jaime, and Beatriz were born. But three children in three years—I suppose she's tired. And even so, she hasn't done what they brought her from England to do."

The count cleared his throat, and for a second time conversation stopped. When it resumed, the subjects were dull and safe: "How are your accommodations? Have you written a letter to your mother yet?"—leaving my mind to continue mulling what had been left unsaid.

I was not too provincial and slow-witted to know what the condesa had meant, about the unfinished duties of Queen Victoria Eugenia— Ena for short. Her firstborn, Alfonsito, was a hemophiliac who had nearly died at his own circumcision. No one was supposed to talk about it, but it was hard to ignore the fact that he lived in his own corner of the palace, tended by nurses and doctors, rarely seen. Something also seemed wrong with one-year-old Jaime, who did not babble or turn his head at the sound of a clap. At least the infant Beatriz seemed healthy enough.

As for Queen Ena herself, she was said to carry herself as gloomily as had her grandmother and namesake. Though only twenty-one, she had a heavy weight on her shoulders. Bourbon heirs had always been scarce—King Alfonso himself had been born just months after his father had died—and the quest for healthy male children had become a national preoccupation.

Toward the meal's end, a footman came to the door and the count excused himself. Changing the subject, the condesa asked, "Your roommate, Rodrigo—is he a good match for you?"

"He says he spends most of his time traveling between Madrid, Lisbon and Paris. I suppose that means I'll have more privacy for practicing."

"How convenient."

I nodded, but I was still thinking about the royal family. "May I ask you one more question?"

The condesa leaned forward, eager to indulge in gossip before her husband returned.

"Do you like Queen Ena?"

"It's not our place to like or dislike," Isabel recited.

The condesa smiled at her daughter gently, then turned back to me. "Even if it were our place, and she were not our Royal Majesty, and she spoke our Castilian tongue with greater ease, I'd have to say...we simply don't know her. That's the problem. No one does."

Pescado frito, Isabel mouthed silently to me, forcing me to focus on her lips.

Taking my leave of them both after dinner, I waited until the condesa had turned away. I took Isabel's hand, shook it awkwardly, and said under my breath: "The Queen likes fried fish?"

"*Frío.* The Queen is a *cold* fish, you imbecile." But she winked at me before closing the door.

My new cello was lustrously varnished, the color of amber. Its sound, however, was somewhat thin and brittle. "It must warm up," the luthier explained. "Every time you play it, you'll be vibrating the wood, changing its sound, helping it to mature like a fine wine." All the same, I was glad to have one familiar and constant thing: my bow.

I had lessons every day with the count in both cello and piano, as well as music theory. Unlike Alberto, a seasoned cellist who rarely played, Count Guzmán was a well-rounded dabbler who could pick up any instrument and play it competently, if not expertly. He had no stifled ambitions or regrets. Even his near-blindness, which had developed slowly over the last decade, didn't seem to dampen his spirits. He could still make out the occasional note or key signature on a page by holding it a centimeter in front of his brown eyes and moving it around slightly. On rare occasions, I saw him study a person or a painting in the same way, putting his face directly up to it and moving back and forth in small, irregular circles, like an insect pollinating a flower.

Most of the time, however, the count relied on his memory and his ears. That was his one regret, he told me cheerfully: that his sense of hearing hadn't become more acute as his vision failed. Wasn't that the expected compensation?

But no, he hurried to reassure me, not wanting me to think him morose. The true compensation was his family. Isabel and the condesa doted on him more every year, just as he needed them more every year. In a royal setting, this kind of intimate servitude was nothing strange— anyone of any rank had someone following after him, refilling his glass or pressing napkins into his lap, or bowing to his commands. "And if you think a blind man—or a king—is the only person who needs a retinue," the count told me pointedly, reading my thoughts, "then you are only beginning to understand the musician's life. A musician relies on people of all kinds: patrons, publishers, the audience. If you've brought any notions from Catalonia about the artist being an independent soul, leave them at the gate—they're rubbish."

Count Guzmán toyed with composition, but most of all he loved to teach. He had tutored many court musicians and even King Alfonso XIII, from the time the boy King was old enough to sit at a piano bench. The scores the count had used with royals and court prodigies were still marked from those long-ago lessons.

"That's where His Majesty would always stumble; counting was not his strength," the count would say nostalgically, listening to me play. "He couldn't wait to quit lessons." Or, "The Queen Mother let me help her with this piece. The *fortes* and *pianos* are all circled to remind her; she had a way of making every measure sound the same."

Had he ever taught the young Queen? Did she play? The count shook his head once, without clarification. Given the little that anyone would tell me, I imagined that if she did play piano, she would play quietly, timidly, without passion. On her wedding day three years earlier, a dramatic attempt had been made on her life. Everyone had marveled that the new Queen had shown no emotion at all, but continued to wave to the frenzied crowds from the palace balcony, her pale blue eyes blank as cornflowers. If she had sobbed, the gossips said, the people would have loved her more. But what did they know? Volume wasn't everything. Barcelona's streets had taught me that.

"Here is something different," the count interrupted my thoughts, extracting a worn sheet of piano music and running his fingers over its wrinkles. "Don't tell me—I recognize the paper. This is the Liszt piano concerto I kept from my last lesson with one of my best students. It was—what? Seven years ago. He never stayed anywhere for long. Anyway, this piece opens with some grueling hand positions. It's not for you, not this one."

"Why is it so . . . creased?"

"That's where he stomped on it."

"Because he couldn't play it?"

I enjoyed the idea that even the count's best student couldn't play everything.

But he corrected me. "Oh no, he could play it. I think he was upset that he hadn't thought to write it."

Youthful brilliance didn't intimidate the count; nothing did. Unlike Alberto, he had a method for everything—unwavering steps he expected students to follow. He didn't spend much time marveling at my lack of formal training. In his experience, most students arrived in poor shape, their training often worse than no music education at all. He set about scrubbing me blank in order to begin our relationship fresh. It was invigorating at first, as any good scrubbing can be, until the flesh becomes raw.

Isabel frequently observed our lessons, as ready as her father to point out my failings.

"Solo, he plays like an angel," she announced one day after I'd played, with the count accompanying on piano. We were in the music room attached to the count's palace apartment, the tall doors drawn closed, the warm air thick with the smell of cut flowers.

"But in duet, or ensemble"—she turned her head dramatically—"it's not his fault, I know. Somehow he is...*stunted* is the word that comes to mind."

I sat up straighter in my chair and tried to look unconcerned.

"Isabel is right," the count said. "You're talented. But you have played alone for too long. Inconsistent tempi, unpredictable dynamic shifts, insufficient communication. They all point to the same thing. You have not learned to adjust to other musicians playing with you."

He rubbed his hand back and forth along his cheeks, his fingertips absentmindedly massaging the barest shadow of new stubble. "What I should do, really, is take him back to the beginning; just the cello, to start—there are problems even there. Best to delay any kind of ensemble work."

Isabel's mouth dropped. "That's the opposite of what I meant! We're playing together in less than two weeks, in the royal salon. He needs *more* duet practice, not less. I'm not an accompanist for hire; he'd best learn to play as equals, and soon."

A maid entered to serve us hot chocolate. I welcomed the interruption and I knew the count would, too; he loved sweets almost as much as he disliked seeing his grown daughter upset. But Isabel continued her protest over the maid's beating of the whisk within the spouted silver pot. There was something artificial in her tirade, but I didn't yet recognize it for what it was: the invented drama of a palace-dwelling courtier's life, neither personal nor truly passionate. And yet my own passions felt inflamed, in response. I would have listened to hours of abuse, if only to watch her chest heave and her fists curl.

Finally the count stepped in. "She is trying to say that a duet is like dancing. You can't step on each other's toes. *De acuerdo?*" He paused for his daughter's agreement. She shrugged, then opened her mouth, ready to lecture me again.

But he preempted her. "Feliu, have you ever ridden a horse?"

"A mule," I said quickly. "I've ridden a mule."

Isabel groaned.

"A mule," the count repeated thoughtfully. "No, I don't think a mule moves as gracefully with its rider. That won't help here."

Finally he said, "I'm not a poet. What I am trying to describe is not just cooperation, but two voices becoming one; not suddenly, but in dynamic stages. Do you understand?"

"Yes, I think so."

After a few sullen minutes, the maid came and cleared the cups. I stared forlornly at Isabel. Even with a thin mustache of chocolate above her lip, she was lovely. Isabel caught me looking and brushed the back of her hand against her face. Then she smiled—finally, one smile! It made me happy and dizzy, all at once.

"I will teach Feliu," she announced suddenly. "Let me have him for a week, and I promise our duet will not sound the same."

"If you think it will help him. And if it will please you," the count said.

"It will please me. But you may not interfere. No one must bother us. This is a matter for artists to resolve privately."

The count tilted his head to one side, the dark orbs of his unseeing eyes fixed on me with what, in earlier days, might have been a puzzled glance. Then he screwed up his face in mock horror. "You're not going to torture him, I hope?"

"Oh, Papá."

Hearing her tone soften, he exhaled, dropping the subject. He patted his vest pocket. "I almost forgot—another addition to our small royal recital! A former student will be in Madrid that day. He is look-ing forward to joining us and hearing you both play."

Isabel, a moment earlier haughty with confidence, now blanched. "Which student?"

"If you must have secrets, then so should I," he laughed. "I think I will leave you guessing."

But we both knew the name of the count's most famous student, the one whom everyone still talked about all these years later, the one who had stomped on Liszt. It had to be Al-Cerraz.

The next day, I entered the count's private music room. Before we ex-changed greetings, I heard Isabel turn the lock. I immediately pulled a chair into place, next to the piano, and began tightening my bow.

"No," she said, and gestured to a brocaded divan at the other end of the room. "Sit down. We barely know each other. Tell me about your village. Tell me about your family."

I was wary, but I began to talk, and soon I was telling her every-thing—about living in Barcelona with Alberto and my mother, about the coast near our home where we'd gone on vacations so long ago, about the strange divide, between people who knew and loved me and thought my music making was nothing unusual, and strangers who seemed to expect great things of me—what exactly, I did not know. I told her I wasn't yet sure where I stood in the world, or what might happen next.

She responded with her own confession. "I've never been afraid of being the world's worst pianist, or the world's best. It's the middle ground I dread."

"Yes," I said, hoping she would continue.

"These days, every woman in the world plays. I recently heard one of Madrid's most eligible bachelors say he plans to marry the first woman he meets who says that she has never touched a piano."

We both laughed, and she laid a hand, gently, on top of mine. I pressed my hand harder into the satiny surface of the divan, so she wouldn't notice I had developed a slight, discomfiting shake. I'd never spent even a minute alone with a young woman behind a closed door. I put a second hand on top of hers, and we sat that way, stiffly, for several more minutes, until I pushed myself to my feet.

"I care for you enough that I would hate to embarrass you," I said.

"You were thinking of embarrassing me?" Isabel replied with a peculiar eagerness.

"By playing poorly, I mean. In front of the Queen Mother. At our recital."

"Oh." Her shoulders slumped.

Recovering, she said, "You must think you're lucky to have found your way to the palace. But the truth is, the court is always desperate for fresh blood. My parents are happy with their routines, but really, a young person doesn't belong here." She smiled coyly. "I see that look. You're probably thinking I don't look so young."

I resisted the urge to take a step back. "No. I was thinking that you're very pretty. Especially with your hair that way."

This comment pleased her. Shoulders lifted, she crossed the room to the piano, her curls bouncing. Then she sat down and played the first measures of the piece we were working on, a Schumann fantasy for cello and piano. It was a romantic piece—overromantic, I thought, requiring lots of hand-flopping excess, though there were a few nice passages where the piano part settled down and followed the cello.

At one point, mid-measure, Isabel stopped and turned. "Schumann was ten years older than Clara when they married, against her father's wishes. I don't think age differences matter, do you?"

My mind was still engaged with the music. I said, "I don't know. I suppose it matters less when the man is older. A middle-aged woman with a young man would seem strange."

Isabel turned back to the piano. But over her shoulder she said,

"Clara may have been younger, but she often said that Schumann reminded her of a little boy."

We started again, but after a few minutes Isabel pushed herself up and strode away from the bench. She paced a few times behind me. I could hear the *spiccato* rhythm of her little hard-soled shoes against the parquet floor.

I'd been too nervous to warm up properly when we'd started; even now, my fingers felt a little slow. So I began with scales, while I waited for Isabel to return to the piano. Instead, she approached from behind my chair. I could feel her standing back there. After two scales, I stopped.

"No, go ahead," she said, and I felt a warm tingle on the back of my neck. Even after she stopped speaking, I was sure I could feel her breath. I closed my eyes and resumed playing.

"You deal well with distractions," she said.

I dug my bow into the string a little fiercely, then found my rhythm again. "When everything is just right, I don't notice the outside world at all."

"Really," she said, and without looking, I could picture the upturned corners of her lips. "Nothing bothers you."

"When everything is right. This wouldn't count—I'm just playing scales."

"Then play something you love."

"All right." And I started the short, sprightly gigue from Bach's first unaccompanied cello suite.

"Solo again—an interesting choice. Not everything can be done solo, you know," she said. And I felt her fingertips on my shoulders.

I was grateful I had picked a fast-moving piece. My back muscles, already tense as I executed the gigue's short bow strokes, tightened further in response to the downward motion of Isabel's hands. Near the bottom of my rib cage, her hands crept forward.

I yelped and jumped to my feet. "This isn't a good idea!" Trying to sound calmer, I continued, "You know, we really should practice our duet. Tomorrow will be better. We can make up for lost time." I stumbled toward the door, holding my cello before me, to hide the physical effect her attentions had produced.

"This isn't lost time, Feliu," she said. But I was already out the door.

Afternoons with the count at his home—and that week, alone with his daughter—were not the only part of my education in Madrid. Count Guzmán and the Queen Mother, who was sponsoring my stay, both believed that a court musician should be immersed in Spain's glories: her arts, her architecture, her history, and even her modern-day government. Mamá, who had been worried about my nonmusical education, would be pleased.

Most mornings after my solo cello practice time, I was dispatched on assignment, to roam, research, and report. I was sent to the Cortes, Spain's parliament, to observe speeches, and to the national library, to read about famous people and events. I visited the mausoleum of King Alfonso XII, the present King's father, who had reigned for only ten years. In the Sala Árabe, at the Army Museum, I saw the sword of Boabdil, the last Muslim ruler of Granada, who surrendered that stronghold in 1492. There was much to learn, though most of it seemed to concern rulers and wars. Enrique would have liked Madrid, I thought to myself. As for me, I wasn't sure.

Barcelona had seemed like a city pushing toward the future. Madrid—dustier, dowdier, hardly a capital—seemed mired in the past. Women coiled their hair in fancier chignons and wore more lace; some men still wore antiquated capes. There was no place in Madrid as open and free as Barcelona's Ramblas. There were public places, certainly, like the Parque del Buen Retiro, where one could rent a rowboat and paddle among the ducks. But the count and his wife warned me to stay away from the lower classes' haunts. They escorted me around the city in a carriage, pointing out the hazards: that's where young men have been knived; that's where a lady never goes; there's the bridge that suicides use—the river beneath it so shallow that the bodies often beached themselves in plain view.

In Barcelona, bombs exploded and dead bodies washed up along the seacoast, yet people there didn't seem half as fearful as the Madrileños. I suppose that in the capital, where the power of the throne resided, people sensed there was more to lose. The fear drove people inside— entertainment was a private affair, lessons were learned in museums instead of on the streets, dramas were played out in private salons. Though café culture thrived in Madrid as well, it seemed less vital.

My favorite mornings were when I was sent to the Museo del Prado, the grand, century-old art museum. There, alone, I would behold the paintings of Velázquez, El Greco, and Goya. Even here the paintings featured battle scenes—like Goya's painting of Madrid's defenders being executed by Napoleon's troops. From the museum I would hurry directly to the palace, trying to hold the images in my mind so that I could discuss the Spanish Masters with my tutor.

"What did the King and Queen look like?" he quizzed me over the midday *comida* after the morning I first viewed the Prado's most famous painting, Velázquez's *Las Meninas*. In my mind's eye, I can still see the canvas edge that runs along the left side of the painting, so that the viewer feels he is peering from behind, glimpsing something more real and candid than a stuffy palace portrait. At the center, framed by deep shadow, is a blond girl, the Infanta Margarita, surrounded by two playmates, two dwarves, and a dog. The King and Queen, who were sitting for a portrait when Velázquez decided to capture the scene, are not in the foreground at all, but are shown only in the hazy background, reflected in a mirror. More prominent than the royal couple is a man off to the left side, who is eyeing the front of the canvas, which the viewer cannot see.

"The King and Queen were small and blurry, I think," I said.

"And Velázquez?"

"Where was he?"

"He was the painter, of course. The man on the left, just next to the children."

"He painted himself into the picture? More prominent than the King?"

"He did," the count laughed. "What do you think of that? The artist more prominent than his intended subjects—do you think that is appropriate?"

I had learned from observing Isabel and the condesa that the count admired strong opinions—to a point. I'd always been opinionated, at least as far as the cello was concerned, but was only just learning to feign verbal confidence on other topics.

"I don't believe it's right. The painter, musician—artist of any sort—should not project himself into the work so arrogantly. He should not destroy the integrity of what he is painting, or what he is playing. The artist is only a servant."

The count nodded, but did not react to my pronouncement.

"And anyway," I said, "I'm sure the King was angry."

"Which King?" Count Guzmán asked.

"The one in the picture."

"But what is his name?"

"Not Carlos. Felipe...the Third?"

"Almost. Felipe the Fourth. You couldn't remember. But you can remember the name of Velázquez."

"Of course! He is famous."

"More famous than a king? Only because he painted himself into the picture?"

"No. He's famous for many paintings, of many places and people, not just the King or Queen."

"I think so," the count said at last. "There was a time when all art was for royalty only, or the Church; all serious music played for them, all paintings made of them. Even Velázquez would have had a hard time imagining it otherwise. But that time is past. I can imagine one day when there won't be a king at all, when a painter, or a writer or a cellist"—here he winked—"will be as powerful as a king."

It was as close as Guzmán ever came to admitting Republican or anti-monarchical leanings. I glanced around the room, searching furtively for eavesdroppers.

"But I thought you said a musician is *not* independent."

The count smiled. "True—and I meant it. Even someone who is powerful is dependent, perhaps even more so. Whenever we need support and acceptance, we are dependent.

"Anyway," he continued, "this question of where the artist stands in relation to his subject, of how much he adds of himself, whether he tries to affect the world he is portraying, how wildly he interprets— that is something to ponder. I think you are both behind and ahead of your time, Feliu—a classicist with modern hands."

I loved the way the count could relate everything to music, and make me feel as if Spain's masterpieces had a personal message for me. I basked in his words, and would have preferred to end our conversation about art there, before I muddled things with another ignorant comment. But then he asked about one more work: the double portrait of the Maja, the Duchess of Alba.

I knew from my museum visit that Goya had painted the duchess twice, in the exact same position, reclining provocatively—one clothed, one nude. When the count pressed me, I had no trouble recalling the latter painting, in embarrassing detail: the way the Maja's pale torso gleamed and her small toes pointed, the orangelike roundness of her breasts. By the time I'd spent several minutes describing the painting, I realized the count was doing more than teaching me. He was using me as his eyes, as an extension of something he had lost. I didn't mind it too much. But I made note of the feeling—the sense of being appropriated—which, in my courtly duties, would become increasingly familiar.

"It's rumored that they slept together," the count said, continuing to relish this day's discussion. "In the nude, she wears a ring that says 'Goya.' More of the artist inserting himself into the picture."

He paused, and belatedly I realized he was waiting for me to laugh. When I didn't, he said, "Forgive my play on words."

"The lesson from Goya?" I asked, to change the subject.

"There are hundreds of lessons, I'm sure. But when you go back, notice how poorly the nude's face is painted. Flat and yellow. So much less realistic than the clothed Maja portrait. This is not a statement against women, Feliu, but it may be a caution for men. Even an artist seems to have a hard time seeing well when a woman is undressed. Remember that."

"Yes, I promise," I said, grateful that the day's lessons finally could turn to grammar.

That afternoon I had my second session with Isabel. She opened the salon door wearing the same simple white dress she'd worn the first time I'd met her, but this time cinched with a bright red sash. My throat tightened.

"Have you thought about me?" she asked.

I thought about the hours I'd lain awake the night before, replaying the day's encounter, regretting my shyness. "You look like the Maja," I whispered.

"Who?"

"The Duchess of Alba."

Isabel smiled slyly. Leading me to the divan, she said, "My father has been sending you to the Prado. Do you mean the painting of the duchess standing, with the little white dog?"

"No, the one where she is leaning back. On a narrow bed. Against some pillows."

"Like this?" She tucked her feet behind her and reclined.

"With her arms up, I think. Hands over her head."

Her smile widened as she tucked her hands behind her hair. The neck of her dress gaped, and I could glimpse the swell of one breast. "Was the Maja beautiful?" she asked.

"She had...small feet."

"Do you like feet, Feliu?"

"Not particularly," I said, voice cracking.

Isabel stood suddenly, flashing a satisfied grin, and strolled to the piano. "Ready to begin?"

We played for an hour. When passion for the music stirred my soul, when the tunnel of light began to blur my vision, I forced myself to focus on Isabel, studying her body for cues—the lift of her chin, the tension in her shoulders, the arch of her back, the sound of a note being extended, waiting. I'd never felt more alert to another's reactions and desires—even if the expression on my face, and in my playing, had all the sophistication of an obedient mastiff awaiting its reward.

After we'd finished playing, Isabel returned to the divan and resumed the Maja pose, gesturing to the floor. I looked around my feet to see what she had dropped. She gestured again, less patiently, until I understood and dropped to one knee in front of her. I lifted my left hand toward her bosom but stopped short until Isabel arched her back, moving herself closer to me, inviting me to trace her loose neckline with one finger.

"They're rough," she said, closing her eyes.

I responded with a quizzical grunt.

"Your fingers."

"Calluses," I mumbled, trying to breathe more slowly. "From pressing on the strings."

She laughed at the animal desperation in my voice. That set me back. But then she lifted the shiny white dress above her knees, and I moved closer.

"So this is what you meant by making up for lost time," she said.

"So this is what you meant by private lessons," I replied, trying to mimic her confidence.

"What if I did?"

I was grateful for everything she knew, and everything she would allow. Neither of us spoke again for several minutes, until her breathing was as ragged as mine.

"The other hand," she moaned.

"What?" I said, reaching for her hands.

"Not mine. Yours," she said impatiently. "Use your right hand."

And with her sighs, squirms, and own fingers guiding me, I switched hands and traveled as far as I dared, under layers of silk and cotton, into places I had not known existed.

At one point, she began to moan instructions, but I didn't comprehend—I didn't want to comprehend—until finally, she switched to musical Italian and barked a command I knew better than to ignore: *"Adagio!"*

Finally, she shivered and her knees clamped tightly, trapping my arm for a moment. I thought I had hurt her, or done something wrong, but her dreamy expression reassured me, and she pulled me up and onto the divan, until I was on top of her.

As soon as my weight was atop her, everything was over. My pleasure lasted only seconds before it was washed away by a flood of embarrassment. I started to roll away and pull my pants together, but she pulled me back.

"Like everything, it takes practice," she said.

"It should last longer."

"Fast is fine once, but now for the slower part. Sonata form."

"So this is still part of the music lesson."

"What did my father say?"

"Oh, please, don't mention your father," I groaned, and I tugged at her dress, trying to cover her exposed breasts, which really did look like the Duchess of Alba's, only softer. But Isabel shrugged off my attempts to clothe her.

"'Not just cooperation, but two voices becoming one.' That is what he said. That is what I am supposed to teach you."

I started to laugh, but her face was serious. "If you don't know when to wait, when to hurry, how to please, you won't be a good lover *or* a good musician."

"Do you care for me, Isabel?"

She rolled her eyes. "Am I not helping you?"

No matter how I tried to elicit a profession of affection she remained disarmingly lighthearted about the whole affair. Finally I said simply, "Can we crescendo again—this time, more slowly?" At last I had found the words that lifted her smile and unlocked her legs.

"I haven't heard much music coming from the salon," Count Guzmán said at dinner the next day. "Is my daughter not keeping her end of the bargain?"

I swallowed hard and said, "She is."

At that moment, Isabel spoke up—"More, please"—and gestured for her mother to pass her the tureen of rice.

"Your appetite certainly has increased," the condesa said warmly.

"Has it?" Isabel said, shoveling large spoonfuls onto her plate.

That afternoon, we were already on the divan together—Isabel's dress askew; all my clothes except for my black socks in a pile at my feet—when the tall salon doors opened. We sat bolt upright and Isabel called out brightly: "We were just chatting on the divan, Papá, but we're ready to play now."

He turned slowly to face us, smiling, no sign of suspicion in his shadow-circled eyes.

"You're breaking your promise," Isabel said teasingly, "but I suppose you can stay to listen—just this once." She skipped across the room to the piano, giving her father a wide berth. Her scent was still in my nose, a flood of complex feminine smells that I hoped wouldn't carry his way. I reached down toward my pants, but realized I'd make too much noise trying to put them on. I looked up and saw Isabel glaring at me, gesturing frantically that I should come and take my seat.

The count declined his daughter's offer of a chair and positioned himself several steps away from us both, the third point in our musical triangle, with his hands clasped behind his back. As we played through the first part of our recital piece, I began to breathe easier, astonished to be surviving this close brush with exposure. Then out of the corner of my eye, I saw the count's face tilt to one side. He lifted a finger tentatively, then lowered it; lifted it again and said, "It's good work. Very fine. But I hear a buzzing—there, against the cello."

Isabel and I stopped playing.

"No," the count said. "Keep going. Don't let it interrupt."

Now I heard it, too—a faint vibrating sound.

The count took one step closer.

"It must be a button," he said, while I continued to bow. That was a common problem: a jacket or shirt button pressing against the cello's wooden back.

The count twitched and stepped closer again. "Feliu—adjust that."

I was sweating now. There was nothing to adjust. I wasn't wearing any shirt—or pants. Or undergarments either.

"We'll skip the repeat," Isabel said over our playing as we neared the end of the piece.

"Don't," the count ordered, visibly annoyed by the sound. Perhaps his hearing was more acute than ours, after all. Or perhaps his fatherly instinct had detected something additionally amiss, compounding the aural imperfection.

He was at my shoulder now, bending forward slightly to bring his eye close to where my shirt should be, even as I bowed, my right elbow on a collision course with his torso.

"We're almost done, Papá," Isabel said, looking over her shoulder as she rushed through the repeat.

It was maddening—nothing was touching the cello, and yet the buzzing was still there. We came to a passage where Isabel played several chords while I rested.

"Perhaps it's the cello itself," I said, leaning forward quickly, hand over the bridge. Then I remembered the garters holding up my socks—the only clothed part of me. I reached down, found the small metal clasp that secured the left garter, and twisted it away from the cello rib. The buzzing stopped.

"There," I said quickly, "just a loose tuner at the bridge. Sorry." And I rejoined Isabel, only a measure late.

The count commented little on our performance, only smiled and wished us continued good luck, then took his leave. Isabel was giddy over the close call, the danger of discovery, the hilarity of my nakedness. She was even more frisky and eager to take our chances on the divan again.

I wasn't as gleeful. We seemed to have gotten away with it, but I couldn't shake the feeling that the count had *known*—that whether or not he had seen me, he had seen *through* me. I already had the sense that Isabel was toying with me, that her game would be a short one, and that I might be indulging one kind of pleasure while sacrificing another: the gratification of a mature and long-lasting mentorship with her father.

Still, our lovemaking really had made me more aware and more accommodating as a musician. I learned to follow Isabel, to chase her, to turn away, to draw her to me. I knew when to hurry and when to delay, how to read pleasure in the movements of her face and fingers, how to satisfy her.

After one session on the divan, I lifted my head from her heart and said, "You were right about learning this way. I promise never to play selfishly again."

She laughed, gasping for air beneath my weight. "Don't feel bad. Some things are difficult to learn, or to teach."

"And who taught you?" I regretted the words as soon as they escaped.

"Taught me...?"

"Piano duets, I mean. Not the other thing."

"Don't worry, Feliu," she said, pushing herself up, and rearranging her curls around her shoulders. "I'm not shy. It was one of my father's students who taught me both things. His most celebrated student, in fact—"

"Don't tell me. I think I've heard of this famous student more than enough already."

"He convinced me that a virgin can understand music only so well. He did the favor for me, and I am doing it for you."

"Favor?"

"Certainly."

I was standing already, pulling on my clothes. "I'm sorry I asked."

"Why are you upset? You didn't think I'd never been with another man, did you?"

"Not that." I balanced on one foot, trying to push the other foot into my shoe without bothering to loosen the laces. "But I don't like to be compared. And I didn't realize this was merely an exercise for you."

"What's wrong with exercises?"

"I suppose it depends on how many people you exercise with."

"What are you implying?"

I grabbed my cello case and bow tube. "If this is how you practice for a duet, I'd hate to see how you prepare for a symphony."

Before she could respond, I slipped out of the music room and closed the door. I heard the sharp thud of flying objects on the other side, followed by her muffled rejoinder. "You're still a child, Feliu!"

Something heavier hit the door, making it tremble.

"Worse than that, you're still a soloist!"

CHAPTER

~ 9 ~

From my apartment window overlooking the hot, flat parade grounds, I watched the preparations for the Queen Mother's concert. Forty men on forty horses—white, with bulging flanks and glossy tails—enacted the changing of the guard. Then the guests arrived, and the tops of the ladies' parasols formed an unbroken sea of shimmering white polygons, winking in the sun.

I had no desire to wade into that decorous ocean until another sight caught my eye. Two silver open-topped motorcars pulled into a corner of the square grounds. I packed up my cello and hurried outside. I had approached to within five or six meters when a driver glared at me threateningly. Glancing around, I recognized one of the servant girls from my floor.

"I thought this was supposed to be a small party," I said to her.

"Bigger now, with *Sus Majestades* back early."

That explained the buzz of activity around the Grand Railings enclosing the parade grounds, the dozens of extra pennant-bearing ceremonial guards, the rifle-bearing soldiers lined up outside the Palace gates.

I hadn't expected to glimpse the King and Queen until October. They moved from one royal residence to another through the cycle of seasons, avoiding Madrid at midsummer. Most recently, they'd been vacationing seaside, at San Sebastián, near the French border. But Queen Ena had wanted to see her doctors in Madrid.

"They say she is making a baby," the servant girl told me.

"But Beatriz is only three months old."

"The *nena* is a girl. They need another boy," she said and walked away, as if to put a safe distance between herself and my ignorance.

The two motorcars were parked at right angles. Behind them, against the wall of the palace, three men stood chatting, cigars in hand, while near them a tall, thin boy in baggy knickers and argyle socks played with some childish contraption. It was one of those stick-and-ball toys, and the tall boy was having trouble spearing the ball, though the three men were giving him what seemed like an excessive amount of encouragement: *"Bien, bien."* "Almost got it." "Bad luck." *"Otra vez."*

Then one of the men said, "Just pretend it's a woman." It seemed a vulgar thing to say to a boy, though it made all four of them burst out in guffaws. The tall boy held his hand to his stomach as he doubled over, laughing; then he used the same hand to slick back his hair. The gesture drew my attention to his eyes, which were large and dark, accentuated by olive-tinted eyelids and above that, a deeply creased forehead.

Walking past the strange youth on my way to the main palace door, I felt the weight of dozens of eyes—the cigar-smoking men, the chauffeurs, guards in three different uniforms. At the door itself, the halberdiers rapped their long ax-topped pikes on the ground. The double-tap startled me, and I passed inside quickly and hobbled toward the main staircase, hoping the guards hadn't noticed me flinch.

I had reason to be nervous this day. Isabel had refused to rehearse with me after our last "lesson." Practicing my part alone, I'd told myself that I would muddle through just fine. I hadn't given any formal recitals; but neither had I learned to fear them. Back in Barcelona, I had made it through my audition with Don José. I'd simply pretend I was playing on the Ramblas.

We were to be the party's second act. The Queen Mother herself would go first, playing a short duet with the count. It had been arranged that the count would present this as a spontaneous idea, bowing low to the ground to beseech her to play, as if he had not been tutoring her for weeks. It was this duty—a diplomatic challenge as well as an artistic one—that had kept him from noticing the discord between me and his recalcitrant daughter.

All went well with the Queen Mother's duet. The applause of three dozen close friends put her into such a buoyant mood that, I dared to hope, even our inadequately rehearsed duet could scarcely threaten it.

The count stood between Isabel and me as we were introduced to the party guests, who were seated in a casual horseshoe of upholstered chairs. I tried to catch Isabel's eye, but she kept her head tilted resolutely away from me.

In the beginning, Isabel pretended she was playing solo and so did I, so that our rhythms and accents were merely out of step. But as the standoff heated up, Isabel decided to play over me, both faster and louder. The composition gave her an edge, because Schumann had loaded it with pianistic hyperbole. Isabel rocked her head and stamped her feet with so much force that she seemed on the verge of falling off the bench. Behind us, a woman gasped. Somewhere nearby, I heard a man with a low, reassuring voice respond, "Very fine—very modern."

I played as ferociously as I could in the shadow of Isabel's angry pounding, trying to subdue her. I brought my bow close to the bridge, working a deep growl from the strings, and I leaned into every stroke, letting my weight help me. At the most frenetic moment in the piece, I couldn't hear Isabel at all. For a fraction of a second I thought she had stopped playing, but when I glanced up, I saw her shoulders still heaving. Continuing to bow thunderously, I scanned to the right, and my eyes fell upon the Queen Mother. Her head was tilted slightly to one side, and her eyes were narrowed in an undecided expression, verging on annoyance.

Next to her, I was surprised to notice, was the tall boy. Now he was suited in formal clothes, although his thin calves were encased in riding boots that looked wrong for a music salon. His jaw was slack, his olive-lidded eyes nearly closed. He looked not just older now, but geriatric. Our sovereign. He may have been an uninspiring young man, but *I* was the fool who had failed to recognize a king.

Though I'd missed a short run of sixteenth notes and Isabel and I were more out of step than ever, I continued to look. Next to the King sat a woman with an oval face, perfectly white, her dark blond hair piled atop her head and her eyes as pale and distant as a cloud reflected in water. I'd never seen the Queen in person until that moment, but I had been told that her eyes hinted at some vacancy within. I didn't believe it. I'd spent enough hours staring at whole notes to know that what looked empty could often hold more than something that looked full.

Just when the music sounded its cacophonous worst, I thought I saw a twitch of amusement on the young Queen's thin lips. But then it was gone, and her face looked milky and dour again. I was still trying to fig-ure out if I'd imagined the smile or really seen it when I came to the end of a rapid descending flurry of notes and dug into my lowest string.

A that moment, a shot rang out. The room erupted in screams and blurry motions. The King threw himself toward the Queen Mother's lap; whether to protect her or to take refuge in her, no one could say. Isabel made one last lurch to the side, slid off the piano bench, and col-lapsed on the floor. Someone yanked open the salon door, allowing two startled halberdiers to peer into the room.

The Queen herself was still sitting perfectly upright, as if she were being held erect by puppet strings. One finger of her gloved white hand seemed to levitate in the air, pointing at—we all craned our necks to follow the trajectory of her gesture—pointing at *me*. Or my cello, any-way. I twisted right and left, pulled the neck of my cello forward, and realized that the G string had snapped. No gun or bomb, just a popped string.

A wave of relief washed over the room, followed by rising chatter and giddy laughter. A guard came to inspect my cello. He examined the popped string, then peered inside the F-shaped sound holes and lifted aside the lapels of my jacket. As the hubbub in the room increased, I saw Isabel slip away. The tip of her nose was red and her cheeks shone with frustrated tears. The duet—thank God—was over, and I did not have to endure any applause, or the lack of it.

"Modern, you say?" I heard the Queen Mother saying above the background clamor, her head still tilted at that undecided angle.

"In Paris, people would have demanded an encore," a rotund man responded. His face was turned away from me, so that I could only see his broad, jacketed back.

"This isn't Paris," the Queen Mother said drily.

"Thank goodness. *Vive la différence.* But if you'd like a third act instead of an encore, I am ready to begin."

"Yes." She reached out to pat his arm with a surprisingly familiar touch while she forced a weak laugh. "Thank you, Justo. I think that would restore order beautifully."

I suppose my life to this point had been oddly, if backhandedly, blessed. Bad things befell me regularly, but often they seemed to work in my favor. From my father's death, I had received a bow; from my mother's doomed pairing with Don Miguel, I was granted flight to Barcelona; in the midst of radical uprising, I was promoted to musical study in Madrid. Now, this failed concert—which should have sent me packing—had attracted the attention of Justo Al-Cerraz for the second time in my life. This time he mistook me for a fellow mischief-maker.

After playing to a charmed audience, he extracted me from the Queen Mother's party and pulled me by the hand down a dark hallway, back to the parade grounds.

"My cello—"

"The count will take care of it. He's the one I am trying to avoid—his daughter, too, actually, but you've assisted me there." He stopped at a bright red car parked alongside the two silver ones I'd seen earlier.

"But he was your teacher. Didn't you come to visit him?"

"I came because the Queen Mother invited me," he said, lumbering up over a dip in the side panel and onto the padded leather bench in front. "She and I have our own history. Will you give me a hand here?"

Could one have a history with a sovereign? A sovereign *is* history.

"She knew I was in Madrid," he continued after he'd squeezed behind the wheel, breathing hard. "I don't say no to royal invitations." He gestured for me to get in on the other side.

"Where are we going?"

"On my personal farewell tour. I don't plan to come this way again. This is my last evening in Madrid—maybe forever."

I hadn't brought an overcoat. The dress shoes I'd borrowed from the count pinched my feet. "How long will we—" I was halfway in, one leg dragging when the motorcar lurched forward.

"Get in!" Al-Cerraz shouted, laughing, and we were off. "This model set the record three years ago. Forty-six kilometers per hour!"

Two halberdiers leaped out of our way and a guard managed to open the main gate just in time for us to pass through without hitting it. On the flagstone parade grounds the motorcar had glided smoothly, but once we hit the road beyond the palace, it erupted into violent vibrations on the loaf-shaped cobblestones. Al-Cerraz gripped the wheel with wide white fingers and clenched his teeth, but nothing could stop his cheeks and belly from shaking.

I lobbed questions at him over the roar of the engine—how long I had wanted to ask a prominent musician so many things! Only every third word transmitted. It was like trying to converse in another language, without subtleties, but between swerves and rattles, the answers came back: "…two hundred seventy-five days…that's touring…the first manager I've ever trusted…Debussy, yes, but…Pedrell, the father of Spanish music…lower spine, if we're not careful…the prize in Rome…the problem with sausages…and then again…" I nodded eagerly trying to organize his words in memory, like little boxes of printer's type, which later—I hoped—could be arranged into meaningful messages. I wasn't certain he was saying anything worth knowing, but I felt lucky all the same—the wind in my hair, horses whinnying as we passed, men and women crowding into doorways along the narrow streets and recoiling as we showered them with clouds of dust. I had envied this man, resented him, but how quickly resentment turned to pride, how easily dislike turned into worship when one felt included.

We turned a corner, the car bucked and slowed, and in the sudden engine-dead silence my voice, barely audible before, emerged as an earsplitting screech: "…she said it was the best way!"

The car rolled another few meters. Al-Cerraz tugged at a glossy black knob and set the brake. He reached into his pocket for a handkerchief and I saw that he was shaking with laughter. "By making love, you said?" He wiped his brow, then brayed a final time and blasted his nose into the handkerchief. "Black snot—that's what you get driving. A windshield would be nice, and a roof. Then again, that would feel like being in a carriage or a train, all hidden away. I still think that motorcars are the way of the future. It fascinates me. Is there any more important question, really, than what will last?"

He said this without a hint of irony, even though his own motorcar had just rolled to a broken halt. Then, returning to the subject that had bridged the car's last gasp, "What gave you the idea that duet partners need to be intimate? Music as lovemaking—what a cliché!" He laughed again, and I looked away, to hide my red face.

"It's not your fault," he continued. "Isabel's, right? And mine—I put that into her head. Of course I did." He laughed again.

Al-Cerraz reached over and ruffled my hair with his large hand. "That's what you need—the windswept look! I hope you don't mind what happened. But why should you? Days behind closed doors with Isabel! I'm sure they were fun while they lasted."

He patted his thighs. There was a long pause. Finally he said, "The count is a good teacher. Stick with him, a year or two at least. Hear him out. Though he, like Isabel, can get stuck on a single motif. Has he told you that you are a modernist with classical hands?"

"A classicist," I said, "with modern hands."

"So there's the difference between us," Al-Cerraz said. "And some warning associated with Goya and women," he remembered, smiling wistfully.

So I was not special; not with Isabel, or with the count. They were reliving with me what they had lived and said and done with Al-Cerraz. I seemed destined to follow in this pianist's footsteps.

Which made me promise myself, at that moment, to focus on being as different from him as possible. Already, I had adopted my own more sober style of playing. That had been instinct, not artifice, but now I vowed to distance myself further from his flamboyance and the antics of so many musicians like him. My face would reveal nothing. I would aim always to channel the music, attracting no attention to myself, focusing on the larger aim…which was? I wished he or someone like him could tell me.

Al-Cerraz studied my face, his eyes twinkling as they watered from the wind and the dust.

"Are you all right? Fernán, was that your name?"

"Feliu."

"Feliu, we must get this motorcar a drink."

"Petrol?"

"Water. It's a Stanley Steamer," he said, peering over the hood to the parched road. "In England, there were creeks at every turn. Where there weren't creeks, there were puddles. But here…" He wiped his forehead again.

"Maybe it's not the best motorcar for these parts," I said.

He bellowed indignantly. "Mercy—I invested in a dealership! But as they explained to me, where there are no creeks, there are troughs, even in La Mancha."

He reached behind his seat, pulled out a rectangular screw-capped container that looked like an oversized flask, and pushed it toward me. "This is why I never drive without a companion. Back one block and turn right—I'm sure I saw a horse trough back there near the lamp-post, where the cabs park. Don't worry about me. I'll guard the car."

Off I went, retracing our route, brooding over what Al-Cerraz had said about Isabel and the count, trying to feel dislike for him, squirming at the recent memory of my pleasure at being asked to join him on this drive. *Fernán*—I said it out loud, bitterly. He didn't know my name. He just wanted a water carrier for his wretched steam machine. *Horse troughs.* I stubbed my toe on a cobblestone and felt a pain shoot into my hip. But someday, I thought, when motorcars take over the world, there won't be horse troughs every few blocks.

When things change, they don't change a little, they change a lot— so completely we can't even anticipate the reversals; what vanishes, what rises to take its place. What would last? Not Stanley Steamers. Not, I predicted, the music of Al-Cerraz.

"I remember a boy," he said to me two hours later, punctuating the statement with flatulence. We'd managed to get the Stanley Steamer restarted, and this was the third *taverna* we'd slumped into—"for a bite to eat," he'd said, though he'd accompanied every crust of bread and bit of greasy meat with at least two glasses of amber liquid.

I leaned as far away from him as my stool would allow. But as soon as I moved, he began to slide, and I had to lean back against his meaty shoulder to keep him upright. The bartender's eyes lifted at the sound of my grunt, which gave Al-Cerraz the opportunity to lift his finger for a refill.

"This boy," he said, "was everything that I am not. I have been trying to find him for years."

I held out my hand to stop the bartender from refilling my glass.

"Met him in a little town. All dust and mule dung and crones dragging their black skirts. You know the place?"

"Of course," I said. "It's called Spain."

"Right. I played there with a trio. He came onstage afterward, carrying the smallest cello I have ever seen."

I sat up straighter.

"His parents were there—pretty mother; greasy father, a show-off. The boy seemed to be in a trance. Stage fright. Boy's father probably beat him. I've seen it in every town. Prodigies..." He paused and stared into space.

"Yes?"

"The boy put this tiny cello between his legs and started to play. And the trance deepened into something I'd *not* seen before. He wasn't even with us on the stage. Carried away. Then—reason why, I can't recall—the father slapped him."

I was sitting rigidly now, neck craning, trying to see into Al-Cerraz's watery eyes for any signs of mischief.

"You're sure it was a cello he held?"

He ignored the question. "Funny part came next. The mother—too good for her husband—was holding something. Walking stick, but thicker. Long and round. And she let loose—astonishing—*crack!*—right at her husband's nose. Terrible mess."

"Maybe it wasn't the lady's husband."

"The point, friend," he said pompously and then paused, his eyes flooding, followed by his nose. He coughed into his sleeve, leaving a trail of slime and boozy tears. I tried to push my handkerchief into his hand but he refused it. "She was beautiful! His protector—a Madonna!"

"And he...?"

"He was in his own world."

"It wasn't a cello," I said. "It was a violin."

"Waiter!" Al-Cerraz thundered.

"It was a violin being played as a cello," I tried to say again.

"You don't understand me," he growled, his strength returning. He grabbed fistfuls of my jacket and lifted me slightly off my stool. I heard the dry rip of bursting stitches.

"You have found that boy," I said, my voice trembling.

"I am trying to tell you a story," he said and shook me once. "He was an angel—an abstraction."

"He's real; he grew up!"

"If we could simply love our music, if we could be protected from everything else, we would be angels, too," Al-Cerraz said, his grip loosening. "I am still looking for that boy, within myself. I am searching for that moment when music is all that matters. There has never been a time when I don't see the audience out of one corner of my eye. Is that woman yawning? Did that man stand to leave? Even alone: Are my fingers moving more clumsily than before? Are my best years behind me? Who will remember?"

He paused. "I am lost everywhere—except where I want to be." He pushed just far away from the bar to spit between his legs. He missed; I could see a shiny patch on his shoe. He reached for his empty grease-smeared glass and held it up. "Here's to what endures...."

I reached out my own hand and caught the glass just as his fingers loosened.

"I am a fraud," he whispered.

"You are famous."

"Sometimes I think the key is to go back to the beginning. But maybe the key is to go to the end."

"You're being melodramatic."

"I don't want to die." He leaned so close to me that one stiff, kinked tip of his thick mustache brushed my cheek. "I just want to disappear. A friend would help me do that—if I had a friend."

He slumped against my shoulder, and I strained to bolster him, his heavy breath in my ear. The bartender, who had stepped closer when he saw me catch Al-Cerraz's glass, motioned with his fingers, rubbing them together.

"Now you must hear me," I struggled to say between grunts, as I pushed my hands into the tight folds of his pockets, searching for his money. "That boy you met, that village..."

But either I couldn't cram my hands in far enough to find anything or the pockets were empty. And the breath in my ear had become a snore.

"You will pay now?" the bartender said.

"He's famous," I said, uncrinkling bills from my own pocket.

"He's heavy," the bartender said, with a pallbearer's practicality. "I'll help you carry him out."

The next day, Al-Cerraz remembered none of it and revealed no trace of a hangover. If anything, he looked fresher than ever as he clasped both my hands in his and gestured to a low chair. He'd sent me a message to bring my cello to the Stradivarius reception room, one of the eighteenth-century chambers on the Palace's northwest side, where prize instruments were kept—various guitars and harps; an odd pair of upright pianos shaped like bookshelves; Stradivarius violins, a viola, and a cello. Once the count had whisked me through this room, but I'd never been invited to linger. Al-Cerraz treated it like his personal salon, even while a guard stood at the door, eyes pinned on us both.

He must have sensed my discomfort, my awe at his ease. He leaned close and said, "The advantage of belonging nowhere is that you manage to feel comfortable anywhere."

"You make it sound easy."

"It is: Don't join anything, sign anything, accept anything—unless it's a kiss. Sometimes a kiss is worth it." He winked at me, then gestured to my cello and asked me to play.

"Better," he said, with a charitable smile. "It was hard to hear yesterday. But maybe I was distracted by all the glamour. Or maybe it was the King's snoring. And that broken string! I won't forget it."

He sat down at one of the uprights and began to play a Spanish piece—rambling tuneful chords, a folksy Aragonese dance. "Can you improvise? Just find the melody—easy, easy. Just play it, enjoy it. Don't think of your lessons."

Playing with him felt easy, nothing at all like playing with Isabel, though I could not tell if that was proof of our compatibility or of his unparalleled sensitivities. "Wonderful," he said at the end, and I found myself smiling back at the way the curling ends of his mustache brushed against his red cheeks. "Now, your choice. Play anything, and I'll follow."

At the end he said, "Good cellists are hard to find—unique cellists even harder. You are . . . sixteen now?"

"Seventeen in December."

"When you have had enough of Madrid—four years, or five—come see me in Paris."

Four years? Long enough that he would forget my name again? He was still a young man himself; he knew that four years must seem impossibly far away. It would have been better if he'd slipped away from the palace, so that I could remember him as a babbling drunk with spit on his shoe who still owed me for the last round. Instead, he left me with the sound of his playing—the bronze bite of ringing bells, broken chords of falling water, a soft drumming tap like a mallet against leather.

———

The botched duet with Isabel did not cost me my allowance from the Queen Mother, but I did lose most of her interest. Nor did the count seem to regard me as he had before. Perhaps Isabel had told him something, or he'd been harboring suspicions of his own. Perhaps he was simply angry that I'd caused him embarrassment. In any case, he seemed bent on punishing me.

This was not the kind of punishment I had craved from Alberto—the punishment of orderly discipline or its opposite, total freedom, either one of which might produce artistic benefit. This was the punishment of humiliation, of disintegration. The count seemed bent on separating me from my own musical style—in other words, from myself.

In the count's view, the Queen Mother's concert only proved what he had told Isabel and me all along; that what I really needed was remedial training, a back-to-basics approach. More scrubbing the raw flesh. He took me back to scales, simple studies—reasonable enough. But he also interrupted me constantly, usually mid-stroke, with an outstretched hand if necessary. My brain would go on singing the note I longed to finish as the count barked his instructions—to start the next bow higher on the string, lower, bow tipped up, bow tipped down. I'd begin to comply, and he'd bark again, finding a new failing. I felt like the subject of an experiment designed to create a stutterer, except it was my bow that began to stutter, instead of my tongue. My right hand began to spasm and twitch whenever I saw his hand reach toward me.

And then there was the left hand, which I preferred to allow to move freely up and down the cello's neck. The count advocated keeping the hand in a fixed location and using extensions whenever possible—reaching back with the first finger, forward with the pinkie—so that by day's end my hand, small to begin with, felt like it had been on a torturer's stretching rack. I thought of Schumann, with his finger brace, stretching his hands and destroying them in the process, ending his concert career.

When the count was particularly irritated with how I was playing, he tried his best to look at me, pushing his face up against my fingers, lowering himself into a crouch so that he could bring his nearly useless eyes level with my left thumb, studying me in his near-blindness, hovering over me like some hunched-over warlock. This was worse than when he pawed at me. It made me feel like he was trying to see something inside of me that no one else could see—some source of my ineptitude and my discontent, some basic character flaw. I would sit still as he ran his weak eyes over me, wanting him to see something good and promising in me, wanting to earn back his favor.

This continued all autumn, leaching away my joy. But my discontent was nothing special; I dared not mention it, or act out on account of it, or in any way publicize my displeasure, when more serious grief was brewing. The entire palace was hushed, contaminated with a melancholia that grew as our Queen Ena's belly grew. The gossip was that she felt worse than ever, had difficulty eating, should not have conceived again so soon.

And then the winter: I'd never been so cold! The wind gusted across the plains of La Mancha, down through the narrow river valley, up the little bluff that led to the palace and around the palace's corners. At night when the wind blew, I could hear a vibrating hum, like a stick rubbed fast against a washboard. It was the wind rasping against the palace's facade, grinding Spanish sand against those countless ribbed Greco-Roman columns. Such ostentation; so little comfort.

One day I caught sight of the Queen, being guided by the elbows along the marble hallway of the main gallery, between her quarters and the King's. She was trembling. Her little paunch, not quite disguised by a flowing gown, was trembling, too. Her pale blue eyes looked like ice that day, and her face looked like cold wax. Her ladies nodded at me as they passed, but the Queen herself showed no recognition of my presence.

Soon after that, workmen flooded the palace, hammering during my cello lessons (more interruptions and distractions; my tic increased). *"Calor,"* the servants whispered. Central heat. The Queen had put her foot down. She who had been raised in gloomy England refused to freeze to death in so-called sunny Spain.

But heat—and spring—were not enough to stem her woes. Her uncle, King Edward VII of England, caught a cold following a wet weekend and, a few days later, died of pneumonia. Only nine years had passed since his mother, the Empress Victoria, had died. The old guard was passing, and their children and grandchildren were taking over. Baby-faced men seemed to run the world. Would they know not to make a mess of things?

Heads of state flocked to England for the funeral from all over Europe, with their medals, sabers, embroidered cuffs, and shiny knee-high boots: King Haakon VII of Norway, Ferdinand of Bulgaria, Manuel II of Portugal, Kaiser Wilhelm II of Germany, Gustav V of Sweden, Albert of Belgium, Frederick VII of Denmark. The newspapers published the royal funeral portrait: Spain's King Alfonso sat in the front row, next to the new English monarch, King George V. King George asked after his cousin, and Alfonso said she was well enough, and sorry she couldn't have come. But it wasn't entirely true. She had wanted to come, but she wasn't at all well. The baby hardly moved.

The weather, too, was strange. People blamed Halley's comet, that streamer in the night sky; another omen. Later, as his power weakened and his paranoia intensified, Alfonso would claim that May itself was to blame. Wasn't that the month when he and his bride had nearly been assassinated? ("But also the month we were wed," Ena tried to remind him.) And wasn't it the month that Alfonsito, their firstborn, had nearly bled to death at his circumcision? ("But also the month that he was born. And he did live," she tried to say, correcting him privately as she never dared correct him in public.)

On some unknown date that month, the royal baby died inside of Ena. The royal doctors refused to operate on the Queen for fear of damaging her reproductive faculties and thus the very future of the monarchy. She had to wait, silent and uncomplaining, for the dead child to be born naturally. The entire palace held its breath. Music lessons and tutorials were canceled for a week. I passed Isabel as she exited the chapel off the main gallery, near the Queen Mother's quarters, and she rested her hand on my shoulder. I was forgiven by her, or at least forgotten, in this sad event that gave her and all the other bored courtiers something to dwell on. *Isn't it terrible?* she mouthed to me, then floated by, down the hall. All of us waited. All of us prayed.

It came out on May 20, stillborn. A boy.

"No vibrato," the count told me.

Through force of will, he had already changed the position of my left hand, and had brought all my bowing experimentation to a standstill. The worst thing was that he was sometimes right. Obeying him, I had improved my intonation, it was true. I had gained a better sense of where my bow rested—its precise orientation in regard to the bridge, its angle as it crossed the string. He noticed things that Alberto had not noticed—the position of my thumb, for example, anchored behind the neck of the cello. He was not correct all the time. But he was correct too often to legitimize a mutiny. And yet I wasn't sure he had my best interests at heart. Isabel seemed to have forgiven me, but he had not. Would my punishment ever be over?

"No vibrato," he said a second time, after we'd started work on a new piece I'd been practicing all week.

"I thought you meant during the first piece only. The warm-up."

"No," he said. "No vibrato at all. You've learned it haphazardly. And it is masking other defects. You are wrapping your notes inside so much ribbon and lace I can't make out if your positions are right, if you're making the corrections we keep talking about."

"It's just…" I stammered, "by now, it's a habit."

"Everything becomes habit. Bad things most of all."

"And I don't think I overuse it."

I tried to sound nonchalant, but inside, my head was spinning. Of all the grounds on which to be attacked! I prided myself on my restraint. I avoided emotionalism. My vibrato was rhythmic and understated and intentional, nothing at all like the wobbly, throbbing vibrato of restaurant violinists and Ramblas buskers.

"You're hiding behind it all the same," he said. "Who is the teacher here, Feliu? Who is the student?"

I had matured. This was a challenge, and I accepted it. Even outside my lessons with the count, even practicing alone, I began to play every note hard, cold, and bright—like a raw winter day, the Spanish sun beating down—no shadows, but also little warmth. And the music did feel different without the vibrato, in a way that I was beginning to grow accustomed to and even to prefer, as one grows accustomed to stronger drink and comes to dislike the sweet wines of youth.

Artistically, this was an essential development, but perhaps I took things a step too far, as was my tendency. I became a bit too sober for a seventeen-year-old. I took my lessons not only from the count, but from the court, and from the Queen herself, for whom self-sacrifice was the highest aim, and sorrow as natural as any song.

CHAPTER

~ 10 ~

That summer, a month after the baby was stillborn, Queen Ena sent for me. I assumed she was doing her mother-in-law a favor, dismissing me from royal service while the Queen Mother herself was away on holiday. Some nine months had passed since the disastrous concert; a year had passed since I'd moved to the palace. Besides composing a wedding song for one of Alfonso's distant cousins, I had done little in my official capacities except to continue studying with the count.

Perhaps, I thought, as I stumbled through cursory greetings—*A sus órdenes, para servirle*—I could prove my talent to the Queen herself.

"If you could hear me play," I began, stuttering through my self-defense as my eyes flitted between her face and the ubiquitous fresco on the vaulted ceiling overhead: classical figures in billowing powder-blue robes, tensed calf muscles and dark, gesturing hands. All that movement, all that drama, contrasting with the face of the woman to whom I spoke—a face of defiant stillness that revealed nothing.

"I *have* heard you play," she said.

"The Queen Mother's concert—"

"You don't have to explain. I've heard you play since. Through doors and across courtyards, but I've heard you play."

There was that twitch again, not a smile but a softening, though her erect posture and thin, unsteady fingers made her look like a deer ready to bolt.

"During my last pregnancy, I was advised to steer clear of music," she said. "For health reasons. Nothing to quicken…" She paused, resting her hand on her chest.

"The heart?" I interjected, wincing inwardly as soon as I'd said it. One wasn't supposed to interrupt a monarch, even one struggling to master a second language.

"The pulse, I was trying to say." She signaled caution, both her lips and eyes narrowing. But there was friendliness in it. It was the kind of look a sister gives a younger brother. "The doctors said—but what do the doctors know? Mostly, they seemed determined to deprive me of pleasure. But the worst still happened. And once it does, no one has power over you anymore."

I waited, listening, thinking of the guard standing at the door behind me, and the statuelike servant off to one side of the room. Walker was her favorite, the only English servant in the palace.

It was from the maids and kitchen staff and doorway guards that I'd gleaned most of what I knew about the royal family, especially the King, about whom many stories circulated. When he went to Paris, he checked into hotels under an assumed name: Monsieur Lamy. Everyone laughed about it. The chambermaids added their own discovery—that the King always traveled with his own sheets. It was said that he loved the look of black satin against his long, thin limbs and sallow skin.

"Next week," the Queen took a deep breath, "we have two birthdays—Jaime and Beatriz, a day apart. And I am wondering: a party for a one-year-old and two-year-old, with a three-year-old attending—what on earth is one supposed to do? The King is in France. The Queen Mother is at San Sebastián."

I said, "All the birthday games I know would make a baby cry."

She looked puzzled.

"The loud noises." I noticed how tired she looked, the faint laven-der shadows around her eyes. "But how about something outside? Something quiet, perhaps with animals?"

"Animals?"

"Burros? Cart rides?"

"There's an idea." She looked away wistfully. "I had a pet donkey, growing up. On the Isle of Wight. He used to help us haul buckets from a deep well. It was two hundred feet deep—at least." She paused. "Amazing how you forget things; how things come back to you."

The conversation flagged, and in the silence I could hear a clock ticking insistently on the mantel behind the Queen's head.

"As for the party," she continued more stiffly. "You could play your cello, next to the cart?"

"Not easily. Maybe some flutists could follow along. The children might like that. What do you think of streamers? In several colors, flut-tering from the cart…"

In the hallway, after I was dismissed, I realized I had squandered an opportunity courtiers were supposed to prize: to get close, to curry favor, to become a favorite of the royal children, to become essential. But I was too distracted to worry. As I walked away, I repeated to myself, again and again, the name of that exotic place as she had pronounced it in her na-tive tongue: "Ay-*íl* ove Wa-*ít*; Ay-*íl* ove Wa-*ít*." There was a melodious-ness to the phrase, to everything she said in English, even when the words ended harshly, without vowels. How could one explain the way such short, sharp words could flow, could sound starkly beautiful? But that was Bach's trick, too. His Germanic music, so measured and re-strained, nonetheless held great emotions and vast mystery.

That day, listening to the Queen speak, I knew that she would like Bach; that she would like how I played it, not in the Spanish way, but in the universal way, without affectation.

———

In his letters, my brother Enrique regularly asked me, rather insistently, if I had gotten to know any girls. I hinted at the affair with Isabel, skipping the embarrassing parts. I tried to make it sound like a conquest. I wrote him about the Queen, too, in a kind of code. I described a palace girl I'd met—I called her Elena—a quiet girl, only a little pretty, not always liked. Trying to capture this half-real new friend on paper felt like tuning an instrument: a careful process of finding the right words, making small corrections, pairing observations into verbal chords, listening for reverberations.

Here was one chord: She looked young, smooth-faced, both full-cheeked and round-eyed, like a child caught just seconds after filling her mouth with stolen pastry. But she also looked old—the guarded expression, the set lips, so like her famous British grandmother's. And here was another: She looked unhappy most of the time, everything about her flat and still and ponderous, but that heavy symmetry could give way in a moment. All she had to do was tilt her head slightly, or stand with one hip jutted from beneath an otherwise-plain ankle-length skirt, to communicate a flash of independent spirit—and in her, independence seemed synonymous with happiness, however fleeting.

But no matter how carefully those chords were struck, they didn't sound properly. The real Queen Ena wasn't oppressed or weak. In fact, she seemed to be the royal family's strongest member and the one most committed to the monarchy. The more I watched her, the less I understood why the Spanish people distrusted her. She was guarding our heritage, cultivating stability, while the King flitted between hunting lodges and polo matches and distant capitals, silly and oversexed, an embarrassing dandy. Madrileños criticized her for being passionless, too tranquil—but her stillness was her power. She was the pole around which everything else spun: the bridge, the sounding post. Everything else could move, could vibrate, because she stayed in place.

The best thing about visiting the royal chapel was that, upon exiting it, one had reason to walk along the gallery fronting the King's and Queen's private rooms, en route to the main palace staircase. One day, I went to light a votive candle in each of my siblings' names, and especially in the name of my new nephew, Enric, who had been born to my unmarried sister five months after I moved to Madrid.

As I headed back down the gallery, I heard my name called. I recognized the accent instantly, but I couldn't quite accept its source. I stepped toward the voice, which was coming from the open door of the Japanese Smoking Room: a tiny, dazzling refuge that was not much bigger than a small bedroom, with a ceiling twice as high. The King's father had ordered the walls covered with bamboo, panels of purple silk, and porcelain plaques depicting Asian fish, birds, and boats. Stepping into the room felt like wrapping oneself in a tight kimono.

Surrounded by all that color and shine, Queen Ena looked small and plain, garbed in a shapeless off-white dress. Her arms hung limply from the dark arms of a cane chair.

"I lost an opportunity, the last time we spoke," she called to me as I loitered in the doorway, unsure of the protocol for entering and greeting her. She waved away my hesitation, gesturing for me to come closer. "You helped me plan the party, but I did not manage to talk you into performing."

Through a side door I could see into the next small chamber—a billiards room, dark-paneled, the green baize of the table glowing under three low-hanging lanterns. I couldn't see the King, but I assumed he must be near, given that these rooms were his. I thought I could smell him, or some man; the smell of tobacco and drink, anyway.

"The opportunity lost was mine," I said. "I talked myself out of an honorable service."

"Everyone makes mistakes," she said.

I added, bowing, *"Al mejor cazador se le escapa la liebre."*

She repeated the words slowly, translating them: "Even the best hunter lets a hare escape. I will try to remember that. Each time the King returns, I try to surprise him with some proof that I am mastering the language."

"You speak it well already. So the King isn't here now?"

"He is away. His work allows him so little leisure."

She looked over my shoulder as if expecting to see someone there, but the hall behind us was empty. "We never have enough time, do we? Any of us, I mean. I suppose one must enjoy what one has. Do you have a good saying for that?"

I clasped my hands behind my back, thinking. *"Aprovecha gaviota, que no hay otra."* Enjoy eating seagull, as long as there's nothing else.

She screwed up her face. "It rhymes nicely, but I can't imagine a worse meal than seagull. You sound like Cervantes's little funny man—like Sancho Panza—spouting those funny *dichos.*"

"Do you have something prettier in English?"

"Goodness, I hope so," she said, wrinkling her nose. "I must. Let me think. How about this?" She enunciated slowly, in her own native tongue: "Gather ye rosebuds while ye may."

For a moment, the words hung in the room. I could picture them quite literally: rising, dispersing, like smoke.

"Please—say it again."

She did. Then she translated it into Spanish with my help, stumbling in her search for *capullo.* But I preferred the English word anyway— rosebud. Already, I could imagine myself including it in a letter to Enrique, to describe the blush of her cheek, the purse of her lips. *Rosebud.* I felt a ticklish heat creep across my chest.

The ticklishness proceeded to my throat, and into my nose. It wasn't just in the walls. And it wasn't just poetry. There was real smoke in the room. At last I traced it to a thin gray column rising just behind the Queen's chair, originating from her hanging hand, curled awkwardly under the chair's polished arm. What piqued my interest wasn't the thing she was hiding, but that she—the most powerful woman in the nation—felt the need to hide anything at all.

"But I'm wasting your talent," she said. "You shouldn't be giving anyone Spanish lessons. You should be giving music lessons."

"Do you play?" I said, too eagerly.

"I don't."

She read my disappointment. "I used to. But I wasn't very good. And where I grew up, silence was the rule, especially on rainy days, when we all crowded indoors. 'Children should be seen, not heard'— perhaps you have heard that English expression."

"You could learn now."

She considered this. "The King's mother—your patroness—is the musical one in this family. It's better, I think, for each person to develop her own strengths."

A man cleared his throat. It was the servant, Walker, behind me in the doorway. I noticed that the Queen's hand curled even more tightly under the arm of her chair.

He said something in English; I caught the words *tea* and *served*.

"No," she said, "the boudoir is fine. I'll be there shortly."

He left, and she turned to me again. "And speaking of language, there is a funny French word—*boudoir*. Do you know that it means 'to sulk'? I hope men don't really think we women sulk in our dressing rooms. Though sometimes I do, I guess." She made a little noise in her throat, a whinnying approximation of a laugh. "Even Madrileños use the word. But I suppose I should set a good example and use the Spanish word, *tocador*."

"But," I said, surprised by my own forwardness, "that also means one who plays an instrument. If you talk about seeking comfort from your *tocador*, someone might think you are talking about your private musician."

"I'd like having a private musician. I'd prefer that to hosting fancy

concerts with lots of people and guards, where the poor King is reduced to snoring."

I'd never been religious beyond the most perfunctory observances,
even in the days when I had spent so much time with Father Basilio. But
I felt myself praying now, with surprising intensity: Please let me teach
you, play for you, do anything for you.

What I said was, *"A sus órdenes,"* bowing low to the ground. *"Para
servirle."* I'd said these phrases before, without meaning anything—
you heard them constantly, all over the palace. But now I felt for the
first time what they meant: to be ready for someone's orders, ready to
serve in any way a sovereign requested.

"Well, you *can* do something for me," she said in a low voice. "If
you'll just fetch me an ashtray, over there. That thing. Yes, attached to
the clock. Is there anything in this palace not attached to a clock?" In
an even lower whisper, she said, "I don't really smoke anymore. The
society ladies have enough already to prattle on about. Who was that
American actress arrested for smoking in public? Ridiculous. Anyway…" she trailed off, looking pensive. "I said I'd quit. I just came
here to smell it. I miss him, that's all."

The ornamental clock had a wide base, with the ashtray mounted
permanently in one side, and porcelain flowers as big as teacups blooming along its base. I pulled at it, expecting to carry it swiftly toward her,
but it weighed too much. I grunted with surprise.

"That's it, bring it here," she encouraged me.

I tried lifting the monstrosity again, but only managed to rock it toward me, a centimeter or so, before letting it fall back on its felt-
bottomed base. Its ticking blended with the pounding of my own
addled heart. Looking back toward the Queen, I saw the caterpillarlike
ash of her cigarette trembling, ready to fall, just a step away. I lunged
toward her with my right palm outstretched.

But I had not steadied the clock sufficiently. Just as I reached the cigarette, taking it from her fingers, I heard a crash and turned to see an exploded galaxy of porcelain shattered against the parquet floor— fragments of shiny red roses and fine white powder and shards of glass and one of the hands of the clock, a meaningless arrow now, pointing toward nothing.

At that moment, Walker cleared his throat from the doorway again, and the stubby cigarette burned to my fingers. I yelped and dropped it. Instantly I covered it with my shoe. Then I closed my eyes, steeling myself for the grip of halberdiers' rough fingers dragging me out of the room.

With my eyes still clenched, I heard Queen Ena's voice. "I don't think it can be saved. I'm so clumsy."

I forced myself to look. There were no guards in sight even now— just Walker with his back to me, his hands on his hips, surveying the mess.

"Perhaps they'll want some of the parts for restoring one of the other King Charles clocks," she said.

He muttered. "It isn't a King Charles. This is a Ferdinand VII, eighteen-twenty or thereabouts."

The Queen's eyelids fluttered. For a brief moment, I thought she might be on the verge of fainting. Then I realized she was only rolling her eyes.

"My God—do you hear that?"

"Yes, madam," Walker said without facing her.

"Silence." She did not bother to conceal her amusement. "A room without ticking!"

Walker left to summon help in cleaning up the mess. When the echo of his footsteps had faded sufficiently, Queen Ena said, "If you won't gossip about my smoking, I won't tell anyone you broke the clock."

I could barely speak, my throat was so tight with embarrassment. "I'm so sorry."

"Don't be," she said. "Charles and Ferdinand were obsessive collectors. There's no way to get rid of their clutter without the occasional accident. Would you be interested in touching anything else?"

I don't think I managed a coherent sentence after that—only a stuttering promise, as I bowed repeatedly and backed my way toward the doorway, to keep our secrets.

"I believe you. I really do." Then she dismissed me.

That's how it started: the first confidence, the first step along a long, discreet road to becoming the Queen's private *tocador*. I hoped she would send for me again right away, but as summer advanced, the heat soared, until even the birds seemed too tired to sing. The King returned and then left again, this time with the Queen and their three children. They had packed heavily, a chambermaid informed me, for an extended stay at San Sebastián. There, Queen Ena loved to swim out from the beach, far into the bracing Atlantic. Two armed and fully uniformed guards would follow her, treading laboriously as their black boots filled with salty water.

Back at the palace, I had my own treading to do—trying to stay dedicated to my lessons with Count Guzmán.

"Now we start again, we build," he announced one summer day as he began to teach me vibrato anew, using a metronome. It had not occurred to me to count the tremor of vibrato as one might count simple rhythms, to control with such precision what had once seemed spontaneous. With his arms he gestured to signify the vibrato's size; how far I should veer from the note being played—wider here, narrower there. "Here," he said. "Draw what I am showing you," and I took notes of his motions, creating a portrait of climbing and falling waves.

I spent weeks following the design of such sketches, and the tick of the metronome, and the arc of his finger in the air—slow at this passage, faster here. When my vibrato lost its rhythm, he signaled for me to stop—again and again. This, I thought, must be what it feels like to be a scientist, to dissect a bird. How could one ever think of it as a flash of feathers once one had seen it stiff on a table, opened up to reveal organs the size of olive pits, tiny bones and tinier veins?

The work was so detailed and so demanding that I paid little attention as July yielded to August, and the royal family returned, settling into their Madrid routines.

At some point late that summer I must have pleased even the unappeasable count, because he closed the metronome's wooden lid and said, "Good enough! You deserve a walk—it's a beautiful day. When is the last time you left the palace?"

He sent me on an errand to pick up some rosin and violin strings at a shop near the Plaza Mayor. I left the palace, still hearing the tick of the metronome in my head, pacing my steps to it, until I noticed what I was doing. If I was going to proceed through life in a march-step, I might as well have joined Enrique in Toledo. With disgust, I tried to vary my gait—a little faster, a casually arrhythmic lope. But being out of rhythm on purpose was harder than being in rhythm. And any kind of jarring gait made my weaker leg twinge. After a while, I gave up. I finished the errand, continued past the royal bakery, stared at the pastries in the window, turned back. I proceeded to a large square, sat on a bench, and watched children kick a ball around the dusty flagstones.

How was it vibrato had once sounded to me? Like honey. How did the cello once sound to me? The deeper notes like chocolate; the highest string like lemon. The resulting emotions: a pleasurable vibration, a painful tension, an opening. Never like a blueprint or mechanical drawing. Never like the tick of a machine.

Of course, there was a different kind of pleasure in understanding that all things could be designed, measured, and documented. An adult pleasure. But I don't think I ever regained my spontaneous approach to vibrato after that year, just as I'd never again have a relationship initiated as thoughtlessly as the one I'd had with Isabel.

Now, when the count and I began to study a new piece of music, we talked for hours before bow touched string, hashing out the details on paper like desert generals at a tent meeting. As we talked, questioned, compromised, I interpreted the count's heavy nodding as respect. One day, after I'd played my part of a new sonata, the Count said, "My daughter could learn something from you—your discipline, your self-control. And yet"—I braced myself—"this piece is still lacking something."

"Yes?"

"Expressiveness."

"Which part?" and I pushed the sheet music toward him, but he didn't reach his hand forward.

"All of it."

I thought he was joking. I laughed once and waited, a pencil in my open palm. It was as if the count expected me to throw the bird we had dissected so carefully back into the air—as if it would really fly, rather than fall back to earth, ruined.

"What would you like me to do, Maestro?"

"Perhaps you could use a break from your studies."

"But my studies are all I have."

"Then perhaps this is your problem. I've done my best to broaden your education, but you're still only seventeen years old. Much as you try to look and act like an old man."

Like an old man? But *he* had reinforced my sober attitude toward music. *He* had turned cold on me after I'd acted my age with his daughter.

"Live with the music for a while."

"What do you mean—*live* with it?"

His voice took a snappish turn. "You think you'll learn everything about the cello overnight? Without struggle? Without trial and error? Nothing is that way."

He lowered his voice. "Make it your own, is all I am saying. The King has requested my services in some official matters. I will let you know when I am available for private lessons again. In the meantime, I've set up a quartet with three of my other students—you'll meet with them each Tuesday and Thursday. I expect none of the trouble you had with my daughter."

I didn't want to part with the count so abruptly. I pushed him for details about his business with the King, but he shrugged off my questions. "You've never been interested in politics before, Feliu. It's nothing for you to trouble yourself about."

But hadn't he told me to take an interest in something other than my cello studies?

"Cultivate some interests," he reiterated. "But don't forget whom you serve. Cultivate innocent interests, I beg you."

I'd been apathetic about court politics. I knew that the Cortes and the King's cabinet changed frequently; I barely managed to memorize a new minister's name before a successor was named, every change alienating some people and enriching others. But I did not know if this was how things always had been and should be, what it said about the King or Spain's future.

Now, two developments fed my interest. One was the count's sudden unavailability and incommunicativeness, which catalyzed my own contrariness. The other was simple excess leisure, that classic fomenter of mischief. Without lessons, I lingered at mealtimes and straggled through the hallways, pausing at the thresholds where chambermaids and court apprentices gathered. I did not ask questions; I simply listened, benefiting from my reputation as a quiet young man whose tongue never wagged.

A cook told me about the King, "He's like a boy who rearranges his toy soldiers again and again, for lack of anything better to do."

"A meddler," agreed the man whose only job was to dust the hundreds of antique jars in the royal pharmacy.

Others used similar terms, criticizing King Alfonso for destabilizing the government every time he intervened in parliamentary matters. They said he was inconsistent and rash, concerned mainly with consolidating his own power. He had long been a fanatic supporter of the army, but his increasingly cozy relationship with the Church worried Madrileños. The Catholic Church had grown richer in recent years; it now owned one-third of Spain's wealth, with investments not only in plantations and railways, but in banks, shipping—even the cabaret business. It sided with employers over workers, and I'd felt its control over the schools even back home in Campo Seco.

"What kind of sin is liberalism?" our catechism teacher had grilled us.

"It is a most grievous sin against faith," we children had answered in one voice.

"Is it a sin for a Catholic to read a liberal newspaper?"

"He may read the *Stock Exchange News.*"

Now, liberals were mounting a campaign demanding that certain unregistered clerical orders begin to pay taxes. Would the King step forward and ask the wealthy Church to pay its share? After all, he had been willing to offend the Church at least once, by marrying Ena, a converted Protestant. If he didn't take a serious stance now—if he continued to treat politics as sport or seduction—then others would step forward to press for change. Anarchist unions were organizing into a powerful *Confederación Nacional de Trabajo.* At the same time, insurrections were brewing in distant provinces.

Palace dwellers noticed that the King vacationed less and inhabited the Palace's reception rooms and marble-floored galleries more. He changed clothes constantly—five times or more each day—so that each time he strode toward some important meeting, it was in a new suit. He enthusiastically attended the military parades that seemed to become more frequent with every passing month.

I had been introduced to him once, in a palace reception line.

"Musician? What section?" he'd asked.

"Strings. Cello, Your Majesty."

"How do you walk with that?"

"I don't, Your Majesty."

The King had a pronounced underbite, like all the Bourbons, and his jutting lower jaw tightened at my response. "Well, there must be a way," he said. "Use a little ingenuity, young man."

The other direct result of the King's new homeland preoccupation was that Rodrigo, my roommate, the architect-apprentice, no longer traveled constantly, to Paris and Lisbon and beyond. Now he was more often at the palace, earning his royal stipend by helping to realize the King's expressed desire to make Madrid more like his beloved Paris. He began to stagger home each night under armloads of blueprints labeled in French.

"Are we to get an Eiffel Tower?" I asked him.

"Who needs a tower? The King wants another *riz*."

I didn't know what a *riz* was. I assumed it was short for *rizo*—a curl or loop—which could only mean, I guessed, some form of palace ornamentation. I couldn't imagine anything less interesting or necessary. It only confirmed for me that King Alfonso was a silly, superficial man and that Queen Ena deserved my most tender sympathies.

The first few times I played for the Queen were uneventful. I brought my cello. I expected her to sit in one of the large royal armchairs and listen to me play. Instead she sat on the nearby piano bench, one arm resting on the piano.

"Are you planning to accompany me?" I asked.

"No. I can enjoy listening more this way, at ease."

"Are you sure?"

She turned to face me. "It's something I haven't gotten used to in Spain—the way that even the humblest servant will talk back to a sovereign."

"Pardon me, Your Majesty."

There was a long pause, but when she spoke again her voice was less stern. "It looks better this way. As if I'm at the piano, taking a lesson. If someone enters."

When I'd arrived, Walker had been standing near the wall, with another guard near the door. But at some hand signal I'd overlooked, they had exited, leaving us alone, the door closed.

I wanted to say, "You are a queen. Can't you do anything you like?" But I remembered the smoking incident. I said, "Forgive my naïveté."

"Señor Delargo, if you were cunning, we couldn't be in this room together. Not alone, anyway."

She moved her hands to her lap and sat with her profile to me, her head slightly bowed. Our relative positions reminded me of being in a confessional, but I wasn't sure who was confessing to whom.

"Please go ahead," she said.

At first I watched her, but only until I lost myself in my own playing. When she lifted her hand, I missed the cue. She stood and repeated the gesture, still facing away from me. "You're dismissed."

I packed up slowly. "Was it satisfactory?"

"It was." But she seemed annoyed that I had asked.

Two days later she called on me again, and I thought, *There is my answer. Don't ask again, just play.*

Her demeanor inspired me. I resolved to be just as strong, to stop asking for approbation. Hadn't that been what I'd wanted from my mother, from Alberto, from the count, even from Rolland? Someone to tell me I played well. None of them had given it effusively, yet I'd kept craving it. Here, playing for the Queen, I finally understood: One must not ask for acceptance. One must assume it, and value actions over words. Did she enjoy my playing? She always asked me to return.

I played for her regularly, and sometimes—only before I played, never after—we talked. I mentioned that my father had died at the hand of insurgents, in colonial Cuba, before I was old enough to attend school. She said that her father, Prince Henry, had died when she was nine, in much the same way. He'd contracted a fever on a military mission to Africa's Gold Coast, and died on the homeward journey to England. He had written to her from Cádiz: "If you are good, you will come to this beautiful country. You will see for yourself how much you will like it and how happy you will be there."

Wasn't that extraordinary? Did I think, she asked, that a father could predestine his child's life in such a way?

I thought of my pernambuco bow stick, a gift from my father's grave, and said: "Absolutely."

She asked me about childhood pastimes in Campo Seco. I told her about the vine-covered hills and the dry wash where I'd been bullied and used my bow tube to fight back. She told me about a game she played with her siblings and cousins, in which the "martyr" endeavored not to cry or protest no matter how the other children beat her.

"Children are brutal," I said, laughing.

"They're less corrupted and more honest," she corrected me, without any trace of a smile.

But these talks were brief, and once I started playing, she always looked away, rotating every week farther round, so that before long she was sitting with her back to me. Even when I'd finished, the silence filling the room between us, she avoided turning toward me. My dismissal was always the same: a wave of her hand. It was the one imperious gesture that reminded me we were sovereign and servant, not intimates.

———

Growing up in Catalonia, where bullfighting was not a tradition, I had no inbred fondness for red capes and gore. In that way I and many of my provincial neighbors were, like the Queen herself, insufficiently Spanish. Madrileños, by comparison, loved the spectacle of the *corrida*. I had heard that the Queen had nearly fainted at her first bullfight, but she attended regularly now, to please her husband, and even more, to please her people.

One Sunday I borrowed my roommate's boxy binoculars and purchased a cheap seat in the sun, one level higher than I would have liked, facing the royal box. I kept my binoculars targeted so resolutely on the Queen that after the first hour my arms ached from the effort, and there were circles of sweat from where I'd pushed the eyepieces against my face.

What I saw confused me. For someone who had winced through her first bullfights, the Queen seemed a rabid fan now. Not a tense or violent moment passed without her lifting her own binoculars, a lighter pair, with brass fittings that flashed in the sun. Other ladies waved squares of lace; men stood to toss their hats and leather *botas* into the ring, hoping the matador would honor them by taking a drink while assistants behind him combed the bloodied sand clean. When the dead bull was at last dragged away, some fans turned to talk to their neighbors, but not the Queen. Even this last bit of business interested her, evidently.

Then the next round began—a fresh bull, a more experienced matador. Dancing and sparring in his *traje de luces*—his tight-fitting, spangled "suit of lights"—he quickly brought the bull to its knees, then stood, spun haughtily, faced the crowd, and just missed being gored as his antagonist struggled to stand again and make a final charge. At this close brush with death, the King himself leaped to his feet. I could not hear his voice amidst the crowd's, but I could see his mouth moving, shaping the joyful cheers as the matador turned just in time to save himself and deliver a final fatal thrust into the bull's wobbling, stained cranium. And still, the Queen stayed glued to her field glasses.

"You must be a true scholar of *la corrida*," said a paunchy man next to me, his eyes reddened from hours of staring into the bright sun.

"Yes? What?" I moved the binoculars just barely, in order to acknowledge him, then set them back against my eyes.

"Those things. For hours, you haven't taken them down."

He wanted to borrow them for the next bullfight, I thought; that's why he was flattering me. But then it sank in. The stranger couldn't tell what I was doing. I wasn't even looking at the bull, but he couldn't see that. I could close my eyes, and he wouldn't even know. I focused on the Queen again—her slim white arms visible beneath lace-edged sleeves, her small oval face hidden beneath the propped lenses. And at last I realized that she was not using the binoculars to watch the bullfight. She was using them to avoid seeing it at all.

The next time the Queen dismissed me after I had played for her, I lingered in the hallway. Ignoring the guard, I pressed my ear against the door.

CHAPTER

~ 11 ~

"Two minutes," the guard yawned.

"What?"

"It's like the sand spilling out of an hourglass."

"Does she do it often?"

"The same every time. Then suddenly, she's done."

I had made of show of refastening my cello case, fussing with the latches in mock frustration, while my eyes grew round at the strange sounds coming from the other side of the closed door.

I peered at the guard, to look for alarm in his face, but the muffled, hiccupy sounds had no effect on him. He leaned his ax-topped halberd against the wall and slid a broken matchstick under his nails, cleaning them.

My pretense of latch trouble was wearing thin. I asked, "Do you think she's all right?"

"She comes out, pushing the pins back into her hair, and asks for Walker to bring her tea in the next room. She likes her privacy. You'd better be moving on."

Grabbing my case, I shuffled down the hall as quickly as my hip would allow.

I felt responsible. But was that responsibility a dull ache, or a warm glow? I toyed with the feeling, pressing on it like a bruise. Did it hurt?

Did it feel good? It *felt*—that was the main thing. After months of inertia and isolation, my music had done something real; it had been received. Now it had a life of its own, and I wasn't sure if that meant I should run away from it or run after it, to make sure it did not make trouble.

I gathered my courage. The next time Queen Ena signaled to dismiss me, I hesitated. From her seat at the piano bench, she gestured again—one flick of her hand, as if she were trying to shake off water. I set aside my bow but stayed seated, resisting the urge to bolt.

Again the gesture, dismissing me.

"Please," I said. "It doesn't seem right to leave you alone."

She turned at last, annoyance flaring, even while the thin skin underneath her eyes grew pink and patchy. "Don't be ridiculous."

I stammered something meant to sound consoling.

"No, don't," she said. "You can stay if you don't talk. It ruins everything."

She turned her back to me again, but she didn't make me leave, that time or the many that followed. It became part of the routine: I would sit quietly, waiting with a thrumming heart and a composed public face that attempted to defy an oddly intimate situation, feeling closer to her at this remove than I'd ever felt with Isabel.

The Queen did not respond equally to everything I played. She was on her guard against the obviously sentimental, and she refused to be swayed so commonly. Saint-Saëns's "The Swan," with its romantic, long-necked slides between notes, did little for her, nor did anything that exploded too early into a theme of menace or melancholy. Once I launched into a Tchaikovsky nocturne and saw her back go rigid. She hated to be told how to feel. She wanted to be reminded of how life itself had already felt, with all its variations and complications.

What moved her most were the pieces that expressed more than one side of an emotion—triumph paired with dark foreshadowing, anger paired with tender acceptance. The first time I came across Respighi's

Adagio con Variazioni, I knew it was for her. Its strong, slow, royal bowings reminded me of how she walked; its gentle diminuendos reminded me of her subtle humor; its faster, rising sections seemed to apologize instead of boast; its most poignant sections were tinged with a regret that somehow contained both anger and comfort. The adagio seemed familiar the first time one heard it; with its undulating variations, it seemed not like *a* memory, but like memory itself—haunting phrases repeated, rewoven, braided with an aching inevitability. The most virtuosic sections came at the end, invariably pulling me back into myself. When I surfaced from the fast, difficult bowing sections, breathless, I saw—from the trembling of the Queen's shoulders—that her breathing had changed, too.

She did not wait for the end of Respighi's *Adagio* to put her face in her hands. As she sobbed, her narrow shoulder blades moved beneath the thin fabric of her dress. The movement made me think of a letter opener sliding beneath the flap of a white envelope—efficient but tense, carrying the possibility of injury. But who would be injured, I wondered: her or me?

I expected the worst when the Queen called for me one day in late autumn. She greeted me with a small, tight smile that seemed to confirm my fears. She had exposed herself to me. She could not afford to have the court know too much about her vulnerabilities. It happened that I was planning to visit home that very week. She could easily use my departure as an opportunity to dismiss me permanently.

Instead, as the door closed behind me, she beckoned me toward her. I came forward with one hand around my cello's neck, the other around my bow, ready to begin playing.

"Put that down. All of it," she said, taking my hands in hers. The small, thin fingers were surprisingly strong and warm. "I have a gift for you."

Still trying to ward off the bad news I thought was coming, I said, "Shouldn't I play first? I'm leaving tomorrow for Campo Seco. I'll be gone nearly two weeks. We'll miss our next meeting."

"I know. This is the perfect time. I have been waiting to do this." She pushed back a lock of hair and shook her wrist, jingling a bracelet she wore there. "You have made me happy," she said.

I noted her use of the past tense.

"You don't believe me," she said. "But you know, it's like when your foot falls asleep, and it gets pins and needles. It hurts so badly and you want to make it worse, pound it out, just to make it go away faster. The last several months have been the pins and needles. Your music helped me get through that."

My brain was having trouble keeping pace with her words, so different from anything I had heard before.

"And something else," she said, straightening her back, releasing my hands for a moment to put a finger to her lips.

"Do you hear?"

I shook my head.

"The clocks—there is no ticking in this room either. No ticking anywhere. In light of the accident last June, our porcelain curator has decided to round up every last King Charles and King Ferdinand object in the palace and perform a massive inventory and cleaning project. It will take several weeks at the very least.

"In other words," she added, smiling, "you have given me both music and silence. I don't know which to thank you for the most."

"You don't have to thank me for either."

"No, I do," she said, growing serious again. "I trust you. In this room, when you are playing, I have felt safe."

"Safe?" I asked. "Are your enemies really a threat, even here?"

"I'm more worried about my friends." She tried to make it sound like a joke. "No, Feliu. Things will be fine."

She gestured toward a nearby chair, motioning for me to move it closer to her and take a seat.

"There are new problems, of course," she said, her voice becoming more businesslike. "The men in the Cortes who resist the King's vision, who would rather have dissension when our country is fragile. It's always fragile, they say. Well, yes, it's true! But whose fault is that?"

She continued, "The society churchwomen who refuse to accept me. The fuss they've made about a cross—the Protestant cross—being hung in the city. As if that is my doing, when I renounced my own faith. They'd prefer we remain in the Middle Ages, with no tolerance at all.

"I'm tempted to ask your opinion about that, coming from a small village. But I won't. What you have given me, Feliu"—she took my hands again, so tightly I could see the white tendons raised over her knuckles—"is refuge from all that. Relief from all that."

She twisted my hands in her hands again, and the heavy bracelet shifted, bouncing light off its multicolored gems: rubies, emeralds, and sapphires in antique settings; a row of large oblong stones dotted with smaller round gems. It was a gaudy piece, nothing at all like the icy diamonds and tiny pearls she usually wore.

"I don't wear it often," she said, noticing my glance. "Never in public. But it has meaning for me. Old things give me comfort. This is a very old bracelet." She held her arm out toward me, displaying it. "How old, do you think?"

I imagined King Alfonso strolling through the streets of Paris or Vienna during one of his trips abroad, a black jewelry box in his hand. "Four years old?"

"Four years?" she laughed. "Closer to four hundred. It belonged to Queen Isabella. Do you know what the history books say, about how she financed Columbus's discovery?"

I shook my head.

"By pawning her jewels. She didn't want to borrow from the Jews."

"This was found in a pawnshop?"

"No," Ena chuckled softly. "This was the bracelet she hid away. The colors reminded her of stained-glass cathedral windows. It was a piece of her that had nothing to do with her sovereign duties. She never wore it in public. I admire that she refused to part with it. A collector would misunderstand this bracelet—he would see it as a symbol of the Spanish conquest. I see it as the opposite. I see it as the symbol of a woman refusing to be conquered."

This was a speech she'd practiced, for which I made an insignificant audience. But I *did* understand. The bracelet was a testament to purity, integrity, and independence. She was nothing like the King, with his revolving-door ministers and complicated intrigues.

She gestured for me to touch it. "Have you ever touched something so old?"

There was an olive tree, just beyond our Campo Seco house, that my mother said was five hundred years old. I'd hung from its branches and rested beneath it, listening to its dry branches creak in the hot wind. But I didn't say that, of course. Tentatively I reached out a finger and traced the gleaming metal surrounding the stones.

She sighed. "I'm not as devout as Isabella. I have never heard God's direct voice. But your music spoke to me. It helped me remember one part of myself, a part of me that existed before I came to Spain or married a king. I want to honor that. Choose one, Feliu."

She wasn't giving me the whole bracelet, just one stone, a small one that wouldn't be missed. She'd have the empty setting and adjacent links removed; it would fit her narrow wrist better that way.

"The mother-of-pearl on your bow gave me the idea," she said. "I thought you could replace it with something more valuable. To remember our time together."

I had no trouble choosing. I looked into her pale eyes and found my voice. I said, "The smallest blue sapphire."

On the train ride home, I snatched only the shortest naps, with the bow tube in my arms, my cheek pressed against the leather. I could imagine the sapphire glowing inside. At one point I had a nightmare that I opened the tube only to see water spill out, as if the sapphire had been a chip of ice and had melted in my feverish embrace.

When another passenger entered my compartment during one of those brief naps and tapped me on the shoulder, my arm flung itself at him like a sprung lever. I awoke to the sound of him grunting, trying to catch his breath. My fist had caught him in the stomach. The edge of a red-roofed building was visible outside the window; beyond that, gaunt cypress trees that looked like tall, thin men until I rubbed the sleep from my eyes.

The train had stopped, which only confirmed my sense that a robbery was underway. *"Jamón,"* the stranger wheezed, lowering himself into the padded seat opposite me. "Sandwiches—they're selling them on the platform. I thought you should know."

He was a gray-haired farmhand, wearing wide-bottomed trousers and unlaced work shoes with flapping tongues. I apologized to him, wiping a slick of drool and sweat from my jaw. By the time I shook myself fully awake, the train was moving again. My stomach was growling, but I'd missed the chance to buy food. He saw the disappointed look on my face and held out a handful of almonds, drawn from his pocket. I ate them without picking away the bits of hair and lint, not wanting to offend him.

"What's in there, anyway?" he asked.

"Surveyor's equipment." I said without thinking. "Railroad detail." I tossed more almonds into my mouth, to stifle my own impulse to keep embellishing.

I told myself I was concerned about thieves. But if so, why was I already planning, on the second train south from Barcelona, not to show my gem-studded bow to my own family? At least, not right away.

I didn't expect them to covet my treasure. Shouldn't I exhibit this proof of royal favor? Didn't I owe it to my mother? Wouldn't it explain who I'd become to Percival and Luisa, whom I hadn't seen once since leaving Campo Seco? Of course I would show them the bow and its new gemstone.

Enrique was the only sibling from whom I hadn't grown apart; we'd continued to exchange at least one letter a month since I'd moved to Madrid. Unfortunately, he wouldn't be in Campo Seco. He'd been posted to El Ferrol, a tiny garrison village in the far north, on the coast. It was an unglamorous posting—the uniforms plainer than the ones he'd worn in military school, the pay entirely inadequate for someone his age, trying to woo a wife. But he was still fond of the military life, and he had close friends—among them Paquito, who'd been assigned the same posting and whose parents happened to live close by.

The swaying train allowed me hours both to worry and to daydream. I recalled the luthier's astonished face when I brought the stone to him, directly after leaving the Queen. His eyebrows had lifted when he heard it was a gift from her, and had lifted even higher when I told him I wanted the sapphire placed on the inside of the frog, facing me, rather than on the outside, where it would be seen most easily by an audience.

Before I'd left the palace for Campo Seco, a messenger had delivered a final note from the Queen. I imagined she had changed her mind and wanted the gem back, but she was writing only to request that I return within ten days. King Alfonso wished me to perform at a public event—he would explain more upon my return. *Para servirle*, I'd responded. What else?

The train arrived in Campo Seco several hours late, at the hottest part of the day. I was the only passenger to disembark. The town was asleep and no one was waiting for me. I was glad, even if it meant limping up-hill with my bags. I'd been away three years. I'd earned money, had a lover, befriended a queen. I'd met—a second time, though he claimed it was the first—the nation's most famous pianist. I'd learned to play the cello. How did everything feel now? Disappointingly familiar: bleached, shrunken, and inadequate.

The glinting foot-worn sidewalks of Campo Seco were even nar-rower than I remembered, barely a ledge flanked by the town's long rows of connected stone buildings. After a block of rubbing my bat-tered suitcase against walls, I gave up and walked up the middle of the cobblestone street instead. Legs tiring, I found myself looking around for an electric tram, only to laugh out loud—Campo Seco had no elec-tric tramlines or even "blood trams," pulled by horses. It was a town for walkers, for shepherds, for bored farmhands tapping the street ahead of them with olive-felling sticks.

I'd never noticed how plain it all was—no tile mosaics or exotic sculptural adornments, as in Barcelona; no columns or vast white flag-stones, as in Madrid. Everything was dark yellow, or a cracked light red. The color of soil. The color of mud. As I passed, the houses' oak front doors—curved at the top, wide enough to fit a cart—looked more than ever like barn doors to me. Passing under a second-story balcony, I heard a softly explosive glottal noise; I thought of a rooting pig, then realized I was hearing snoring. Someone was taking his after-noon nap above me, with the doors thrown open.

My family's door was just as barnlike as the others. When Luisa opened it, she shrieked and buried me in kisses, then tried to race me up the stairs to the main floor, just as we'd done as children. But now she was too wide. I stepped back to let her climb ahead of me, and she bunched up her skirt and scaled the stairs with exaggerated steps, mock-ing my gentlemanly gesture. Walking behind her, I noticed the dirt on her bare feet, the thick yellow pad of her cracked, calloused heel and the width of her calf, flaring muscularly from her Achilles tendon.

Upstairs, I dug into one of my bags and pulled out the white gown I'd bought for my nephew Enric, finished at the bottom with a satin ribbon.

"*Lindo!*" Luisa called out with delight. Then taking it in her hands, "But it's so tiny!"

"The storekeeper said it would be just right for a baptism."

"For a one-week-old's baptism, but not for a one-year-old's."

She continued to hold it up, as if the fabric might widen if she stared at it long enough.

My mother came and put her arms around my waist. "That's what she gets for waiting."

"Mamá," Luisa protested—and I did not need to hear the rest, to know this argument had waxed and waned for a year, sustained by ir-regular letters from the baby's father, an atheist, serving in Morocco.

"Keep it for the next baby," came Tía's leathery voice from a dark corner—the most optimistic thing I'd ever heard the old lady say.

"Have you heard from him?" I asked Luisa, under my breath.

"Not lately."

There was an awkward pause, and then I was nearly knocked over by Percival, who had grabbed me from behind.

"You're skinny!" my eldest brother shouted, looming over me.

I struggled free. "You're blue." His loose white tunic was speckled with paint. There were smears even on his large ears, which protruded from his stubbly scalp, all close-shorn except for a large black forelock over his forehead. "Have you become an artist?"

"I have."

"I heard nothing about it!"

"My exhibition finishes tomorrow." His lips were twisted into a braggart's pout. My mother was smiling.

"Finishes? You mean closes? Where?"

"Here, in Campo Seco. I am the next Picasso."

"I had no idea. Mamá, Luisa—why didn't you mention it in your letters?"

Tía sat in the corner, fanning herself stiffly, scowling at all of us.

"All that music has left you blind, Feliu," Luisa laughed. "Look up!"

I did. The ceiling was the same color as the paint flecks—pale blue, except for the exposed dark-wood beams, just as it had always been, in this and every room. The sky-blue surface, freshly painted, should have looked familiar. I'd stared at it for years.

"Your old room is the only one that's still wet, and the smell is strong," my mother said, ladling the food onto dishes. "You'll have to sleep out here, on the floor."

"If you can sleep on a floor, given what you're used to," my brother added. "We hear the palace beds are so high off the ground, you get nosebleeds."

I was still catching my breath, still laughing, but there was something else in my voice; I heard it myself as it slipped out, an off-key note. "Percival—you're not a painter?"

He pushed my shoulder a little too hard to be friendly. And then, to make up for it, he pulled our father's old chair away from the table, gesturing for me to take the place of honor, though he was older. I stalled, unsure. Mamá and Luisa called out in unison, "La comida está fría," and their combined voices woke the baby sleeping in the corner. I reached out a hand, waving to catch his attention, but his eyes were deep, wet wrinkles of fury. Luisa smiled apologetically and carried him to the table, where he bawled through the dinner blessings. Mamá tried to hurry the routine but Tía's mouth kept moving long after the rest of us had crossed ourselves.

I kept waiting to feel more comfortable in my home, more comfortable with my family, but the feeling never materialized. The low point came during the second course, as we worked our way through the gluey pink rice and rubbery shrimp. At a grunting, suckling noise, I looked up, thinking it was Tía extracting the last bits of meat from the tails. But it was Enric. Luisa was nursing her red-cheeked baby at the table. As he sucked, one tightly curled fist punched first at the air and then, with more satisfaction, at the soft white drum of her breast. She continued eating, lifting her fork each time over his flailing arm. A part of one dark nipple was visible, level with her plate.

I stopped eating.

"You said they starved you on the train," Mamá protested. "Where's your appetite?"

"It's good, Mamá. I'm tired."

"Tired? You need to eat. Have seconds. After all that travel."

"Travel is the problem," I said. "It unsettled my stomach."

"Percival, pass me his plate." She held out her hand.

"No, Mamá. I'll have some more wine. See? A half-glass more."

"You can drink, but you can't eat? Is that what court life has taught you?"

Luisa was still filling her cheeks with rice; the baby kept letting go of her nipple and then finding it again, pushing his face into her breast. Luisa sighed. "He can't latch on properly. He's all stuffed up with a cold. Do you think he'll be all right for the ceremony tomorrow?"

"He'll be fine," Tía said, her mouth full of rice.

"Everyone has it," Mamá said. "And with the heat—what misery. The church will be cool, though. He'll sleep through most of it."

I cleared my throat. "Does she have to nurse the baby at the table?"

Luisa ignored the comment, but my mother's face darkened. Percival looked at our mother, then cast a sidelong glance toward me. I felt everyone's eyes on me, expecting an apology.

"Can't she go into another room?"

My mother set down her fork.

"It's not very discreet—that's all I'm saying. You asked me what happened to my appetite."

Mamá wiped her mouth with her napkin. She took a deep breath. "How—and where—does Queen Ena nurse her infants?"

"I haven't seen her do it," I stammered. "Maybe someone does it for her."

Percival snickered.

"She certainly has many babies," Mamá said. "Close together, and not very healthy, so we hear. If she isn't nursing them herself, perhaps that is the problem."

"Can't we talk about something else?"

"I nursed you at the table, Feliu," she said. "In the church, in the street, on the stair."

She was reminding me of my beginnings, putting me in my place.

"Please, Mamá—"

"I wouldn't look to royalty for lessons in how to live," she said. "I'm glad you're doing well in Madrid, but don't forget—it's not real life, living at court."

"Actually, I've received a surprising honor," I started to say, wondering how best to mention the sapphire without seeming to boast.

My mother seemed not to hear. "Watch and learn and prosper. But don't lose your head."

I persevered. "Not so much an honor, as a kind of reward..." But it was coming out all wrong. "I suppose," I tried again, smiling weakly, "you'd call it more of a gift."

My mother's stern eyes met mine. "In life, there are no gifts. Do you remember the free violin lessons?" Her voice wavered. "Do you remember the piano?" She tossed her napkin on the table and left the room.

Luisa broke the long silence that ensued. "*Have* you gotten to see much of the Queen?"

"The back of her head, mainly," I said.

Percival laughed. My self-deprecation had earned me brief entry back into the fold. But I knew I wouldn't tell them about the sapphire now.

Hours later, Percival shook me awake. I reached toward him in the dark, felt the thick coarse fabric of his sleeve and smelled something like turpentine. It turned out to be rank home-brewed liquor—stronger and less skillfully brewed than my father's regional liqueur.

"Get dressed."

"Why are you wearing a coat?"

I sat up and banged my head. I'd forgotten I'd gone to sleep under the dining-room table, feet splayed toward the open balcony doors. From the street, I heard a light whistle, followed by stifled mirth: Percival's friends, waiting for us.

Outside, I stood at a distance while Percival concluded, in muffled whispers, some long-simmering argument with one of the other men—was that little Jordi? And Remei's cousin, too? I heard my old nickname, Cerillito, and Percival saying that he'd hidden a wheelbarrow near the church, to aid our escape; if I couldn't run fast enough he'd push me in it. I didn't press for further details. I was more concerned with straining to hear what had been said about me, and finding satisfaction in Percival's insistence that I come.

Under the footbridge someone had stored three lanterns and a pile of fat sticks. When the first lantern was lit, I finally saw the faces. The flame leaped, the shadows settled, and where I expected to see full cheeks and tousled hair, I saw red eyes and trembling Adam's apples, protruding above the edges of tightly tied bandannas. These were not boys, they were men, and they did not look merely mischievous. Laughter had petered out into nervous chuckles, and then into anxious throat-clearings punctuated with barked commands, issued at half-volume. Jordi wrapped a rag around a stick while he told us that back home, his son was coughing flecks of blood and his wife was distraught; he couldn't stay away long. He drained the bottle Percival had brought and threw it hard against one of the bridge's wooden pilings, where it shattered. I was still thinking: *Little Jordi is married? He has a son?*

"Percival—where are we going?"

"I told you," he said. "The church."

"What are we doing there?"

He turned his back to me. I heard Remei's cousin say Father Basilio's name. He accented the last symbol and lengthened it—Basili'oro, "Basil of the Gold."

"Father Basilio isn't rich," I said to the others' backs. "He doesn't even eat meat."

A man called Quim started lighting his rag torch and the others flapped their arms at him, telling him to save it until they were on the other side of town. He dropped the torch and stepped on it, struggling to suffocate the flame.

"I don't mean just on Fridays. I mean on all days."

Quim swore under his breath. A gurgle erupted from another man's throat—a forced, drowning laugh.

"He doesn't have a housekeeper," I continued—that was a polite word for a live-in girlfriend. Most of the priests had them.

No one heard me.

"We used to bring him—right, Percival?—we used to bring him tomatoes."

"We'll give him tomatoes," one of the others muttered.

"Why waste tomatoes?" someone asked. "Use cobblestones."

I said, "If this is about money, you're going to the wrong place. You should see Father Basilio's socks!" But my attempt at humor came out as a squeak. In Madrid, I had grown used to turning heads as soon as I pulled my bow across a string. Here no one listened to me.

Only Percival cocked his head in my direction, granting me a profile backlit by the flicker of Quim's lantern. "The Church is sitting on a fortune," he said.

"But our church isn't *the* Church."

"They refuse to pay taxes, while our neighbors are losing their farms—except Oviedo, of course." That was the duke, the one Don Miguel Rivera worked for. "He's twice as rich as when you ran off to Barcelona." He said it as if the two things were connected: the rising power of the aristocracy and my pursuit of a musical career.

Percival turned back toward the others. The huddle tightened; I stood outside of it.

"Father Basilio will recognize you," I said, pulling on Percival's sleeve. "How can you do this the night before your nephew's baptism?"

Percival spun and hovered over me. He laid his hands across my shoulders, stooping so that his forehead touched mine. "Basilio will stay inside," he whispered. "He knows from the last time. These fellows won't hurt anyone. They're just sending a message."

"It's wrong," I said.

"You're just soft on the priest."

"Not him—it could be anyone. There are better ways to do things. There are better ways to send messages."

Percival said, "You'd like us to talk to someone in the Cortes? Someone handpicked by Oviedo? Someone the Rivera brothers do favors for?" He pushed away from me and forced a chuckle. "Or do you mean the King? Maybe you're right. Go talk to him. We'll wait here." When I didn't speak or move, he said, "What have you ever discussed with the King? Horseracing? Whores? Don't pretend you have his ear. Our kind of people never have his ear."

"Please, Percival." I said softly, ignoring the impatient glances of the others. "You don't have to be involved."

He shook his head slowly, grabbed my ears and made my head swivel in time with his. We were boys again, but only for a second.

"*Somos o no somos?*"

"*No somos.* We should stay out of this mess."

"Stay out? We're in it."

"Not me."

"You want to see the bulls through the barrier, eh? No risk?"

"I don't want to see anything," I whispered. "I'm not going."

"They'll wonder about you. *I* wonder about you sometimes, brother. Which side are you on?"

"I'm not on any side. Percival—you shouldn't be doing this." I reached out to embrace him, but he stepped backward, into the darkness. The lanterns had been snuffed—Quim's torch, too. The smells lingered—oily, soaked rags, the acrid smell of Quim's burned shoe. The group was slumping away from me—uneven footsteps, clattering along the stony riverbed of the dry wash. Then they scaled the riverbank, cleared a small hill, and vanished.

I fought sleep the rest of the night, waiting for the sounds of Percival's return. An hour before dawn, I heard footsteps on the stairs, and surrendered to confusing, long-delayed dreams. In what felt like minutes, the house was bustling again. Luisa was kicking at my feet, extended beneath the table, and my mother was dragging the blanket from my bare legs and chastising me for sleeping too long on an important day.

The walk to church was agonizing. I held back, delaying everyone, while my mother clucked sympathetically about my legs, a ready-made excuse. Down every alley and around every turn, I looked for signs of the previous night's malice. The scorch mark I saw darkening a fine stone house was really just a long morning shadow. The windowpane on the school building had been cracked a week earlier, my mother informed me, by boys playing *pelota* in the plaza. I was imagining the horrible shouts of men with torches while Mamá mused, "It's funny to say, but it's almost pretty, the way the cracks catch the early light. It looks like a dew-covered spiderweb."

Coming around the last corner, with the church tower in view, I saw a pile of white robes, a collapsed figure in the street. I gasped and tripped into Mamá's side, steadying myself against her arm. But it was only a sheet blown off a balcony clothesline. A young girl waved down to us from the balcony and then appeared at street level a moment later, to retrieve her muddied linen while her unseen mother moaned above us, lamenting the wasted effort. The little scene made Luisa laugh; she had been walking just ahead of us, with baby Enric in her arms, both of them radiant, as if there'd never been a more perfect morning.

Percival had taken another route. Avoiding me at the house that morning, he'd found an excuse to leave early by volunteering to stop at the bakery to pick up the special pastry that had been ordered for the occasion. Or so he said. I rehearsed what I would tell my mother if Percival never showed up—if he jumped on a train bound for Alicante or Cádiz, and was never seen again. As we crossed the plaza, I was still shaping the words in my head when I heard Luisa say, "There he is, coming with the pastry box. I want to get inside and settle the baby before the others arrive."

No graffiti, no broken glass—just the cool church, the smell of dusty darkness and the flicker of candles. Perhaps the boys—the men—had decided instead to hike into the hills, unearthing hidden bottles. Perhaps they had wobbled all the way to the shack of ill repute where Juanita, the aging orphan girl, lived.

My thoughts were interrupted by a tap on my arm: Father Basilio. From one side, his smile looked normal and welcoming. Then he turned. The left side of his face drooped. Swelling half-closed one purple eye. A vertical gash ran just in front of his ear.

"I must..." he said in a low whisper, his voice strained.

Mamá, standing next to me, turned and saw his face. "Father! What happened?"

"An accident. It's nothing."

Ignoring her alarm, intent on his message, he persevered, pinning me with one beetle-bright eye while the other remained an unfocused and watery slit.

"There is a name I need to tell you—"

Heart pounding, I steadied myself to hear the recriminations.

"Because you will understand the importance," the priest continued. "You have the position now; you will tell the court of Madrid."

He expected this to become a national matter? I looked around, panicky, for my brother. He was sitting to one side, relaxing in the church pew, demonstrating oblivion with a well-practiced poker face.

"That they should never forget"—and here Father Basilio gestured dramatically with his robed arms—"Scarlatti."

I froze, trapped between the priest's grand gesture and Mamá's confused stare.

"Domenico Scarlatti!" the priest said again, feigning offense at my flustered ignorance. He started to laugh, but the movement quickly became a grimace, sealing his swollen eye completely.

I explained to Mamá, "Scarlatti. He was the Italian composer who came to the Madrid court in the 1700s."

"Will you do that for me?" he asked. "Remind them. Just remind them." His eyes rolled slightly upward and refocused over our heads. At first I thought it was a reaction to pain in his face. But it was only a form of relaxation—a habitual escape from a deeper pain. He lifted a finger from beneath his robe and began to mark a silent, spry rhythm, as if he were imagining the harpsichord, actually hearing it, erasing his pain note by note, in soothing, measured echoes. He did not want Mamá to ask him about his face. He did not want to tell me who had hurt him. He wanted to think about his music, to imagine it in his mind's ear, to let it rise and swell and keep him company in this town of disloyal parishioners. Surely he'd seen their faces the night before.

As suddenly as his finger had started marking time, it stopped. "Will you?" he said again.

"Of course."

"No one honors him anymore. In Spain, his works are being forgotten. Perhaps if they had a special royal concert, or named something after

him. Perhaps a new building, or at least a statue...We shall talk again,"
he continued. "I would love to hear you play, one of these days. You
didn't bring your cello? What a shame. But now—here they come."

Father Basilio gestured toward the open church doors, where six
elderly black-clad women filed into pews, fanning themselves all the
while. Behind them came Don Miguel Rivera in black jacket and open-
throated white shirt. He gestured grandly to an open seat, reserved for
the short, stout second wife he had finally married, a year earlier.

"Don Rivera has made a special contribution in honor of your
nephew's day of honor," Father Basilio said. "He is a pillar in this
crumbling town. As you may one day be. God be with you, Feliu."

By the next day, I was feverish and congested. The strain of travel and
three sleepless nights had weakened me, and accepting several kisses
from bubbling, fussing Enric had sealed my fate. I spent the rest of my
visit in bed, coughing, light-headed, miserable—and grateful, because
this forced reclusion kept me from seeing any more of Campo Seco.

I spoke to Percival only once about that night: "I'm glad it wasn't
any worse."

He said, "It isn't done. Quim and Jordi were afraid of being locked
up during their harvest jobs. You know Rivera and the Church—*a cal
y canto.*" Lime and stone; tight. "But when the grape harvest is done—
two weeks from next Friday—they'll finish what they started."

"What's the difference waiting? Rivera will still see that they're
punished."

"Not with olives starting. He'll spare men for grapes, but not for
olives."

"And Father Basilio?"

"He's had his warnings. But you've seen his expression? In the
clouds, *hermanito.* In the clouds."

CHAPTER

~ 12 ~

On the train back to Madrid, climbing away from the coast and onto the dry La Mancha plain, my sniffles eased, my mind cleared, and I felt a keener appreciation for my present life. I kept my head up, smiling at the halberdier, as I passed through the main palace gate. Opening the door of my apartment, I called out to Rodrigo. Near Atocha station, I'd bought a small box of chocolate truffles for my roommate—my way of kindling a friendship I should have cultivated a year earlier. To whom else could I confide the disappointing nature of my visit? He would understand how the streets back home shrank, how odors deepened, how family ties wore thin.

But when I pushed open the apartment door, I discovered that Rodrigo was too busy packing to accept my embrace. He thanked me for the chocolates but didn't open the box.

"Is this yours?" he said, holding up a burgundy silk cravat for inspection.

"I don't think so."

"Fine," he said, and tossed it into a trunk overstuffed with shirts and pants. He filled his arms with books, looked left and right, and then proceeded to push them on top of the wrinkled clothes. The room was almost bare already. He'd removed a lithograph from the wall, the one that showed the construction of the Eiffel Tower, half-finished. On his nightstand, three patches of dust-free wood showed where his framed family photos had stood. His pin-striped mattress had been stripped of its sheets. A flat black bug hobbled out of a rip in the fabric. Rodrigo picked it up and squashed it between his fingers.

"A souvenir," he said. "When someone asks me what it was like to live in a palace, I can show them this, to prove it's really just the same."

Rodrigo gestured for me to help him close the trunk. I sat atop it; he fastened the final latch and looked up, to catch me staring.

"You finished your project?" I said.

"Yes—but who cares? What does a building matter? We have a Republic!"

"Who does?"

"You haven't heard? Portugal!"

"King Manuel is dead?"

"Monarchy is dead. What do you care about our King? Anyway, he isn't dead, he's in Gibraltar—let him stew there. We have a new government. Braga, the literature professor, is heading it."

I'd never heard of him.

"Can you believe? In my lifetime!"

I kept one hand on the trunk. "Maybe you should wait for things to settle. Aren't these situations dangerous?"

"They'll need men like me—builders, planners. There will be a constitution, economic programs—as soon as they get the cannons cleared away."

"But what about your project here in Spain? If you stay, you'll be rewarded."

"Feliu," he said disdainfully, "liberty *is* my reward."

When he leaned low to look under the bed, I palmed the box of chocolates. He didn't appreciate them. But on his way out the door, dragging a valise behind the halberdiers carrying his trunk, he looked around, caught my eye, and realized what I had done.

"Isn't liberty sweet enough?" I said.

"Almost." And he grabbed the box out of my hand.

I followed at a discreet distance and watched the guards struggle down the stairwell with Rodrigo's trunk. I was planning to return to my room, thinking a cool sponge-bath would help me relax and get my bearings, when a third guard tapped me on the shoulder.

"His Majesty will see you."

"Did he say why?"

The guard smirked. "Follow me."

King Alfonso was taking tea, seated in a chair that was too low for him. He sat with his legs apart, knees high, thin fingers hooked awkwardly around a diminutive teacup. Queen Ena was with him. She acknowledged me with a stiff smile.

The King asked, "Have you heard the news?"

"Yes, Your Majesty."

"My men tell me you just came off the train. Were the people speaking of it there?"

Before I could answer, the Queen whispered into his ear.

"You were in Catalonia?" the King asked. "Has the news reached that far already?"

"They're always a few days behind," I said. "I'm sure they'll hear soon."

"Of course they will!" he said, slapping his thigh. His giddy smile confused me. "This will put Iberia on the map. No one can say we are behind the times."

The Queen nodded her head almost imperceptibly, encouraging me to respond.

"The world changes quickly." I tried to maintain an even tone, with no hint of distress or undue interest.

He paused for a moment, fingered his thin mustache, then smiled even more broadly. "Yes, exactly so." He stared ahead, dreamily.

This, I thought, was a strange form of bravado. The King seemed not only unconcerned about the Portuguese monarch's fall, but buoyed by it, for reasons I couldn't fathom.

He said, "The average gentleman in Paris thinks he knows Spain. He knows nothing about it. He imagines knights with barber-basin hats and cigarette-factory workers and filth. Does he understand that a man such as yourself plays Bach, Wagner, all the greats; that a man such as myself speaks many languages; that a guest wishing to make a telephone call in Madrid might wish to do so without leaving a building, without even descending the stairs?

"The point is," he continued, "the world will be watching us this week. And for a misunderstood country, that can be only a good thing."

The mention of telephoning confused me, and I struggled to make sense of what the King was saying. Yes, it was probably true that the world would be watching Madrid. In Lisbon, a new government would expect recognition. Antimonarchical organizations within Spain might be jockeying to rouse their supporters, to imagine the possibilities closer to home. For the first time, sitting in the palace, I let myself dwell on the possibility that Percival's night mission had been more than a local scuffle. Perhaps instead it was a stray spark, a sign of larger fires burning elsewhere. In Madrid there was only smoke. It was harder to see and understand things here, at the center of things, than anywhere else.

The King said, "We must have the correct spirit about change, don't you think?"

I moved my lips. It was enough.

"Then you're with us," the King said, and pushed himself out of the too-small chair, shaking out one booted foot. "My wife was correct.

She suggested you were the right person to perform for the occasion—you and your fellows."

"Your quartet," the Queen mouthed.

He winked at her. "I thought perhaps a singer. Operatic. But then she said, 'Do you want them to remember her voice or yours?'" He laughed.

"The occasion?" I asked, still struggling to understand why he'd want to sponsor a celebration honoring the Portuguese king's fall from power.

"The grand opening," King Alfonso said. "El Hotel Ritz de Madrid. Two years in the making and ready at last."

"A hotel?"

Finally it became clear to me. This was the "*riẓ*" Rodrigo had been working on, and as far as the King was concerned, its completion was the news of the moment, overshadowing the tumult of a neighboring government's fall.

"If people will insist on comparing, I don't want them hearing gypsy music. I'll want—well, you know. Nothing from a *ẓarẓuela*. Who is the one, my dear? The song they were playing when we first danced at Buckingham Palace?"

"Beethoven," the Queen said. "Minuet in G. Don't be silly. You remember."

"Is that it? Hum it for me."

She looked around awkwardly and worked her mouth, as if she were preparing to dredge up enough saliva to swallow a very dry cracker. Then she whistled the first two bars.

"That's it," he said. "Like that. Music for light toes, not for heavy heels. No thrumming or drumming of any kind. Friday evening. By then, the news will have flowed to every corner of Spain. Even your distant relatives will know that Madrid is no second cousin to any capital. A telephone on every floor. A water closet next to every one of the better bedrooms. Do you know that one of my architects here thought that was wasteful? But the world changes, just as you said. Lucky for me, that upstart is going home to Lisbon and I won't have to stomach his complaints any longer."

I was preparing to take my leave when three men in tight breeches and ruffled shirts filled the doorway, lingering unannounced, with the guard blocking their entry.

"Let them in, let them in!" the King barked at the guard, and then to the Queen, "Are you sure, *mi cielita?*" When she shook her head, he turned to me. "And how about you, young man—would you like to ride with us today?"

"Horses?"

"What do you think, geese? *Cierto,* horses!"

I dug my hands into my armpits and glanced wildly around the room until the Queen rescued me.

"His leg, dear," she said quietly to the King. "A slight infirmity." My face reddened. "You be off, have a grand time, and I'll have a final word."

The King and his *amigotes* cleared away, their rowdy voices echoing in the marble hallways outside the reception room. She sent one guard away on an errand and asked the other to stand outside.

"I might have been able to ride," I said. "It isn't really so bad, anymore."

She seemed not to hear. She was eager to finish the conversation, to fill in the gaps, and she spoke in a torrent, as if she expected the King to return any moment.

The Queen explained that she would not be attending the Ritz opening. She had received an honorary award from the Red Cross, newly forming in Spain, for her support of hospitals and nursing. The Red Cross ceremony would take place in Toledo; she would not be back in Madrid in time to make the Friday gala.

"It's a convenient excuse," she said. "Every other society lady will be there, for reasons I can't imagine. After all, what does a fancy hotel mean? Only that their husbands can rent a local room for"—she shook her head with distaste—"But you will be there, Feliu. You will be my eyes and ears."

I presumed she wanted me to watch who danced with whom. The idea of eavesdropping unnerved me. But at least I understood it, because I could imagine the kind of envy and protectiveness that prompts a loving woman to spy on her man.

She gave me a detailed description of the woman I was supposed to watch—a duchess with dark hair and green eyes.

"You've seen her in the palace before—at Royal Masses, sometimes on the arm of the Bishop."

"Will she be wearing black, like all the *Doñas Negras?*"

The mention of "Black Ladies" made the Queen wince. It was a nickname we gave all the pious society women who made a vain display of their black garb. They weren't widows, though they seemed eager for the attention that robust grieving might bring. They looked forward to confession the same way the King and his men looked forward to polo or cards. Having turned the eye of princes during the week, they seemed to enjoy the special challenge of turning the eyes and ears of priests, calling out at unexpected moments, *"Ay-de-mi!"* when the religious spirit swelled their breasts.

"The ladies wear their black on Sundays, Feliu," the Queen said. "They'll be more colorfully attired for this event. The duchess, I've been told, will be wearing a pale blue dress."

"What if she doesn't?"

"She's just purchased it, through the mail, from Paris," the Queen said. "She'll wear it."

My job, the Queen explained, was to make sure the duchess didn't leave the hotel ballroom.

"But I'll be busy playing."

"That's the point. As long as you play, she won't leave. She fancies herself the belle of the ball. She does not like to miss a single dance. She will monopolize the King all night if he lets her."

"And that's all right?"

"In that room, in public, it is fine. If they leave the room together"—her voice faltered—"that is intolerable."

I awaited further instructions.

"Anyway," she said, "if anything goes wrong, a minister will be there to take the next step."

"A minister?"

"The most trusted man in the King's cabinet."

"Then the King knows this plan?"

"He could not be protected if he knew; and besides, we are protecting him from himself as well. That's more than you need to hear."

"Why not have the minister keep an eye on this lady?"

"He'll be coming and going, talking with guests, moving from salon to salon with his own important duties. He can't look over his shoulder every minute—and if he did, it would look peculiar."

"Forgive me," I said. "I can't say I understand this." How could I explain that everyone knew about the King's infidelities? I couldn't see how one more tryst would tip the moral scales.

She glared at me irritably. "The Church is refusing the new tax. It's no small sum. The extreme clericals are stronger than ever, and the liberals are losing patience. The King can't please them both. I'm not sure he can please anyone." After a deep breath, she continued. "The duchess and her husband are vocal opponents of the new tax. If the King indulges her, people will make assumptions—perhaps correct ones. If he chooses that path, well...I hear Gibraltar has become crowded since the Portuguese Republicans took Lisbon.

"This isn't about passion, Feliu. This is about influence. We are simply making sure the sides are balanced."

My mind's eye flashed on an image of Percival, backlit by a smoky red halo: *This is your chance to show them what side you're on.*

The Queen said, a little testily, "This isn't complicated. Are you having doubts?"

Percival, nodding, his face marred by jumping shadows: *These fellows won't hurt anyone.*

The Queen said, "It's the duchess who will be responsible for her actions, not you. You'll be playing music—that's all."

Then her voice changed, straining toward lightness. "And how is the bow doing? Fetch it and the cello; play me something. Perhaps I'll hear a new sparkle in it."

In fact, it was harder to play that day. The addition of the gem and its inlaid setting, a small ring of silver, added a subtle weight to the frog end of the stick. It was just a question of adapting, I told myself— every bow had its own peculiarities. And maybe I was still recovering from the illness I'd contracted in Campo Seco. But my bow stroke was the aspect of my playing in which I took the greatest pride; flexibility and a light touch, I felt certain, would be remembered as my trademark.

I had two days until the Ritz opening. I summoned my chamber group, in which I had emerged as the informal leader. We pulled together a program with an emphasis on danceable rhythms, which would leave me lots of freedom for surveying the crowd. The morning of the Ritz opening, I picked up a suit that I had left at the court tailor for altering before my trip to Campo Seco. "It's been ready three weeks," the tailor chastised me. "I was going to donate the suit to charity. I thought you'd left the country."

Three weeks! Time had flown. In Campo Seco, the grape harvest would be completed by now. Any night Percival and the others might visit Father Basilio again. But I wasn't home anymore. I had a new life here, a musical life, among people who needed and appreciated me.

The night of the grand opening, a half-dozen national flags fluttered outside the hotel's entrance. Inside, the polished wooden floors glowed with reflected chandelier light. Our quartet set up at the front of the Sala Real, a long room with lustrous white walls and ornate moldings. I took a seat angled toward an enormous square mirror that covered most of one wall, so that I could watch the crowd while feeling protected from it.

We worked our way through some simple Haydn as gowned women and tuxedoed men filled the room: a few dozen, then a hundred, then two hundred, by my estimation. During our first break a boy handed me a clear drink on a tray—gin—and I swallowed it fast, without thinking. Just as the juniper lit up my nose, a man whispered into my ear from behind, "That boy—he'll be the one to send for me, if that's necessary."

I turned to meet the face of the messenger, but the man was already moving away. Another man stepped into his path, saying, "Excuse me, Don Pérez." Pérez—that was the minister. The gin boy stood to the side of the mirror, playing with the pearly buttons on his white gloves.

When the King was announced, we struck up a rendition of the national anthem. Toasts and speeches followed: a cheer for Paris with the French lead architect lifting his glass, a louder one for Spain, and deafening applause for the King. I drank another slyly delivered cocktail during these, and started regretting it when the blazing wall sconces danced in the mirror. Endeavoring to focus, I studied the reflections for a blue dress. There was midnight, and there was turquoise, and there was a satiny purplish-blue that made me think of mussel shells. Only when the guests were applauding the final speech did I spot pale blue ruffles cascading to the floor, and above them, the deep V of a bare narrow back, the midline cleft as straight and deep as a well-plowed furrow. I felt as if I could reach into the mirror and run my fingers down her spine. I shook myself from the trance and raised a finger toward the boy.

"Message for the minister?" he said, breathless.

"No," I yelled, making him jump. "*Otra ginebra.*"

The number of guests had doubled again, so that the dance floor was a constant murmur of apologies—"Pardon my back"—each time a shoulder was turned toward a stranger. The tapestry-covered chairs that lined the sides of the room went unused. Everyone was too excited to sit.

The violinist touched my sleeve, recalling me from a daydream. We struck up a waltz, and the center of the room became an agitated whirlpool, while the fluid edges did their best to pull back, to make more room. The King danced; not with the duchess, but with an older woman whose soft upper arms flapped as she spun. I kept my eye on the duchess, who stood to one side, talking with a circle of women, all elegant and young. Were these the other Doñas Negras, stripped of their dour black husks? The room was growing warmer by the minute. The ladies' faces shone.

Suddenly I noticed the hole in the reflection, the blank spot that had been pale blue. Just then, I spotted the edge of the duchess's dress, trailing out of the doorway and into the hall beyond. The Queen had assured me the duchess would stay to dance, but already she was slipping away. I wasn't sure what to do next. It didn't make sense to alert the minister when the King himself was still in the room.

I nodded to the rest of the quartet—keep going—set my cello aside, and nearly tripped off the stage. The gin boy looked toward me but I waved him away. Down another hallway, a tight turn, and the tail of the dress again. Then, just as I made another turn, the huff of a closing door. I stood outside it, breathing hard. I rested my hand against the golden handle. Suddenly, the door pulled away as someone opened it again, from the other side.

I backed away to the swell of women's voices and clouds of powder.

"Ay-de-mi!" a portly woman shrieked. "The men's is down there!" Deeper within the perfume-scented sanctuary, feminine laughter erupted.

I stormed away, face flaming. Passing the men's lavatory, I continued down the red carpet to the main exit and found myself standing outside the hotel, drinking in the cool night air. I reasoned that I could spare the time; the duchess would be indisposed for several minutes at least. Outside, I waited for the gin fizz in my head to recede, the buzz in my ears to quiet. I looked up at the velvet sky and the stars, and felt a momentary peace. Then I looked back toward the Ritz, to the light of chandeliers and sconces dancing in the windows. The windows had steamed slightly, so that every orb of glittering light had its own halo. Suddenly they looked like torches to me; torches flickering, borne by a mob. I inhaled quickly.

Where would the men of Campo Seco be now—my old schoolmates, my old neighbors? Out of the dry wash where they had gathered, a group twice the last group's size. Having escaped punishment the last time, they'd be more brazen now, and the ambivalent ones would have joined them. They'd be heading downhill, strides lengthening.

I felt a tug at my sleeve. It was the gin boy. "Come back, the violinist says."

"Yes, I will."

But I was still trying to remember and imagine each block: first, they'd pass a tool shop. Then a community spigot—maybe one of the men, thirsty, would stop to fill a leather bag. On the next block, they'd pass the closed newsstand, and the café. Maybe one of their wives or relatives would be sleeping lightly, and would call out to them, "Look at you all! Come in. I have some soup left, if you'll come off the street."

The boy tugged again. "The violinist. He said—"

"I'm coming."

Back inside, another waltz was coming to an end and the audience was applauding the footwork of the King and his dancing partner, yet another elderly lady who had her hand to her chest, catching her breath. He smiled distractedly, a thin-lipped smirk, while his eyes searched the room. The duchess had returned and stood alongside the far wall, her face no longer shiny, two small reddish-brown curls fixed just in front of her ears.

The violinist lifted his eyebrows and leaned toward me. It was more than a look of reproach. He wanted to know what we'd play next, since my exit had prompted a departure from the program. Men mopped their brows and ladies fanned themselves, waiting for the next dance to begin. The King bowed to several guests and made his way obliquely—shoulders hunched, face fixed in concentration—toward the doorway. From the other side of the room, the duchess headed in the same direction.

I felt dizzy still, and indecisive. The dizziness would pass. The indecisiveness would take root, snagging dark ideas in its sharp-edged branches. I had advised Percival to steer clear of intrigues. I had looked down on Alberto for being in the wrong place at the wrong time, allowing his music to be a backdrop for something sinister. I had been moved by the Liceo's mottoes and had accepted the Queen's sapphire, believing it to be a symbol of purity and apolitical devotion—and perhaps she had meant it as such, at that grateful moment. But look how easily things became muddled. Look how impossible purity was, outside of Bach's elegant measures.

And yet: What, really, could they do to the duchess? Nothing rough—she was a lady. And what would they do to the priest? Give him a second black eye to match the first. Frighten him back to Italy, perhaps.

The gin buzzed in my head and the heat in the room seemed to grow. I remembered Quim trying to extinguish his torch and pictured him swatting it against a drapery this time, or smothering it in one of the cloths hanging off the altar, while another voice said, "Just let it burn."

Someone else: "But the school next door."

The first again: "There's no one in it now. Besides, what good did we learn there? Our catechism? 'What kind of sin is liberalism?' 'A grievous sin.' 'And what kind of liberal newspapers may one read?' 'Only the *Stock Exchange News*.'"

The men would be laughing at that; it was almost enough to make me laugh now. Then I imagined Father Basilio coming down the stairs in a white nightshirt, calling out in a tremulous voice, "I know who you are." And my own brother, Percival, responding, "So? You always did."

In the gilt-edged reflection to one side of my cello chair, I could see that King Alfonso and the blue-gowned lady were heading toward their private reunion. The duchess, enveloped in an aura of mock humility, was ravishing. But what else does one do in this world except take advantage of one's natural assets? Besides, shouldn't it take more than beauty to persuade a king? Shouldn't it take more even than a private conversation with a bishop, or with a landowner, trotting side by side on fine horses through the woods?

The duchess was closest to the doorway now, only a few strides away, and the King was smiling on one side of his face. I'd never disliked him so much as in that moment.

"Minuet in G," I mouthed toward the other three players, and scarcely gave them a moment to understand before I was playing the first two notes—a slur on the A string. By the fifth note, my fellows had joined in.

I looked in the mirror. The King had stopped. Everyone was looking at him, anticipating him leading the noble dance. He was looking toward the stage. He had recognized the tune. He was remembering dancing to it with Ena, before she became the Queen. Perhaps he also remembered how she laughed at his jokes, how she hid her face in her hands when he recounted the gaffe he had made, explaining to a London crowd he was sorry for being constipated, when he'd really meant to say only that he had a cold. He remembered the lightness of her step, and her mention of loving the smell of orange blossoms, after which he'd sent her an entire orange tree, all the way from Spain to England.

The King would not exit the ballroom as long as the minuet played. It would be too dishonorable, even for him. We played to the repeat, and then to the end. The others reached the final note and paused, each one of them waiting with their bows resting on the strings, while they all looked to me. I started over. They were professionals; they joined me seamlessly. If the King simply stayed in this room, then nothing would happen; wouldn't that be the best thing?

The flames were leaping over the altar now. "You were always a gambler," I could imagine Father Basilio saying to Percival. "I am betting you won't let this building burn. If we get water, if we wake everyone, we might still put it out."

"Aren't confessions confidential?" Percival said. "Some priest you are."

Another voice, from the back of the church: "Stone won't burn easily. It's all the claptrap he's worried about—the vestments and such. And the money, hidden somewhere."

My mind wouldn't stop inventing the scenes, following the torchlight, trying to guess who would be saying what, who might stop things and who would advance them. But what about Father Basilio—what would they do to him? I prayed: Percival, walk away; let the Father walk away. Go home.

The second repeat of the minuet was coming to an end. It closed with a frilly eighth-note, followed by an eighth-note rest. The anticlimactic ending made it easy to return *da capo* again, turning it into an endless loop. We could play it all night if we wanted to, though people were beginning to notice. The dancing crowd had thinned, and for the first time all evening, men were sitting in a few of the chairs alongside the wall. We were spoiling the party, or perhaps only allowing it to wind down to its natural end.

My bow was heavy in my hand. I wiggled my ring finger and pinkie over the frog, a subtle flex, just to reset them more comfortably. The imbalance was bothering me still. We came to the final eighth-note rest and I paused—no longer than the rest required. But the first violinist interpreted the movement incorrectly. He thought I wanted a break. He took the lead. Ahead of me, he pushed his bow into the solo opening of another piece: Mozart.

I looked up. The duchess was gone. And the King.

I let my bowing hand fall. The boy was instantly at my sleeve, "*Otra ginebra?*"

"No. Get the minister."

From one of the church's back closets, Jordi would have emerged, his arms tangled in ropes. I recognized them. They were the ones Rivera and his brother and the other men had used to move the piano. I remembered them coiled like snakes in the church's side door. "Here," he'd be saying to Percival. "We'll lead him through town, that will be enough." And they were wrapping the rope around the priest's neck while his eyes flickered right and left, searching for a shamed face, someone who would stand up and choose, someone who might save him.

I couldn't sit there without playing. I waited for one musical phrase to end and then slid into the next, trying to cover my shaking with a strong vibrato, until our music was interrupted by the tinkling of silver spoons and fan handles against glasses. Someone waved his arms from the center of the room: Minister Pérez, of course. Flanked by the duchess, red-cheeked, and the King, pale and sullen, like a young boy often warned and finally caught.

"Here he is, here he is," called a voice, and a fourth figure joined them—the duchess's husband, the Duke of Montalbanil, who had been in the adjacent Salon Goya, which had been set up discreetly for cigars and cards. He looked flummoxed and annoyed.

"It is appropriate," Señor Pérez boomed, as the crowd quieted, "to choose this evening to bestow a special honor, on behalf of the King and Queen. When else would so many close friends of the duke and duchess be present?"

There was a chorus of jubilant "Hear, hear!" from the far corners, and a scattered suspicious whispering from nearer the center, where the more perceptive guests stood.

Minister Pérez was well prepared. He pulled a medallion from his jacket pocket, attached to a blue ribbon. More whispers, as everyone leaned forward, trying to understand what the medallion represented.

"The duke has so many fine natural qualities," Pérez intoned. The duke frowned. King Alfonso smiled queasily. "Often he has expressed desire to rule over more expansive lands." Only the duchess was smiling sincerely, a sweet, puzzled expression on her upturned face. "And so, on the King's behalf, I am authorized tonight to grant him a great honor. He inherits the title of Duke of Ortiz, and dominion over the isles of Puerto Cruz and Verillana. To take residence, and do the Crown's bidding, immediately...."

The whispers escalated. The duchess's eyes widened. The King reached a hand toward the duke, who accepted it, with mouth open and jowls faintly trembling.

I turned to the violinist. "Where are—?" But he'd had enough of me and my disappearing acts that night. The violist was more forgiving. He leaned forward and said, "Fly specks—little dry islets, southwest of Morocco. Uninhabited. Once a penal colony, I think."

A week later, two items in the newspaper caught my eye. The first mentioned that the King had resolved again to press the Church to pay taxes. Several incensed patrons of the Church were quoted, expressing their consternation that the King had not "come around" as they had hoped and expected he would. Several liberal groups that had opposed the King now congratulated him in a lukewarm, cautious fashion.

The other item was smaller, but of much greater interest to me. It reported an incident in Campo Seco—one of the few times our town would be mentioned in the national press. There was no mention of a fire, but there was mention of several deaths. The priest had been hanged by an unknown group of vandals in the town square. Three unidentified peasants had been executed by the Civil Guard in response. I scanned quickly again, looking for names. They weren't provided. Peasants' deaths didn't merit such detail.

I allowed myself to hope and dream that Percival was not among the men caught. I tried to hold open an uncorrupted place in my heart, a place full of soothing uncertainty, at least until I heard the facts from home. But that uncorrupted place had already sprung a leak; no matter what I tried to pour into it—anger, fear, self-pity—it kept emptying and shriveling, folding back upon itself. If I had stayed in Campo Seco another few weeks, if I had not raced back to Madrid to serve the Queen in a task that bothered me still, I could have kept an eye on my brother. I had reneged on a family responsibility with the pretense of nonintervention. And only so that I would be in the proper time and place to help intervene in other matters, equally tainted.

None of it should have had anything to do with me in the first place. I wasn't an outlaw. I wasn't a court opportunist. I was only a musician. *Only* a musician. How many times did I repeat that unsatisfying phrase in my mind? At least until the letter came, confirming the worst, informing me there would be no funeral, that I should not visit, that Percival's body had already been put to rest with other shamed corpses outside the cemetery gate.

I requested an audience with the Queen. She kept me waiting for three days, busy with other things—medical visits, I later heard. I asked her to accept the return of the sapphire.

"You don't care for it?"

"I don't deserve it. I don't feel equal to your confidences. I am not sure I can continue to serve you in the way you expect."

"But Feliu, it was a personal gift." Her face was blank. "You're not mixing up the affair of the other night with this symbol of our friendship?"

I didn't know how to answer, or what to think. In the silence that passed between us, I noticed the sound of ticking—not one clock but three in the room, not synchronized.

She followed my glance and narrowed her eyes. "Yes, they're back from the restorer—every last one, plus an antique scrounged from Vienna to replace the one that broke. All with shiny new parts inside."

When I started to speak again, she interrupted. "Keep the stone. I won't take it back. I continue to trust in your services."

At that moment, she knew me better than I knew myself. Because I did want to keep her gift. I did want to serve her still, not because I believed in the monarchy, not because I believed in a king without integrity, whose views—conservative one day, liberal the next—could be manipulated so easily without regard for Spain's future. I wanted to serve her because of who *she* was: a struggling soul with whom my own slightly off-pitch sense of self could harmonize, passing for true.

Then she told me her latest news, which only her closest attendants knew.

"I'm with child again, Feliu. And you know what that means. I must be very careful—no wine or coffee or chocolate; no strong emotions. No music. That's what the doctors advise."

PART IV

The Road to Anual

1914

CHAPTER

~ 13 ~

"Are you permanently attached to that seat?" said a voice behind me.

I couldn't make out the face, only a shock of thick dark hair in the rust-spotted reflection above the weathered headline—CATASTROPHE IN SARAJEVO—with a blurry, yellowing photo of the assassin, Gavrilo Princip, being dragged away by several policemen.

"How long have you been sitting there?" the stranger tried again.

"I'm still on my first."

"I doubt that."

He was even closer now, pressing against the back of my chair to let another man pass. When he reached over my shoulder to signal for a drink, I noted the sharp clean line of his shirt cuff and the heft of his arm. I could smell something on him—lavender, perhaps—that was aggressive in its floral prettiness.

I ignored him and lifted a finger toward the aproned barkeeper.

"I think you've been sitting several hours," he persevered.

"Listen—"

"Maybe even years."

"If you're in a hurry—" I said, turning.

The words caught in my throat. He laughed and clapped me on the back and finally embraced me, squeezing my thin suit jacket. Even after he let go, I could feel the spot on each triceps where his wide fingertips had pressed.

"*Dios santo,*" I gasped, catching my breath, "I thought you were in Paris!"

"I was, until a week ago."

"You promised you were never coming back to Madrid."

"Did I? I wish I could keep that promise."

Fine red capillaries snaked across his cheeks, but from a distance, they would only look like the hearty bloom of indefatigable youth. Everything about him, from his shoes to his wax-tipped mustache, shone.

He was studying me as closely as I was studying him. I opened my mouth and realized, after a hard swallow, that I had nothing to say.

The barkeeper set down my drink. Al-Cerraz reached over and grabbed it before I could, and gave it a sniff. "I forgot how cheap the liquor is here. I can't let you drink this! We'll find ourselves a better bottle somewhere."

I reached out to rescue the drink but Al-Cerraz had already pushed it, along with a coin, into the barkeeper's hand. "Coffee instead, please—two of them, *cortados.*"

I said, "You didn't leave because of the fighting?"

"It wasn't the war itself I couldn't stand, it was the whole festive atmosphere—one big party, the whole city engaged in debauchery, and young boys running around with wine bottles, hanging on their sweethearts, telling them they'd be back in two weeks. Two weeks!"

"Well, maybe…"

"They'll make beautiful targets in their bright uniforms. Here." He gestured for me to join him at an emptying table on the other side of the café, closer to the entrance. "The worst of it was the music. Three days of it. Bands playing in the streets, people dancing and singing like wind-up toys. If there had been a moment of quiet, people might have had a chance to think." The bartender came around and wiped the table for us. Al-Cerraz thanked him. "They say music is a dangerous aphrodisiac. It's nothing compared to patriotism. Anyway—how long have you been trying to grow a beard?"

"What do you mean, trying?"

He wrapped a heavy arm around me again and squeezed. His fingernails were manicured, glossy, with shiny white half-moons rising from trimmed cuticles. Suddenly I was aware of how long it had been since I'd laundered my shirt.

"This wasn't the first place I looked for you. I tried the music school, the theater. Then I thought, maybe some of the finer restaurants—they're not too bad, if you don't mind tinkling spoons. Personally, I refuse to compete with flan for attention."

"I have a few private students."

"Then I thought, maybe he's gone to America! Carnegie Hall."

"Not all of us are looking for fame and fortune."

"I can see that."

"Listen..."

"I'm listening, Feliu—tell me everything!"

"The letters," I managed to say with effort. "Didn't you get them?"

He made a few false starts, then smiled sheepishly. "I'm hopeless at writing. Ask anyone."

"But seven times? Eight? I figured the address was bad, but I had nowhere else to write."

"I'm here now. You can ask me—tell me—anything." And he leaned forward, bearded chin resting in his fleshy palms.

"Forget it. If you're here to find out about the latest intrigues, you're talking to the wrong man. I'm not with the court anymore." When he didn't react, I added, "The Queen asks to see me every few months, though I no longer play for her. Any local dandy spends more time there than I do. If you're setting up royal residence, you'll have the entire spotlight to yourself. I never had much of it, anyway."

"No, you just caught one bright spark." He bumped the table slightly, chuckling. "I hear it left a shiny spot on the inside of your bow."

A shaft of light had penetrated the bar's entryway and was dancing on a mirrored pillar next to the table. "You know," I said, squinting, "it's good to see you. But I think I'll go back to where I was sitting. Sun's in my eyes. I feel a headache coming on."

"The sun's in your eyes?" He laughed again, jostling his full cup. The saucer beneath was close to overflowing.

"You don't need the dark, you need something to eat. Away from here. I insist."

I hedged, thrust my hand into my pocket, felt the last coin there, and thought of the empty apartment waiting me.

"*Vale.* But I'm not fetching any water for your car," I cautioned.

"Water? There's no need—but that gives me a marvelous idea."

He didn't mean the Stanley Steamer; he'd replaced that long ago, before souring altogether on automotive fads. By water, he meant the *estanque,* the nearby Retiro's pond with its paddleboats and lawns for picnicking. This August day it was nearly deserted, the food stalls and little puppet theater shuttered against the midday sun while a few employees napped in the shadows, waiting for evening's cool reprieve. The only other park stroller was a shifty-looking man in a threadbare cape—perhaps a failed courtier like me—tilting his ear toward the marble statue of the King's father as if he were listening to the dead monarch's secrets.

Al-Cerraz rattled the window to rouse the sleeping rowboat attendant and slipped a folded bill between the bars. Soon we were floating on the dazzling water, next to a line of ducks too hot to flee. I hadn't thought I was hungry, but when I smelled the grease-spotted bags he'd loaded into the boat, filled with bread, sausage, cheese, and fruit he'd bought along the way, my appetite returned. I listened, sleepy and full for the first time in days, as the pianist expressed his distaste for Stravinsky's *Rite of Spring*, his tentative interest in jazz, his catalog of every famous Spanish musician and artist living in Paris. "Anyone and everyone you can think of!" And then, catching himself and endeavoring to be more kind, "Well, not everyone. A lot of has-beens, come to think of it."

He talked to me about music and life in England, Italy, San Francisco, and New Orleans—about everywhere, it seemed, but Spain. Perhaps I'd assumed wrong. Al-Cerraz wasn't settling back into court life here, he was just passing through. Spain was the last place in the world that interested him, and he was a man who demanded to be interested, inspired, at the center of things, where everything was new. Yet he hated war—even the most remote hint of it, the sight of bandages, any hint of tinny bugling. And so, he assured me when I asked him directly, he was home to stay. Spain, he predicted, would stay neutral in the war, not upon any moral high ground, but to dig itself out of its economic slump. With the rest of Europe in ruins, its tottering industries might have a chance—as might its performers.

"We'll take the trains," he was saying. "Not with our own private car, not this time—anyway, traveling with a piano is overrated; why rehearse with a better instrument than you'll get to play at the concerts themselves? But first class we'll manage, traveling light. The cities, of course, but the smaller towns, too, on the way. You'll have the energy for that. As my beautiful mother always said, hard work and a harder bed keep an artist young."

I had nodded off, lulled by the gentle rocking of the boat. "Trains?" I rubbed my eyes, yellow spots dancing on my inner lids.

"You're probably wondering about the violinist. He's adequate. He's had the same questions about you, of course—as did Monsieur Biber, but I've reassured him. The first week is always a trial, but after that—"

"Reassured him?"

"That you'll perform to our standards."

"Who says I'll perform at all?"

"Biber asked what you'd want in terms of fees. I told him you'd understand what the life is really like—steady work, few vacations. I told him you'd be fair."

"Fair." I closed my eyes. "As fair as not answering the letters I wrote you?"

"Yes, yes—about coming to Paris."

"So you *did* read them."

"And look—I was right! It's no place for a musician. Not now."

"But you didn't explain that. I couldn't have known you were ignoring me for my own good."

When he failed to answer, I closed my eyes. He discarded his jacket and his shirt and rowed in his undershirt, making lazy circles in the sun. I heard the snap of the oarlocks. "Feliu, I went to your apartment first, before I found you at the café. I saw how you're living."

"I'm not interested," I said.

"You were seeking opportunity; now you're rejecting it. You don't consider this a good offer?"

"Too good, and too sudden. Over the years, I've developed a taste for independence—and a distaste for favors."

"'Over the years!'" he snorted and stood up. The rowboat lurched. I leaned forward and put my arms over the gunwales, trying to steady the boat while he balanced on one beefy leg, tugging at his shoelaces. "You're rather young for that sort of talk!"

My face over my knees, I willed the boat to stop rocking. I could hear more than see: the snap of a knee garter; the clatter of a dropped shoe. One black sock landed in my lap.

"Say no more," he said. "Disagreement is bad for digestion. And indigestion is bad for swimming."

The boat leaned hard and then righted itself so violently that I gasped. He splashed and was gone, under the surface. I heard a few protesting quacks when he came up for breath, several meters away.

"Come in!" he called.

When I didn't answer right away, he called back, "Never mind. It's wonderful. Don't do yourself any favors."

I watched him float on his back, his belly rising as a smooth white island above the surface. His undershirt was taut and nearly translucent against his chest, whorls of black hair visible beneath it. His large pink toes flexed above the opaque surface of the water.

"There are only two places in the world where I feel weightless and at peace," he called to me cheerfully, his irritation already purged. "This is the second one."

He took his time returning to the rowboat. Pulling himself back aboard, he glistened like an otter, diamond-bright drops of water nesting on his matted mustache, beard, and gleaming black hair. Water streamed from his rolled pant-legs while he lit a damp cigar, its leafy smolder doubling as the breeze shifted in my direction.

"I'm feeling a little sick, actually," I said.

"I told you a swim would make you feel better."

"I'm not a strong swimmer. I like the water, but..."

"Too much sun." He puffed away. "You never asked me what the first was—the first place I feel at peace."

"Maybe we could switch sides," I said, wanting to get away from the smoke. "I'll row us back."

"Not at the piano, if that's what you're thinking."

I wasn't. I still remembered him confessing years earlier his unease at playing, his self-consciousness on the stage—if that had all been true, rather than an exaggerated, wine-soaked lament.

"Aboard trains. That's what I meant."

"I see," I told him, but I was more focused on our balance in the boat. Holding each other by the forearms, we tried to execute a shuffling dance, working our way around each other while the boat lurched.

We had nearly stepped around each other when Al-Cerraz started to speak; then he shouted suddenly: *"Huy!"* The cigar had slipped out of his mouth. It was floating, like some chamber-pot detritus, in the tea-colored pond water. He leaned over, as if to retrieve it. I began to yell. Then my own mouth was full, and I was sinking, weighted down by all my clothes, darkness all around me. I kicked hard and came above the surface, gasping.

I could hear him laughing from the boat. "*Cálmate!* It's not that deep—just over your head!"

I went down again, felt the springy surface of weeds under my feet, kicked up, and breathed.

"Use your arms!"

Down again, another light bounce, and the agonizing tickle of inhaled water.

"Fool! Swim!"

Every time I came up to the dazzling surface, I saw the shadowy underside of the rocking boat, but nothing else—no sign of an out-stretched hand. He was too busy trying to fish his cigar out of the water.

"Stop flailing!" he shouted again, barely bothering to look my way.

"I have a bad..." I started to say, sucking in water. I sputtered, "...leg—hip, really."

"What's a hip got to do with swimming? Look at me—I could swim to Africa!"

For a second, my fury overwhelmed my fear; somehow, that helped. Finally, I controlled my breathing and started pushing the water away from my face and kicking more evenly. A slippery piece of grass brushed my cheek, but I kept the rhythm. In just three or four more strokes, I was at the boat, reaching for the gunwale.

"See?" He hauled me in. "Not so bad, was it? I knew you couldn't have grown up near the Mediterranean and not be able to swim." A pause. Then: "You owe me a cigar, you know."

I spit, coughed, and finally retched until I managed to vomit over the side. Al-Cerraz turned away.

"Look what you've done," I said afterward, gasping, as I sprawled in the boat. "Imagine the filth I've swallowed."

"Oh—certainly. It was the pond water that did it—"

And the cigar smoke, I was thinking.

"—not the half-bottle of swill you'd drunk before two o'clock today. Or the hundreds of bottles before that."

"I'm not a drunk," I snapped.

"Good. I'm glad we got that question out of the way. Are you suicidal?"

"Why would you say that?"

"Your landlady said you spend a lot of time sitting on the suicides' bridge."

"That's rubbish."

"I'm glad to hear it."

Several glum minutes passed.

Finally he said, "You can see I don't put others first—there's no worry about that. So here's how it is. It's no favor to you. It's a favor to me. We have a dozen concerts already booked, and our French cellist ran off to Belgium, to sacrifice himself for *la guerre*. Fine, if that's what he wants."

He added, "You're not the first cellist I asked. You're the third. That's not because I don't think you're immensely talented. It's only because you're inexperienced and unknown. In semiretirement at— what—twenty-one?"

I glared at him.

"Be offended, if it will help you feel better about it. This isn't a great deal for either of us, but I'm too broke to live without touring. I've been paid to compose an opera based on *Don Quixote*, but it's gone nowhere. I can't remember the last time I had a good night's sleep." He perked up. "But the trains will help that. They're the perfect cure for insomnia."

I was too tired to speak. Sourness burned in my throat.

"You're afraid of getting wrapped up in something," he continued. "Makes no sense at all. You've got nothing to lose. But put it this way: If you had only a month to live, would you try touring with us?"

"Possibly."

"Well, then—" He pointed to a sign on the shore: NO SWIMMING IN THE ESTANQUE—RISK OF CHOLERA—BUREAU OF PUBLIC HEALTH.

"As for me," Al-Cerraz said, "I never catch anything. A terrible scarlet rash whenever I eat shrimp, but besides that, *nada*."

Within a week, I was preparing to board a train and say good-bye to the capital that had been my home for five years. Al-Cerraz was correct. I had nothing to lose. Despite my skepticism about the pianist, despite my initial pretenses of aloofness, I couldn't fight the tingle that mounted as the train approached, vibrating the platform. As jaded as I'd become in Madrid, I still believed it was possible to climb aboard a train as one person, and step off it as another.

I encountered our French violinist for the first time on the platform, crowded with people and suitcases. He swept by me, glancing around and through my legs, muttering into his thin blond mustache. I reached out a hand: "Feliu Delargo." But he circled me and walked back the other way, past Al-Cerraz and his five massive trunks.

"To him, you are not a person," Al-Cerraz explained. "You are someone with luggage—fortunately, not too much of it, since we are traveling heavy already."

Al-Cerraz nodded at the porter who, with the violinist's help, was directing the flow of our baggage into the train.

"He can be excessive with *ritardes*, and he once lost all memory of a Franck sonata we had performed a hundred times. But he has never lost a piece of our luggage. I introduce you to our violinist and chief transportation coordinator, Louis Gauthier."

Gauthier did not look up at the sound of his name. He was still immersed in discussion with the porter as the stationmaster walked by, ringing a handbell.

"Come on. He will be the last to board," Al-Cerraz continued. "And then he'll spend the next hour studying the railway timetable. And he will get off first at every stop, to calm our fans."

"Fans? Are you serious?"

"I think he must have played with trains as a boy," Al-Cerraz continued. "When he is very good, we let him ride in the locomotive."

In our compartment, Al-Cerraz put one arm around me. "I know this country better than anyone else alive. Bottom bunk all right?"

"That's fine." I'd never traveled first class. Captivated, I studied the small sitting room that would transform, at the turn of the porter's key, into a bedroom: the red carpet, the round table tucked between two chairs, the diminutive washbasin in one corner. It was immaculate and elegant, for the moment; less so as Al-Cerraz hung a sausage from the tasseled curtain rod over the picture window and set a woven garland of garlic in the marble washbasin.

"Since I was a very small boy, traveling from town to town, three hundred days a year, I learned to love this life," he continued. "The cradlelike rock and sway of the train, the hospitality of our countrymen, the gentle hearts of our countrywomen." He winked. "You will find that, as long as you keep moving, there is no end to the delights awaiting you. But you must keep moving, Feliu. Even when the heart skips; even when the view blurs."

I had seen so little of Spain, apart from my home coast and the capital, that for the first months of our 1914 tour, the place names alone were a new kind of music. Segovia. Burgos. Valladolid. And between those fabled places, hundreds of smaller hamlets, places that appeared on few maps and didn't need to. Each village had its own source of pride as the birthplace of a saint or Renaissance poet, or as the place with the sweetest grapes, the best-trained horses, the most talented leatherworkers.

The train rattled along its narrow tracks and the last few years fell away, shrugged off like a heavy cape. My health and color improved. My mood lightened. To make up for the reclusive gloominess of my recent past, I felt that I now deserved some pleasure. And who better to find it with than Al-Cerraz, who attracted the best and choicest and prettiest of everything, and who enjoyed life with such appetite, and no guilt?

Our trio had a natural chemistry. Gauthier was a tall, lean, light-haired serious man who cloaked his feelings beneath a wispy mustache and a smirk, providing a contrast to Al-Cerraz's clownishness. On the train, he most often took a horizontal position, reclining in his bunk as he wrote to each of his nine sisters, who were scattered between Paris and Alsace. As the eldest, and the only boy, he'd had many responsibilities, he told me in our first days together. He'd grown more committed to his violin when he realized that his parents would never interrupt him to carry wood or dress a toddler as long as he was practicing. In the moments when he'd stopped playing and not yet been redirected toward a chore, he'd learned to embrace ephemeral leisure without delay. I'd never seen a man more eager to sleep—or more able to leap from a state of sleep into instant readiness, as soon as duty called. No wonder Al-Cerraz had come to rely on him to keep track of luggage, schedules, and communications with the manager, Monsieur Biber.

It was Gauthier who first explained to me how little money touring actually made. For large city engagements, we sometimes were paid in advance. But small towns were a gamble. Whoever had arranged the show—a cultural league, a women's group, a music-loving town leader—assisted with promotion through the local posting of flyers, and paid us only after we played, based on their generosity or their success at fund-raising. When our income far exceeded our expenses, we paid ourselves and took an extended weekend—even the occasional week—off near the tour route. We never took off enough time to go "home," which satisfied me; I had no desire to return to Campo Seco or anywhere else I'd lived, and at least while the Great War raged, Gauthier and Al-Cerraz felt the same way. When our income dipped, we had to do without, living simply until the next, more profitable run of shows. As our audiences found it harder and harder to pay, Al-Cerraz began to subsidize our concertizing for weeks at a time.

"But why would he do that?" I asked Gauthier once, when Al-Cerraz was off by himself in the smoking car.

"He tours to feed himself." Gauthier reclined on his bunk with a folded newspaper on his lap.

"But when we're losing money, how can he feed himself?"

"Not with food," he said, pulling thoughtfully on his blond mustache. "He feeds his ego—and, I hope, his imagination."

Gauthier saw my baffled expression. "He can only afford to subsidize us because he gets money from Brenan." That was Thomas Brenan, the patron who had commissioned Al-Cerraz's *Don Quixote*. "I don't think he wrote a single note while he was in Paris. I'm sure he thinks time in Spain will enhance his creativity."

"Do you think he'll really compose anything?"

"He's always talked about it. First, his father was to blame for getting in the way. Then his mother—"

"Which one?" I interrupted.

Gauthier laughed. "You mean the one who is dead, the one he wishes were dead, the one who is a saint, the one who was a courtesan, or the one who takes half of whatever money he's got left at the end of each month?"

"Who is she, really?"

"I don't know. All I know is that he has dined out on anecdotes about her—and about everything else—for his entire life. Perhaps he'll never compose anything but stories." And with that he closed his eyes.

Gauthier had other ambitions. His fantasy was to retire early to a French Polynesian island and to spend the last third of his life in a hammock, undisturbed. I could imagine his balding, age-spotted pate growing ever browner, like a coconut, and his wispy blond mustache shifting like a grass skirt in the South Pacific breeze. To that end, Gauthier aimed only to save a little money every few weeks, tucking it into his carefully guarded violin case. He was already in his late forties, and did not expect any more fame or attention than the modest quantity he'd already attained.

Gauthier and I rehearsed daily in our train car. Without a piano, Al-Cerraz could not join us, but that suited his natural inclination, which was to save his energies for his audiences. As the violinist and I played, Al-Cerraz would listen, rocking lightly back and forth, just an arm's length from my moving bow. Sometimes he'd appear on the verge of falling asleep, but suddenly, his eyes would fly open: "There! Can you try...?" In his own mind, he could hear himself playing with perfect clarity, fused with our parts; Gauthier and I had the disadvantage, since we couldn't hear or imagine him as well. But it was impossible to worry, when Al-Cerraz did not. And at each performance, we found our harmonies, adapted our dynamics, and made impromptu bowing changes.

I had not yet recorded, of course, and Al-Cerraz had made only a few records by this time. But that was not how most villagers knew him. They had committed his trademark performance pieces to memory, preserved with great mental discipline since the time of his most recent visit.

As we pulled into each town, a self-selected music enthusiast—an *alcalde*, or the wife of some eminent merchant—would ambush Al-Cerraz as he stepped off the train. In a fishing village on the Cantabrian coast, it was a heavyset woman draped in a stiff and intricately patterned brocade gown one size too small. Thus confined, she nonetheless managed to sing wordlessly for close to a minute in a loud and passionate voice that made the carriage horse awaiting us take a few uncertain steps backward, ears flicking. I didn't recognize the song until Al-Cerraz announced, "Yes, Schubert! How long has it been, Señora—?"

"Rubielos," she said, bowing low. She remained there for a moment, catching her breath until she could answer, "It has been six years."

As we stepped into the carriage, an elaborate antique resurrected from a local museum or someone's barn, Al-Cerraz whispered, "There is always a Señora Rubielos."

Sometimes this archetypal aficionada hummed Chopin, or whistled Liszt. Sometimes she had waited four years, or eight. Her rendition might be a faithful mimicry, in a town where at least one person knew how to play the piano well, or had managed to lay hands on a score. More often, it would be mangled and fragmented, blended with some other work. But invariably the enthusiasts were earnest, delivering Al-Cerraz's notes back to him as if to prove his listeners' loyalty during the maestro's absence. They were like the New World natives we were told about as children, who upon hearing the word of Christ from a shipwrecked priest, chanted it into an amalgam, scarcely recognizable and yet still sacred to the Conquistadores arriving years later.

Al-Cerraz explained it to me this way: "In the deserts of the south there is a plant that requires rain only every few decades. Some say it will live without water for a century. But when the rain comes, it blooms. Feliu, we are the rain that comes to these towns."

In return, villagers opened their hearts and doors to us. As part of his onstage patter, just prior to his final encore, Al-Cerraz would describe the homesickness that plagued his heart, the great longing he had for a simple home-cooked Spanish meal. Hand signals would fly between mothers and sons; young boys would dash for the exits. Through open doors, as Al-Cerraz's encore relaxed into its final diminuendo, I was certain I could hear the protesting squawk of chickens pressed to the slaughter block.

Ideally, we would arrive at a small town at midday, proceed directly to an afternoon or early-evening performance, then repair to a bar for an hour until the locally chosen Doña had our dinner ready. Between courses, Al-Cerraz would regale his hostess and her guests with stories. After dinner, if she had a piano, he would play more encores, no matter how poorly tuned or ill-repaired the instrument. If keys were missing, it only increased the suspense as Al-Cerraz improvised around them, aping consternation, his black shock of hair more unruly with each passing hour.

He seemed to enjoy playing at a village hall more than at a city music palace, and he relished playing in a private house crowded with steaming bodies most of all. If a villager appeared with a guitar, Al-Cerraz would compete with it, mimicking the sounds of strummed chords by playing his own broken chords on the piano. If a boy produced some sort of shepherd's pipe or whistle, Al-Cerraz would accompany it, making it sound like the foundation for some elaborate concerto. If a woman commandeered the attention, stamping out some complicated Andalucían rhythm with her feet, Al-Cerraz would pause, listen, and finally join in, mimicking the rhythm. Then he would back just one step away from it, so that they continued to play together—hands and feet—in a tricky syncopation of escalating speed and intensity until one of them surrendered, sweating and laughing uncontrollably while the whole room erupted with earsplitting applause.

He had said we were the rain, as if these villages were bone-dry, without music or culture save what we delivered. It seemed to me that we were simply the spark, in places already rich with kindling. In such places lived the Señoras who revered foreign composers like Chopin (as Chopin's own Polish countryfolk had not revered him), and there were villagers who celebrated—and played—their own native folk music. And there was a sense, which my own town had lost sometime between my father's generation and mine, that Spain could have both: be European and Iberian, look back and look forward, preserve and innovate.

"It's remarkable," I told him once as we took the air outside a rustic house one evening, moments after he'd accompanied a trio of farmers with their handmade instruments.

"What is?"

"The way you perform with them."

He finished swabbing his face with a handkerchief, then looked at me curiously. "I wouldn't call it performing. I'm just being a good guest. They say 'How do you do?' and I answer, 'How do you do?'" He didn't recognize the value of his talent, which allowed him to listen and mimic, distinguish and hybridize, changing accents and rhythms as we traveled from north to south, east to west. He thought it was a liability.

"They're just parlor tricks, refined from the accidents of birth," he said. "I have a sensitive ear. It not only detects, it collects, traps, and clogs. If the nation of Spain ever falls silent, I'm sure some doctor will take a scalpel to my inner ear—or better yet my brain—split it open, and perish as an avalanche of sounds burst forth."

He smiled mournfully, then clapped me on the shoulder with abrupt, effortful heartiness. "I know just what you need!"

Back inside the main *sala*, Al-Cerraz slid onto the piano bench and pounded out several introductory chords to get everyone's attention. Then he stopped and called out, "Men, find a partner!"

I pressed my back against the wall.

"You as well, Feliu!"

Suddenly there was a slim, feminine hand in mine. Al-Cerraz launched into an Aragonese *jota*. Men unbuttoned their collars. Women grabbed thick handfuls of skirt with one hand. Bodies began to hop around me. I don't think anyone except the puzzled lady with whom I'd been paired would have noticed my inactivity if only Al-Cerraz would have kept playing. Instead he stopped mid-measure, laughing, and announced to the crowd: "Forgive my partner! He makes a formidable obstacle on any dance floor."

All heads turned toward me.

My eyes must have flashed, because Al-Cerraz said quickly: "Forgive *me*, I should say. I am a man whose heart beats in rapid triple-time. Whereas my cellist"—and here Al-Cerraz began to play a simpler, slower melody—"lives to a statelier beat."

Later that evening, he gestured across the room to the woman with whom I had danced. "I've already told her that you need some air. And that you have a fascination with aqueducts."

"Aqueducts?"

"Medieval bell towers. Ancient granaries. Every town has some architectural feature on the outskirts, something they like to show off."

"But shouldn't we—"

"You'll notice"—Al-Cerraz breathed heavily into my ear—"Gauthier hasn't been seen in an hour. I myself have an interest in choir stalls. This lady"—he angled his head toward another young woman leaning against the piano—"has offered to take me to see the local cathedral by moonlight."

"I'm not very fond of strolling," I said. "I'd prefer to find a quiet place to sit."

He whispered into my ear, "Stroll only as far as necessary, then."

"I wouldn't know what to say to one of these girls."

"The less the better."

"But I'm not sure—"

"Listen," he interrupted, backing away to lock eyes. "If there is any reward to be gained from a lady in this room, it won't be gained by what you say. She's already heard you perform. That's the only reason she is interested in you now.

"These," he continued with emphasis, "are the perfumed hours. The music lasts a little while, the roses in their hair a few hours beyond that. And then…" he made a fluttering motion with the fingers of both hands, tracing the invisible lines of some dissipating magic.

"I thought you were interested only in what lasts," I mocked.

He looked at his hands, still floating in the air, as if they were unfamiliar objects. "The eternal." He studied his left hand. "And the ephemeral." He studied his right. "Yes, you're correct. It is a contradiction. Unless it isn't. Unless I find some way to contain these intangible, sublime moments within something that will outlast everything—even you and me."

He held himself like that for a moment, and then he exploded with self-mocking guffaws. "Such lofty ideals! All that the great philosophers ever wanted was beauty, and we have a dozen examples of it in this room."

"And truth…" I said, but he was already walking toward the woman leaning on the piano, leaving me standing opposite my former dance partner.

She wore a sleeveless gown, one size too large—perhaps a cousin's, pulled from a dusty wardrobe earlier that day; perhaps a sister's, traded in exchange for a week's worth of chores. I could see the pin at each side, under her bare arms, where she had pulled in and secured the fabric, and closer to her hip, through a small tear, a hint of some lace undergarment—perhaps borrowed as well. She saw me staring and stood straighter, raising both arms over her head to rearrange an ebony comb in the back of her wavy chestnut hair.

Just before I went to take her hand I said again, to no one but myself, "They wanted beauty—and truth."

But there weren't always young pretty women in abundance during those early years; or lavish parties, or even chickens. Sometimes the audience—small or large, finely dressed or plain—was missing altogether.

We arrived one night in our second year at a manor house in the far south. We had been picked up at the train station by a taciturn man with a wagon, the least-enthusiastic welcoming committee we'd had in some time. At the house, there were a dozen people, rather than the sixty or eighty we expected. The mood was peculiarly tense. I asked the wagon driver if a harvest was underway. The man, whose eyes were hidden under a sweat-stained fedora, fumbled nervously with the handkerchief tied around his neck. A better-dressed gentleman at the front of the room spoke up. "No harvest. We didn't plant this season."

Following the performance, there were no encores, and no post-concert festivities. The wagon driver gave us a ride back to the town center. Iron gates covered the shoe-repair shop and one of the town's two bakeries. The pharmacy was boarded over. We ate sandwiches at the train station, where we finally learned from the stationmaster what had happened to the townsfolk. With seed prices high and crop prices low, word had spread that most laborers would lose their jobs. Fearing reprisals, landowners and the local civil guard had trucked two loads of farmworkers away from the town—carted them three hundred kilometers west and left them there.

"What, like unwanted kittens in a burlap sack?" Gauthier said.

"I won't have this!" Al-Cerraz said sharply, and I turned to him with interest. Despite his fame in Spain—his access to reporters and high society ladies and artistic opinion-makers—I had never known him to attach his name to any cause. Perhaps he simply hadn't been incensed enough.

"I won't have this," he repeated—but he was not referring to the laborers. "I won't have my time and energy wasted." He turned to the railway table, and then to Gauthier. "Is there an earlier train out of here?"

That second year of touring, a reviewer in one of the larger cities made first mention of my contributions to the trio. By the end of the next year, a good quarter of the reviews praised my playing first; a smaller number offered first attentions to Gauthier, which still left the majority to fawn on Al-Cerraz.

By 1917, Gauthier was rarely mentioned at all. "It's only because you're French," I tried to console him, though he refused to act as if he needed any consolation. "The war, you understand. Everyone defending their own."

"If anything, my nationality should gain me sympathy," he said. "Don't your countrymen appreciate that we're fighting in your stead?"

But that wasn't how Spaniards saw it. We endeavored to remain neutral in the war. As Al-Cerraz had predicted, that neutrality offered benefits, and a prestige Spain hadn't enjoyed in our lifetimes. New diplomatic and business offices opened in Madrid, Barcelona, Bilbao, and elsewhere. Coal mining and steel production surged. Industrialists profited from the opportunity to supply what the rest of war-torn Europe could not.

And yet, though we had read and heard that these riches would eventually fill even poor men's pockets, the reverse seemed to be true. Inflation drove prices up, while workers' wages—and army officers' fixed wages as well—remained stagnant. The Spanish-American War, in which my own father had died, had left the countryside impoverished. And now this "prosperous" peace somehow did the same.

Talk of economic policy rarely invaded the first-class parlor cars. But the proof of changing times hung just outside the train windows, providing glimpses for those who chose to see. The houses looked emptier, the horse-drawn wagons fewer and farther between. Some train stations looked abandoned. Others were curiously crowded, with people who seemed only to stand and stare; never departing, never arriving.

In the small towns where we performed, the "perfumed hours" lost their easygoing charm. An evening stroll with a young lady, whatever her station in life, often led to overeager conversations about the prospects for life in some other corner in Spain. I was asked frequently whether I intended to marry, and if so, where I would settle, and whether things were better off there? Kisses were offered with greater urgency; addresses were pressed into my hand more forcefully. Where my fellow musicians and I had once represented a romantic dalliance— a moment beyond time and reason—we now seemed to represent some greater reality: the chance to escape into a better situation.

"I know this country better than anyone else alive," Al-Cerraz had said. But what did he know, if what he had nearly always seen were people in their weekend best, depleting their stores and their cellars? I felt like we were seeing not real places, but stage sets, constructed to last just until the train moved on, billows of locomotive steam curling the paper facades of pretend buildings, the blue boxboard sky propped overhead, everything ready to crash as soon as pulled out of view.

"Keep moving," Al-Cerraz had advised, and we did. But as we left each village, we seemed barely to outpace the groping hands we left behind.

Our train rides between performances began to seem interminable, especially as we stopped playing some of the smaller venues, traveling farther between towns and cities that would pay us. On top of that, there were more delays, particularly in the south, where debris littered the track and uniformed men patrolled the stations, looking for signs of revolutionary activity.

Three men were one too many for a compartment as narrow as ours, even after the beds were folded away. I tired of Gauthier's ceaseless smoking. Al-Cerraz was irritated by my morning routine of Bach, followed by an hour of scales. He could have gone to the dining car, but I think he liked to talk over my practicing, assuring himself a captive audience for his ritualistic morning laments, which were usually about the state of his mind, his heart, and his gastric system.

"You've heard of creative juices," he said one day as I bowed a minor scale. "Mine are overproductive. With insufficient outlet, they are dissolving my organs from the inside out. It's all from lack of artistic opportunity." Anyone who lived with our pianist could see the cause of his periodic discomforts: rich foods, sausage, cigars, espresso, wine. Our compartment smelled like a delicatessen, with an entire leg of air-cured serrano ham hanging from the ceiling, stale loaves of bread tucked into the folded bed platform, liquor bottles and empty anchovy jars accumulating in the washbasin.

Afternoons, I read musical biographies in German, French, and English, to continue advancing my language skills. Gauthier buried himself in our business, organizing the receipts and records he would forward to Biber. Al-Cerraz stretched out on his bunk to compose, he said, though I suspected he was composing only obsequious letters to his patron. Eventually, the heaviness of Gauthier's and Al-Cerraz's sighs drove me out of the compartment and into the passageway, where I would stand alone, eyes fixed on the passing landscape of terraced hills and crumbling barns.

"Trouble finding your compartment?" conductors asked in train after train; or, "Dining car open for another few minutes, if you hurry." Then they'd leave me to watch as the cars glided through these tranquil scenes, disturbing only the clouds of black birds that alighted, startled, from yellow fields. As we made our way south, gray slate roofs gave way to red; dark, water-stained walls to white. The sun shone, but from behind the glass, I could not feel it. We passed a grove of olive trees, and I remembered how the bark had felt against my fingertips, the cold ground against my back, the branches dividing blue sky overhead as Percival, doing the hard physical work that my own infirmity prevented me from doing, called down to me from his precarious perch, "More here? Feliu, pay attention—cut here?"

Some days it felt as if the world beyond the train windows were more real than the one within, that the acts of eating and talking and sleeping and playing in constant motion placed us outside of normalcy, saved us from reality—which made us doubly saved, since to live in neutral Spain during the War to End All Wars was in itself a form of salvation. But if we were saved, then why did the real world, even in its impoverished state, seem so much more enchanting than our private refuge?

Constant travel had made it more difficult to correspond with Enrique, but the occasional letter reached me. My brother was still living a bachelor soldier's life, and he was beginning to feel not only underpaid but unappreciated—unable to settle down with any real comfort, respect, or purpose; unable to attract a wife or start a family. He'd come back to El Ferrol from a two-year tour in Morocco without much to show for it. His friend Paquito had suffered a near-fatal stomach wound during his own African tour, but this close brush with death had yielded considerable rewards. Paquito had been promoted to the rank of major and had earned renown as a fearless man of extraordinary good luck. Enrique's friend was determined to go to Morocco again, and to return with either "*la caja o la faja*"—the coffin or the general's sash.

A general's sash didn't seem to be in my brother's future regardless of where he was posted. To cheer him up, I did my best to describe the itinerant musician's life for him, exaggerating both our adventures and discomforts and poking fun at my musical partners and their quirks.

It was a few months before Enrique's response reached me: *You are right when you blame AlCezzar* [his spelling] *for not seeing the Poverty and Ruin around him.*

Had I done such a thing?

You told me he only goes to the Parlorcar with the large picture windows at night and I can imagine why. Have you noticed when you ride in a Traincar during the day you can see out? But after sunset when it is brighter inside the car than outside the window becomes a Mirror? He

prefers his own image to that of the world. That is how our current lead-
ers are. They are just as self-centered as your Pianist.

It embarrassed me to read such unkind things written about Justo,
whom my brother had never met. But it was my brother's uncharacteristic bitterness that concerned me more. Perhaps he only needed someone to dislike or blame, as an outlet for his undeserved disappointment
and frustration. And so I tolerated the barbs in one letter after another
about this "piggish AlCezzar," and even "this enemy Moor," to which
I felt duty bound to respond that Al-Cerraz's ethnic identity relied
upon a distant ancestral connection, perhaps a wishful fabrication at
that.

Now you write to say that he is not a Moor. That makes him a Liar. It
does not surprise me at all.

I wrote again, explaining that Al-Cerraz was more complex than I
must have portrayed, and perhaps nobler as well—that his greatest
passion was truly music, not himself. That he could be childish, but he
could also show maturity. That he could be frivolous, but that he was
faithful to his fellow musicians.

I was relieved when Enrique dropped the personal attacks in favor
of larger topics. He wrote back:

You were surprised at the criticism I levied on the Government but make
no mistake. Our Military while esteeming Authority Loyalty and Re-
spect does not necessarily side with those currently in power. It is not
a contradiction to say that we career soldiers are both the greatest
standard-bearers of Tradition and also the only force for real change.
What that change will be I cannot say.

   When you and I were both enanitos *together it impressed me that*
you knew your Destiny. That day you saw the cello played you said that

was your instrument and we laughed at the seriousness in your little man's voice. But what I didn't tell you that day or any other was that I wished I had my own Star to follow, the way you had yours.

Some of us can be great and some of us can only recognize greatness. Some day a more worthy leader will rise up from our ranks and hopefully I will recognize him, perhaps I have already, just as you recognized your own passion.

Siempre,

Enrique

That letter awaited me in Córdoba, where we spent a long weekend, along with a second from Enrique, announcing that he had been promoted, at long last. Encouraged, he had decided to accept Paquito's advice to seek another posting in Morocco, under his friend's leadership.

Don't worry for me. Paquito and I will look after each other.

Also waiting in Córdoba were a telegram and a package from Thomas Brenan. Al-Cerraz's patron telegraphed every three months or so, requesting updates. Until now, Brenan had seemed perversely pleased by obstacles and delays, as if such inconveniences foretold an even more brilliant result. But the continuing European war was taking its toll on even the optimism of the rich. For the first time, Brenan warned Al-Cerraz that he couldn't afford more advances without some evidence of progress. "Prove to me," he wrote, "that in four years you have accomplished something."

On the train later that afternoon, Al-Cerraz filled the stale air of our compartment with cigar smoke. His listlessness matched the stark, dry scenery around us as our train labored through a scrubby mountain pass, rocks bouncing from the rail bed. Addressing no one in particular, he said, "It's ironic, really, that our own countrymen don't respect us enough to support our art. And the man who does hasn't visited

Spain for twenty years. He doesn't have to, does he? He has learned everything from Spanish literature. He wants his name immortalized as a patron of Spanish music. Your English is better than mine, Feliu. Read this."

He leaned forward and handed me a manuscript that he'd extracted from Brenan's package. The title page read, "Libretto for *Don Quixote.*"

"Your patron paid someone to write the libretto?"

"*He* wrote the libretto. Tell me how bad it is."

I scanned for several minutes without getting past the first character's recitation, a long-winded, rhythmically unvarying solo that read like something from a children's book. "It *does* seem to rhyme."

He thrust out a hand to take back the manuscript. "It rhymes. *Vale.* No problems there."

Ignoring him, I flipped toward the middle and tried to read again.

Al-Cerraz grabbed for it more insistently. "It doesn't matter what he's written. It's been done already, a hundred times."

"A *thousand* times," I corrected him distractedly, still reading. "But maybe if you took more time away from touring—more than just the odd week off now and again. You'd have time and quiet and a good piano—"

At that moment, the train shuddered. Gauthier fell toward Al-Cerraz's lap, then regained his balance. We all looked at each other, surprised for a moment, but nothing more seemed to happen, and the train banked smoothly into a curve. Just as reassured smiles began to spread, a second jolt hit. Metal screeched against metal as the train braked to a halt. Gauthier lost his balance again and hit his head with a dull thud. But that didn't stop him from being the first to run outside.

Five minutes later, he was back. "That first bump might have been some sort of failed explosive."

Al-Cerraz said, "An exaggeration, don't you think? I'd wager it was debris."

"If so, debris artfully placed," Gauthier replied.

Outside in the hallway, two men were arguing. We opened our door to find the conductor interrogating a man who didn't have a ticket. The porter was suggesting they put him off the train immediately. The conductor wanted to confine him and turn him over to authorities at the next station. The man himself seemed confused; he continued to pat his pockets and search for words of explanation in broken Spanish.

I was considering intervening—it didn't seem right to leave a man out here in the middle of nowhere, with nothing but rocks and bushes, not even a gnarled tree for shade—when Al-Cerraz stepped in front of me to flag down a passing serving girl carrying a tray of sandwiches.

"We'll have some of those," he said.

"I can't," the girl replied. "They're someone else's. But I can't find the door."

"What's the number?" Gauthier asked.

She cocked her chin downward, indicating a ticket in the front pocket of her apron. "It isn't a number, just a name. But I can't make it out."

Gauthier reached toward the apron. "I will try to read it for you," he said, his French accent noticeably thicker.

She wrinkled her nose. "No, thank you. Are you movie stars?"

"Movie stars? What a treasure you are," Al-Cerraz replied.

"I recognize you from your picture on a flyer at one of the stations."

"How clever. And what is your name?" He was interrupted by a knock at the door. I opened it to find another serving girl, stockier than the first, but fair. She stepped over the threshold, attempted a quick smile, and then said to her friend in a low voice, "Felipa—you still haven't found it?"

The girl shook her head.

"So—it's Felipa," Al-Cerraz said. "It gives a person nearly magical powers, to know another person's true name, all the more so when it is hidden. I had my own name changed when I was scarcely twelve—"

"You changed your name?" Felipa interrupted. "That's terribly glamorous. Dolores—they *are* movie stars!"

"I don't believe it for a minute," Dolores said, glancing around the compartment at the empty tins and bottles and the scraps of food.

Felipa, still holding the tray high, began to whine, "It comes out of our own pay if we can't deliver it."

"Someone will buy it," Gauthier said.

"Not this much. Not if it goes stale." Her lips turned down as she shaped the last word.

"Well let's just eat it then—all of us," Al-Cerraz said. "Don't worry, we'll pay for it. But only if you stay."

"I've got to set this down," Felipa said, arms starting to tremble under the weight of the tray.

Al-Cerraz ran a finger along the front of her apron, tickling her waist as he tucked some money into her pocket. "Do you promise...?"

I'd watched Al-Cerraz flirt countless times but there was a manic, dogged quality to this flirtation that was all the more inappropriate given how many immediate problems begged our attention: the upsetting letter from Brenan; the train's sudden, mysterious halt. I looked to Gauthier, thinking he would help me put an end to this impromptu party, but he was playing his customary role, following Al-Cerraz's lead.

"I will be the gentleman," Gauthier said to Felipa. But instead of taking her tray, he lifted only one sandwich. With pinkie finger extended, he took a bite from the middle, then tossed the rest out of the half-open train window.

Dolores spoke up: "I haven't eaten all day! If you're just going to waste them..."

"You'll get these girls fired," I said.

Al-Cerraz replied, "If they're fired, they'll live with us, in here. This compartment could use a woman's touch. They can stay with us for a few weeks at least."

"He's joking," I said. "We get off in just a few hours." But Felipa gave me a sour look, as if she were angry with me for spoiling the fun. Then the train started to move again and she lost her footing, landing in Al-Cerraz's lap. Her face registered surprise, uncertainty and, finally, resignation.

"If I'm too heavy, you'll have to tell me," she said, shifting into a more comfortable position on his knee.

"Heavy! I should think not," he replied, and he settled his arm lightly around her waist, crooking one thick finger under her sash to loosen it.

Dolores leaned in closer to Gauthier. She said tenderly, "Do you realize your head is bleeding?"

The train moved only a few hundred yards before it stopped again. The corridor clattered with the sounds of many footsteps. The porter knocked at every door, calling out in an efficient, unworried voice, "Everyone out! Off the train!"

Felipa and Dolores exchanged glances. Al-Cerraz sighed, then gathered an armful of sandwiches and a small blanket from a pocket above one of the folded-up bunks.

Small clusters of passengers milled around the sandy wasteland just beyond the tracks. The foreign man who had been arguing with the conductor and porter had been reunited with his wife and two children; he kept a protective arm around the younger child's shoulders, glaring at the train staff anytime they drew near.

Al-Cerraz spread the blanket over a steep and scrubby slope and anchored it with his rump, his back to the train. He gestured for Felipa and Dolores to sit, then called to an elegantly dressed lady picking her way across the rocky terrain with the help of a closed parasol. The serving girls exchanged nervous glances as the lady approached, unwilling to fraternize with well-heeled passengers so openly, where everyone could see.

"Please, stay," Al-Cerraz lamented without rising, his arms outstretched, as Felipa and Dolores mumbled farewells. "Oh, come now, look at the view! Everyone together, looking out over the valley. And look, our new arrival has had the forethought to bring a parasol. This is like that beautiful painting— what is it called, Gauthier? *A Sunday*...?"

"*Un dimanche après-midi*..." Gauthier said, still standing.

"At some island..."

"*à l'Île de la Grande Jatte.*"

"That's it."

The lady had reached the blanket in time to hear the last of this exchange. "Weren't they gazing at water in that painting?" she said. "We have no water here. How do you do?"

Al-Cerraz smiled. "We have a blue horizon, though, if you look far enough and squint." He patted the blanket. "Come, sit down. Make yourself at home." He did not notice the departure of Dolores, who had made her way along the tracks to the back of the train, or Felipa, who was backing away slowly, confused by the mention of an island when there was no island in view, a painting she'd never heard about or seen. He was entertaining this new guest, swept along by the tide of good fortune that had brought her to his shores.

"An artist recognizes a setting, a moment," he was lecturing the lady, who had introduced herself as Señorita Silva. "An artist of *life* does the same thing—we are here, the weather is fine, why should this seem like an inconvenience?"

The lady glanced over her shoulder. "But I *was* concerned about how abruptly we stopped."

The conductor and a man in greasy overalls were walking down the tracks, in the direction we had been traveling. A group of male passengers watched them go, then formed a tighter circle near the locomotive, scratching their heads and wiping their brows as they talked amongst themselves.

Al-Cerraz reached out and tugged me down by the trouser leg. "Are you traveling with any friends?" he asked Señorita Silva. "Perhaps someone who would enjoy meeting my shy, impolite friend here?"

She answered distractedly. "With my sister. But look where those men are heading. On the tracks—does that look like a log to you? There aren't many trees about. I suppose they used the brakes just in time."

Al-Cerraz shook his head forlornly. He refused to look in the direction she was gesturing. "We have food, a blanket, shade if shade is needed, sun if sun is preferred..."

Gauthier offered tentatively, "I'll go see what it's about, if it will make everyone feel better."

Al-Cerraz slapped his leg with satisfaction. "There—our expert. An engineer at heart."

When Gauthier was out of earshot, I reached for a sandwich and took a bite, chewing moodily. I said to Al-Cerraz, "When I wanted to help talk to that foreign man on the train, you didn't volunteer my time—or your own."

"I fathomed," the pianist enunciated slowly, trying to impress this latest lady with his diction, "that you were going to get embroiled in some sort of political discussion with the train staff. Not a technical one."

Señorita Silva tilted her head toward me, fingering a pendant around her neck. "Are you very political?"

"He is a cellist," Al-Cerraz said.

She narrowed her eyes playfully. "Is that like a communist?"

Al-Cerraz reached out to extract a burr from the knotted laces of the lady's boot, allowing his wrist to graze the knob of her stockinged ankle. "I put these well-trained hands at your service."

"Are you a doctor?"

He laughed. "A doctor! Doctors are butchers. They lay their hands on living things and prod them toward death. I touch things that are long dead and bring them to life."

She pursed her lips together, suppressing a smile. "A riddle."

He plucked another burr from the underside of her hem. "These little devils have a way of crawling into dangerous places. I promise only to feel for them, not look..."

Her face registered no shock, though I'm sure mine did. He was seducing her as swiftly as he had attempted to seduce Felipa. If she walked away, there would be others. If I walked away, he wouldn't notice. Even with onlookers mere meters to either side, he would move his hands under her skirts, just because he enjoyed a challenge; it distracted him from his troubles nearly as well as playing the piano.

"There now," he said.

"A little higher," he said.

"Now, if you'll close *your* eyes," he said.

And his last rambling words: "My belief is that people simply choose to be unhappy..."—before the startling explosion which brought the impromptu picnic to an abrupt end.

"As soon as we reach a station, I will contact his sisters," I told Al-Cerraz later, as we contemplated the four bodies amid the wreckage of wood and burnt fuses and wire. Two hundred yards away, where the undamaged train awaited, there was no sign of the disaster, except for the fluttering tatters of singed cloth. A woman was crying, back near the train, but her sobs were indistinct hiccups swallowed by the warm wind.

Gauthier's family would want to know what happened. How would I explain?

"Anarchists," a man next to me muttered. "People who want our entire country to fall on its knees."

A younger man next to him reacted with offense: "You don't know that. It could have been our own Civil Guard."

"Wrecking a train?"

"Wrecking reputations, more like."

I didn't care, then or later, who'd done it. I just wanted to know how one could explain to nine sisters how their brother, who had avoided nearly every malady of those times—including both war and influenza—could suddenly and unthinkably have perished.

I turned to Al-Cerraz. "Do you know all of the sisters' names?"

"It is possible that he is only unconscious."

"That isn't possible, Justo. There's nothing you can do. Let me take you back."

But he was gripping the shoulder of another train passenger, a man in a dark suit who had brought blankets to cover the bodies. He was telling the stranger, "When we bothered him too much, he'd lay an arm over his head, just like that…"

I pulled on his sleeve.

"…he'd pretend to sleep…"

I pulled harder, but he wouldn't leave until he'd finished explaining.

"…I think he pretended not to mind things, when really he did."

And from the measured insistence with which Al-Cerraz spoke, I realized—finally—that he was talking about himself.

CHAPTER

~ 14 ~

We escorted the violinist's crated remains to the French border. The box would make a slow and circuitous route to Paris, a lower priority than the soldiers and matériel making its way to and from the western front. We also sent his two trunks and his violin, but not before lifting the neck out of the case and looking into the rosin box beneath, to see how much Gauthier had managed to save over the years toward his Polynesian retirement. We hoped it would be enough for the funeral, with perhaps some additional assistance that his sisters would appreciate. But when we lifted the rosin and the tiny polish cloth beneath, we found only three crumpled bills, barely enough to buy a new set of strings.

I watched as Al-Cerraz opened his own billfold and emptied it, then retrieved a small cigar box from his largest trunk and emptied that.

"Is that everything?" I asked as I watched him roll the bills, fit them carefully around the violin, and push hard to close the case.

"Everything and nothing," he said.

"I have a little more." I reached into my own jacket, but he waved me off.

"We'll need it."

At San Sebastián we inquired about escorting the crate and trunks on into France, but the stationmaster said, "There's no point in it. At Paris they'll just ask if you're 'essential.' First, you're Spanish."

"I maintained an address in France for years," said Al-Cerraz.

"And second, what did you say were your professions?"

"We're musicians, sir," Al-Cerraz fumed.

The stationmaster returned his ticket pad to his pocket.

For three weeks we holed up in a hotel room in Bilbao. The staff was deferential, but only until word got around that the IOUs we had scattered around town weren't being paid. Then we were back where we started; worse, actually, with the money from Brenan having dried up.

I asked Al-Cerraz, "Don't you have savings somewhere, from all that earlier touring and recording?"

His chin sagged toward his chest.

I remembered the Stanley Steamer franchise and all the other passing infatuations. "Investments?"

He sighed.

"Dare I ask if your mother is doing any better these days?"

He mumbled, "No better than yours, I'm sure."

"Would Biber give us a loan?"

Al-Cerraz covered his face with his hands. "Gauthier was always the one who wrote to him. Gauthier did everything."

"I don't mind taking on additional duties."

"I don't want to think of duties. I don't want to think of anything. Please stop. I can't think."

Our best option was to tour again, but we had no trio now. We did not even have a duet.

I played a solo recital in the hotel restaurant to earn some kitchen credit and a few more nights in the hotel manager's good graces. That night I placed my cello near Al-Cerraz's bed, where he had reclined through the dinner hour, and played a new score I had purchased in the city. It was a furious, yearning piece—insistent, emotional, difficult to ignore. I sight-read it for forty minutes, beginning to end, with only the briefest pauses.

The next morning I returned to the third movement—the Andante—and repeated it several times as Al-Cerraz washed lethargically and picked up the hotel phone to order a small lunch of *patatas bravas* and meat-stuffed cabbage. When the food came, he picked at it, then crawled back into bed, with the blanket up and around his ears. But later he asked, "Who was that by?"

"Rachmaninov."

The name stirred him. "Rachmaninov."

The next day, he asked me, "Arranged for cello?"

"Composed originally for the cello. Cello and piano."

When he didn't respond, I added, "G Minor, from 1901."

"It's vaguely familiar."

The third and final day, when I played it again, he said, "I didn't recognize the first two movements the other day. They sound so bare without the piano."

"Of course. It's Rachmaninov. He composed it for a friend, a cellist named Anatoly Brandukov. But he couldn't help giving the piano the best part."

"You have it? The complete score?"

"I do."

And we were performing again; slowly at first, in the north of Spain, as Al-Cerraz allowed his spirit to be revived by the work of rehearsing new compositions and arranging old ones, filling in the missing violin parts with more challenging cello accompaniments. The absence of our partner cast a shadow over our first performances. But at the same time, it forced a clean break with old habits. We could not play by rote, nor we could we mimic other trios' arrangements.

We had to innovate, and as the months passed, our sound matured—though, in respect for Gauthier's passing, we steered clear of self-congratulation. Instead, we protested more than was necessary about the difficulties of coordinating train schedules and counting luggage. One day, just after exiting a train, Al-Cerraz discovered he had lost an entire trunk carrying some of his childhood memorabilia, including early copies of a march he had written when he was six years old, as well as a postcard photo of his mother which he'd never let me see. Tallying the losses, he dropped to his knees, and began to gasp and cough into his hands while other passengers hurried around us. I didn't know what to do, how to help—other than to stand by as Al-Cerraz grieved the disappearance of these talismans, proofs of his mother's youthful beauty and his own precocity. But there was a benefit to the mishap. Al-Cerraz had been groping for evidence that, logistically, we could not manage as well without Gauthier. This dramatic demonstration allowed him to rage a final time about our violinist's death, an emotional purging that made room for a deeper artistic truth: that we played far better without him.

We didn't intend to remain a duet, but it proved hard to find a compatible substitute violinist. The first we fired after a month, when he refused to play the flyspeck villages that Al-Cerraz and I continued to visit when we could, between more profitable city engagements. Next came a slew of hardworking violinists with insufficient talent or talented violinists with insufficient stamina. Biber wrote, beseeching us to choose someone young, attractive, or recently "discovered" in order to boost ticket sales, especially in the larger cities. But we weren't interested in gimmicks. We accepted our musical marriage, "For better or for worse," as they say.

And there *were* many "betters": ovations, attention from the press, letters of interest from recording companies. Financially, we regained a modest footing, able to get by comfortably as long as we continued to perform—which Al-Cerraz would have done even if no one paid him, once he'd shaken off his deepest gloom. He returned to sending his mother a little money each month, even without Brenan's further assistance.

But those are financial details. What I remember best from those times is the music itself. When it succeeded, we took hold of the audience's attention, working it from a distracted, unshaped mass into spun beauty, passing the fine strands back and forth until we wove together something grander, not only music but memory, too—the particulars of past and present, stretched taut across a loom of timeless ideals. Harmony. Symmetry. Order.

The strength of that weave is what anchored me, while Al-Cerraz took a greater pride and fancy in how our sounds evoked the tapestry's edges: the soft fringes of the natural world just beyond our playing. A current of warm air, scented with orange blossoms. Blue shadows, lightening with the rising moon. Or rather, the imagined beauty of those things. Poets claim the moonlight is warm, but that warmth is only in the mind's eye.

Our styles were different. Our aims were different. During our best times, it didn't matter. We had become, finally, more than the former prodigy Al-Cerraz, with accompaniment. We had become a true *conjunto musical:* unified, complete, and whole.

Revived as he was, Al-Cerraz remained a more sober man overall. I know he was fretting about the *Don Quixote* commission. He still hadn't managed to compose anything of value, whether for a patron or for his own satisfaction. Even the November 1918 armistice did not overjoy him. To him it meant that the rest of Europe was awaiting his return, unless they had forgotten him. Either possibility seemed to fill him with anxiety.

By December we were traveling a northern route between Spanish cities, picking up telegrams at every stop, turning down offers to play

in the south because Al-Cerraz wanted to remain ready for the slight-
est flurry of interest from north of the Pyrenees.

Finally, word from Biber came: "Cancel Burgos and head east. Biar-
ritz en route, then Toulouse. Three concerts booked, more planned."

"East?" Al-Cerraz took the telegram from my hands. "He means
northeast! He means France!" He kissed the telegram, then kneeled
down and attempted to put his lips to the sidewalk, or as close as he
could get before his waist refused to bend any farther.

I reached for his elbow. "That's what you do when you get to a
place, not when you leave one."

"Toulouse!" he shouted, taking my arm and struggling to his feet.
"*Now* the war is over! He wrapped both his arms around me and
squeezed. "Perhaps Marseilles after that. Then Paris." He dropped his
arms and his voice. "*Mon Dieu,* I need new shoes. Oh," and he splayed
his fingers and regarded the nails with disgust. He twisted to look over
one shoulder, trying to gain a view of the back of his frayed suit jacket.
He kept turning, like a dog trying to bite its own tail.

"Come on, Cinderella," I urged him. "We need to check the train
schedule. There will be a dozen better places across the border where
you can shop and get a manicure."

He looked horrified. "You do not arrive and then *dress.* You dress
and then *arrive.* What if someone hears I'm en route and comes to meet
me on the platform?" Then he switched to French, slipping into it as
easily as he'd slipped into the Retiro pond that day, and leaving me
nearly as stranded. English was my second strongest tongue; German
after that, owing to my fondness for biographies of Bach. Still I caught
the gist, as he gushed through pursed lips about certain theaters, the
parties of Madame Lafitte, a restaurant in Bayonne.

"Five years," he told me, as we waited at a café across from the train
station, an hour before we were due to depart. A mostly uneaten croissant rested on the plate in front of him. He'd pinched at it repeatedly,
blanketing the table with buttery flakes. "Nearly an eighth of my life.

And this," and pushed the plate away, but only by a few centimeters. "I can't eat it. Too rich." A server began to approach, but at the bovine swing of Al-Cerraz's head over the plate backed away.

"I'm sure everything has changed," he said.

"I'm sure it has."

"Who will remember me?"

"They asked for you. Biber got the bookings. *Tout le monde* is waiting for you, waiting for everything to be back to normal."

"*Tout le monde*," he repeated, and began to push fingerfuls of croissant into his mouth, covering his beard and thick mustache with crumbs.

That night, despite the train's soporific rocking, Al-Cerraz didn't sleep well.

"What did I say about *Rite of Spring?*" he whispered, then barreled out of the bottom bunk to stand next to me, his mouth level with my head. I rolled away from him and told him to ask me in the morning.

"When I came to see you in Madrid, and found you in the bar," he persevered. "We went to the park. I told you about Stravinsky. About the premiere, and the riot it caused. I agreed with the detractors. Do you remember?"

I rolled back and felt his steamy breath on my face—no smell of liquor, only the sweet staleness of long, dark hours. "We talked about a lot of things that day."

"I wasn't fair. I was narrow-minded."

I thought for a moment. "You told me how you'd heard jazz, that same month in Paris, and loved it. See? You weren't narrow-minded. Go to sleep."

Silence. But I knew he was still there. His fingers, resting on the edges of the bunk, pulled it downward. Rolling slightly toward him, I could feel the pressure of the guardrail against my leg. After several minutes, I must have fallen asleep again. His next words interrupted a dream.

"I can still hear . . ." he whispered.

"*Hmmm?*"

"The catcalls. Debussy—he was there, pleading with the audience, telling them to calm down and listen. The dancers couldn't hear the orchestra. Ravel was in the audience, screaming '*Genius! Genius!*' at the top of his lungs while a veritable brawl broke out. Those two men recognized what they were hearing. They weren't threatened by it."

"Next time, listen to men like Debussy and Ravel."

"You know why I didn't?"

When I didn't respond, he answered the question for me. "Because of Ravel's *Rapsodie Espagnole*—1908. And Debussy's *Iberia*—1910. I heard them both. I saw them performed. I bought the scores. I was a Spaniard in Paris, and every French composer was writing Spanish music—my music!—what I should have written, if I had been more focused, more forward-thinking, more willing to abstain from the instant gratuitous pleasures of performing, of being admired . . ."

I was wide awake now. "The French are always writing picture-postcard music about Spain. Bizet started it, before you were born."

"Yes. Precisely. Picture-postcard. But what beautiful postcards. And what Englishman doesn't hope to meet some exotic Carmen dancing outside a cigarette factory when he vacations in Andalucía?"

I waited for more, but when he didn't continue, I offered, "Rimsky-Korsakov. *Capriccio Espagnol*—what, 1887? 1888?"

"Must have been. I think I was five years old."

"Just so you don't blame the French."

I stared into the darkness, listening to him breathe, until he said, "Perhaps the well is dry."

I sat up on one elbow. "It's just exoticism—writing about some far-away, folkloric land that's easier to capture than your own. The way the Russians love to write about the Orient, for example."

He wasn't listening. "They have created a Spain more real than our Spain; their art has transcended our reality."

"That's a dangerous thing, transcending reality. Look at Don Quixote—he was beaten to a bloody pulp."

Al-Cerraz groaned. "Please, not Don Quixote. If I were free of Don Quixote, I might dare try my hand at some other kind of composition."

"But haven't you tried?"

"Not really. Not in years."

"But you *do* keep a notebook."

"Yes, I scribble things in a notebook, when I can't get a sound out of my head. It's not to help me remember. Sometimes, it's the only way I can manage to *forget*. But that doesn't make me a composer. The difference between my notes and a finished opera is like the difference between a grocery list and a novel."

He expelled the weariest of laughs. "I don't think on large scales. What Spaniard does? We can't even fathom true nationhood—'I am a Galician, you are a Basque, he's Catalan, she's a gypsy.' I mean, look—look at how we eat! We can't hold a thought long enough to plan a dinner. Instead, it's tapas—an olive here, a bite of fish there, now I'll switch to meatballs." He laughed again. "Feliu, are you awake?"

"*Mmm.*" I had closed my eyes again.

"Compare it to the Germans—everything to them is epic. Heroic. The strength, the character!"

"Too epic," I mumbled.

"What?"

"They overreached. They lost the war. They're finished. You're always asking, 'What will last?' Not them."

"I don't know." He sighed. "Sometimes I can't even see the connections between one moment and the next. I don't have any mythic stories to tell. I can barely understand the story of my own life. How did I get to this?"

"You were apologizing about Stravinsky."

He snorted. "No. My *life*, I mean. How did I get to *this*?"

A pause again. The sounds of the train. The soprano of steel wheels gliding over a new pattern in the track, as we sped without stopping through a village station, the platform cloaked in darkness except for one mist-haloed station lamp—a low, flickering star, here and gone.

"I have sinned, Feliu. I have erred. I have been envious…"

"You still are."

"I have been vain…"

"We will be playing tomorrow near a church. You'll have no trouble finding a priest."

"I don't"—he stuttered—"I'm not—the kind of man to make confession."

"You just did. Now, please. I was sleeping."

I felt the weight of his fingers leave the mattress, then from beneath me came his voice one last time: "Thank you, Feliu."

For me, those first European months provided an effortless introduction to some of the world's greatest music halls, on the arm of a musician already beloved. The French, the Swiss, the Italians—they did remember him, and they were even more eager than he to forget the war years and to embrace art and entertainment anew. Long lines of automobiles queued up outside the halls and theaters we were playing. Ladies arrived in backless evening gowns and soft knee-skimming skirts. Headlines carried news of war reparations and hunger, but at the parties hosted for us after major city concerts, talk focused instead on movies, fashions, and America's experiment with Prohibition.

"Will you play in America next?" a lady in Nice asked Al-Cerraz.

"I'm sure we shall!" He raised his glass to the room.

Yet whatever relief I had been able to provide to Al-Cerraz in our midnight conversation seemed to be dissipating. "In Spain, I was able to feel I was doing a service," he confided to me when we reached Paris after a five-city tour. "Not here, where there is a concert every night of the week, and a play, and an art opening; and everyone has records, and radio. Well, it's the modern age. It's freeing, in a way. And did you know, Madame Lafitte has a mustache now? She wears that hobble skirt, the Poiret number, but I think it was lovelier when I couldn't see her ankles so plainly. And the oysters at Bayonne—*oof.* Better in memory, perhaps, than reality."

"Perhaps if you'd had merely a dozen, instead of four dozen."

"I suppose it couldn't last forever," he sighed. "The Belle Époque is over."

The Belle Époque was over, but in Paris, *Les Années Folles*—the Crazy Years—had just begun. A strong dollar drew American writers and artists to the Left Bank. Women bared their breasts at nightclubs. Men attended street parties in the spring without clothing, their bodies painted in gleaming colors. At night, jazz blared in the alleyways. During the day, on the streetcars, young girls rolled down their stockings, hiked up their skirts, and leaned out the windows, singing, "Oh, how I hate to get up in the morning!"

The world was new again, or seemed to be. In Paris, it had become fashionable to thumb one's nose at anything conventional, to take nothing seriously, to parody everything that had gone before. The lingering trauma of the Great War had invited a regression into childishness, complete with Dada-ist baby babble—a prolonged metaphysical giggle.

But a giggle doesn't satisfy, and even nude costume balls lose their novelty with surprising speed. Beneath the glamour, surrealism, and silliness, people hungered for eternal excellence. They clamored for Beethoven and Bach, for Paganini and Liszt. They clamored for Al-Cerraz and me.

The gossip columns reported our appearance at Gertrude Stein's Sunday salon. We drew a crowd in the modest Salle Thérèse, its stained-glass windows still boarded up from German shelling. We sold out the larger, grander Théâtre des Champs-Élysées and elicited a massive standing ovation that continued to build even after Al-Cerraz reentered the stage, peaking only after I reentered and stood at his side, bowing together.

He took my rising stature in stride. We toured fifteen more European cities, many more damaged than Paris had been; many waking only slowly to postwar life. But we always returned to Paris. In no time at all, we were the top classical billing there. We were asked to play on the first anniversary of the death of Claude Debussy, who had passed away during a week when the city was being bombarded, and whose casket was carried through deserted streets. Now, finally, Debussy could be properly honored. We performed a special arrangement of the French composer's *Claire de Lune,* and then led a procession to the Cimetière de Passy, where Debussy's grave sat under a bower of chestnut trees, with a view of the Eiffel Tower.

After the crowd dispersed, I suggested to Al-Cerraz that we cross the city and visit the grave of Gauthier, something we had not yet done. It was March, and the trees were in bud, but in the mist they still looked skeletal, their branches black with rain. We found the cemetery, the name of which I no longer recall. We found the groundskeeper, and with him spent a good hour looking for the grave, confounded by the sheer number of new plots, filled with victims of war, influenza, and starvation. By the time we found Gauthier's rectangle of earth, it was nearly dark. There was no stone yet, no trees, not much of a view. At my feet lay an old bouquet of flowers wrapped in a disintegrating cone of tissue paper, the exposed rose petals blackened with age.

"Where are the other flowers?" Al-Cerraz demanded. "Where is the tombstone?"

When I didn't answer, he asked more insistently, "Where are his sisters?"

I responded, "Where were *we?*"

We stood shivering in the rain next to his grave, quietly; neither one of us prayed.

Finally Al-Cerraz said, "Which shall it be?"

I thought he meant Right Bank or Left—we hadn't yet decided where we'd go for dinner. Earlier, we had discussed heading to a café in Montmartre to watch a local pianist and composer named Erik Satie, who—dressed always in his gray velvet suit and bowler hat—entertained diners with his melancholic piano miniatures.

But Al-Cerraz wasn't talking about Satie, about Left Bank or Right. He was talking about the two graves we'd visited that day, and how we imagined our own future resting places.

"Like Gauthier's—bare and forgotten? Or like Debussy's?"

"I don't think it matters much to them," I said.

"It matters," he said, voice cracking, "to me."

It is a testament to our friendship that Al-Cerraz stayed in Paris as long as he did. Our roles had reversed. He, the cosmopolitan who had endured Spain only because of the war, felt ready to return and commit himself again to the more serious, unprofitable work of composing a Spanish work—not only because Brenan still expected it of him, but because, in Al-Cerraz's mind, destiny did.

I was the one who had grown accustomed to comfort, to Left Bank cafés and international salons, to my slowly rising reputation, without which—I assured myself—I couldn't really help Spain, anyway. In 1920 he agreed to one more European tour with me, though it proved to be a nerve-racking season for him.

On a summer night in Lucerne, fifteen minutes before curtain, Al-Cerraz burst into our shared dressing room, looking pale and distraught: "He's here—in the audience!"

"Who?"

Al-Cerraz groaned. "Thomas Brenan."

I sat down and withdrew my bow and a polishing cloth from its case. "That's fine. We should invite him out after the concert."

"Invite him *out*? I can't see him. I can't go on."

We argued until the stage manager knocked. I tried to calm him. "He's not expecting you to hand over a finished *Don Quixote* score tonight. He just wants to hear you perform. He has a right, Justo. He has been very generous to you."

"It doesn't matter." He removed his cuff links and dropped them into an empty coffee cup, then began to unbutton his dress shirt.

"Pretend he isn't there."

"I won't be able to focus."

"Justo, you owe him something—"

He stopped and turned to me. "Haven't you ever resented a debt? What of that gemstone in your bow—have you produced anything worthy of that?"

I gripped the frog of my bow protectively, feeling my thumb pass over the sapphire.

"It wasn't payment, it was a gift."

Al-Cerraz continued, "What about the bow itself? When your father gave it to you, did you give anything in return?"

Under my breath I answered, "My father was already dead when I received it."

"All the more reason."

Through the thin dressing-room door, we could hear the shuffling of feet, the bouncy echo of moving seat-backs, the coughing, rustling, and shifting of an audience preparing for the concert ahead.

Al-Cerraz said, "In Madrid, you said you'd developed a 'distaste for favors.' Do you remember that? You should understand my situation better than anyone." He leaned over the sink and started to dry-heave.

"You aren't really sick."

He paused for a breath and wiped his dry lips. "Explain to the audience. Tell the stage manager. And make no exceptions: I'll see no one after the concert."

I walked out to a packed house, twenty-four hundred seats in six golden tiers all facing me in a chandelier-lit horseshoe.

I stood next to my cello chair and announced Al-Cerraz's cancellation stiffly, as if I were reading from a piece of paper, though I held nothing in my hand but my bow. The auditorium echoed with murmured disappointment and some seats bounced up as a few people squeezed out of their rows and up the aisles. I had expected worse.

The audience settled, waiting to see what I would do next. I could still cancel for myself as well; the contract said as much. I stood under the lights, enveloped by warmth and silence and the humidity of the gathered crowd, all those expectant breaths. If I decided to play, I would have to change the program. There weren't many choices, without accompaniment of any kind. But while my head thrummed and stalled, my hands, or my heart, decided to go ahead. I sat down, pulled my bow across the string, and began to play the Prelude to the first Bach Cello Suite.

After the second ovation, I slammed the dressing door closed behind me. Al-Cerraz had heard the thunderous applause; he saw me grinning and hurrying to change from my sweat-stained dress shirt into a dry, clean one. He said, "There's no point putting that on yet, when you're so heated up."

I tried to open a window at the room's far end; it was painted shut.

"You can't be finished, with that much applause still going."

I found a towel and scrubbed my neck with it.

He tried again. "You certainly look better than you did an hour ago. I feel better myself." He shook the brown vial the doctor had given him. "But only a little. Maybe I should have doubled the dose." When

I still didn't respond, he teased, "So I've created a monster. Now you'll want to be a soloist!"

I didn't understand what I was feeling. I had enjoyed playing solo, even with the greater burden of carrying the show, even with the awareness of thousands of scrutinizing faces just beyond the lights. Even now, the energy of my performance coursed through me. I was terribly thirsty. Sweat continued to drip down my spine, dampening my new shirt, soaking my waistband, where my leather belt chafed. I didn't want to sit down.

The theater manager brought me a bottle of champagne. I swigged at it, then passed it to my partner—leaving him to worry about how it might affect his sedative-addled mind. Another arrived, courtesy of a fan who had been waylaid by the determined stage manager, and we drank that, too. But still, the adrenaline didn't settle; I felt ill with the weight and heat of it, as if there was some force building in me that could not be expressed.

The next night Al-Cerraz again refused to play, worried that Thomas Brenan might have returned. I went on alone.

In Amsterdam, too, Al-Cerraz refused to play. This time, we were able to give advance notice, and the concert was publicized as a solo performance. The first-night crowd filled the hall to an acceptable three-quarters, and the next night—after a laudatory review in the city's major newspaper—the hall filled completely.

That second night on the Amsterdam stage, I forced myself to look out in the audience as the curtain rose. As I introduced myself and explained the music I would be performing, I stood with feet widely planted, my cello and bow well behind me, next to my chair. My stance looked like confidence. It began, in fact, to feel like confidence.

I drew another ovation that night. Among those standing was a figure in the royal box, a spotlight revealing an unremarkable-looking

man with sideburns and a dark suit, bowing to me and then to the audience at large. All eyes turned toward him, and the applause continued, now directed in the gentleman's direction as well. It was later
explained to me that he was Prince Hendrik, husband to Queen Wil-
helmina of the Netherlands. The audience had applauded us equally, a
fact that inspired in me an unbecoming giddiness that lasted for hours.
I remembered Count Guzmán saying that someday a cellist could be as
powerful as a king. But, I hastened to remind myself, I was not powerful at all, only popular. They were not the same thing.

What had Alberto wished for me? Not only to be good, but to *do*
good. Was I doing anything at all besides entertaining people, and perhaps also inhibiting my partner from the serious work he wished to do?
I was less than powerful. In fact, I was becoming imprisoned by my own
simple desires: to be liked, to be cheered, to be comfortable, to live in a
city of lights that had no connection to any person or place from my past.

I had a dream that night of following a man down a hallway. It was
Prince Hendrik, dressed more regally now, in a military uniform. He
pushed open a door and entered; I followed at a discreet distance. He
walked toward a woman sitting on a black bench, her back turned to
me, and whispered in her ear. Then he disappeared. I advanced closer
to the woman, certain now that she was waiting for me, that I had
something to say which she must hear. But she wouldn't turn around. I
could not reach out and touch her. And though I called out, she
wouldn't respond to my voice.

We had one more Dutch performance, in Utrecht. Two hours before
the curtain, Al-Cerraz received a telegram from Thomas Brenan, saying the patron was back in London now, and greatly distraught that he
hadn't been able to see Al-Cerraz play.

"*Gracias a Dios!*" Al-Cerraz shouted to the puzzled messenger who
had delivered the telegram to our dressing room, and began to dress

immediately. That night we played a concert that thrilled the audience and disappointed several reviewers who noted, as I did, that Al-Cerraz had played so loudly and demonically that the cello could barely be heard.

Only two concerts remained on our tour, and both were in London, a week and a half away. Al-Cerraz made no mystery of his plans. He would come to London, he said, just to make a good show of it. Knowing that Brenan might appear, he would wait until the last minute and play sick again.

From our Dutch hotel, I corresponded with Biber, who was growing testy about Al-Cerraz's cancellations. After London, he couldn't promise any more bookings until Al-Cerraz was certain he was well. Unless, Biber wrote, I wanted to go ahead and make a few solo bookings?

"You wouldn't," Al-Cerraz said, after I'd handed him the letter. "Would you?"

"I don't think so," I said.

In London, the theater manager made it clear that he was alert to Al-Cerraz's habit of canceling, and he insisted on having a doctor visit the pianist at our hotel the day before the concert. Al-Cerraz, fond of the sedative he had received in Lucerne, expressed a complete willingness to cooperate. He asked me, "Will a psychiatrist be able to prescribe something for relaxation?"

"*Claro.*" I thought for a second. "They're sending a psychiatrist this time? Not a physician?"

"What's the difference, exactly?"

"I guess you'll find out. If your career as a pianist falls apart, perhaps you'll find work as an actor."

"But I *am* sick," he protested.

"Yes, yes, I know," I said as the hotel door closed between us.

I had my own London plans. Sir Edward Elgar had heard about my solo concerts in Switzerland and the Netherlands. He asked me to visit him at a friend's house in the city, and to bring my cello along.

The renowned British composer was in his early sixties—a dapper Edwardian with tidy white hair, sharp cheekbones, and a mustache that covered all but the bottom edge of his lower lip, so that it was hard to tell if he was smiling. I felt comfortable with him immediately. There was something in his accent and bearing that reminded me of Queen Ena—even more so as he conducted most of our conversation from a piano bench.

"The world in which I was raised doesn't exist anymore," he said at one point. The crow's-feet around his eyes deepened as he attempted to smile. He added, "You've been to Berlin?"

"I have."

"I had many German friends. People in our line usually do. Music doesn't stay behind borders very well."

I mustered the courage to ask, "Did you lose someone in particular?" I didn't have to add, "In the war."

He cleared his throat; I saw his heavy mustache twitch. "We all lost something, didn't we? We lost two thousand years of civilization."

I had heard from other colleagues in musical circles that Elgar, who had been so prolific in his earlier life, had spent most of the time between 1914 to 1918 in a depressed and unproductive state. He talked about his troubles with his health, and said how much he owed his wife, Alice, who made up composition paper for him, marking the ledger lines by hand, saving him hours of drudgery. He did not mention that she was seriously ill. In fact, she would be dead within a month, and he would never compose seriously again.

"But," he added now, "I will share with you something I did manage to accomplish during the war—the one important thing." He brought out the score for his Cello Concerto in E Minor, premiered by the London Symphony Orchestra just the year before.

I hadn't yet heard the concerto myself, only heard of it. I knew the premiere had been a disaster. The cellist hadn't had adequate rehearsal time, and the critics had panned the performance. Yet Elgar revealed no lack of confidence in his own work. He felt the concerto would be one of his most-remembered compositions, much finer than his patriotic works, truer to his own reflective and subdued nature, much truer to the state of the modern world.

"Play it for me, if you will," he said.

I looked at the cello part of the score and read the opening measures, a somber solo passage highlighted with four difficult, dramatic chords. I bowed the passage then stopped, amateurishly. The opening had sounded like a desperate cry descending into a low-pitched, agitated sob; I felt I had played it poorly. "That sounds rough to start," I apologized. "I suppose without hearing the orchestration before it..."

"No. There is no orchestration before it. That's how it begins."

Before I could go on, he said, "I chose the cello for a reason. Of all the instruments, it is the one that sounds most like a human voice. I would ask you to play humanly, that's all."

I did not need to ask him for more direction after that. I had never played a piece so fully imagined, in which the cello not only took the lead but competed with the orchestra at times, as if to shake the other musicians by the throats, to make them face injustice and despair. The concerto had lighter movements, too, just as my afternoon with Elgar had lighter moments. He had laughed, during a break from my cello playing, as he told me how he'd once worked as a bandmaster in a lunatic asylum. "I was only a little younger than you are now," he'd said. "You may not feel you are young. Believe me, you are!"

Nevertheless, it was the concerto's dark parts that stayed with me. And the Elgar I still see in my mind is pensive, nodding almost imperceptibly at my interpretation from the piano bench, a companion in sorrow and confusion. Except that he had found a way to give voice to his confusion.

Once my cello was put away and Elgar had set a tea tray between us, I found it harder to make conversation that afternoon. He described the single recording he had made of the concerto in 1919, and said that he wanted to try again soon, in the expectation that acoustic technology had improved. He hoped I would spend some more time in London after my tour was finished, and work with him to record the concerto again.

"I will consider it," I told him.

He set a slightly shaky hand on my shoulder in response to my quick answer. "*Will* you?"

When I didn't respond immediately, he leaned closer, studying me sympathetically. "When you were playing my concerto, something in your face changed. You went away. I interpreted it as a good sign. But when you finished playing, I did not see you come back. Where were you, Mr. Delargo?"

"In my own country," I said honestly. "In Spain."

Elgar did not ask me again that day about recording the concerto. I think he understood that much as I loved it and even though it had moved me—perhaps *because* it had moved me—I wouldn't be in a position to record it that year.

Even in his grief, Elgar had seemed perfectly sure about three things, in descending order: the power of music, the voice of the cello, and me. I respected his creation without reservation. But I was not sure about any of those three things.

"You are a young man," he told me when we parted. "For me, it's all I can do to grieve for a bygone world. Your generation needs to help shape a new one."

Back at the hotel, I expected to find Al-Cerraz fretting about the upcoming concert, or else reclining languorously, thanks to psychiatric tonics. Instead I found him ready to pounce on me as soon as I entered his room.

"I should have tried this ages ago," he enthused.

The visit with Elgar had tired me, and I'd spent the long walk back thinking. I wasn't in the mood for another of Al-Cerraz's foolish enthusiasms. I reclined on his bed and watched him pace and gesture manically.

"Hypnosis," he explained, before I could ask. "The composer's cure!" He reminded me that hypnosis had allowed Rachmaninov to break through a dry spell and produce his second piano concerto. He beamed, "Dr. Key explained why I love to swim so much."

Thinking of Freud and wanting to humor my friend, I said, "Because the ocean reminds you of your mother's womb?"

That stopped Al-Cerraz in mid-stride, finger extended, considering. "Good thinking. But what he said was this: The ocean is silent." He paused, with a smug expression on his face, like a doorman waiting for a tip.

"Yes?"

"So that's it. I am seeking silence. I am trying to escape from music."

"Trying to escape. That's why you insist on touring about three hundred days a year."

"Well," Al-Cerraz paused, "I am like an addict, both attracted and repulsed."

"I can see that. I've felt that way toward people."

He didn't catch my insinuation. "The doctor said I need to get it out. I need a cassis."

"No, that's a liqueur, from currants. He must have said 'catharsis.'"

"*Eso es.*"

"But what kind of catharsis?"

"One of composition, my sublimated passion."

Sublimated—that was not an Al-Cerraz word, either.

"I think when one sublimates," I ventured, "one takes a coarse desire—for food or sex or something else biological—and redirects it toward something loftier. You've done the opposite. You've spent the last
ten years channeling your artistic drive into coarseness."

"Regardless," he said, "Dr. Key said I should compose a great work."

"That's what you've been saying for years. So you finally get to
work on the *Don Quixote*."

Al-Cerraz evaded my glance. "Actually, we had a stimulating session. I began to tell him about how I missed Spain; he has never been,
but he mentioned the Alhambra. Next thing, I am telling him that this
is what I've always longed to write—a masterpiece about the great
Moorish fortresses of Andalucía."

"I hope you weren't just trying to please him."

"What do you mean?"

"By reflecting back his own interests—his own perceptions. It's
only a suggestion."

"But why would I try to please him?"

"Because he was an audience."

"Hardly—"

"An audience of one. It is sufficient."

Al-Cerraz changed the subject. "Next—you will be proud of
me—I met with my patron."

"With Brenan? Already?"

"He came right here. You are sitting just where I told him."

I looked around for signs of struggle: broken bottles, shredded letters, fistfuls of hair.

"I told him about my self-discovery. And he is also interested in a
symphonic work about the Alhambra. He understands that I need to
pursue my own inspirations, as soon as possible."

"That's wonderful, Justo. You are finally free."

"*Eso es.*"

He had been pacing the entire time with such heavy footfalls that I expected a maid to come knocking on the door with a complaint from the room below. Finally, he took a seat next to me, on the bed.

"It certainly buys me time," he said, looking suddenly winded. "That is the important thing."

"How so?"

"The Alhambra work, due in two years. *Quixote*, two years after that—and I don't even have to use Brenan's libretto, if it doesn't inspire me." He looked away, saving me the trouble of hiding my incredulous expression. "It's perfectly fair, considering the support he has given me."

"So," I said, choosing my words carefully, "now it's double or nothing."

He repeated the phrase aloud, and I winced to see it sink in. "Of course, you will come home with me," he added.

I was touched that he'd called Spain "home." If our needs hadn't coincided, perhaps we would have parted ways then. And perhaps it would have worked out better that way, in the long run. But fate and friendship had run an intersecting course.

"After our London concerts," I answered him. "Then we'll go home, Justo. You'll find your Alhambra. I hope we both will."

CHAPTER

~ 15 ~

At the main plaza in Granada, two buskers were strumming guitars and shouting *"Allah!"* in the old, uncorrupted style. Farther up the street, outside a teahouse, hookah-smoking customers were listening to a dark-skinned man playing a rebec—a kind of pear-shaped Renaissance fiddle. I saw Al-Cerraz tilt his head toward the sound, then look around impatiently, waiting for me to catch up. The day's heat was building; there was no time to lose.

We had played a concert of Bach and Haydn that morning—marble music in a city of carved wood and flowing water. But that had been only a prelude to Al-Cerraz's real mission here, which was to visit the Alhambra, the fortified Moorish palace that rose from Granada's north flank, just beyond the city's hilly edge.

We hadn't come directly from England. I had spent some time at the university in Salamanca, teaching several master classes while expanding my social and political connections beyond the world of music, as my meeting with Elgar had inspired me to do. Al-Cerraz, still enthusiastic about his visit with the hypnotist, had lodged in a lady friend's villa in Málaga, composing. He had instructed Biber to book a concert in Granada—but only one. He was finished with relentless town-to-town touring, he said. Additionally, he'd heard his mother wasn't well and wanted to visit her directly after our trip.

Our morning concert had gone well enough. As an encore, we played a repetitive Spanish folk tune, one of those beautiful picture postcards, and this was applauded with great sincerity by half the audience and hardly at all by the other half. I understood the latter group's reaction. It was a catchy tune, but so musically undemanding that I caught myself yawning in the middle of it.

"You see? Some love those trifles, but that's all they are," Al-Cerraz said now as we climbed a narrow road beyond the city center, in the direction of our hillside hotel. "For years, nationalist composers have relied on folkloric dances as a base, but without tapping the real spirit—and worse, without moving forward, without true synthesis or innovation. Manuel de Falla knows. Consider *Nights in the Gardens of Spain*. He doesn't quote every folkloric element, he simply distills the local essence. The Andalucían spirit. He'll fill our ears with theory, no doubt."

"Fill our ears?"

"When we meet him."

"Is he expecting us?"

"No. But his house will be a convenient stop on the way to the Alhambra—the place I must finally see, if my intuitions are correct."

"Wait. You've never visited the Alhambra?" Al-Cerraz had spoken of it so often, with its fabled rooms lined in *azulejo* tiles, its domed halls and elaborate arched doorways, its gardens and fountains, I thought he knew it well.

"No need to lecture," he said.

When we approached our hotel, I veered toward it.

"You're not coming with me?" Al-Cerraz asked. "To the maestro's house, and up—what is it, a kilometer to the Alhambra gate?"

"Maybe only a half kilometer, but it's vertical."

"Feliu," he scowled. "This is research. This is *history*." He lowered his voice. "I don't want to boast prematurely, but I've been experimenting with Andalucían rhythms—I can't promise you won't hear a little flamenco in what I've done—but...I'm saying too much." He looked up the street, to the unseen Alhambra screened by stony walls and lush foliage. "Please come with me."

When I still didn't answer, he tucked his chin down into his neck. "I would have come with you, had you asked."

I groaned. But I agreed to accompany him after I had dropped off my cello.

Back outside, I found Al-Cerraz waiting at the curb, a hand on his hamstring. "These streets are so steep, it's paining my legs just to stand."

"You asked for it," I said. *"Adelante."*

An hour later, Manuel de Falla answered his own front door. The formal white suit he was wearing gave the appearance of a man expecting company—but not our company, as Al-Cerraz's profuse and bumbling apologies made clear.

The venerable composer held silver dumbbells the size of baby rattles in each hand. They had been made with springs in the split handles, so that he could squeeze and execute small curling motions at the same time. Al-Cerraz sprang forward to hug and kiss him. With his hands occupied, Falla couldn't defend himself, though his grimace made it clear he didn't appreciate the attentions. We discovered later he had a horror of germs and any manner of physical contact.

Falla was pale and skeletal, each contour of his skull visible beneath the taut skin of his face. His only remaining hair, a rim of light gray stubble just above each ear, contrasted with his bushy black eyebrows and his black bow-tie, a sort of third eyebrow. His eyes were small and dark, with sleepy lines etched beneath them. A mechanical smile made the small, snaking veins at his temple bulge, and brought out the apples of his cheeks, but only briefly.

Through the force of Al-Cerraz's personality, we earned entrance to the courtyard, where we sat stiffly on white metal patio chairs. Falla sat down next to Al-Cerraz, crossed one leg over the other, picked anxiously at his own pant leg, stood again, and went inside. While he was away, a woman entered the courtyard, bearing a tray. "You interrupted him during his routine," she said. As she bent to push a drink into my hand, the heavy black cross around her neck knocked against my cheek. "It takes him three hours. He had an hour left."

Al-Cerraz perched on the edge of his chair. "Three hours? That's his work routine?"

"That's his toilette," she sniffed, and then vanished back into the house.

After a few minutes Falla returned, still squeezing the dumbbells. The sun was shining fiercely into the courtyard and he had put on little round glasses with bright blue lenses.

Al-Cerraz broke the silence. "I'm afraid we've somehow offended your maid."

"That wasn't my maid."

"Forgive me," Al-Cerraz said. His face never flushed, but two spots on his neck, just below his beard, darkened with embarrassment.

"Sister Maria," Falla said, fixing us both with that opaque, blue-lensed stare.

"Does she come from the convent each day, or live with you all the time?"

"Not *a* sister, *my* sister. Maria del Carmen."

Al-Cerraz patted his lap. "Well. I suppose I should explain that I'm a pianist."

"Of course. I know your work, I've seen you play—three times," Falla said, the corners of his large mouth twitching. He ticked them off on his fingers: "Cádiz. Madrid. Paris."

Al-Cerraz smiled at me and settled more deeply into his chair. "I am interested in composing—not suddenly, not impulsively. Really, it's been my aim for years," he continued, and I let my attention wander around the courtyard until, several minutes, later, the words "Don

Quixote" brought me back into focus. Al-Cerraz was laughing, while Falla sat motionless.

"It's just ridiculous, what others want us to do—repetition, imitation. There is no interest in originality. If there were, we'd let these old themes rest in peace." The pianist shook his head, rattled his glass, and raised it to his mouth.

Falla picked at his pant leg. "I, too, am composing a work based on *Don Quixote.*"

Al-Cerraz froze, holding his glass in front of his face for a prolonged moment to shield his unsettled expression.

"It takes the form of a puppet play," Falla said.

Al-Cerraz's discomfort exploded into laughter. "Puppets!" He looked to me. "A puppet play, did you hear? The maestro is pulling our leg."

Falla didn't laugh.

Al-Cerraz cleared his throat. "It's going well, then?"

"It's nearly complete."

The sister entered the courtyard with a fresh pitcher in her hand. She refilled our glasses dutifully, without making eye contact, as if she were watering plants. My bladder was full, but I busied myself emptying a second tall glass.

Falla rose and exited the courtyard again, without explanation, squeezing a dumbbell in his hand as he walked. Al-Cerraz reached inside his vest pocket, pulled out a flask, and poured a healthy slug into his lemonade, nearly overflowing the glass. Just as he replaced it Falla reappeared and took his seat.

"Of course, there's also something to be said for timeless themes and timeless places," Al-Cerraz ventured. "I mean, consider Andalucía itself—the history here! The deep feeling! Anyone who listens to *Nights in the Gardens of Spain* can feel it, hear it, smell it." He was warming to the task. "The perfumed opening—I can see the moon shining against the stone walls. The first broken piano chords—I can hear the water running, that great Moorish irrigation, bringing the jasmine-scented gardens to life! The tense violins—"

Falla uncrossed and recrossed his legs, shifting away from us. "My intention was never to be quite that pictorially descriptive, in the limited sense."

"Of course not," Al-Cerraz said.

The composer muttered inaudibly.

"Perdóname?" Al-Cerraz asked.

"On the rue de Richelieu," Falla repeated. "In Paris. I picked up a booklet, just a little thing, with some pictures. About the Alhambra."

"And it led you here, to do your research?"

De Falla paused; I could hear the dumbbells squeaking, like little trapped mice.

"I moved here after writing *Nights,*" he said finally. "I did not need to see the Alhambra in order to conceive that work."

Al-Cerraz and I stood outside Falla's house, surveying the cobblestone road that led steeply upward, and the vines on the walls flanking the road. The plants seemed to have grown thicker and greener in the last hour, encouraged by the day's deepening humidity.

"Does this mean you don't want to see it now?"

Al-Cerraz sighed.

"I don't see why you're upset. He is a Romantic, like you. 'Imagination as the supreme faculty'; didn't you praise a philosopher who said that? So Falla relied on his imagination of the Alhambra."

Al-Cerraz ran a hand through his hair. It was damp from perspiration, and the result of his distracted raking was a crazed, spiky look. "Feel, and dream, but first—observe. Whether it's poetry or painting or music, there has to be truth. The Impressionists didn't invent the idea of light—they observed it."

I rubbed my neck and felt coils of sweaty dirt forming. I wanted to say, "The Alhambra was just an idea. Music's real truth isn't in its story or imagery. Music's real truth is in its deeper structure—balance, control, proportion, all those elements that nineteenth-century pianists started tampering with when they disrupted meter and harmony in favor of extreme expression."

But it was too hot, so instead I said, "Come on."

"I don't feel well," Al-Cerraz said.

"You want to find something to eat?"

"No."

This wasn't Al-Cerraz at all.

"Go on," I said. "Let me hear it."

"What should I say?"

"I don't know. Say he's no different from Debussy. Say we might as well just give it all away." I raised my voice: "Let the French tell us about sunny Spain—let the vendors of the rue de Richelieu sell us their little pictures of the Alhambra!"

"Is that how you think I'd react?"

"Isn't it?"

When I realized he had no more to say, I reached for his arm. Much as I longed to head back downhill to the hotel in time for a siesta, I found myself pulling Al-Cerraz uphill instead. After a few feet he held up a finger, patted at his jacket, found the flask, and offered me a sip.

"*Seguro,* in a moment," I said, and stepped closer to the wall to relieve myself.

Al-Cerraz shrieked, "You're urinating against the maestro's house?"

I waved a hand at him. "This isn't his house—it's the city wall. What's got into you?"

Al-Cerraz watched the yellow trickle run downhill, along the shingle-lined ditch. Then he nodded with disgust, took another swig from his flask, and started walking uphill. "Come on," he called back to me, "the day's already a lost cause. I will bring my mother something from the Alhambra—that will make her pleased to see me, for a little while at least."

At the first switchback, we paused. Al-Cerraz's face blazed red. My shirt clung to my back.

"You know," I said, "in all these years, I don't think you've ever mentioned your mother's name."

Al-Cerraz paused for a moment, then, too tired to obfuscate, he replied, "Her name is Carolina Otero."

"La Belle Otero? The dancer?"

"Dancer, cabaret artist, courtesan—and worse."

"You shouldn't say that."

"She wouldn't deny it. Vanderbilt, the American—that was her first big catch. Then the Kaiser, our randy little Alfonso, the Shah of Persia, a Japanese emperor..." he paused, breathless. After a minute he added, "She might have kept it up a little longer, if not for her illness."

Something in my expression must have indicated distaste. I was imagining what kinds of diseases a courtesan would have.

"Gambling," he explained. "That was her illness."

"She had a house in Nice, once," he continued. "Now she lives at a hotel. In her prime, she lost millions. She got sloppy. She'd take any lover who would pay her debts. Once she became common, shahs and emperors had no use for her."

I whistled through my teeth. "I've seen her picture, the one where she is wearing that tall headdress and the costume..." I stopped. "Well, she must have been much younger then."

At the next switchback, Al-Cerraz leaned over, his hands on his knees, face blanched. "My heart's beating too fast. I need water."

A boy was passing, heading downhill. "The Alhambra," I called out to him. "Are we almost there?"

He nodded and kept going.

We continued, and a tall red wall rose on our left, then two towers, but no gate. "I'm sure we'll come to an opening soon."

Al-Cerraz stopped again, and leaned heavily on his uphill leg. He let out a desperate laugh. "Maybe I should have stuck with a French postcard."

At last we came to a gate and passed through it, onto more level ground. That seemed to give him renewed energy. "I'm going to pick a rose for my mother when we get to the gardens. It will cheer her. There's the palace. I think I see a way in."

A man approached us and offered to be our guide. Al-Cerraz handed him a coin and told him to go away. We entered the Nasrid palace together, walking from one silent, cool, unlit room to the next, under arched doorways, admiring the mosaic-tiled walls, the slim pillars framing hallways, the elaborately carved ceilings, the wooden grilles as finely cut as lace.

We came to a long rectangular courtyard with overgrown hedges on either side and a shallow reflecting pool in the middle. "There's your water," I laughed. It was dark green, opaque with algae.

After a while, I said, "Why isn't your last name Otero?"

"She wouldn't let me use it."

"Wouldn't let you?"

"She'd already left us by the time I started touring. My father and his second wife raised me. My father, the cuckold, would have gladly had me use her last name, despite the sordid implications, but she wouldn't agree to it. She didn't want anyone knowing she'd had a child."

"I'd think she'd be proud."

He stared at me blankly. "Exclusivity, competition, independence— first lessons in being a courtesan. So, I went nameless for a while."

"As El Nene..."

"Until I wasn't a nene anymore, and I had to choose a real name. My earliest memories of my mother—my only childhood memories of her—are of her telling me stories that took place in the desert. Full of oases and harems." He paused. "She had presented herself as Andalucían, the daughter of a gypsy. My father said she was really from the north—the daughter of an umbrella salesman. Which story would *you* choose to believe?"

"You could have used your father's last name."

"Not exotic enough. I'd learned something from my mother's success. Do what is necessary. Between umbrellas and mystery, choose mystery."

This was different from his typical stories. It had no punch line or happy ending, and it added no luster to his persona. But for all it lacked, it rang truer than anything he'd ever told me.

I followed him through a doorway into another dark room with an ornate, horseshoe-shaped window. From a distance, it looked all gold, but that was only the late-day sun coming through the opening, setting the carved wood aglow.

"The name Al-Cerraz was my idea. It sounded right to me. I believed in my heart that I had Moorish roots." He stared into the distance, a green sea of cypresses. "I always believed in some kind of ancestral memory. I believed that this place would feel like home."

"Does it?"

He didn't answer.

I busied myself studying the tiles on the wall, arranged in endless repeating eight-sided stars. I reached out to rub a hand over them. When I turned back, Al-Cerraz was gone.

I found him later, at the top of the Alcazaba, after I'd spent a good hour following an endless progression of stone steps that circled a decaying core. Al-Cerraz was at the citadel's highest, farthest corner, sitting on a crumbling rectangle of stone, surrounded by the weathered rocks that had once been walls, benches, and the floors of cell-like rooms in which long-ago soldiers had slept, close to a signal tower. I saw the flash of metal—the flask being lifted a final time, backlit by the setting sun. In the city below us, white buildings glowed, separated by the spiky tops of palm trees.

"A drink for my troubles?" I said when I reached his side.

"Last one," he said, and handed it to me.

"I'm sure it's against the rules," I said after I'd barely managed to wet my lips. "Drinking amidst Muslim ruins."

"Rules—that's what we need." He sounded tipsy. "*Por ejemplo:* children should be named after their parents. And people shouldn't try to be what they are not."

We watched the sun set. I tried to imagine the Moorish battles of five centuries ago. I conjured up the clash of soldiers and the shouted orders of the Nasrid rulers, guarding their final Iberian stronghold. I imagined horses and banners and harem girls with kohl-lined eyes.

After a while, I asked, "Did you get the rose for your mother?"

He laid an arm across my shoulder. "Did you know? They didn't plant roses in the Nasrid times. That's what a lady told me, in the garden. There's roses now, a few of them, nothing to write home about. And mossy fountains. But it's all fake, really. I can't see the point in it. This whole place," and he lifted his other arm to encompass the breathtaking view of red-rock ruins. "All fake. It does not move me one bit."

"It isn't fake, Justo. I think you're angry at your mother. Or else Falla's story confused you. His representation of it may be imaginary, but this is real. Just look around you."

"No one lived here. No one loved here. If they did"—his voice broke a little—"I would feel it."

I said, "You'll find your inspiration."

The sky lost its bronze warmth, lightened to a pale yellow, and then slipped toward gray; the red walls darkened. I stood up, ready to go, when Al-Cerraz tugged at my arm.

"Falla got the little book on the rue de Richelieu, but that's not how he came up with the opening theme. He said it came from some out-of-tune notes he kept hearing a blind violinist play outside his window when he was renting a house in Madrid, of all places." He forced a little laugh. "Isn't that funny?"

"I don't get the joke."

"I didn't tell you the second part. There was another musician sharing the house. Amadeo Vives. You know Vives? He put the notes in his piece, too—a *zarzuela* number he was working on. They realized it only later. One old busker, inspiring two maestros!" This time he laughed uncontrollably. Then he wiped his eyes and shook his head. "Falla said the world is full of music already. He said: '*Listen.*'"

"And?"

"And," Al-Cerraz said it louder, "*listen!* As if that's helpful advice."

"But Justo, you *do* listen. You have an amazing ear. You've said so yourself: Your brain is a huge repository of melodies and rhythms from all the places we've traveled. Isn't that right?"

"Falla knew," Al-Cerraz whispered. "He knows my secret. That nothing in here is real." He banged a fist against his chest. "Nothing in here." He banged his fist against his temple and winced. The action drew my eye to the dark hair pasted against his head in that spot. I'd taken it for sweat. It was blood, from a nasty cut, the wet edge of which ran just inside his hairline.

"*La osa!*" I leaned toward him and held a hand out toward his face, but he leaned away from me. "What did you do?"

"Fell."

"Where?"

"On the steps."

"Don't you know to put your hands out when you fall?"

"My hands? Are you deranged?" He tucked his fists into his lap protectively and cocked his head. "How can anyone listen when there's not a quiet place in this whole goddamned world?" And he squinted his eyes and covered his ears, as if to block out the crash of cymbals.

I listened too, but could hear only the faintest rattle—a breeze far below us, rustling the blades of a palm tree. But then, there—where was it coming from? Behind us: notes as light as distant birdsong at first. Then louder. It was a boy singing, voice high, jumping an octave, falling back, nonsense words repeated. Then he switched to a whistle. It *was* birdsong—or rather an imitation of it. He was whistling a folk song about springtime that I remembered from my own youth. It brought a smile to my face.

"It's just a boy," I said, relieved, and reached up to pull Al-Cerraz's fingers away from his ears. "Justo, do you remember the time in Madrid, years ago, when you told me a story about a boy playing a violin placed between his legs—and you said you wanted to be like that boy, immersed in music? There are two things I've always meant to tell you. One: You *are* immersed. Your entire heart is in your music, all the more so when you're playing for a few people instead of in some stuffy concert hall."

He looked dubious. "And the second thing?"

"That boy was me."

"I don't believe it." But a small smile had formed on his lips.

I slapped my leg. "You knew it all along, didn't you?"

"Maybe yes, maybe no. I *did* know that we were destined to perform together." His smile faded; he grew serious again. "But I was destined for many things. That doesn't always make them happen."

The boy came up the stairs toward us slowly, alternately whistling and singing. As he approached, I saw that he was dragging one leg behind him with every step. I watched him advance toward us over the rooftop of broken stone, hopping up and over a low ruined wall with the alacrity of an injured pigeon that has adapted long ago to a broken wing and still manages to get its share of plaza crumbs. This was the same boy we'd seen on our way to the Alhambra gate, but I hadn't seen him before—hadn't noticed his leg; hadn't seen his face lit up with song. I couldn't stop staring at the boy's dust-covered shoe, split at the side where it dragged against the ground, and his open face, crowned with disheveled black hair, now directly before us.

"Father says you shouldn't be here now." The boy's chest puffed importantly. "Father says he is closing all the gates."

When we didn't respond immediately, the boy lost his brio and let his chest cave inward again. "You don't want to spend the night here," he said more quietly, directly to me, with real concern in his dark eyes. "There are ghosts."

"We don't mind apparitions," I said jovially, reaching out a friendly hand toward the boy's tousled hair. Al-Cerraz's booming voice stopped me.

"Don't tell me when to go," he threatened the boy. "If I'm not ready..."

He pushed himself to standing, legs spread shoulder-wide to support his bulk. But he wasn't fully upright before his legs wobbled and he reached for my shoulder.

"I'm ready now," he said. "Help me."

"Of course," I said. "Always."

CHAPTER

~ 16 ~

Something changed in me that evening, in that ancient place that had failed to move Al-Cerraz in the way he had expected. I tried to settle into that feeling, to prolong it, remembering above all the image of the boy, his song and his light step, the sense of hope and self-acceptance it had inspired.

Al-Cerraz visited his mother in Monte Carlo, before returning to his lady-friend's villa in Málaga. I accepted an interim post as a symphony conductor in Salamanca. Conducting was something I'd never even thought of doing, and now I found myself enjoying it, intellectually, physically, and emotionally. And what a relief to be in control, yet out of the spotlight, or at least sharing it with other fine musicians.

Somehow, this respite from my own ego dissolved barriers around me. Instead of staring at the country through a train window, I found myself walking daily around that ancient scholars' city. I attended lectures—on subjects other than music, no less. I had no idea where our country should go but I attempted to educate myself, remedially, on how we had arrived at our current situation: led by a weak king and an ineffectual parliament, pulled various directions by the army and the Church, which together threatened to have more power than any of our democratic institutions. When a group of university professors sponsored a two-day conference at which various liberal groups debated current events, I accepted their invitation to perform at the concluding dinner. It was the least I could do. Even though my reputation had grown considerably in the last decade, I still saw my role as a citizen first, a ceremonial figure second, perhaps a well-recognized advocate of certain reforms (none of them particularly radical and certainly not antimonarchical)—always off to one side.

I began to accept dinner invitations, allowing myself to be seated next to young, eligible women. Over Easter, I rented a cottage in the mountains and invited my family to visit; Mamá made excuses, saying Tía needed daily assistance and it was too hard to bring her. But Luisa came with Enric, and I reflected with satisfaction that I was beginning to have a normal life, as best I could imagine it.

Enrique wasn't there, of course. He had arrived in Morocco by way of ferry to Algeciras, handpicked by his friend Paquito—now known as Paco—to help lead Spain's new Tercio de Extranjeros. The Tercio was a mercenary legion, modeled after the French Foreign Legion. While Al-Cerraz was covering his ears, alarmed by the sound of a young boy singing, Enrique and Paco had been screaming at the top of their lungs into the hardened faces of two hundred recruits: common criminals, malcontent Great War veterans, dangerous thugs, pathetic misfits. They were telling these men that their lives had been worthless, but that they might have a new life, as long as they were willing to pay for it with the ultimate sacrifice. "Consider yourselves *novios de la muerte*—bridegrooms of death!"

Sitting in the Alcazar with Al-Cerraz, I had not been able to imagine what a medieval battle really felt like, let alone a modern-day battle in those lands just a short boat ride across the Strait of Gibraltar. I could not imagine what desert thirst felt like; the monotony of scrub-covered dunes; the terror of approaching hoofbeats; the smell of cadavers left for six weeks in the sun. Clouds of flies. The sticky awfulness of sand-soaked blood. What did I even know of real purpose and real camaraderie, or of its essential ingredients, sacrifice and self-denial? Nothing—that's what my brother would have said.

I could imagine, though, that my brother felt the sense of purpose he'd not felt in peacetime, while polishing his saber in El Ferrol. Better to be an *africanista* than a *peninsulare,* especially when the folks back home didn't appreciate a career soldier's efforts. In Morocco, unlike in Spain, there were opportunities for fast advancement, and also opportunities to change the course of history. It was the beginning of something terrible and new—for one soon-to-be-lauded *africanista* hero at least, my brother's friend, whom Enrique might not have befriended in the first place had not the runt reminded him of me.

Regarding this time in my brother's life, I know only what I read later from books. That may sound like a boast, but there is no boast in it. Who wants to read in cold print what one should have read in a man's own hand—or, better yet, heard from his own living voice?

I read that Enrique was one of his battalion's best mapmakers. He never went anywhere without the compass he'd inherited, the same day I'd inherited my bow. I read that he had helped route fresh water from the nearby mountains to the barracks. Certainly, there were legionnaires who tortured prisoners and brandished Moors' heads on pikes—they even presented a duchess, a philanthropist dedicated to nursing, with two heads cradled in a basket of roses.

But not Enrique—I won't believe it. And not most of the thousands of regular soldiers who inhabited that godforsaken place—endless square kilometers of parched terrain that we'd spent years struggling to keep. They did it to make up for losing Cuba and Puerto Rico way back when—that's how Enrique had explained it to me once. One disaster spawns another, and another, on down the years; *da capo,* back to the top, again and again.

———

I invited Al-Cerraz to visit me several times, but he said he was too busy, which I interpreted as a good sign. Not far away, in Segovia, the director of a music festival beseeched me and my duet partner to play. I was willing, but Al-Cerraz didn't even answer the director's telegram. Two more invitations arrived, from León and Ávila. These were convenient for me, but Al-Cerraz said he couldn't tolerate the distraction. Our manager wrote to ask if we were adopting some new strategy, trying to enhance our reputations by becoming reclusive. If so, he wrote, it was working. We were more in demand than ever.

Finally Al-Cerraz agreed to visit me—not to perform, but only to share a dinner, a play, and a walk around the university. He teased me about my pride in the city and accused me of becoming a homebody. I reminded him he'd spent the same nine months in Málaga, to which he said, "Oh, but I haven't noticed. I rarely leave my room, in the mansion's quiet wing; even the maids forget I'm back there. I didn't even emerge for Carnaval. One evening I asked my hostess, the Doña de Larrocha, if we might watch any of the processions together, and she laughed and said I'd already missed them—every last party."

I tried to talk him into staying another day, but he begged off, even when I promised him a grand dinner in his honor. Walking with him to the train station, I asked, "Will you keep turning down concert requests?"

"Only until I'm done. It's very close now. I'll be finished by summer. In fact, it's now that I need your help, to premiere the work. It's for solo piano—a suite. I may orchestrate it later. For now, I'm just hoping to find a really grand venue for it."

"Certainly. The symphony hall here—"

"No," he bowed his head apologetically. "I was thinking of Madrid. A royal premiere."

"That would be something."

"I have the Queen Mother's ear, which might not hear so well anymore. You have the Queen's. I was hoping you'd help me arrange it. It should be a night of several acts, to keep the press from asking too many questions about my part in it. They'll be expecting Al-Cerraz the performer of Chopin and Liszt, not Al-Cerraz the composer. I want the audience to have an open mind. I want them to be surprised."

"I don't get to hear a preview?"

"It's an autobiographical work. You've been with me for years—that's your preview."

"So you're writing about indigestion and mischief."

He didn't smile.

"Give me the title at least." It was a warm spring night, and breezy; a girl with fashionably short-cropped hair chased her cap down the street; it looked like a bird's nest that had tumbled off a tree. The alleyways were full of students looking for the entrances to dark, cheap restaurants. I was feeling jocular. "So this is a fantasia of the Alhambra—a reverie of Andalucía? Tell me."

His face darkened. "You're mistaken. After our last trip, I started over completely. It's nothing of the kind."

His touchiness surprised me. "I'm sorry, Justo. I'm looking forward to it, that's all. It will be a new start for you. Just as you've said."

A month later, I sent him the word for which he was waiting:

The perfect opportunity has presented itself. Better than Madrid, and fully royal. King Alfonso is planning a great public event on July 25 at Burgos, to coincide with the Feast of Santiago.

I followed it almost immediately with a second letter:

The King, I hear, will also be making a speech honoring El Cid, whose remains are being translated to the Burgos Cathedral. Word is that he will use the same platform to extol our troops in Morocco; evidently he is counting on his latest favorite, General Silvestre, to produce some good news worth celebrating by that date. You wanted a "night of many acts"? This one will have a half-dozen at least, only a few of them artistic.

I paid a visit to Queen Ena. Modernity had caught up with her; her hair was bobbed and crisply waved, and her skirt had risen one or two centimeters for every year since I'd last seen her. She took my hand in hers, asked after my family, mentioned that she'd seen my photograph in the newspapers many times. It didn't seem to bother her that I had become publicly associated with political causes that did not necessarily favor her husband's positions.

Tired as she looked that day, Queen Ena seemed excited about planning a national party. Special Masses were scheduled in more than one location, and arrangements for the evening's concert were made: this cathedral, that hall—no, better an entire square, given the thousands that would be expected. Diplomatic invitations must be sent. The rail schedule must be adjusted. And more entertainment—would that be all right? Another musical prelude wouldn't overshadow our plans? Not at all—medieval *cántigos* by a children's choir before the classical concert, the more the better. And all to set the stage for what I hoped would satisfy my partner—my friend. Had I ever called him simply that?

I planned to play two cello pieces, the first solo, the second with piano. Justo asked if I didn't mind having someone else accompany me, just to draw a clearer distinction between my performance and his original work, to follow. The Queen Mother was bothered by this—Spanish musicians were like fashion accessories to her, to be mixed and matched at whim—but Queen Ena helped to placate her.

One week in advance I wrote to him: *We haven't rushed you? You are sure you're ready? You are satisfied?*

His immediate response:

As satisfied as a cat dragging home a bird in its mouth. The satisfaction of instinct brought to fruition. Of course, we all know that when the cat arrives, the lady of the house might give it quite a beating. The audience's response can never be assured. But yes, Feliu, I am satisfied—as satisfied as I know how to be.

That week, the newspapers reported that General Silvestre, who had cultivated a reputation as daring, was marching his men forty miles across the desolate Rif highlands, from Melilla to Alhucemas, to suppress Berber tribesmen and occupy the area. King Alfonso was eager for a victory. He'd grown impatient with his minister of war and had decided to direct operations himself, over the heads of the War Office.

I traveled to Burgos two days early, to arrive before the royal procession. Stepping off the train, I went to buy a newspaper. There were none available. After checking into my hotel, I found a café. Near the back of the room, a circle of men were arguing violently, one of them holding up a newspaper and smacking it with his open palm. Another man reached up to take his arm and spilled a cup of coffee. A chair tipped as a third man tried to evade the flow. An explosion of swearing erupted.

"Excuse me," I said, barely audible above their shouts. "Abd-el-Krim? Are you talking about the Berber chieftain?"

"Another disaster," one of the men said to me and pushed past my seat, his pants soaked. Did he mean the spilled coffee, or something that had happened overseas?

I heard Silvestre's name, and then King Alfonso's, appended with a few unrepeatable words. "Anual?" I asked, trying to intrude upon their fiery conversation. "Where is Anual? Please? Damn it!" And I banged my fist on the table, making the silverware jump. "May I see that, please?"

I wrested the newspaper from a young man's hand and spread it out on my own table, soaked as it was. The headline read: THOUSANDS

POSSIBLY DEAD....TERRITORY GAINS SINCE 1909 LOST OVERNIGHT. AC-
TION CONTINUING....

I walked back to my hotel, stopping at every newsstand along the
way. One newspaper carried no reports at all, only a puff piece about
the King's planned festivities. Another newspaper's banner headline:
TRIBESMEN ON THE RAMPAGE. I held the coffee-soaked newspaper in my
left hand, and this one in my right, unwilling to discard either, hoping
that somehow they'd cancel each other out, that the news from Morocco was simply wrong.

The details filtered in slowly over the next two days. Garrison after
garrison, slaughtered—by the thousands. Other garrisons remained
under siege, without water, forcing the trapped men to drink their own
urine, sweetened with sugar. Some soldiers who had managed to escape
had deserted the army. Silvestre himself had either killed himself or
been murdered. Could it all be true?

OVERCONFIDENCE, LACK OF PREPARATION BLAMED, said the left-wing
papers. REPORTS UNRELIABLE, said the right-wing papers.

On July 25, St. James's Day, I met my partner coming off the train:
"Justo, have you heard?"

He walked past me, anxious to count his trunks.

"It seems to get worse by the hour. They're saying it's the worst defeat Morocco has ever known. Some young men made a scene in the
Plaza Mayor last night, throwing rocks, breaking glass, but the Civil
Guard cleared it out quickly. Justo—we have to do something about
this."

"The King hasn't canceled the festivities, has he?" Al-Cerraz asked.

"No. For his own safety he should, but I think he's trying to put a
brave face on it."

"Thank goodness," he said, and headed off the platform, guiding a
small army of porters. At the waiting car he added, "It would be just

my luck to have this premiere wrecked by a battle in—what is this place called? Anual?"

"It's not one battle."

He opened the car door, started to get in, then stepped back. "You know what Jesus said about the poor—that they'll always be with us? It's like that. Morocco will always be with us. This is the most important night in my life."

"Please," I said. "I think we should—"

He wouldn't listen. "No matter what happens, everything changes tonight," he said. "Now get in."

The rest of the day was a blur of frantic preparations. Streets blocked off. Cameras clicking. Hammers pounding all day, constructing the stage in the square just under my window. I sent a message to Queen Ena, begging to see her. Instead of a letter, I got congratulatory flowers in response—flowers!

And then I was in the square, the sky darkening, a lower false sky of twinkling lanterns strung in zigzags above my head, the spokes of streets fanning out from the square packed with people as far as the eye could see. Voices rumbled ceaselessly.

King Alfonso and Queen Ena sat to one side, on their own higher dais, strung with lights. The royals were formally announced. Applause, at first tepid, then wilting, while the rumble rose and overtook it—catcalls and that one repeated word: "Anual! Anual!" I could feel the collective anger like a vibration under my feet. Alfonso ignored the jeers, stood smiling, and said a few words that faded before they reached my seat. He lifted an arm in my direction, introducing me. The rumble quieted; applause erupted. Someone shouted, *"El Rey!"* Confusion. I looked around. Applause again. *"El Rey del Arco!* The King of the Bow!"

They were cheering for me—and insulting the King. But still he smiled—shrewdly—one side of his mouth lifted, under that thin dandy's mustache. He lifted an arm again, as if to join the throng, as if to command them to do what they were already doing. The crowds pressed forward, and despite the cordon of soldiers pressing back, I could feel the platform beneath my feet tremble.

I tried to acknowledge the crowd with a wave. I stood and faced the King, bowing to him. Where was my cello? Back inside, at the end of a protected corridor that ran from the stage into a hotel where Al-Cerraz was waiting, warming up on a second concert grand inside the lobby. It wasn't like him to warm up. First, though, came the children's choir. I was meant only to introduce them.

I said a few words. No one could hear me. The children began to sing. When the crowds quieted, I darted back into the hotel.

"We have to do something." I laid a hand on the piano to get Al-Cerraz's attention. "At least *say* something. To go along with this party, as if nothing has happened—it's the worst thing we can do, endorsing all this."

Al-Cerraz stopped playing. "All what? Who knows what's happened?"

"It's our responsibility."

"This"—he gestured to the piano—"is our responsibility. There will be more bad news tomorrow. Let them forget their cares tonight. Or do you want all those people to take over the stage and pull the King and Queen down with them—and probably trample us, too?"

I paced back and forth. "We cancel the rest of it. Send everyone home, peacefully."

"Cancel it? You've lost your senses."

I sat on the edge of the piano bench with my back to him and buried my face in my hands.

He said, "A moment of silence, is that what you want? Nothing political. Just silence?"

"They say it's Silvestre's fault, and Alfonso's fault—this was all just an arrogant demonstration, revenge against the parliament."

"Cálmate."

A young woman from the hotel shuffled toward me, breathless. "It's a telegram for you, Señor Delargo."

"He'll take it in one hour, after the concert," Al-Cerraz said. "He needs quiet."

"It has a military stamp. From Africa," she said.

"Africa!" I jumped to my feet.

"It's from"—she squinted at the form—"Francisco Franco."

"Franco? I don't know him." And my stomach lurched. "Oh, Francisco—Paco, she means. My brother's friend. Paquito."

"Don't read it now," Al-Cerraz said, but I already had it in my hands.

The crowd outside was cheering for the children, momentarily assuaged. They exited the stage and filed into the hotel past me as I read the telegram. It informed me that my brother Enrique, the last of my three brothers, was now among the dead.

I told Al-Cerraz my plan, and he—a genius at music, oblivious to more basic and practical matters, even simple multiplication—said nothing, only shook his head and turned away, battling his own demons.

Onstage, I held up my hand until the crowds quieted. I explained the news I had just received. I said I would have rung all the city's bells if I could. But failing that, I intended to play one bow stroke for every soldier dead, as far as we knew.

Each meditative, unadorned bow stroke took perhaps a second. Sixty of them in a minute. There was respectful silence for the first few minutes, then a rising tide of whispers. Some angry shouts erupted; more jeers toward the royal dais; a shot into the air from a guard. But I wouldn't give it up. One bow stroke each second. Over three thousand in an hour. The open D string, unvarying. Al-Cerraz hadn't done the calculation, and neither had the crowd.

By the end of the first hour, my shoulder ached, but I hadn't built up stamina all those years for nothing. The crowd reacted in different ways, as people will. Some walked away peacefully, bored, disappointed. Some gave angry catcalls; a bottle missed my head by centimeters. A third of the crowd, at least, remained, some unable to leave without knowing how the drama would end; some struck with grief. A woman at the front of the crowd started wailing—a primal wail, out of time with my bow strokes, a terrible syncopation.

Heavily guarded, the King and Queen left their dais. Someone—who, I don't know—stood behind me and put a hand on my shoulder. I lost track of the strokes; no one could count them all; they outnumbered the stars. But that was the point. That was precisely why I couldn't play, and couldn't let Al-Cerraz play. All that death, my brother's included. I couldn't bear the thought of everyone overlooking the scope of the tragedy, absorbing and accepting it, allowing the next week's news to overshadow what had happened. True silence might have been even better, but I hadn't learned true silence yet—only this. A protest of monotony. Three hours passed before I stopped.

When I stumbled into the hotel, eyes blurred, I couldn't understand what I was seeing. Then the shapes resolved. It was the grand piano, lid open, with the bench tossed inside—my partner's frustrated demolition attempt. The musician who had been chosen to accompany me was asleep on a couch in the corner, head tipped back, mouth gaping. The girl who'd delivered the telegram was sitting on the marble floor, mascara streaks on her cheek.

I didn't see Al-Cerraz again that night, or for another eight years.

PART V

La Niña Bonita

1929

CHAPTER

~ 17 ~

My secretary sat on the edge of my desk, reading me the mail as I
shaved over a bowl in the corner, preparing for rehearsal:

*My daughter and I greatly enjoyed the article of August 15, in
Madrid's* ABC. *It reminded me of the felicitous similarities between—*

"Is that the same woman who sent me her daughter's lock of hair?"
"The same."
"Skip that one, please."
Rita speared the letter dramatically on the phone message spike.
Then she ripped the edge of the next envelope and blew into it. "Here's
one from the same reporter who interviewed you for *Diario de Bilbao.*"
"Why doesn't he call?"
"He did. Four times. You haven't called him back. He included
some clippings with his byline."
"Not more 'Portraits of Courage'!"
"I liked that one he did on Colonel Franco, the same issue he did
you... Are you all right?"
I dabbed at my neck, wincing. "*General* Franco," I corrected her.
"They were good photos—both of you," she continued, oblivious
to my expression. "He was clever to put you together, with all the

quotes that sounded so alike—humility and *Patria* and neither one of you liking public attention or politics to begin with."

I groaned.

"I don't see why it bothers you." She sighed. "Did you see that other article last month, about him and his wife, in *Estampa*? I hated her dress. Black crepe—it looked like a nun's habit. But Franco seemed nice. He said his real 'inclination' was painting. That's good, right?"

"The frustrated artist—I don't believe it."

"Why don't you like him?"

I pressed my lips together and made a last swipe at my neck.

"If he writes to you again, will you write him back?"

I mumbled into the hand towel: "The reporter?"

"Franco."

"What leads you to believe he's written to me?"

Rita had worked for me a year. I'd given her permission to open the current mail, but not to pry into my old correspondence. Now she pretended to study her painted nails, lined up along the envelope's edge.

"I'll call Bilbao," I said. "I promise. Next, please. The letters on the bottom are a week old."

She squeezed the pile to her chest. "We could just throw them away, and tomorrow, start at a café instead, take the morning off. Your matinee performance isn't until two."

I tried to look stern, but she didn't notice.

I liked Rita: the sound of her slow two-fingered typing, and the way she faced the big black machine with hunched shoulders and a brooding expression worthy of Beethoven. I told her that once, and she said, "How can you know what Beethoven looked like? He's dead, isn't he? I mean, I suppose there are drawings, but drawings can lie…"

"His death mask," I interrupted her. "I've seen it in Germany."

"Oh." She shivered. "Even dead, he looked mad?"

"Not mad, just preoccupied. Maybe frustrated."

"Are all musicians that way?"

"Of course not, Rita. Look at me."

She had whistled and turned back toward her typewriter without comment, chin tipped up and eyebrows lifted, her forehead effortfully smooth.

I didn't even mind the way she left cheese rinds and apple cores on my desk. I caught myself smiling when I picked them up, and then I had to reprimand myself: When had I come to find sloth charming? There had been a time when sausage casings in sinks and orange peels on a compartment floor were enough to make me fume, but that was long ago. Maybe I found her charming *because* she reminded me of past irritations, in tolerable quantities.

"Any letters from old colleagues?" I asked her, as I did at least once a week.

"No. And no phone calls either."

"That's fine." I concentrated on my cuff links. "Next week, possibly."

One of the files Rita kept for me was full of clippings documenting Al-Cerraz's career since the Burgos concert. Six months later, he had managed to premiere his work at a smaller venue in Toledo, to a disappointing review from the one critic who attended. A year later, he'd tried again with another series of compositions, but although Rita had found a small preconcert announcement, she hadn't been able to locate any review at all. The next time he performed, it was at a concert honoring Liszt; and the time after that, at a concert featuring new Russian works. He was back to playing other men's music, no doubt a concession to financial realities.

My own financial situation was more comfortable than it had ever been. Between seasonal conducting, regular touring and sales of my first three records, I had earned more in 1929 than ever before. Besides my mother, to whom I dispatched a regular stipend, I had no one on whom to spend my earnings. If marriage and a normal life had seemed on the horizon eight years earlier, that horizon had grown less visible under the hazy storm-clouds of current events.

Following the 1921 Burgos concert, my acquaintances had divided into two camps: those inspired by my spontaneous protest and those enraged by it. I'd hoped the attention would blow over, but debate about the disaster at Anual only inflamed my minor role, giving the public something to glorify or ridicule while they waited for a more meaningful conclusion that was slow in coming. Two years would pass before the government's official investigation into the tragedy closed. In the meanwhile, every social occasion had seemed fraught with the threat of ambush. I'd dated one young woman only to find out that her father despised me for my Anual stance. I'd dated another whose entire family adored me, but more for my high political profile than for my status as an a artist, or as a man.

In 1923 a special commission was ready at last to present its investigative report to the Cortes, analyzing how our forces in Africa had been recklessly overextended, and by whom. Just before the report was due to be released, General Miguel Primo de Rivera staged an army uprising in support of King Alfonso, the man expected to bear substantial blame. Alfonso supported the uprising, allowing his supposed protector, Primo de Rivera, to assume the role of dictator. Our King had merely traded one kind of shame for another. Unwilling to take responsibility for Anual, he had rendered himself a ceremonial vestige—monarch still, but reduced to a shadow life while another man held the country's reins.

I imagine that Ena felt disgraced by Alfonso's surrender. She had contacted me once by letter, just after Anual, to ask me to return the gift she'd given me. I wouldn't.

She had followed up a year later with another letter, no less aggrieved:

You've gained fame for your disruptive gimmick and your current pub-
lic stance. I believe it's clear you are no longer a friend to the monarchy.

I wrote back:

There is a technical issue to consider. I am comfortable with my bow as it is, and I don't see any reason to take an artistic risk merely to satisfy your sensibilities. Besides, I refuse to be stripped of an honor bestowed upon me in less-troubled times.

But my formal tone was a bluff, meant to disguise the pain in my heart. I'd never found a better audience than the Queen, and I'd never found a substitute for her elegant and compassionate company. Years later, I would keep a newspaper photo of her from the day she fled the country. Alfonso was already abroad, leaving Ena to bring up the rear, with mobs not far behind. In the photograph she is seated on a roadside boulder, commonly dressed, looking forlorn but resigned, and openly smoking a cigarette—no longer beholden to public opinion.

One of the few people to emerge unscathed from the Anual *desastre* was that little soldier, my brother's friend, who returned from Morocco a national hero, having managed to spill Berber blood on a battlefield strewn with mostly Spanish corpses. Because of the Anual inquiries, he wasn't promoted immediately, but he was honored with military medals, feted at Automobile Club luncheons, and profiled endlessly in the newspapers—even newspapers that were hostile to the military as a whole. Franco represented the noble soldier untarnished by the ignobility of war itself—an emblem of order, loyalty, and survival. The adulation, he claimed, ran contrary to his greatest wish, to continue to serve his country yet "pass unnoticed."

Yet he had wanted me to notice, to know the precise details of what he'd done, to approve. He had heard as much about me as I'd heard about him. He was aware that Enrique's lifelong kindness toward him had been a proxy for Enrique's love for me. He said as much and thanked me for it in the letter that came two months after the telegram telling me of Enrique's death.

The letter went on to detail what Franco had done in honor of my brother, whom we had both adored. Pursuing the Berber leader Abd-el-Krim, Franco and a handpicked band of Legionnaires had decided to wreak vengeance on Moroccan villages along the way. They set houses blazing and killed old men, women, and children—"baby Moors"—without mercy. There were many more details, in a neat, unvarying handwriting that never revealed emotion or even fatigue. What disturbed me most was how much they had enjoyed it, and how much Franco felt I needed to know and enjoy it alongside him. The job was "difficult but pretty," he wrote me. "Know that I did it in your brother's name, and in yours."

Coming on top of my grief for Enrique, that sickening letter wrecked my concentration and addled my brain. It wasn't that I had decided on principle not to perform, it was only that I couldn't. The staff lines blurred together. The notes danced on the page, and took wing like flies—the battlefield flies that gather in clouds where there are too many bodies to bury.

But when, after Anual, I canceled my early-autumn concerts, the reporters started phoning, and the photographers came to take my picture. No one listened when I said I had headaches and blurry vision; that I was canceling only for September, and planned to resume by October or November, at the latest. They wanted to believe I was protesting, still; that I had some plan; that alongside the governmental inquiries some drama might emerge to give the disaster satisfying closure.

I felt guilty when I played poorly, distractedly, my heart insisting that this was not a time for musical pleasures and escapism. I felt guilty when I didn't play and the reporters came, showering me with undeserved attention. I finally returned to a regular performance schedule, but the attention didn't diminish. Just as a poor reputation is hard to correct, so is a heroic one. The more humble and resisting I tried to be, the more my humility and resistance was praised. I despised Franco for benefiting from this mess, but my career was benefiting, too.

And truly, there was no small pleasure in being a successful soloist and conductor, in demand across Europe. Never before in the history of Spain, or perhaps of the world, had a cellist's name been known by the average man. Every year that decade, my fame increased. My mail swelled with honors, invitations, and requests. Young musicians beseeched me for favors. Political organizations requested my support. It was hard just to keep track of it all. Yet even as my fans multiplied, old friends slipped away. I had not heard from Alberto in years. It had been even longer since I'd heard any news of Count Guzmán and his family.

And, since the Burgos concert, I had not heard from Al-Cerraz. Given the fieriness of his exit, and the debacle of his later debut, I did not dare contact him. In my mind, it was clear he would have to make the first move. Surely he couldn't stay angry with me forever.

I was almost ready to go out the door when I heard Rita squeal and hop off the desk. "Here it is! I knew it would come someday. Maestro, come see!"

With great effort, I ignored the thick piece of stationery she held out to me until I finished tying one of my dress shoes. She saw my hesitation, came around the desk, and pressed the letter into my hands. "It's from America! An invitation to play at the White House!"

"Oh," I said; and then louder, for Rita's benefit and my own, "Oh my! That's wonderful. Of course it is."

"Well," she said, puzzled by the catch in my voice, "you deserve it."

"Of course. Yes. Write back directly. Tell them I accept, with pleasure."

I visited Washington, D.C., in late October of 1929, six months into President Hoover's first term. At the formal dinner that preceded my concert, I could not manage to eat more than a few bites, due to mild nervousness, but I performed to my and my hosts' satisfaction. I was looking forward to the postconcert reception, where I hoped to have a chance to ask the president his thoughts on how one should best help one's own floundering country. Hoover had a heroic reputation among Europeans for the relief work he had done privately during the Great War, particularly in Belgium.

But it was impossible to get a private word with the president that night. Everyone was too distracted by "Black Thursday" the day before, when the U.S. stock market had taken an alarming dive. Gentlemen hooked fingers under their cummerbunds or pulled at their bow ties, nodding morosely at talk of liquidations, speculation, overheated markets, and other terms wholly unfamiliar to me. The only mention of my home country came in a broader reference to Europe, when one of the Rockefeller ladies lamented the thousands of foreign investors who had abandoned Wall Street in favor of investing in their own recovering national markets.

The climate was no different on the steamer I boarded the day after the concert, eager to return to Spain, where I had a new recording contract waiting for me. At every meal, my fellow first-class passengers discussed the weekend financial reports, dreading the reopening of the stock markets on Monday. By Sunday evening, panic had engulfed the ship. At dinner, two older men started to argue about finance, until a white-haired woman between them stood up, twisting the double strand of pearls over her wide bosom as she called out, "Can't we find anything else to talk about? I don't believe I can stomach any more of this."

The man next to her reached for her hand, but she refused it. Another couple a few seats down started bickering about whose idea it had been to travel to Europe in the first place. Someone said that the ship should turn around. A fourth person blamed the coming crash on pessimists and naysayers—"people like yourselves, who can't sit tight and let the market adjust." The dinner ended without any exchange of physical aggression, but just barely. We heard that one of the men from the table had reported to the ship doctor with chest pains.

The ship's captain approached me later that night. "I hear you performed at the White House this week. What can I do to convince you to play a concert on board?"

Before I had time to answer, a junior officer tapped the captain's shoulder. A long line of guests was requesting use of the ship's radio, he said. Telegrams to and from brokers were overloading the ship's communications staff.

After his subordinate left, the captain turned to me again. "Tomorrow night, if you could. It will give the passengers something else to think about. I can't control an entire ship full of anxious Wall Street barons." He added, "Even without the crisis, it would be foolish of me not to take advantage of the musical talent on board. We always have a few actors, a few writers, but two celebrated musicians from the same country isn't so common."

"Two?" I said.

"Beg your pardon—not to put you both in the same category. Though I'm told the other fellow is quite famous, or used to be. He recognized your name immediately."

"It couldn't be Justo Al-Cerraz? The pianist?"

"That's him."

"But why haven't I seen him on board?"

The captain leaned closer, lowering his voice. "He's in second class. I said I'd give him a better cabin if he wouldn't mind playing a concert as well. He said I should ask you."

At that moment, another junior officer approached. While the two men conversed, I turned away, my throat tight with emotion. *Ask me?* I was surprised Al-Cerraz was willing to speak with me, much less perform with me.

"The Empress Lounge has an excellent grand piano," the captain resumed. "The last concert there was jazz, but I think you'll like the acoustics. Do you want to see it?"

I didn't hear the rest. I was still trying to imagine what I should say to Al-Cerraz, when we turned a corner into the lounge and saw him there, fingers hovering just above the keys.

Al-Cerraz swung around on the piano bench, clasped my hand, and held it for a moment. I had time to study him: jowls, a little heavier and redder, forcing his earlobes to jut at right angles away from his head; hair as thick as ever, but streaked with silver. His mouth widened into a smile, and I felt my body relax, from the shoulders downward, all except for one knot in my stomach. Could forgiveness really come so easily?

"What are the chances?" I managed to say.

He confessed, "I'd say the chances were good. I read about your White House appearance and knew you were traveling back to Europe on this ship."

I did not ask him why he'd never written or called; he avoided the same questions. Instead, he told me about some small concerts he had played in Philadelphia and Boston, and in South America before that. "I considered staying in New York another month, but my finances are a little rocky, let's say. So I figured, as long as I'm heading home…"

"You're not one of the investors affected, are you?"

"Every investor is affected. My broker didn't bother to return my call on Friday. It was easy to get a last-minute steamer ticket. There were plenty of cancellations."

A shroud of bad luck still seemed to hang over him, but he appeared to be taking the news astonishingly well. "What lasts?" he asked rhetorically, as he had so many times before. Then he laughed. "Good looks, rarely. Money—never."

"And friendship?" I asked cautiously.

He fingered his mustache. "Sometimes. I suppose I'd put it in the same category as love: flawed and messy, and of questionable duration, and yet somehow irresistible."

The concert, on Monday night, reminded me of a palace affair. Twelve rows of straight-backed chairs filled the generically elegant room. We offered a simple program: Massenet, the Franck we'd played all those years ago with Gauthier. Eight years hadn't diminished how well we played together. And it was so much easier to reconcile without speaking. I appreciated, as I hadn't appreciated in years, the power of music to transcend the mundane, to satisfy complicated emotions, to provide a shared language when words failed.

When we were finished, the assembled passengers called for an encore, which we supplied. Then they called for a second one. Al-Cerraz, who'd always favored small audiences such as this one, promised to play again, but first he launched into a speech about his love of ocean passages and his memory of his first one, when he stowed away to Brazil at the age of seven. I'd heard it before, never quite the same version twice. This anecdote opened the door to other recollections of a former prodigy: being pursued by the authorities through Caribbean isles, befriending a port-haunting woman of ill repute who helped him earn his passage back home. I was thirsty now, and ready for the performance to be over, gripping my bow tighter the longer he talked.

The audience's laughter punctuated something Al-Cerraz had just said—I'd stopped paying attention—and suddenly, he sat down and started to play again. It was Saint-Saëns's "The Swan," a piece that had never been one of my favorites, and I missed the opening cue. In rushing to catch up, I must have dug in hard, with my bow hand off balance. Suddenly—alarmingly—my hand was empty. And the bow, arrow-straight and sure, was flying through the air, sprung from the tension formed between my hand and the string. A gasp escaped the room. Al-Cerraz finished a measure and turned.

I waited for the laughter to come. These same rosy-cheeked passengers had proven capable of it; the men with their hands over their tight vests, and the women with their hands at their flushed necks. But then this awkward breach had opened, breaking the spell.

I knew I should say something. Al-Cerraz would have made the right quip, the right pun, and somehow even in the back row, where his voice wouldn't have carried, or even the middle, where his thick accent wouldn't be comprehended, still they would have laughed—or at least exhaled. But I couldn't find the words. And anyway, I was more worried about my bow. I couldn't begin to imagine what I'd do if the stick had snapped, or the sapphire had come unlodged and rolled under some matron's heel, camouflaged among the stray bits of send-off confetti that were never completely swept away from one sailing to the next.

I rose from my chair and pushed my way through the silence. I was halfway to the first row when a young woman stood and—leaning over a stooped gentleman seated in front of her—bent toward me.

She was pretty, with a light olive complexion and large dark eyes close-set on either side of a long, slim nose. She had dark hair, a lock of which had fallen loose from its comb. In a room of gowns, she wore a plain long-sleeved dress with a prim, scalloped collar, above which I could see her throat pulsing like a trapped sparrow.

That quiver betrayed her. If I hadn't seen it, I would have believed she was perfectly composed. Her right arm came forward and my eyes followed it, tracing the long, thin wrist. Just before I reached her, she nudged one finger into the crook of the ebony frog and let the bow swing a swift ninety degrees to nearly vertical—a surrendered pistol, a compass needle swinging to true. Then she lifted the bow slightly upward, toward me.

That's how I knew. Someone who had never touched a bow would have wrapped an awkward fist around it, spoiling the hair; or lifted it heavenward in two flat palms, like an exotic sacrifice.

I muttered my thanks. She leaned toward my ear and whispered, "Now"—and she paused and wetted her lips self-consciously—"Now you have their perfect attention."

Not *our* attention, but *their* attention. A small conspiratorial detail. Violinist was just a guess— the right one, as it turned out.

For perhaps the first time in his life, Al-Cerraz took the realistic, rational view. She was just another passenger—one among thousands. He accused me of hitting her with my bow on purpose. As if anyone, save Cupid, could have such perfect aim.

CHAPTER

~ 18 ~

"You don't believe me?" I said to Al-Cerraz the next day on the second-class deck. "There she is. I'll prove it."

I approached the young woman and we exchanged introductions as if the evening before had never happened: What a shame to have gray days when sun on the open sea must be spectacular, and wasn't it surprising how far from land gulls will fly. Looking skyward, she confided she didn't care for the ocean, actually. She'd felt queasy the whole trip.

I asked her in English, "Did you bring it?"

"Bring what?"

"On this crossing—did you bring your instrument?"

"What instrument?" She tucked her slim fingers under her armpits, forearms flattening her already small, high breasts.

"Please," I said. "If I say 'violin' and it's viola, you'll never speak to me again—and vice versa. I don't understand the problem about violas, but I know not to make a joke of it. Make it easy for me. Tell me what you play."

She unlocked her arms and dropped her hands slowly. "I'm sorry if my English isn't good."

"It's perfect. Better than my—what is your native...?"

"I don't speak Spanish," she said, avoiding the question.

"Any French?" Al-Cerraz butted in.

"Only a little, sorry," she said. "German?"

"Whatever tongue, we'll make you answer," I said, and Al-Cerraz's eyes widened.

"We're on our way home to Spain," Al-Cerraz interrupted, rescuing her from my inquiries. "And you?"

At this she hugged herself again, tucked her left cheek close to her shoulder, and stared at the rail. Then she spun on one low heel and walked away.

"Well done," I said.

He shook his hairy head and held up his palms. "*You* were the rude one."

It was the Beethoven ladies who were able to enlighten me, at least in part. I'd met the two elderly women on my rambles through second class, and we'd already had several discussions about "new music," as one of them called anything composed after her mother's birth year, 1820. The young lady was from northern Italy, they informed me. They stumbled over her last name ("About seventeen syllables long— no wonder she introduces herself by her given name") but her first name was Aviva. They knew for certain that she had had proper business in the United States, some kind of special visa, an invitation to play violin with the New York Philharmonic. Yet no sooner had she arrived in New York than she had turned around and booked a cabin to go back on the very same ship.

"Do you think it's stage fright?" said the darker-haired lady—the one who preferred Beethoven's early period.

I said, "I don't think that's it. If she had a foreign job offer, she must have had considerable experience performing back in Italy."

"Exactly," the other matron said. "I think it's a personal matter. Perhaps love."

"Yet the skin on her finger is evenly toned," the darker-haired matron interjected. Seeing my puzzled expression, she explained, "She has not recently discarded any ring."

The other lady countered, "Perhaps she never obtained one."

Al-Cerraz appeared a short while later, claiming he was already bored with his tablemates, who had spent all of luncheon discussing the latest vanished billions. "They're calling this 'Black Tuesday,'" he groaned. "First Black Thursday, now Black Tuesday. The entire week is a massive, ugly bruise."

"What do you think about a concert?"

"Another one?"

"A different one. A trio."

The captain was willing to close off a small parlor for us, long enough to allow us to audition Aviva. Though she showed up with her violin, she demonstrated no eagerness to remove the instrument from its case. Al-Cerraz tried to put her at ease, encouraging her just as he had encouraged me, the first time we'd played together at the palace in Madrid. He could be wonderful that way, when his mind wasn't preoccupied by appetite, ego, or thoughts of the distant future.

Still, our small talk lagged, and Aviva still seemed disinclined to play. With a pang of desperation, I said, "This is quite an opportunity for you, if you don't mind my saying so."

She cocked her head. "I'm perfectly aware of your reputation."

Al-Cerraz heard the stridency in her tone. "Don't mind him. Please—this crossing is dreadfully dull. Do it for me."

"I'll think about it," she said.

"No thinking," he said. "Just say you will."

I wanted her to perform, but not just because he'd beseeched her. "Take your time, Miss—"

"Just think about it," Al-Cerraz interrupted. "It isn't much to ask."

She nodded and gripped her violin case, eyes on her shoes. When she turned to go, Al-Cerraz winked at me, then started to shuffle through the sheet music he'd spread out on the piano's lid.

He called to Aviva, "*Au revoir.* Perhaps we'll see you on deck later. Could you close the door after you?" Then to me, louder: "Actually Feliu, if you have just a moment." He stopped shuffling and pulled out a sheet, squinting at it. "I don't think I've found the pulse of this particular work."

In all our years together, Al-Cerraz had never petitioned me for any kind of interpretive advice. He didn't typically read from sheet music, either. He might study it away from the piano, but when he played, it was nearly always from memory. Now he had a seat on the bench and pulled up to the keyboard. "Just listen." His hands flew over the keyboard.

"I don't recognize it."

"Fauré, D Minor," he said, over his frenetic playing.

"You have my part?"

"On the piano."

"Why didn't you say so?"

As I went to retrieve it, Al-Cerraz shouted over his shoulder, "Shut it, please. I won't have the outside world hearing something I haven't yet perfected." I realized he was addressing Aviva, still lingering in the open doorway.

But of course he had perfected it. He had launched into Fauré's restless opening with complete confidence, his hands conjuring the sound of a rapidly tolling bell, hitched to some wave-tossed buoy, sending out warnings across a dark seascape. The agitated music begged for something—but not for anything that Al-Cerraz or any pianist could provide. Music in hand, I took my seat and joined in: and there, ah, the relief provided by the cello—a slower, surer melody, like a ship cutting through those agitated waves, holding steady against the wind and the spray.

The two parts together were magical, but they required a third to complete Fauré's vision. I was so busy following my own music that I didn't see Aviva take a step back into the room and extract her violin from its case. She joined the trio just as the violin's melody twined with the cello's, then rose above it, cleaving the darkness. She had no trouble leading me, using the bold harmonizing strokes the piece required. But later in the movement, it was as if she suddenly realized how high she'd climbed; some vertigo set in and her energy waned a little. She continued to play masterfully, in a way no audience would have criticized; but she had succumbed to some self-imposed limit.

And yet she looked contented when we finished, all of us breathing heavily as the final notes echoed across the room, inhibitions erased by the sheer physical challenge of working through an unfamiliar piece so quickly. Aviva stood next to Al-Cerraz, laughing now. "Next time, you'll let me tune, I hope!"

"Next time," Al-Cerraz smiled. "Those are the words I like to hear. You've played it before, I take it?"

For the first time it registered with me that Aviva hadn't needed the sheet music.

"I performed it two years ago," she replied.

I said, "I'm not familiar with it. When was it composed?"

"In 1923," Al-Cerraz guffawed. "Feliu—you must keep up with things!" And then back to her: "But he's lost in the 1600s, half the time."

It didn't matter—not the teasing and one-upmanship that followed, not the trivial banter as the euphoria of a wonderfully executed movement faded. We had seen what Aviva could do, and perhaps a little of who she was.

I sought the captain's permission to give a concert the last night before reaching port. I explained that we knew it was strange, assembling an untried trio of musicians in such record time.

"Strange? Record time? Not at all. On this ship, I've married passengers who met just days before. Seems to be some people's notion of romance, to hurry things along. Besides, the passengers loved your first concert. Anything that will keep them out of my radio room is much appreciated."

Furthermore, the captain said, having a trio concert with Aviva would be a kindness to her.

"A kindness?"

"You do realize she doesn't have any money, don't you? A patron paid for her westbound ticket so that she could save what little she had to get herself set up in an apartment. But then she spent all of it coming back. Unlike most of the people on board, she was broke even before Black Tuesday."

"I didn't realize."

"Well, we've got some music fanciers on board. I'm sure we can arrange to do something for her. Nothing as crass as passing a collection plate, don't you worry."

When we told Aviva the news, she tried to dodge the concert one more time, halfheartedly. "I don't have anything to wear besides this," she said, lowering her eyes to the same prim, scalloped-neck dress she'd worn the night Al-Cerraz and I had performed.

I wanted to say that clothes didn't matter, but Al-Cerraz was our showman. "We'll find you something better," he told her, pinching the sleeve of her dress.

It turned out that the Beethoven ladies' young niece, who was traveling with them, had a green gown that she was willing to take in at the waist. Wielding a pincushion, the two of them crowded with Aviva into Al-Cerraz's large cabin—he'd taken the captain up on the offered upgrade—while Al-Cerraz and I hovered near the doorway. One of the ladies held the sleeveless gown in front of Aviva's torso. Aviva turned to look at me, lips parted, eyebrows tilted upward in an expression of confusion, nausea, or both.

Then the door closed.

"She was fine at rehearsal," I said.

"I don't think she's nervous about playing, I think it's just the attention. And maybe the dress. It's somewhat revealing. One of the ladies told me she grew up in a convent."

"Not fair, is it? You and I aren't planning on wearing anything revealing."

"Thank goodness," he said. "People don't want to see any more of me than they already do. As for you—you're invisible. Don't argue with me. When you're playing, you hardly look up from the floor. There's not much to see but the slump of your shoulders and the shine of your head. But they'll be staring at her, one way or the other." He added, "*You* stare at her, even when she's not playing."

After a few minutes, it dawned on me that we both looked like nervous bridegrooms, pacing outside the door. I, for one, chose to leave.

And regretted my decision deeply, when I returned an hour later.

Al-Cerraz's cabin door was closed. I figured the volunteer seamstresses were gone by now and Aviva was finishing her toilette. I put my ear to the door. There was some knocking and bumping, and then Aviva's voice, high and strained: "It hurts."

"Hold still," came Al-Cerraz's voice, followed by a grunt. "I'm not going to tell you again."

Perspiration sprang from my temples, chest, and armpits; even from the soles of my feet.

"It doesn't feel good—please!" she said again.

"Maybe it has to hurt. That's what my mother said." His mother, the worn-out courtesan? *Dios mío.*

I started to knock, but then I heard Aviva say, "I want to put my clothes back on."

My knuckles hovered against the door; my hand paused above the knob. Why couldn't I act when it mattered most? But this was Al-Cerraz. Granted I'd witnessed many of his countless seductions, in small towns across Spain, but he'd never take a woman against her will. Or would he?

I heard him groan again. Please, I thought, just hit him. Kick. Scream. He's hopeless, once he's flat on the ground. Just push. But no sound from Aviva.

The back of my hand brushed the door, faltering. I cleared my throat loudly: no scuffling response inside. Then a sharp feminine yelp.

Without thinking, I grabbed the doorknob, turned, and fell forward. The door hadn't been locked. Aviva was sitting awkwardly on the edge of a bed in the green gown, hunched forward, while Al-Cerraz knelt on the floor before her, grasping one of her slender arms. They turned to look at me, but only for a second. Then Al-Cerraz resumed what he was doing, grunting and pulling. And what was that in his hand?

"Aviva," I said. She winced and looked toward me, but she didn't spring to her feet or burst into grateful tears.

"Hold still," Al-Cerraz said again. And gave the half-lemon another turn, grinding it onto her elbow.

He leaned back on his haunches. "Maybe milk would have worked better. I remember my mother using milk, too. At least I think I do. Haven't you ever seen a lemon before, Feliu? And shut that door."

"He won't rest until he's satisfied with my appearance." Aviva extracted her arm from Al-Cerraz's grasp. "Now look. The skin isn't white—it's all red."

"Better than black." He laughed. "Now we know why she didn't want to wear a sleeveless gown. She has a tomboy's arms, dark and rough as wood from all those years of climbing trees."

"Walls. We'd climb the convent walls, I said."

I closed the door and leaned against it, weak-kneed.

"He's teasing me, Feliu." She looked uncomfortable using my first name, but there—she had said it. "I hate my arms. They're too hairy from the elbows down—like a little monkey, a teacher once told me. I can't believe I'm talking about this. I've never gone without sleeves in my life." Now she was laughing, holding her red elbow and laughing.

"And this," she pointed to a little gold cross at her neck. The same niece who'd loaned her the gown had insisted on loaning her jewelry, too. "I didn't want to offend her, but I can't wear this. How did I get mixed up with you both?"

She laughed again, then stopped herself, hand patting her neck as if she had swallowed a fishbone. But my expression must have looked even more pained. She reached a hand toward me: "Mr. Delargo, are you all right?"

The concert was a resounding success, followed all too quickly the next day by our arrival in port. Before we knew it, we were walking down the gangplank and into the darkened harbor on clumsy, sea-adapted legs. In a waterfront café we attempted to delay our final leavetaking. Al-Cerraz went in search of a long-distance telephone service. Dark fog blocked our view of the water. Aviva and I sat inhaling the damp air, which smelled of fish and fuel.

The night before, after the concert, some of the wealthier passengers had crowded around her, asking about her plans. The captain had hinted that she was bound for Germany, a report that she'd confirmed reluctantly. She'd barely gotten the words out before they pressed bills upon her, praising her performance and saying it was the least they could do to further her career.

Now, over coffee, I pushed her for details, which she provided just as reluctantly. "My contact is Herr Weill. He had offered a job before, and I realized, when I reached New York, that I should have taken it."

"That's something. Isn't it?"

"Yes, but it doesn't start for six months. It begins just ahead of the school year. I'll be touring from school to school with the national music-education program."

We sat for a while without speaking, until I finally said, "I still don't understand. You had a great job waiting for you in New York, starting immediately, and you'd already traveled all that way. Why change your mind?"

She rested her cheek in one hand. "That's a long story."

"I've got nothing to do until Justo gets back."

She bit her lip, considering. "May I ask you a question?"

"I'd be honored."

"It may be a question you hear all the time."

"I don't mind."

"Why the cello?"

I paused, rubbing my chin.

"You don't have a stock answer?"

"I suppose I do. If I were trying to gain your sympathy, I'd tell you I was weak as a boy and needed an instrument I could play sitting."

"That isn't true?"

"It *is* true, but it's a stock answer. If I were trying to be flirtatious— and I'm not—I'd say it's because the cello is shaped like a woman."

"But that's still a stock answer."

"Yes."

"It's all right if you don't want to tell me."

"I *do* want to tell you." I cleared my throat and pushed my coffee cup to one side. "I want to tell you that the cello has the most human voice of any instrument—Sir Edward Elgar once told me that. I want to tell you that it reminds me of my mother's singing before she stopped, and my father's humility—or what I remember of it. That when the playing goes well, I can't tell where I end and where the cello begins. But what I most want to tell you—"

A man squeezed past our chairs and Aviva tapped a spoon against the table nervously, waiting for the stranger to pass. Before I could continue, she said, "You're much more talkative when your partner isn't around."

"He has a way of talking for both of us. And he hasn't really been my partner for about eight years."

"He's very charming."

I tried to suppress a twinge of irritation. "What I most want to tell you," I continued, my voice lower, "is that I don't always know *why* I play the cello. I tell myself various reasons, but I don't know whether they're rational, or true. Sometimes I wonder whether we have feelings and then invent reasons to fit them—or have reasons, and then invent the feelings."

Aviva was staring into her cup determinedly. "But you're something of a statesman, aren't you? In public, you seem to know exactly why you do everything you do."

I pressed my fingers against my temples and chose my words carefully. "Yes, that's right. I've managed to give that impression." I tried to laugh. "But—do you know?—I've lost my train of thought. I was really trying to talk about you."

She shifted in her seat.

I persevered, "What I meant to say was—I was attracted to you when we met because you *do* seem to know why you play your instrument."

She bowed her head slightly at the compliment.

"I've seen ambition before, of course, and focus—but rarely have I seen perfect focus without professional ambition. Am I insulting you?"

"No."

"Did I answer your question?"

"A little."

"Will you answer mine?"

She looked up. "Which one—about why I play, or why I turned back from New York?"

"I thought I might get lucky," I said. "I thought one answer might lead to the other."

"I don't think it will. Not today." She squinted out into the fog, which obscured all but the fuzzy white lights of ships docked for the night. "Why is Justo taking so long?"

"Anytime someone recognizes him, he'll stop and chat. It can take him an entire evening to cross a town square, if he's in a good mood."

"Why should he be in a good mood? It seems he has lost his money, like all the Americans."

"He's in a good mood because we met you."

She looked away. "I'd like to say a proper good-bye to him. I'd like to say a proper thanks and good-bye to you both."

"But until then?"

She sighed deeply, set her cup aside, and put her hands in her lap. "I suppose it's easier to tell this kind of story to someone I'll never see again...."

She was born in 1910, she said, to a musical family in an Italian mountain village near Bolzano, on the Adige River, closer to the birthplaces of Handel, Mozart, and Bach than to Rome. Innsbruck was a hundred kilometers away by train, Munich and Salzburg another hundred kilometers beyond to the north and northeast, though she never saw those places as a child. Her family was poor, and poorer yet after her parents died—her father in the war, her mother from tuberculosis a few years later. Unlike most of the other children she knew, she was an only child. She lived alone with her grandmother until the age of thirteen.

That's when the music teacher came—the one who first recognized her talent, and persuaded Nonna to let him show her off, in small recitals in Verona and Brescia and later Bergamo. Aviva wouldn't say his name even now, not because she'd hated him—quite the contrary. He loved music history, and he'd told her stories about all the Italian virtuosi; he took her for carriage rides even when they weren't touring. He backed her up against the wall of the little room in his house where she sometimes slept, when they'd gotten back into town late from a performance, and made charcoal marks on the wall to show how much she'd grown. He held out his hand and pressed it against hers, marveling as her slim fingertips grew beyond his, rising crescents that, with every new half-centimeter, might stretch to reach new positions without shifting. He did not make her feel guilty for growing up, as her grief-stricken and ever-fearful Nonna did. He filled her with hope.

She was fourteen when he took her to Bologna, to perform for a family that was interested in sponsoring her. They left before dawn in a horse-drawn carriage, Aviva peppering him with questions as they bumped along in the dark.

"If they bought me a violin, would it really be mine, or theirs?"

"Theirs. But you'll be the one to play it. It doesn't matter."

"Remember Paganini? He borrowed that violin for a concert and loved it so much he refused to give it back."

"Paganini could get away with such things," he said, but without any severity. She knew he liked to hear her talk about the gaunt maestro, whose impossible-to-play caprices were among her teacher's favorites. And it wasn't just Paganini's music he worshipped, but the man himself. Her teacher had a hundred-year-old snuffbox from Vienna with Paganini's scowling, hollow-cheeked face on the lid, under a thick coat of lacquer.

"Will they send me to a conservatory?"

He squeezed her chin without answering, and it occurred to her that she shouldn't sound so cheerful about being sent away, beyond the reach of his tutelage.

"One more question?"

He yawned—effortfully, theatrically. In truth, he didn't look fatigued at all. One hand was cupped tensely over her knee. His own narrow legs were clenched together, kneecaps tight against the thin shiny cloth of his trousers.

"Go ahead."

"Will they mind that I'm not Christian?"

"We won't mention it."

"And if they find out later?"

But in the end, the question of religion never would even arise. She would play terribly that afternoon. Signor Magione would agree to lend her a slightly better violin and ask to see her again, to discuss her future education, when he visited Bolzano on business in six months' time. Perhaps, he said hopefully, she would have matured a little more by then.

As it turned out, in six months she would have matured too much, and she wouldn't be able to play for him at all.

But all that was still to come. First, her teacher had a stop to make, at a graveyard in Parma that he was raising funds to improve. She knew he was a member of various men's associations and active in all sorts of civic and Church-related causes, and she assumed that he had a personal connection, perhaps family buried there.

The morning still felt like night: A pale moon bulged low on the horizon, the unkempt grass was stiff with frost. The cemetery gate was locked but her teacher drew from his vest pocket his own key, a benefit of his philanthropy. They made their way between the stones. He didn't speak. She searched for his surname among the inscriptions, wanting to be helpful by spotting the correct section first. But he knew where he was going and didn't need her help.

They arrived at another small black picket gate—a separate key, drawn with great ceremony from a separate satin-trimmed pocket. Beyond the gate stood a large marble mausoleum. Four stone steps led to four columns, a pedestal, and the bust of a gaunt-cheeked man. Niccolò Paganini.

"The devil himself," she whispered under her breath, and stooped to read the inscriptions, wondering if it was her comment about the maestro and his violin that had put the idea of coming here in her teacher's head. She turned to thank him and to make her way back down the stairs, but he stood in her path.

"Don't you have family to attend to?" She gestured hopefully to the rows of humbler gravesites surrounding them.

"Only this"—and he forced a smile—"my spiritual family."

She put her hands behind her back and rocked on her heels, looking around the graveyard. She counted the seconds, watching out of the corner of one eye to see if he made a move to pray. But he continued to look straight at her, at the front of her overcoat where the buttons joined. Then he sat down on the topmost step and took a jackknife and an apple from his pocket. She watched as he began to peel it, in a long, unbroken strand.

She turned back to the pedestal. "Why doesn't it say he died in Italy?"

"Because he didn't. You saw more than one date, didn't you?"

She nodded.

"In Nice, as he was dying, he refused the final sacrament, so the Church wouldn't sanction his burial, nor would it allow the local church bells to be rung. So his body was kept unburied for five years. Does that bother you? Here, here." He handed her the peeled apple and put his arm around her shoulder. "Actually, can I tell you something? I've seen part of him, his unburied part, in a jar of formaldehyde. A man in Berlin has it. It's shriveled now, but then whose wouldn't be, after all that time? Given his reputation with the ladies, it's no indication..." And his voice lowered, as if he regretted the turn his story had taken. If his lecture had been designed to comfort or seduce, it was a failure.

Seduce. Yes, somehow she understood—even as her teacher finished describing the long-delayed burial, the subsequent disinterment and transfer of the remains, and the second, more elaborate burial he had subsidized, along with a group of others who worshipped the Faustian genius—that he had brought her here to seduce her.

The details didn't matter, and she had tried to forget them as best she could. The marble was slippery and cold. The stairs were narrow. Her head bumped against the pedestal seven or eight times, and she had a staggering headache by the time they reached Bologna. Back in the carriage, he had offered her his handkerchief, but she had looked at it blankly until he gestured to her skirt. Then he realized he had forgotten to lock the gate.

By the time he returned, she had her eyes shut, feigning sleep. She could feel his eyes on her as the sun rose, burning off the morning mist, but she didn't stir, even when her shoulder and neck screamed with stiffness, even when he eased her hand into his lap. Now the sickening effort of her charade was as hard to shake than the memory of what he had done at the cemetery.

He made no attempt to repeat the event. For the next few months he returned to his usual kind self, attentive during her lessons, encouraging despite her poor performance for the Magiones, ready to correct a tensed shoulder with a paternal hand or an awkward angle with a tap on the wrist. Then—overnight—he stopped touching her, stopped even looking at her. It took another month before Aviva grasped what had happened, and in another month Nonna understood, too.

The teacher took back the Magione violin.

Two weeks later, he returned, told her to pack, and took her away. He brought her to a convent even farther into the mountains, near the Austrian border. He explained that she would be allowed to live there, alongside some other unfortunate girls. When she started to cry, he reminded her that music thrived in surprising places—consider the Conservatorio della Pietà, the Venetian orphanage where Antonio Vivaldi, the red-haired priest-composer, had led an outstanding choir and orchestra of foundling girls.

"Does this place have an orchestra?" she said, looking up at the crumbling walls surrounding by treeless, boulder-dotted grounds.

"No."

Before he left, he whispered, "If it's a boy, name him Niccolò"—the only time he'd acknowledged her condition.

She spat on the ground between them.

A foghorn blasted in the distance.

"Ever since, I've hated Paganini. Whenever I hear those arrogant caprices, I think of him trying to stick his inhuman fingers where they don't belong—if you'll forgive me for the image."

I swallowed the last sip of my cold coffee.

"Please," she said. "You're not saying anything."

"It's a terrible story."

"You're shocked by it."

"I suppose I am."

"You don't believe in honesty?" She leaned back in her chair.

"No—I do." I paused and took a deep breath. "It reminds me of something that happened to someone very dear to me. Something I've never been able to put out of my mind."

She studied me, teetering between defensiveness and trust. "I'm not claiming it's an uncommon experience. I don't think about it most of the time. I wouldn't think of it all, except..."

She trailed off, looking over my shoulder. Al-Cerraz was standing at the far side of the café, waving to us from the counter.

"I suppose nothing can be done."

"In most cases, no. In mine—possibly."

She seemed to be waiting for me to say something, to ask something. Perhaps she was only deciding how much more to divulge.

"Is there some way I can help?"

"No," she said flatly. Without turning, I could sense Al-Cerraz's approach in her changed expression, her squared shoulders and forced smile. "It's something I need to take care of. Maybe immediately, maybe in a year. In any case, it is the reason I couldn't stay in America, after all. I'm sorry I haven't answered your questions very well."

And then he was with us: a hand on my shoulder, a puddle of coffee on the table as he bumped it, the strong smell of lavender, the booming voice that drowned out the last of Aviva's words.

"It's true!" he bellowed. "According to my broker, I don't have a cent!" He squeezed Aviva's arm. "At least you have the fifty dollars that matron on the steamer gave you."

Aviva nodded politely, switching from German to less-confident English. "It's better than nothing."

"That settles it, then," Al-Cerraz beamed. "We'll be poor together!"

I was not poor; I had more work than I could manage. Just before my American trip, my record label, Reixos, had asked me to do a fourth recording. They had suggested an accompanist for the project, but it wasn't anyone I admired. I didn't expect the record to sound half as good as some of my concerts—certainly not as good as the two concerts on the ship.

I said to Al-Cerraz, "An idea has just come to me. Would you consider recording?"

I would like to say, all these years later, that I was trying to help him financially, or that I was making amends for the Burgos concert. But I was only acting on impulse, moved by the memory of how we had sounded and the ease of our last week together. And there was another force acting upon me as well.

I added, "Aviva could record with us. At last we'd have a trio."

"You can't just decide that, can you?" Aviva asked. "Doesn't your record company decide these things?"

"Reixos will be thrilled."

"Biber will be even more thrilled," Al-Cerraz interjected. "We'll have to let him know where we want to play after the recording comes out."

I stammered, "Yes, I suppose we will. But I do have my own manager now."

"I can't let mine go," Al-Cerraz explained to Aviva, ignoring me. "Lifetime contract."

"And I have a secretary," I said. "I should try to reach her."

"A secretary?" Al-Cerraz howled. "Don't answer all those letters—that's what I say. Let the manager handle the bookings and ignore the rest. Inaccessibility is one of the keys to long-lasting fame."

"You misunderstand me," I said. "I haven't tried to become more famous."

"Oh, of course not..."

Aviva glanced from one of us to the other, following our rising voices and sharpening tones. We were only warming up, but I suppose she'd never lived with other musicians. She'd simply have to adapt, I found myself thinking—and realized, in that thought, how quickly I was accepting this new arrangement, how easily I could envision the coming year: first a recording, and then a short tour in Spain, perhaps another across Europe.

With far less certainty, Aviva stood, smiled, and began to thread her way between our piles of mismatched cases and trunks. "Let me think about this. While you're both here to guard the castle, I'll go clean myself."

"Fort," I corrected her automatically. "And 'freshen up,' in English. Never mind. Take your time."

When she was out of earshot, Al-Cerraz eyed me gleefully. "Well, this is a big risk for you. Touring with someone new is one thing—but recording? Right away? You won't shake her off too easily after that."

"Since when do I shake people off?"

He cocked his head, studying me, then chose his words with uncharacteristic caution. "We don't know much about her."

I knew something about her, more than he did. But I knew I couldn't share it, because it was the only advantage I held over him. If he knew what I knew, if he spoke better German or Italian, they would be inseparable within days—I was sure of it. With luck, I would always know her a little better. With luck, he would keep his hands to himself.

"I'll say this politely," he tried. "You realize there are far easier ways to get a date."

"A date?" I laughed. "This isn't about a date."

"Then what is it about?"

"It's about music, of course. We sounded brilliant together on the ship, all three of us. If you don't agree one hundred percent, then say it—but I know you agree. I know you heard it. She's everything we wanted in a trio partner ten years ago: fresh, energetic, appreciative, skilled but malleable—"

"You're doing this for music," he repeated, testing me. "When have you ever done anything just for the music?"

I might have argued with him then, but I saw a shadow pass over his face—emotion dangerously near the surface. I knew then that the Burgos concert was still with us, that he still held me responsible for damaging his composing career. He wanted to forgive, I believed he did. And even more, he wanted to move ahead, to perform and to be inspired.

"I left behind so much of my sheet music in Germany," Aviva lamented one day later that autumn, at an outdoor café in Segovia.

The three of us had a day to spend in the city, before heading southeast to a recording studio in Madrid. My label had agreed we should record the Dvořák Piano Trios, which we'd been rehearsing for most of November. We'd already accepted some engagements following the recording sessions, but we knew we'd want a broader repertoire for those concerts.

"Eventually, we'll all need more trio music," Al-Cerraz told her. "I know the perfect place. But first"—he gestured across the street to a woman's dress shop—"take as much of the day as you need. I don't mind giving you a loan until Reixos pays us."

I said, "He means that *I* don't mind giving you a loan."

Al-Cerraz continued, "Feliu and I will pick up some scores and meet you later, for lunch."

She shot him a dark look.

He pressed some money into her hand, oblivious. "Don't skimp."

Al-Cerraz and I were finishing our second coffees with a city map laid out between us when Aviva emerged from the shop and crossed the street toward us, carrying two large bags.

"Done," she said, collapsing into a chair. "Now, there's a Brahms Trio in C Minor I haven't performed; that should be easy to find."

Al-Cerraz stared at her bags.

She tucked them farther under the table. "What about the León concert in December? Do we pair the 'Dumky' with another Dvořák piece, or do something entirely different?"

"Something different," I started to say, then stopped, watching Al-Cerraz lower his head, with theatrical effort, under the table. Snagging the handles with his pinkies, he pulled the shopping bags back into view.

"Did you actually try them on, or just point to the window display?"

Aviva extracted a white box, opened it, lifted a red belted dress to her chest, and then stuffed it back into the bag. "Two others," she said. "Same style, different colors."

Al-Cerraz pinned me with an imploring stare. When I didn't pick up the argument, he persevered solo. "No alterations required?"

"The belt has notches," she said flatly.

"Length?"

"They don't drag on the ground, if that's what you mean." Aviva turned the city map around so that she could study it. Al-Cerraz cleared his throat heavily, but she ignored him. Without looking up, she said, "Now where is that music shop?"

I knew there was no point in telling Al-Cerraz that Aviva wasn't a female Gauthier. He could see for himself that she had no difficulty standing up to him.

At least he wasn't a chauvinist. He had paid as much attention to his own appearance in the last few weeks as he paid to hers. Our very first week off the steamer from America, he had started dyeing his silver-streaked hair, so that now the dyed patches gleamed blue-black in the sun. The change was so transparent, it made me laugh. But I dared not tease him about it. Al-Cerraz *did* look younger, and in the months that followed, he seemed healthier as well. He ate better, complained less of his digestive problems, and retired early, with notebook in hand. Privately, discreetly, and without a patron dominating his efforts, he was composing again.

Onstage, Aviva had a contrary style that could not help but attract attention, even while her mannerisms defied charm. She was about ten centimeters taller than I was, and rarely wore high heels. Playing a duet with Al-Cerraz, she stood near the piano, in a surprisingly wide-footed position, as if she were preparing to push a heavy cart through a muddy, rutted field. In trio, she typically sat, but even sitting, she managed an athletic stance, with feet squarely planted, spine straight, and head forward, as if ready to leap off her chair at any moment.

That sense of impending flight mirrored the hesitation she'd displayed on the steamer. Always, there was the sense that she was saving herself for something—or someone; that any given concert, no matter how dutifully performed, was merely a way station. And yet she never said so. Like most prodigies, she was still eager to please—if not the audience, whom she barely noticed, then at least Al-Cerraz and me.

Most of the violinists I'd known saved their virtuosic displays, their enthusiasm and energy and most focused vibrato for the thin, high strings—the high register where the violin soars and sings, beyond the easy pitch range of viola or cello. Aviva tended to play high notes starkly—brushed pewter instead of silver, a beautiful effect. But she saved her best artistic effects for the low register. Plunging in, she planted her feet, bowed her head, closed her eyes, executed her widest vibrato, her most expressive bowing. Her facial features and thin arms radiated fragility, but her posture and her sound could only make one think of hard physical labor. Once, watching her play out of the corner of my eye, I was struck by the image of someone sinking into deep gray-green water, not thrashing but pushing forcefully and purposefully against the water's weight, motion slowed by the chill. In that cold darkness she seemed most focused and at peace.

Violin concertos would have been a perfect vehicle for her, if she'd ever wanted to solo with an orchestra instead of playing in a trio. But as much as she enjoyed hearing other solo violinists perform, she claimed to have no interest in that sort of debut.

Once in Toledo, during our first winter's tour, I invited Aviva to a Sibelius concert.

"Is Justo coming along?"

"I couldn't get more than two seats together." I was a terrible liar.

She looked concerned, on the verge of refusing.

"You know how he is," I added quickly. "It's a concerto with orchestra. No starring role for a pianist. Besides, how could he sit still when he isn't the one playing?"

Aviva sat during the Sibelius concert with her eyes closed, her hands folded in her lap, while the soloist on stage played high, flutelike passages so soft one could just barely hear them above the orchestration. The effect produced was one of Scandinavian mist, weaving a spell of mass hypnosis.

I took the opportunity to study her profile from the corner of my eye, daring myself to move my arm closer to hers, to let our shoulders touch, to reach out for her hand—adolescent challenges, at which I failed completely.

During the intermission, a man behind us complained that the solo violinist was too weak to play with a full orchestra. "It's nothing like the record," he complained to the lady on his arm. "It's as if the sound was turned off. At the end, the bow was still on the string but I couldn't hear anything."

He carried on about the acoustics, the ticket prices, and the stature of the soloist until Aviva finally turned and said, "Perhaps he didn't care if you could hear every measure. Perhaps he was playing those last few notes just for himself."

"That's ridiculous," the man scowled. "It wasn't played correctly at all. I've got the record at home—"

"Then go home and listen to it," Aviva said, leading me away to the bar, where she paid for two vodka shots with her own money, and handed one to me. When the end-of-intermission bell rang and I hadn't so much as sipped mine, Aviva lifted it lightly out of my fingers and downed it herself, in one easy swallow.

"Sorry," I said. "I was thinking about something."

"Not about that amateur critic, I hope. We can change seats, if we need to."

But no, I'd been thinking about what she had said about the Sibelius soloist—that he might have been playing for himself. Aviva herself often seemed to play that way. And yet her playing did not seem to fulfill or energize her—if anything, she looked more drained as the music proceeded. At the beginning of a concert, Al-Cerraz was tense and desperate for silence; at the end he was gregarious and hardly willing to leave the stage. Aviva was the opposite. She began each concert relaxed and ready and ended limp, vanishing from the stage before I had stepped out from behind my cello. Her rapid exit did not seem calculated, but it did have a predictable effect: The audience cheered even more loudly, insistent on encores, refusing to let her disappear.

Aside from our musical performances, I remember that first tour as a series of images: Al-Cerraz down on his knees on a black stage floor, behind the curtain, not scrubbing Aviva's elbows this time, not proposing to her (as I'd thought at first, with my heart in my throat), but retrieving a lost earring. I nearly collided with him as he knelt there, the glittering rhinestone stud cradled within the thick crease of his palm. I was used to seeing him stand next to women on tiptoe, all the better to peer down their décolletage. I'd never seen him on his knees before a woman, and certainly not twice in a span of six months.

It wasn't that he treated Aviva as a special object of romantic esteem. He continued to treat all women with equal gallantry, opening cab doors and surrendering preferred café tables from one city to the next. But only Aviva merited his tender, quieter gestures. The way he pushed her hair out of the way, off her forehead. The time, standing on a train platform together, that he reached a thumb behind her ear to rub away a smudge while Aviva stared off into the distance, unbothered by his familiarity. Perhaps all I was seeing in him was the development of a brotherly demeanor, after a lifetime of acting like a spoiled only child. Or perhaps that was wishful thinking. Nothing had happened between them, but that didn't mean it would never happen. Perhaps I was living on borrowed time.

Sometimes I played worse when I played with Aviva, distracted by thoughts of what we'd all do after the concert, or the next day. Perhaps we would rent a car and tour the countryside. Perhaps we had planned dinner at an elegant restaurant, where I hoped through some alchemy of the soul that I would find a way to become more noticeable than Al-

Cerraz, more gay, taller in my chair, more comfortable in my clothes, in my own skin. But usually, when the time came, the alchemy failed. Listening to Al-Cerraz charming Aviva across the table—charming everyone in the room, even the waiter bringing us champagne courtesy of some music fan several tables away—I would slip my hands into my jacket pockets and remember one of my earliest selves: the boy who had chocolate at his fingertips but refused to eat it, refused even to touch it.

Didn't it make sense to wait, to be restrained? Hadn't Aviva herself said she needed to address her past first—perhaps immediately, perhaps within a year—to make things right? I had known other women like her—women like my mother and like the Queen, who had been pushed hard by men, or by circumstance. The more I thought of her that way, the farther I nudged her out of my own grasp, on a pedestal raised so high that even a taller man would have had trouble reaching her.

And if I occasionally played worse because of Aviva, many more times I played better. Once I stepped onto a stage to play Saint-Saëns's "The Swan," and Al-Cerraz, catching my jaded expression at the prospect of playing that romantic, shopworn piece yet again, mouthed, "Think of her." I did. I pictured Aviva as she was at that moment, waiting for her entrance backstage, pinning up her hair as a stagehand finished buttoning up the back of her new custom-made gown. (At Al-Cerraz's insistence, she had advanced finally beyond cheap ready-made dresses.) I let my bow trace that image of her, imagining her long waist, the tiny white cloth-covered buttons between her shoulder blades, the line of her collar, her bare neck. I took my time with the duet's sliding notes, my wrist flexing to connect them smoothly, to blend up-bow into down-bow. Gradually I let my vibrato widen, until I sketched the thin final note and let it fade, as gracefully as a swan's silver wake. Applause rolled across the room in undulating waves; tremendous applause. It was accompanied by that rarer thing, a quick approving nod of Al-Cerraz's head from behind the grand piano's open lid. Afterward, he whispered to me, "I *knew* you'd learn to play that piece, sometime or other."

By the spring of 1930, Biber was forwarding various new requests for our busy trio: the chance to perform on radio with the BBC Symphony Orchestra; a fall music festival in Paris. Aviva reminded us that she'd be returning to Germany for the school year. As a trio, we had to decline any appearance that couldn't wait until the following summer. Our lack of availability fanned the flames of interest. How could we decline all performances in fall and winter, the height of the music season?

A Madrid magazine featured Aviva, alone, on the cover: *La Mujer Misteriosa*. The mysterious woman. The article inside speculated about Aviva's sudden emergence in the world of classical music. An enterprising reporter had tracked her earliest recital notices in some small-town Italian newspapers and found glowing descriptions of her in a Munich society column. It was hinted that she had performed privately for a prominent fascist.

Al-Cerraz had picked up a copy of the magazine at a train station, and now he passed it to me in the parlor car. "I bought it without even looking! If I'd noticed, I would have taken several copies."

I held it out to Aviva, but she lit a cigarette and looked away.

"Our talented girl, playing for Hitler," Al-Cerraz fawned, but Aviva did not laugh. Instead she said stiffly, "Nowhere does it mention Hitler."

"She's right," I said. "I hear Mussolini loves the violin."

This time Aviva said nothing.

"I'm only joking, Aviva."

Al-Cerraz persevered: "Mussolini?"

Still she didn't answer.

"Then it's true! Was this with an orchestra?" Al-Cerraz asked.

"Nothing so formal."

"Oh, come now—*please!*"

"I was eighteen," she relented. "It was an audition—something a friend had arranged, which I couldn't cancel without offense. One half hour."

We questioned her more closely on the timing, trying to stitch together what little we understood about the year before we'd met her, when we knew she had moved from Italy to Germany.

"He has the most amazing head—like one of those enormous Toltec stone heads they find in the Mayan jungle," Al-Cerraz said. "That left hand he keeps on his hip must be some kind of structural support, to keep his top half from tipping."

"Tell us about the music," I said.

She sighed through a cloud of smoke. "I was on my own for the first time, after leaving the convent. He was looking for a nanny. A nanny with musical talent. His little boy, Romano—just a baby, then, very sweet—showed a fascination with music, especially piano music. But you know, that was just a pretext. Il Duce wanted a private violin teacher in the house, for his own pleasure, someone on call."

"So then he does play the violin?"

"Absolutely. He's known for it, just as he's known for reading a canto of Dante every morning—a champion of Italian culture. With the violin, it's fifteen to twenty minutes, every day, or—" She paused.

"Or...?"

"Well, all right. I'll tell you one small thing, then we change the subject. Do you promise?"

Al-Cerraz wouldn't promise. I glowered at him threateningly.

Finally she relaxed long enough to sketch the scene for us: the official residence of Villa Torlonia, the music room with its gramophone and stacks of Verdi and Puccini records. Mussolini closed the curtains and locked the door whenever he practiced, and made it clear that no one was allowed to disturb him for that sacred twenty minutes when he relinquished the nation's helm and lost himself to music.

"But how did he play?" Al-Cerraz demanded.

"I don't know," she said.

"What do you mean, you don't know?"

"He put on a record—a record of a solo violin, playing études. He held the violin to his chin for a moment or two—"

"That chin! I'm surprised he didn't crush the violin!" Al-Cerraz interjected. I shushed him.

"—as if he were producing the sound on the record," she continued, undaunted. "But then he set it down. And began flirting."

"Aha!" Al-Cerraz laughed. "So it's a ploy. He doesn't play."

"No—he does. My friend who arranged the meeting, another violinist, once played a duet with him. Mussolini plays when he likes. But he also has an insistent wife, many children and counselors and, more to the point, a long line of mistresses coming and going to that music room all the time, and it seems that twenty uninterrupted minutes is just the requisite interval."

Al-Cerraz was delighted.

"Anyway," she continued, "I'd had enough life experience by that point to communicate my...lack of interest. I did play the violin for a few minutes, at the end, but I had decided already I wasn't interested in the position. There was no need to make use of the defensive weapons I'd brought for the occasion."

"Weapons?" I asked.

"Stiletto heels. You know I don't like to wear anything but flat shoes, but this was a special occasion."

"*Brava!*" Al-Cerraz said.

But I was bothered. "You didn't mind performing for a dictator?"

"I wasn't interested in the position."

"But even in that half hour; you weren't sickened to face that man?"

"Friends," Al-Cerraz interrupted. "Please."

"He is the leader of Italy. Anyone with that kind of power has some skeletons, I'm sure. But I'm sorry—Il Duce has been Il Duce for all of my adult life."

"This is a man who murdered people from the very beginning— his socialist opponent in 1924, just for starters."

"I was fourteen years old in 1924," Aviva said. "It wasn't a good year for me either, you know."

"Skeletons don't begin to describe what are in that man's closet— fresh corpses, more like." My voice sharpened. "Every time that man makes a political decision, someone dies."

"I think *I* would have preferred to die that year, myself."

"Friends," Al-Cerraz interrupted, "what are you talking about? Can't you hear yourselves? You're talking right past each other."

I persevered, "You're aware of these things, Aviva. How could you not be, when you plan to go to Germany and perform with Kurt Weill and Bertolt Brecht? They're just the sort of musicians the Nazis hate."

"The Nazis interrupt theatrical performances. With noise, with threats, with stink bombs—even with chamber pots. If they actually want to attend our performances, I won't deny them for a moment. It might do them some good."

"You don't draw a line about whom you would play for?"

"Anyone," Aviva said. "Or no one—it's all the same. It's not any one particular audience I am trying to reach. I have my own reasons."

Al-Cerraz gave up on stopping the conversation and tried to steer it away from my grasp instead. "I think," he said, nodding genially, "that I would have to convince myself first that the person wasn't a monster. I'd have to see his human side—everyone has a human side."

"Nonsense," I said, but already I felt terrible. I had not meant to start an argument with Aviva.

She stood. "Gentlemen, you've tired me, and the day has just begun. I'll be resting in my berth."

"If she only ate a little more," Al-Cerraz mumbled after she left, nibbling the leftover crusts on her lunch plate. "What did she mean, about wanting to die in 1924?"

That week, after a concert in Lisbon, the three of us went to a night-club. We were tired, and we had yet another train to catch the next day, but a local patron of the arts had invited us, and we felt it necessary to accept. To a fast-paced jazz band, Aviva danced with the patron, a Sen-hor Medina. Then she danced with Al-Cerraz, as Medina hovered nearby, ready to grab her hand again.

Instead, she took the seat next to me, her cheeks flushed, her collar-bone shining. She shouted, "I suppose you hate this music."

I shouted back, "No, I don't hate it."

"Well, then?"

I laughed. "You're expecting me to dance? I've finally worked my way up to waltzes, but any faster and I'd never walk again."

"What?"

"Never mind," I shouted, smiling, indicating the music.

She moved closer, so that she could speak directly into my ear.

"Does it hurt?"

"What?" I said, though I had heard her.

She leaned closer. Her hair touched my cheek. "Your hip. Does it hurt?"

"Sometimes," I said. From the first time we met, Aviva had been more sympathetic about my infirmity than Al-Cerraz had ever been. Since she had joined us, there had been no more mad dashes to concert halls, no bullying to walk farther or carry more, no forced swims. She had accommodated me without speaking, without even asking—until now.

"Have you seen a doctor?"

My forced laugh was swallowed by the roar of the nightclub. "It happened at birth. There's no point." I turned back, with my ear next to her lips, to hear her reply.

She cupped her hand against my cheek and leaned close. "Why are you punishing yourself?"

I did not move. I did not dare even turn, because then she might move away, or worse, I might see that what I had heard as tender sympathy was really only curiosity.

"You don't have to live with pain." Her hand was still against my face.

When she didn't say anything else, I reached up and took her hand, holding it there as long as I dared.

She whispered something. It sounded like: "Come outside with me." But I didn't want to move, didn't want to gamble this moment for another that was less certain. And all the while, my eyes tracked across the table, counting the emptied glasses, feeling my heart thud in my chest.

"I won't ask again," she said.

Just then, the song ended and Al-Cerraz collapsed back into his seat, with Medina not far behind. "Won't ask what?" our Portuguese host asked, panting and smiling.

Aviva pulled her hand away from me and sat up straighter. "For another drink, of course."

"Shame on you," Al-Cerraz said, hitting my back. "Letting this gorgeous girl get thirsty while we were away."

"Interesting," Dr. Gindl said. "But not unusual."

This was two weeks later, in Switzerland. I had laughed at Al-Cerraz for dyeing his hair to impress Aviva. But I was trying to impress her, too. I intended to follow her advice. And perhaps I had even higher aims. Perhaps I imagined that I might find a way to dance with her someday.

I told the doctor, "It doesn't give me too much pain, except when—"

"It will," he interrupted. "You're thirty-seven, you said?"

"—an occasional twinge…"

"In the forties, the arthritis tends to accelerate. You bear weight on your left side, do you? The pain may become considerable. Later on, you'll want a cane."

Up until now, I had been smiling, attempting to mask the discomfort I felt as the doctor manipulated my leg.

"Dysplasia of the hip," he said, lifting and rotating my thigh one last time, sending a hot ache into my groin. "The head of the thighbone doesn't sit properly in the socket of the pelvis. Go ahead, you can sit up now."

I did so, slowly.

"A difficult breech birth?" he asked. Then, seeing my incomprehension: "Rear end first?"

I nodded.

"Fairly common result. Caught just after birth, it could have been splinted."

He kept a hand on my knee. "Anyone discuss childhood surgery with your parents?"

I shook my head.

"Well, that's fairly recent. Special footwear is important—I'm sure you've experimented with that. Exercises are essential."

"It does fatigue easily."

"All muscles fatigue—and then they become stronger. You're from the countryside? I trust your parents kept you busy as a youth—running, carrying, working that leg. There's nothing to be gained from letting the muscles wither. A century ago, people were more ignorant. They would have kept you as inactive as possible—and made a weakling of you in the process."

When I turned away from him, he said, "I do hope it hasn't hindered you."

My jacket was across the room. I climbed down from the examination table and walked toward it, as evenly as I could, ignoring the pain lingering from the manipulation. I was almost out the door when he said, "For the pain, you could try this." He handed me a small brown vial from his bag.

I read the label. "Isn't this very strong?"

"It does the job."

"I don't think I'd feel comfortable taking it. My hip isn't that bad."

"It lasts only four to six hours. Some patients require it to sleep. There's nothing shameful in it."

I was thinking of the people I admired who had accepted discomfort and surrender in their lives; but I was also thinking how their hopelessness had tainted my own life. I felt ready to move beyond those memories. Aviva had said pain wasn't necessary. I wanted to believe her.

Aviva's twentieth birthday, later that spring, coincided with a concert in Milan. We bought her a set of matching luggage, to replace the small wicker valise that Al-Cerraz had, at first glance, mistaken for a lunch box. At a restaurant following the performance, we toasted her health and Justo gave her a pair of fine leather gloves—a sneaky addendum to the gift we'd bought together, allowing me no time to match it.

Later that night, after Aviva and Al-Cerraz had returned to their own hotel rooms, I wandered off by myself and found my way to a bordello where, after the requisite services had been rendered, I spent some part of the predawn paying extra for my buxom, yawning bedmate to keep me company. She darned socks while I rambled on about birthdays and age differences and the proper age for marrying.

"Twenty isn't so young," the not-so-young damsel informed me.

"Soon she'll be gone. When I see her next, she'll be twenty-one." I couldn't bear to say Aviva's name aloud in this disreputable house.

"Let her out of your sight that long, and for certain she'll be married when you see her again."

"No. She's a musician—an entertainer."

"I'm an entertainer," the woman said. "I'm married."

I must have glanced nervously toward the door. She laughed. "You met him already when you came in. He took your money."

"Besides," I said, searching the rumpled bedclothes for my trousers, "she's not likely to find a husband. There are complicating factors."

"Previously married?"

"No."

"Ruined reputation? Non-Catholic?"

I stared at her. "Both. How did you know?"

She laughed. "What other problems would a pretty young woman have in Spain?"

"She isn't Spanish. She'll be living in Germany soon."

"Well, then." She plumped the pillows behind her and resumed her darning.

"What does that mean?"

"In my better days, I spent a summer in Berlin. I worked in a *variété*—you know, a cabaret? We had every type there: unmarried mothers, gypsies, Jews, an American Negro—God he was beautiful, as shiny purple as an eggplant. It was a very open-minded place. More open-minded than here. I don't know why I left." She frowned at the door, then turned the same scowl on me. "She won't be judged harshly, if that's what you're counting on." *Fool*, she wanted to add—I'm sure of it.

She asked, "What line of work do you do, anyway?"

"What do you think I do?"

A tasseled red scarf covered the bedside lamp, infusing the room with a pink glow. She tugged it off suddenly, and blinding white, stomach-turning light flooded the room. From her regally supine position, she squinted at me, as if seeing me for the first time.

"Some kind of bureaucrat, I'd say. Or a plumber. Those little hard spots at the end of your fingertips remind me of the lines at the end of pipes—what are they called?"

"The threads."

"Right. See?"

I didn't tell her she was wrong. But the rest of what she'd said stayed with me. I hadn't meant to rely on Aviva's past or her identity to improve my own chances. I wasn't counting on anything. One of the things that attracted me to her was her determination, her clear sense of purpose—a purpose that was leading her away from Al-Cerraz and me.

A few days later, we took her to the train station. Weill had asked Aviva to join the school-music program rehearsals for *Der Jasager,* a short children's opera he'd written, beginning in May. She promised to return to Spain during the first long school break, the following summer.

As we stood on the platform, waiting for the train, Al-Cerraz asked her, "You're not fond of this fellow, are you?" Damn Justo for his new-found paternalism; bless him for his inappropriate curiosity. It was, of course, what I wanted to know, too. Weill was formidable: only thirty, successful, evidently brilliant, and Jewish.

"Herr Weill?" She screwed up her face. "He's married to Lotte Lenya, the beautiful actress! I love his violin concerto and all his theater pieces. But—with that cue-ball head? Those glasses? The way he sprays spittle when a musician misses the pickup? Sorry—no."

Which meant that I still had a chance.

I felt less secure a moment later, when Al-Cerraz said, "But you know—I'd like to see this 'school opera.' Why not? I'll come along for a few days, if it's the same to you."

I swiveled toward Aviva, studying her face for ambivalence, so that I'd have a reason to talk Al-Cerraz out of his plan. But she was digging in her handbag, seemingly unbothered by the notion of sudden company.

"We've been together for half a year," I ventured. "A break might be good for all of us, artistically speaking. Absence makes the heart grow fonder, don't you think?"

Al-Cerraz said, "No one's making you come along."

The train blew into the station, rattling our platform. Passengers crowded around the doors immediately, pushing past us with their bags.

"Our luggage is back at the hotel," I reminded Al-Cerraz.

"You didn't think I'd escort her at this very moment, did you?" But I could see him warming to the idea. He smiled. "Why not? I can buy a toothbrush anywhere. Maybe that composer friend of hers will lend me a nightshirt. If I walk around in his clothes, perhaps his success will rub off on me."

Aviva was smiling, too, tickled by Al-Cerraz's sudden eagerness, or perhaps by my discomfort. She shook my hand coolly, then said to Al-Cerraz, "I'll wait for you onboard."

He waved and started walking toward the ticket window, talking to me over his shoulder. "Just tell the hotel to hold my bags. Three or four days should do it. It's a shame to come back at all—maybe you could have them forward the bags directly to Spain."

"I'm not your luggage handler," I said to his back, but he was busy talking with the ticket seller. "And I'm not your chaperon, either. I won't feel pressured to come along, just to keep you out of trouble."

He finished his business at the window, thanked the ticket seller grandly, and then turned around. "Keep *me* out of trouble? Why would I ever want you to do that?"

CHAPTER

~ 19 ~

"This deserves celebrating," Aviva said when she saw me on the train, and began rummaging in her purse again until she pulled out a flask. She sent Al-Cerraz to the dining car to fetch three teacups while I basked in her festive mood. When he returned, she poured a healthy dram of amber liquid into each and held hers aloft. "To Feliu's first spontaneous act!"

I hesitated, stung by the caustic edge to her tone, which undermined the brief elation I'd felt at her evident pleasure upon seeing me. After a few minutes, Al-Cerraz said, "I'll finish that if you don't." With effort, I drained the cup, feeling the burning in my throat turn to warmth.

"It's not my first spontaneous act, by the way." I patted my chest.

This only made Aviva laugh. She dribbled more liquid into our cups and toasted me: "To Feliu's second spontaneous act!"

When Al-Cerraz set down his empty cup and looked my way, I drank again, quickly.

"I had a dog like that, when I was a kid," he said. "A skinny mutt. Almost hairless. His ribs stuck out so far that if you rubbed a wooden spoon against his side, you got a washboard sound. He was a living instrument. We were terrible to him."

Aviva was fumbling through her purse again, not listening.

Al-Cerraz looked directly at me, "He wouldn't finish the food in his bowl, but if you went near it, if you shook the bowl"—here he grabbed my arm playfully—"then he'd nod his head as if he were waking up out of a daze. He'd start growling at us. Then he'd start eating. He seemed not to know he was hungry unless he thought you were hungry."

Aviva pushed to her feet unsteadily. "That's terrible, teasing a sweet dog."

We watched her struggle with the compartment latch and then catch her low heel on the threshold of the doorway. She freed it, regained her balance, and stepped into the hallway, en route to the ladies' room.

Al-Cerraz reached out a hand to pull the door shut again. He leaned toward me, holding my attention with a meaningful look. "The silly dog didn't know he was hungry unless he thought *you* were."

"Yes, you said that."

"He was kind of a runt. I guess he was lucky we'd taken him in because he didn't have much of a survivor's instinct. We had to teach him to fight for what he wanted."

I lifted Aviva's flask off the seat where she'd left it, shook it, and confirmed, gratefully, that it was empty. "You seem to think this anecdote is an excellent metaphor for something. But I'm a little more interested in our friend's welfare. For someone who was eager to start her new job in Berlin, she seems nervous."

He clenched his eyes shut, exasperated, but he didn't pursue his topic. "Well, a new job can make a person nervous."

We stared out the train windows, waiting for Aviva to return. "There is someone waiting for her in Germany," I said after a while. "Someone besides Weill and the school-opera people."

"Yes?" I had his full attention now.

"There must be a good reason why she turned back from America, a reason she's never told us completely."

"Completely?"

"Something she doesn't want to talk about."

"I think you might be right," he said slowly.

"We shouldn't be waiting for some tabloid magazine to tell us all her secrets."

"Right again."

"So why haven't you asked her? You're not afraid to say anything."

"Because she trusts you, Feliu."

I was about to protest, but he interrupted. "She adores me. But my dearest, thick-skulled partner, she trusts *you*. Find out who she is and what she's hiding, before we lose her again."

I'd traveled to Berlin a number of times in the last decade. Even as the Great War receded into history, the city retained its ravaged appearance. Postwar development meant more smokestacks and blocky tenements, iron railings and chain-link fences, sober flat-topped buildings meant to inspire city dwellers toward modernity. When I called it ugly, Aviva disagreed. She said she found it refreshing to be somewhere so clearly on the way to becoming something else.

"But what is it becoming?" I asked, looking out the window at the gray city outskirts.

Aviva had been told to come to the apartment of a woman named Frau Zemmler, who was involved with the school-opera project. Al-Cerraz and I checked into a guesthouse on a residential street in the Bayerische Viertel, or Bavarian Quarter. We agreed to rendezvous the next day at the theater where Aviva would be meeting Weill, Brecht, and their young students.

When we showed up late the next morning, the rehearsal was already under way. A man with round wire-rimmed eyeglasses and a polka-dotted tie—that would be Weill—sat in the front row. He called out lines and directions toward the stage, where a dozen adolescent musicians stood or sat, most of them in shorts or knee-high skirts and

identical white school blouses, instruments on their laps, thin legs swinging, restless hands scratching scalps or twisting braids around fingers.

Three seats down from Weill, Aviva studied the score in her hands,
pointing out a line to Bertolt Brecht, instantly recognizable in his
slouchy leather jacket.

Aviva was the first violinist and concertmaster, and I understood
why Weill had chosen her for that position. She was as talented as any
young touring soloist, but without a soloist's pretensions. She would
inspire the other musicians and set a high standard without becoming a
prima donna. She was only a few years older than the youngest company musician, but could discuss everything from orchestration to
adolescent discipline with Brecht, Weill, and Frau Zemmler, the brown-
suited chaperone in charge of feeding and tending the troupe.

Aviva saw us enter the theater and lifted a hand to indicate Weill,
who turned and nodded curtly. Brecht touched his hatless forehead,
taking advantage of the gesture to scratch discreetly at the edge of his
crew cut. Visitors to the theater made them nervous. The Brown Shirts
had made a mess of their last collaboration, *Mahoganny*, at its premiere
in Leipzig, and again the previous month, when Party members in the
opening night audience of a new production at the Frankfurt Opera
made so much noise that one could barely hear the singers onstage. The
Nazis called all of Weill's work "degenerate," but they hadn't yet made
a move to disrupt *Der Jasager*.

I took a seat a few rows behind them. Al-Cerraz scuttled to the side
of the stage and returned with a score and a program explaining the
opera.

The program informed us that *Der Jasager* was based on the
fourteenth-century Japanese Noh play, *Taniko*. In Brecht's version, a
group of students undertakes a perilous mountain trek in order to visit
an esteemed scholar. A younger student begs to go with them, in order
to obtain medicine for his sick mother. The teacher-guide acquiesces,

but not before warning the boy of an ancient custom: Anyone who can't keep up—who endangers the group by faltering—must be sacrificed.

Al-Cerraz snorted under his breath. "Am I reading this correctly?" He pointed to a line in the program.

I translated for him, from German into Spanish. "Yes—'hurled into the valley.' Now, please."

He whispered, a touch too loudly: "Where are the costumes? I hope they have some marvelous Japanese costumes."

"I don't see any."

"At least makeup. What do you call that white-faced look? *Geishas*—that would spice things up."

"*Tranquilo, por favor.*"

"Sorry."

To one side of the stage, some hastily written signs leaned against the wall. One of them read, simply: "Mountain."

He stage-whispered again, "These Berliners are very literal."

"I imagine they'll add set design later."

"I hope so. Take away the costumes and the sets from most operas, and all you have left is screaming."

"No wonder you had so much trouble writing *Don Quixote*," I whispered back. "You don't even *like* opera."

I jabbed at the program, and continued reading. The students proceed up the mountain. The younger boy becomes ill. The opera—only slightly more than half an hour long—ends with the boy consenting to the ancient custom and sacrificing himself for the societal good. He is *Der Jasager*, the Yea-sayer, and the school audiences would be prompted, as the theater curtain closed, to reflect and discuss: Should he have said yes?

Al-Cerraz followed my finger to the end of the description. He snorted again, loud enough that Brecht turned and glowered at us over his shoulder.

Three more children entered the stage, wearing signs around their necks. The signs read: "Boy." "Mother." "Teacher." Al-Cerraz burst out laughing.

Aviva appeared suddenly next to us. She reached a hand toward Al-Cerraz, touched his neck, and gave him a sly, warning smile. "Quiet, please. We are rehearsing."

The smile she directed at me was less warm and far less secure. "Please don't make any judgments until you've heard and seen the whole thing. Tell me you won't."

"Of course I won't." I scowled at Al-Cerraz. *He* had been the one laughing, not me. Why did she always expect me to judge her harshly?

The musicians played well for a school ensemble, and the orchestration provided no cause for snickering. I knew little about Weill's work, but this was spare and haunting, a Germanic interpretation of lyrical Orientalism. I detected nothing trite in it, nothing overblown or kitschy.

Al-Cerraz wasn't equally impressed. From the corner of my eye, I could see his head shaking, subtly at first, and then with vigor, animated by barely suppressed critical urges. I watched him puzzling over the roundlike lyrics from the score, overlapping strains of a simple sentiment: "*It is important to know when to be in agreement. Many say yes, and there is no agreement. There are many who are not asked, and many agree with what is wrong. Therefore: it is important to know when to be in agreement.*"

He muttered into my neck. "Is this a speech, or is it a riddle? It isn't a song, I'm sure of that."

After they'd made it through the work, with much pausing for direction from Weill, he invited the students to take seats on the stage's lip and accepted a cigar from Brecht. "Your reactions, please?"

Silence.

Weill smiled and tilted his head back, peering through the bottom half of his glasses. "Don't be shy. Speak up."

I felt Al-Cerraz move forward in his chair, balancing on its padded edge. I put a steadying hand on his leg and whispered, "Not you."

Finally one of the students spoke. I recognized him as the alto sax player. "The story, sir. It's horrible," he said, querulous voice breaking.

Another thin young voice added, "Yes, murderous!"

Brecht, smiling, puffed on his stubby cigar and Weill nodded with satisfaction, tapping his pen against the notebook in his lap. They leaned their heads together for a minute.

A student clarinetist cleared his throat and called out from the stage, "I think the boy's suicide was an honorable action, actually—I mean, if you'd like another opinion, sir."

Weill looked up. Brecht exhaled and slitted his eyes against the cloud of smoke. There was an awkward silence, until Brecht spoke: "Good. Very good. Just because this is a didactic work doesn't mean it's propaganda, after all. There isn't one correct reaction. A small number of audience members might misunderstand the theatrical intent, and find the Yea-sayer's actions heroic. That's fine. Thank you."

The young baritone who had played the Teacher raised his hand. "Herr Brecht, please—if I may add a word. Personal sacrifice is sometimes necessary, particularly in these troubled times."

"That's your feeling, is it?" Brecht said.

"Yes, sir."

"And by sacrifice, you mean the ultimate sacrifice? You think the boy was right to take his own life, simply because he couldn't keep up with the others?"

"I think so, sir. That was the ancient custom, after all."

Weill wrote in his notebook.

Al-Cerraz whispered to me, "I've heard that anything goes in Berlin—but I didn't know it meant this. They've taken an ironic story and turned it into an idiotic one."

Next the harmonium player added her public comment, along the same lines as the clarinetist, followed by two members of the chorus and the tall girl who had played the lute. The consensus swelled; even one of the violinists reneged on his label of "murderous" and joined the crowd in arguing that the opera's main character had taken the moral high road and deserved our praise.

Brecht nervously worried the brushy edge of his hair with a flat palm. Weill sighed, "Perhaps we'll have to make changes."

Later, at a café, Aviva asked us, "It wasn't an ideal first rehearsal, was it?" She unpinned her hat, crushing it in one hand and leaving the top of her uncovered head a mass of curls.

"They played remarkably well," I started to say. I reached out to smooth her hair but stopped as soon as she turned, my hand hovering for a moment before I tucked it underneath the small round table. Around us lay the refuse of a half-finished meal—dishes of eel in herb sauce, green beans, gherkins, and hard rolls.

Al-Cerraz, his breath foul with the smell of pickled herring, leaned hard into both of our faces. "That's the problem when you use musical theater to send messages. It's like that children's game of telephone: It always comes out wrong by the time it reaches the far end of the room."

"I don't think the original was quite so simplistic," Aviva said. "The Japanese version ended with the boy's spiritual resurrection. Brecht took that out."

Al-Cerraz grumbled, "Well, he would, wouldn't he?"

I asked, "What do you mean?"

"He's a Marxist. He took out religion. He left in all the parts where the mother worries about the boy's food and clothes. It's all about labor and capital now, don't you see?"

Aviva said apologetically, "He took out a lot." I pushed a plate toward her, but she ignored it, draining her glass instead. "His assistant, Elisabeth Hauptmann, talked to me at the rehearsal. She made her own German translation. Hers included a line where the boy's sick mother tells her son..." Aviva faltered.

"Go ahead," I said. "What did it say?"

She laughed at herself. "Never mind."

"No. Go ahead. Just the general idea…"

She sat up straighter on her stool, steeling herself. "It said, 'You were never out of my thoughts and out of my sight longer than it takes a dewdrop to evaporate.'"

Her eyes darkened and seemed to grow larger, trembling under the glassy lens of emotion. I looked around for a clean napkin to hand her.

But Al-Cerraz snorted, "Longer than it takes a dewdrop to evaporate? *Dios mío.* Between that and Brecht, you have your work cut out for you, my dear."

We continued to talk long into the night about *Der Jasager*. Aviva gave Weill and Brecht credit. They had said at the rehearsal that they would keep working on the opera, altering it according to students' suggestions. They would attempt to remove traces of martyrdom and to introduce complications that made the "ancient custom," while no longer called such, more sensible and legitimate. They would try, above all, to make the boy's forced suicide seem less savage, even while they wanted audiences to react to it with some degree of horror. That was the point, after all. They claimed they wanted audiences to think, but they were bothered that the majority of students might think the wrong thing, might agree to mindless "yea-saying" that only reinforced the authoritarian tendencies the opera's creators were hoping to challenge.

Aviva explained, "Brecht's already talked of writing a counter-play, a sort of parallel production—*Der Neinsager*—to make his original intentions more clear."

Al-Cerraz sneered. "The Naysayer. The Yea-sayer."

I asked, "What does Weill say?"

"He says the music should stand on its own. There is no need for any supplemental texts."

Al-Cerraz raised his glass. "Hear, hear."

"Besides, the music itself is antiauthoritarian," Aviva said, raising her finger to the bartender as she spoke, evidently quoting from Weill again, if the false confidence in her tone was any indication. "A grim chorus; triumphant solo melodies. The audience should know to root for the individual."

Al-Cerraz raised his eyebrows. "Well, I wouldn't go that far. I wouldn't count on the audience knowing whom to cheer for, based on what I saw today."

I reached a hand toward Aviva's wrist. "Are you sure you want another?"

She squirmed away from me, smiling across the room at the waiter approaching us, a towel over his forearm, a stoppered bottle in his hands.

"*Mineralwasser, bitte,*" I suggested with a nod in all directions, but the suggestion made little impact; Aviva ordered her own glass of *likor* instead.

Al-Cerraz said, "Can you imagine Beethoven saying, 'Listen to this measure. This dotted rhythm here tells the workers they should meet at quarter-past nine to smash all the machines'? Nonsense. *Der Jasager, Der Neinsager*—it will not stand the test of time."

Aviva downed her freshened glass and set it down. "Anyway, I'm here. That's all that matters, really."

When the hotel bar closed, we hired a cab and escorted Aviva back to Frau Zemmler's house, then walked back to the guesthouse by ourselves.

I asked Al-Cerraz, "Didn't you see, at the bar?"

"What?"

"She got teary about that line from the opera."

"Not our stoic girl." But then he reconsidered. "Something about dewdrops."

"*Eso es*. That's what the mother tells her son. She thinks about him every minute. That's how Aviva feels. She can't forget him."

"Who, Weill?"

"No."

"Brecht?"

"No!"

"Frau Zemmler? I've heard some strange things about these German women, I'll admit. They don't follow the rules our Spanish women follow. At some of these cabarets—"

I slapped him hard on the back, torn between aggravation and gratitude for his clowning.

"No. I am saying that Aviva misses her baby."

"Her baby," he repeated, stopping dead in his tracks, all playfulness extinguished. Without turning, I could feel the slump of his shoulders, his eyelids growing heavy with disappointment.

That night, I finally told him what I knew, what Aviva had told me at the harbor café, about her music teacher and Paganini's grave, and being left at the convent, pregnant. He was astounded by the story, but even more astounded that I hadn't revealed it to him earlier.

"The baby was born? It lived?"

"I assume so."

"Where is it, then?"

"I don't know."

"Does she?"

"The way she put it…"

"And then? And then?" he kept saying, incredulous that I hadn't pressed to know what happened later. "It couldn't be any more personal than what she'd already told you. Good Lord, Feliu—you're an ass."

"I was worried about her feelings," I said.

"You were worried about *your* feelings. You don't want any complications. You like playing the priestly role—Father Confessor—

someone whispering into your prim, sexless ear, as long as what they say doesn't require you to take action."

"I'm hardly a religious man—"

"I'm not talking about religion, I'm talking about authority—the kind that likes to keep everything how it is and everyone in their place."

"That just isn't true."

"It's the last thing I'd expect from someone with your—leanings." He stopped and ran his hands through his hair. "Do you remember that 'Mysterious Woman' article? There will be more like that one. We'd better know more about Aviva than what some malicious journalist has to say."

The next morning, I knocked on Al-Cerraz's door and got no answer. I went to the rehearsal hall, but Aviva hadn't shown up for work. I sat in the back row of the hall, sweating in my overcoat as I listened to the young choristers' falsetto, more annoying with every refrain: *It is important to know when to be in agreement. Many say yes, and there is no agreement.*

After an hour, Aviva hurried in, hair disheveled, a run up the back of one stocking. She winced as she passed quickly by me, face half-hidden in her coat collar, but I caught the mascara smears under her eyes. Weill's assistant approached, took Aviva's coat and led her backstage. When she emerged, her face was clean but redder, fiercely scrubbed.

For another hour I waited, my throat tight. When the rehearsal ended, Aviva took her time in apologizing to Weill, then made her way slowly to where I sat, in the shadowy rear.

"Justo spent the night," she said, refusing to look directly at me. My worst fears were confirmed. In one night of swift and decisive passion, Al-Cerraz had surmounted my months of hesitation. Seeing my expression, Aviva said, "It isn't what you think, Feliu. We argued." She began to sob, the tears dripping from her red nose into the fur of her coat collar. "Don't be angry with me, too."

I cleared my throat, struggling for composure. "Why was he angry?" To my own throbbing ears, my voice sounded aged and strained, as if I hadn't spoken for days, as if I'd lived alone for years.

"Because I wouldn't tell him," she said, and leaned into me, her wet cheek against my own, the tips of her collar soft against my eyes. The embrace provided the perfect blind for my sudden burst of relief.

"He already knows about your teacher, and the pregnancy. I told him."

"That became clear," she said sharply, then softened again. "But there is more, and it's not his business."

"Of course it isn't."

"He'll want to advise me, and I can't bear advice. I can't bear anyone's questions. I have one idea, but it's mine, and it's all I have. If he laughed it away, I think I'd fall apart."

"Of course."

She pushed away, rubbing her face with the back of one hand. "Justo thinks that one yes means a yes to everything."

I felt the tightness take hold again, the hollow ache of fading relief.

"He's used to getting everything he wants—you know that."

"Please," I said, taking her hands in mine and squeezing. I saw her eyes grow wide as she struggled against the pressure of my hands. "Don't tell me any more about what you and Justo did."

"Well, at first—"

"I don't want to hear this." I swallowed hard as a pain gripped my chest.

"You're overreacting. We didn't do anything. We talked—*he* talked. Into his own glass, by the end. Are you listening to me?" she said, noticing the fist clenched over my heart.

I closed my eyes.

"You're different, Feliu. You have principles. And you don't push."

"Promise me you and Justo aren't lovers."

She wrested her hands away from mine. "That's all you care about?"

"At this moment, yes."

She reached a hand up to smooth her hair. "Fine. I promise."

My head sank to my chest. I felt as if I'd just played a double concert, the worst of my life.

I stayed in Berlin through the summer. Within days, a letter arrived from Al-Cerraz, postmarked from Málaga. He asked me to assure Aviva that he wasn't angry, only worried. He looked forward to our tour the following summer. I replied immediately, reassuring him that nothing had changed with the trio, that we'd all be together again as planned. As long as he stayed away, I reasoned, whatever had passed between them could be forgotten.

In the meanwhile, I told him, I was enjoying an impromptu vacation. I planned to visit several museums, analyze some historical scores, improve my German—all things I *did* intend to do, as I wrote them. What I ultimately desired I wouldn't have been able to explain, to him or to myself.

What another man might have accomplished with overt action, I tried to accomplish with the same dogged determination that had allowed me to master the cello. I relied on long hours and repetitive motions. I refrained from making physical advances upon Aviva, even when opportunities presented themselves, reasoning that I had earned her trust so far by leaving her alone. I waited and followed. I listened. And over the next month, Aviva told me her story. After rehearsals, we met at bars, and later, in my hotel room, where she would relax, sometimes in a chair in the corner, hands wrapped around a glass, head nodding as I played the Bach suites for her.

I stopped once, just as her glass was tipping into her lap. I reached forward to catch it, set it aside, and said, "Justo always hated when I practiced these on the train."

She shook her head and wiped her chin, pretending to be wide awake. "He was envious."

"Of what?"

"Of your single-minded devotion."

Al-Cerraz's letters continued to arrive frequently. *How is Aviva?*

She is fine, I wrote back.

How are you both?

She and I are fine, I wrote, and in later letters, more forcefully, *We are fine.* I did not mention her drinking, which seemed if anything to increase, here in the land that reminded her daily of her unfinished task. I was haunted by the thought that Al-Cerraz would have handled all this better—would have handled *her* better. I thought of my mother pressuring me to choose among my father's gifts. "I don't want to get it wrong," I'd told her. "You will be wrong, sometimes," she had said—and she was right. I had been wrong many times, always when it mattered most.

And yet I could not seem to change course. If anything, I became a caricature of myself, even *to* myself: cautious, stern, dogmatic, ascetic.

When Aviva drank, refilling her glass even before it was empty, I switched to water. When she came out of my bathroom wrapped in a towel, wet hair streaming down her pale back, I turned away and busied myself in a corner, sorting through letters. When she decided to talk, I listened, hands in my lap, face impassive. She did not want sympathy, I told myself. She did not want physical love.

I did not touch her even when she fell asleep on my bed, head on my lap, whispering in German to herself as she nodded off: "*Es macht nichts.*" It does not matter.

In the mornings when we left together, the guesthouse matron would turn a blind eye. We'd go to a café on the corner where I'd order her *Katerfrühstück,* a "hangover breakfast" of sausage and herring. But she rarely touched it, and I gained a few kilos before I learned to order only enough for one.

I heard most of Aviva's stories not during the evenings, when she turned silently inward, but during these headache-plagued mornings-after, when she became more verbose and acidic, angry at herself and therefore willing to invite discovery. Repeatedly, she asked me not to judge her. But why did she tell her stories to me instead of Justo, except that she did want to be judged?

Judaism, Aviva told me, was not what set her apart at the convent near the Austrian border where her violin teacher had dumped her unceremoniously. Where she was raised, Jews and Catholics intermarried occasionally. In the convent, the sisters treated her with compassion and did not try to convert her.

As she soon discovered, pregnancy did not make her different, either. First she was shown to her shared room in the attic, where she set down her valise and the battered violin case that held her first instrument (vastly inferior to the borrowed Magione). Next she was taken to the main hall, where the other girls sat at long benches that paralleled even longer tables, doing piecework sewing. Sister Luigia clapped for the girls' attention. In a disorderly wave, the girls pushed themselves up, some supporting themselves with hands on the table or hands on their lower backs, and Aviva saw that every last one of them was carrying a shameful burden, just like her. Only a few bothered to smile.

Sister Luigia was a music lover. After dinner, she asked Aviva to perform something on the violin for the other girls. Nausea had plagued Aviva for her first trimester and was only barely beginning to recede now. Smells still bothered her, and the convent was infused with them: mold, though the nuns and girls spent part of each day scrubbing the floors; garlic, which she had once loved, and sour, overcooked squash, which she did not; iodine and peroxide wafting in from the overcrowded infirmary. Aviva told the nun she felt too ill to play.

Many of the girls had come from well-off families in the south, but class meant less here than practical knowledge. The girls at the top of the pecking order were invariably among those farthest along in their pregnancies. They regaled and taunted the others after bedtime, as they lay in darkened attic rows, with the knowledge gained by their greater experience: how it felt to be so far along that the baby kicked your liver and forced the air from your lungs; how one could distinguish false contractions from real. A select few served as helpers in the infirmary. They alone knew what happened during labor and in the first few days following childbirth. Aviva didn't want to hear about it or think about it.

Sister Luigia again asked her to play the violin, a week later. And again a week after that. "I see," the nun said, in a quiet moment alone. "Humility is a virtue."

"I'm not humble, Sister," Aviva said.

"Then play for us."

"I can't."

"You mean, you won't."

"No, Sister. That's not what I mean."

A month had passed since she'd last played—the longest she'd gone without playing since she'd first picked up the instrument. By now everything about her felt different. Her hair was thicker, dryer and less curly, her fingers too fat to wear the simple ring her mother had left her. Veins sprang up on the back of her calves. The hair on her forearms darkened, but not nearly so much as the alarming stripe of dark skin that extended from her navel toward her pelvis, like an arrow from God, pointing to the place where all the trouble had begun. While some of the girls whispered clandestinely about their changing bodies, Aviva was sure that none of them had a stripe like hers; perhaps it was Paganini's mark on her. Each night, she faced the wall while undressing, to conceal it. It was easy to believe she would never be herself again. Nothing felt right, nothing mattered.

She wasn't depressed to the point of complete inaction. She ate a fair amount: pasta and soup and root vegetables, as mindless as a grazing cow. At the nuns' request, she sewed and washed floors; cleaned, dried, and ground herbs; scrubbed potatoes. She rarely talked, because there was nothing to talk about. One night, the girl who slept in the bed next to her asked in a whisper after lights out what Aviva would name her baby, but Aviva could hardly think what to say. The nuns would decide the babies' names, just as they would arrange the adoptions. She pretended to be asleep.

Each day, the nuns granted the girls free time to read magazines, stroll the vegetable garden, pray, or nap. Aviva didn't care what she did, as long as she could do it alone. All the other girls who were at her stage—five or more months along—had been talking about the first quickenings they'd felt. One girl likened it to bubbles popping just under the skin's surface. Another said it felt longer and more continuous, like a slithering snake. Aviva hadn't felt anything. The other girls knew, she was certain; it gave her an aura of contagious bad luck. Even though no girl would be allowed to keep her baby, none of them wanted to lose it to death—not at this advanced stage, anyway.

Two more weeks passed. A nun examined her without comment. Now she was entering her third trimester, still growing, but without any sign of movement inside. Perhaps her baby *was* dead. The nausea had long since passed, but a sourness remained, the metallic taste of sorrow. Two new girls, each in their first trimester, came to the home, and Aviva joined them in scrambling up the convent wall to view the hills beyond—a tricky task, with bellies pressing against the stone wall. They returned with scratched legs and arms, blackened elbows and knees, and Sister Luigia punished them each with a day's solitary confinement. What had they been thinking? Did they realize what might have happened if they had fallen?

As new girls entered, others graduated. A bossy redhead from Firenze had spent her last month reveling in her superior girth and know-it-all status, until the evening her contractions started. They began at lunch, continued through free time and afternoon chores and vespers. Even from the chapel, all the girls could hear her moaning in the infirmary next door. The nuns attempted to keep straight faces, but all the girls' eyes were wide, listening to the moans escalate into screams—even profane curses—to which some responded by crossing themselves and others by covering their mouths, to stifle panicky giggles.

Aviva didn't feel so well herself. Listening to the screaming, her pulse beat faster, and a deep pain rippled across her abdomen. During free time she began to think it was her time, too, even if the nuns had said it wouldn't happen for two months more. She rocked back and forth with the pain until she couldn't ignore it anymore. Then she walked toward the screams and moans to the infirmary. Rounding the corner, she saw red and purple, two nuns holding down the girl's arms, her open legs, silver bowls glinting everywhere like some awful blood sacrifice.

Despite the pain, she managed to climb the stairs to the attic bedroom faster than she'd ever climbed them before. In the room, she took out her violin without thinking, an automatic motion practiced thousands of times. In the infirmary, her ears had flooded with white static, and she fingered several measures without hearing the sour din she was producing. Suddenly the white curtain of noise parted and she realized she hadn't tuned the neglected thing; it sounded wretched. She twisted a tuning peg, heard the wood of the neck groan in protest, and then the pop of the A string. She fumbled through the case and realized she'd brought no extra strings. Useless. Then she would play without the A string. The second string went the way of the first. She laughed out loud for the first time in recent memory, and mouthed a message to Paganini himself: I know this is the trick you loved best. But I can't play an entire piece on one string. Leave me two at least. The last two held: E and G.

Her violin teacher had encouraged her to stand with heels touching and toes apart, like a ballerina in first position, but she ignored that now and spread her swollen feet shoulder-wide, planted at an ungainly right angle. She rocked side to side as she played, feeling the weight of the baby nestling deep down into her pelvic bones. Her violin wasn't louder than the screams still issuing from the infirmary below, but it was a welcome distraction, a point of focus. At some point, the girl downstairs stopped, but Aviva kept playing—even an hour later, when the nun's handbell rang, calling all the girls together to share with them the bad news. The girl from Firenze was well enough, but her baby had died, and though no one had wanted it, every girl felt death's hand brushing too close for comfort.

Aviva felt no guilt in not rushing to join them then, or at the ensuing chapel service; there would always be bad news, there was no hurry. For now, she felt stuck to the floor—not glued but pierced—as if an iron shaft had descended through her pelvic bone, numbing the pain there and anchoring her to the floor, easing her need to rock. During a Vivaldi sonata, when she had played for perhaps two continuous hours, she felt the first stirrings of the baby inside her. Not deep in her pelvic bones, but higher up, just under her right ribs. Looking down, she saw the fabric of her jumper move, an elbow or knee pushing against the surface, followed by a deeper, indefinable gaseous shift, smooth and yet unexpected, like an ice cube rolling in a glass. "Vivaldi woke you up, not Paganini," she whispered. "I'm glad."

From that moment forth, she played every day. One girl complained that Aviva's use of the attic during free time infringed on others' rights to nap, but several other girls stepped forward to say they liked the music, and Sister Luigia allowed it to continue, even climbing the stairs to listen on occasion. Another nun brought her new strings after a trip to town. The strings were appreciated, but the praise meant nothing to Aviva; she would have preferred to play alone. Or not really alone, because she knew now for whom she was playing. Her baby never failed to move when she played—a percussive pummel, a sudden stretch that took her breath away, a slippery shift that gave it back.

One night two weeks before Aviva was due, the girl in the next bed whispered to her again. "I'm going to name mine," she said. "I will insist on it."

"Against the rules," Aviva yawned.

"I have a boy's name chosen and a girl's name, though I'm sure it's a girl. I won't push unless they say they'll agree to use it on the forms. The sisters will agree."

"Won't push?" Aviva laughed into her pillow. "You'll be dying to push. It's like going to the bathroom; that's what Elena said."

"That's disgusting," said the girl, and rolled away.

But she did not sleep, and neither did Aviva. A shutter was drawn over the attic's only window, but she could see the bright glow of a moon beyond the slats, until the moon had moved and the slats gradually darkened. Aviva whispered across the room, "Why do you want to name it? You'll never see it again."

"Maybe in a few years, maybe later, when I'm married and have a family, and I'll be shopping for a hat somewhere, and a beautiful young girl will enter the shop with her nanny..."

Unlikely, Aviva thought, but she had asked.

"...and I'll recognize the shape of her eyes, or her nose," the girl continued. "I'll pretend not to know her but I'll ask her to tell me her name. They'll place her only among good people—that's what the sisters have promised. And if I get along with her mother, I might ask her to tea."

From across the darkened aisle, a voice shushed them both.

"But what if the new mother decides to change her name? Parents can do that."

The girl pulled her sheets to her chin and answered with exaspera-tion, "I'll choose a good name. It will fit her, and they won't change it."

"But how do you know it will fit your baby if you've never seen her?"

More shushing, aggrieved now.

The girl's insistence dismayed Aviva; it made her feel as if she'd spent no time considering the future. Certainly, she'd felt she had no future just a few months ago; but now that she was nearing pregnancy's end, the baby felt disturbingly real. When it nestled its hard round head against her abdomen, she could place a hand there, and it was almost the same as rubbing a fully developed baby's head; she could almost feel the fine hair, the soft skin, almost smell it. She longed to watch her baby's eyes open. She longed to see the small clenched fists that had been playing dotted rhythms against her lungs.

The nuns didn't allow the girls to nurse their babies. Following birth, mother and child were separated. Some preselected babies were delivered directly to wet nurses hired by prospective parents, upper-class couples who concealed all signs that the babies had not been born to them. Other babies were moved to a second home, where they were raised through early infancy and adopted out in less-predictable fash-ion. All the girls had agreed, upon entering the convent, not to attempt any contact with their children.

But how not to forget, how to forge a bond, leaving open the possi-bility of later breaking that agreement—that was the question. A name was nothing, the first thing another person could take away. She would have to give her baby something more lasting.

Aviva's family had changed its surname once, attempting to assim-ilate into the region where her parents had settled. She had been told her great-grandmother's maiden name, but couldn't recall it. She had never asked her great-grandfather's trade. The nuns' rules aside, her sense of family was foggy, eroded by her parents' early deaths, disloca-tion, simple forgetting.

And yet consider how lovingly her music teacher, scoundrel that he was, had tended Paganini's grave. Consider what she herself knew of Vivaldi, eight generations removed from her own life. Aviva's memory of her own mother was a still portrait—the shape of a woman standing, hands on hips, in an open doorway. But Vivaldi was a living presence to her, a life that continued past that door, with whom she could spend a day, a season, a year. Playing the violin part of *Le Quattro Stagioni*, Aviva could sit on a rain-drenched hillside next to him, or walk in the paths of goatherds and laugh upon finding them asleep beneath a massive tree, their light snores accompanied by the buzz of sun-drunk flies. Those who loved his music need never be alone. And so she played the same measures again and again for her unborn child in those final two weeks, standing for hours until she thought her pelvic bones would split under the deepening weight.

The baby was taken away, but not adopted out immediately. Three months later, when Aviva moved away from the convent, she knew only that it had been a boy, and that the nuns had listed his religion on the form. She hadn't thought they'd do that; surely it lowered his chances of being placed into a good home.

She tried to put the idea of him behind her. She moved south to Bologna and spent two years studying violin and piano with a Madame Borghese, who also arranged a place for Aviva with a local family, in exchange for occasional help with their four children.

As her eighteenth birthday approached, her career prospects improved. Several people seemed to think she'd make an ideal musical nanny—thus, the short interview with Mussolini. But Aviva was not interested in tending others' children as a lifelong pursuit, and Madame Borghese had higher hopes for her as well. Aviva spent a season performing solo recitals and began to garner favorable publicity, publicity that might increase, Madame Borghese implored, if only Aviva would dress better, cultivate more eye contact with the audience, narrow her stance slightly, and so on, listing the recommendations that Al-Cerraz would echo in a year or so.

At an intermission during one of these recitals, in Padova, Aviva spotted Sister Luigia in the audience. To her surprise, she was happy to see the music-loving nun.

"When we last knew one another, you would not accept requests," Sister Luigia said. "Play one for me now."

"The program is already established," Aviva said, confused.

"As an encore, then. I will wait."

Aviva leaned closer and said, "The encore is established, too. Madame leaves nothing to chance."

"You can't allow yourself to be spontaneously inspired?"

"Madame doesn't believe in spontaneity." Aviva tried to smile. "Which is for the best. I am not consistently inspired."

Sister Luigia frowned. "No requests for an old friend? Well, what can I do? Punch is no substitute, but I'd accept some at this moment."

Aviva hesitated. Madame didn't allow Aviva near the refreshments table, for fear of something—a ruined dress, or the temptation of marzipan, which might lead to sticky fingers or the temptation to imbibe, which might lead in turn to a full bladder at the wrong moment. But Madame, immersed in a discussion with a small circle of well-dressed women, had her back to the two of them.

When she returned with Sister Luigia's punch, the nun did not immediately take it. Aviva stepped closer, and held the cup forward again. Only when they were toe to toe did Sister Luigia reach forward, wrap her hands around Aviva's and say, "You play too well for this local audience. Madame must know it, too. Is there a reason you haven't gone to Rome, or to Paris?"

Aviva nodded.

"You're feeling bound to your past, aren't you? You're staying around in case you catch word that he finds no home." Her grip tightened around Aviva's. "He *did* find parents. Two and a half is old for that—no one wants a child who is old enough to remember, who can speak. Your child didn't speak, actually—that was the problem, the appearance of a delay of some kind. But a very special Jewish gentleman came and took an instant liking to him."

"Tell me more," Aviva whispered, just as she saw over the nun's shoulder Madame's group breaking up, the accompanist entering the room.

"I said you played well—and you did, *certamente*, but I sensed hesitation. It was technically impressive, of course, but I remember how you played at the convent once you were willing to play—through the roof, like a bird! I thought I should say something. My intention was to help you to stop worrying, to free yourself—"

"What do you mean, he doesn't speak?" Aviva interrupted.

"That's not uncommon in a group home where children aren't often spoken to. Dear, I'm upsetting you. I didn't mean to. He's a clever child. And with pretty hair—light and curly, like a cherub. Doctor— the Jewish gentleman—spent an afternoon with him. They went for a walk; they played the piano..."

"Played the piano?" Aviva saw Madame glancing around the room for her.

"There is a piano in the orphanage. The boy liked to pick out notes, or sit under the piano with his head against the wood. I'm not saying he's a prodigy—nothing of the kind. But he has an affinity. He was hiding under the piano when the doctor and his wife first came to us. They might have overlooked him if the doctor hadn't sat down for a moment, to try his own hand at the keyboard."

Madame Borghese was at Aviva's arm, awaiting an introduction.

"Sister—tell me where; at least name the province."

Sister Luigia nodded her head in wordless acknowledgment of Madame. "I really cannot."

"You cannot, or you *will* not?"

The nun recognized her own words returning to her. "Truthfully, I cannot. It's unfamiliar to me."

Madame dropped any pretense of politeness. She put an arm on Aviva's shoulder and tried to turn her, forcibly.

"Unfamiliar? Is it that far away?"

"*Gut* and far," she winked. "You need not concern yourself with it anymore."

Gut, is that what she had really said? And far—not Austria, then, but Germany, perhaps one of the northern cities. A Jewish doctor who liked the piano. Upper class, musically inclined, living in a richly cultured, tolerant place where Jews were well assimilated. Better even than the region where she'd been raised. A homeland without limitations, the best that one could wish for her child. So she could be free now. She could live and travel as she pleased.

Why, then, with so many choices, did she end up six months later enrolled in the Magdeburg Music Conservatory, two hours west of Berlin? She spent long weekends exploring the surrounding towns, feeding birds in plazas, watching nursemaids pushing prams, observing schoolchildren lining up outside local bakeries. She spent money that was meant for musical scores and staff-ruled composition pads on train tickets and restaurant fare: a few sausages and many more beers. She found herself waking, in a daze, in roadside inns on Monday morning and thinking: music theory—missed again. That, in addition to the poor marks she received in the required *Volkslied* singing class, left her on probation at semester's end. She had no intention of rehabilitating herself. It was easier to leave.

The Friday before she intended to inform her adviser, she performed in a student quartet. A small man with an impressively round, balding pate and large lips listened from the back of the room, his fingertips pressed against his left temple. It was Kurt Weill.

The next afternoon, when they happened to meet at a café, he asked what she had been thinking about as he'd watched her play. "A child," she said, without elaborating. Her confession caught her by surprise; she hid her face behind a cup. But something about the answer pleased him. It reminded him of the work that was foremost in his mind that week, an opera for and about children.

Weill told her that he hadn't had a rigorous musical education, either. His father was a cantor, and Weill himself had started composing songs at the age of sixteen, without the benefit of formal conservatory training. He did not ask her what her ethnic background was, but he seemed to know, and he made a cautious remark about feeling as uncomfortable among Zionists and zealots as he did among pompous, assimilated German Jews. When she asked him what kind of Judaism he *did* believe in, he said, "The simple kind: innocent belief."

Weill got her hired on to play in the orchestra pit of a local production of his musical play, *Die Dreigroschenoper, The Threepenny Opera.* His career had exploded, and he had multiple projects boiling at all times—new compositions under way, others in rehearsal, or thriving in established runs. That year, *Die Dreigroschenoper* alone was performed in various cities over four thousand times. Weill was like a big puppy that hadn't yet grown into its oversized feet, suddenly endowed with celebrity and access to every musician and conductor in Europe, still incredulous at his own success and the consideration, both positive and negative, that his work was attracting.

When the Magdeburg run ended, he discussed future opportunities with Aviva. She did not know why he took the time to offer her advice and to recommend her for auditions, all the while admonishing her that many of the jobs were technically and creatively beneath her. Among these was a position as an adult lead in the school opera he'd mentioned—repetitive, low-profile labor for anyone who had a chance at a solo or ensemble career, he warned. And a lot of time on the road—he intended to take *Der Jasager* to schools throughout the country.

She didn't feel she deserved the attention, and in a lucid moment, she admitted that her decision to come to Germany from Italy had been rash. America would be a better place for her, she argued convincingly one night over too much schnapps. He seemed to agree. The next day, he sent a strongly worded telegram on her behalf to the New York Philharmonic. Within another week, she was headed across the Atlantic, but her resolve weakened during the voyage. On the day Al-Cerraz and I met her, she had decided to turn back. Always, she was counting in the back of her mind how old her son would be, in the event she ever did meet him: four that year, in 1929. Five years old now, in 1930. Not a baby anymore. Old enough for school.

No matter how Aviva spent her evenings, she always made it to rehearsals and performances the following day. But I witnessed the growing strain on her, which seemed to intensify in the fall, as *Der Jasager* finished its Berlin run. I was glad to leave the city—Babylon on the River Spree, as they called it then. Weill and Brecht had already detached themselves from the project. Soon Aviva and Frau Zemmler would head to a series of smaller cities and towns, to help rehearse the youth orchestras at each school, spending three or four days in each place before moving on.

One September weekend before Aviva left Berlin, I talked her into a final outing. We took the express train to Wannsee, a large inland lake southwest of the city. From the sandy beach, we watched small boats sail past each other. Hardy bathers frolicked and splashed in the cold lake, dancing between spirals and ribbons sketched by the wind. But not Aviva—I never even saw the suit she wore beneath a large black robe.

We rented a large wicker bathing chair and curled inside, out of the wind. I watched her tremble, the thinness of her forearms and wrists emphasized by the robe's wide sleeves. The acrid scent of wet wicker will forever remind me of the specific and peculiar discomfort of trying to be merry in the wrong place, at the wrong season.

I had meant to leave Berlin in the fall, when Aviva did. Instead, I tagged along from Brandenburg to Leipzig, from Nürnburg to Stuttgart and on across Germany, a shadow figure carrying Aviva's violin and my own cello, which I played in hotel rooms—never in public. I lurked behind coatracks, resisted introductions, ducked away from the impressed whispers of local music teachers who recognized my name. I helped set up music stands. I distributed programs. I turned away from cameras. I refused to sign autographs. No doubt people thought Aviva and I were lovers. And why wouldn't we be? An attractive and talented young woman, a revered older man with a formidable reputation. Perhaps they saw the shadows under Aviva eyes and thought we had stayed up all night, reveling in decadence and depravity. That we had never kissed or embraced passionately was harder to explain.

After each school-opera performance, Aviva went from classroom to classroom, giving short instrumental demonstrations, allowing the youngest students to watch a violin string vibrate up close or handle a felt-covered hammer that had been removed from the inside of a piano. She watched the face of every child, studying this one's response to the mention of a piano, that one's reaction to the violin, especially when she played Vivaldi. She appraised noses and eyes, reached out a finger to pat a curl, quizzed children on their favorite animals and foods and—when a teacher was distracted—on their birthdays, each and every one.

She watched them while I watched her. I told myself I should return to Spain, but her intensity fueled my own. I pretended that her search was metaphorical: She felt guilty for abandoning a child and so had dedicated herself to educating all children. But watching her in the classroom day after day forced me, finally, to abandon my own delusion.

She fully expected to find her son. Long after she tired of *Der Jasager* and students' puzzled reactions to it—"Why did the boy kill himself?" "Couldn't someone else have gone for the mother's medicine?" "Why do we have to watch a Japanese play in the first place?"—she clung to the job because it allowed her to continue her search.

"I'll find him," she told me one night, nearly asleep, her head in my lap.

"There are tens of thousands of children."

"I meet hundreds of them each week."

"My brother once told me that my mother used to sing to us, when I was just a baby. But I don't remember it." Though even as I said it, an image formed in my mind: Mamá's dark head, bowed over mine, singing just under her breath as I nodded off to sleep.

"I played for him every day," Aviva said. "He heard Vivaldi before he tasted milk."

There was no reasoning with her, so I simply watched and waited, as summer turned to fall, and fall to damp, cold winter. My hip throbbed. I knew the warm, dry climate of southern Spain would lessen the pain, but I could not leave her. Once, after a particularly bad night, I tried the morphine tonic Dr. Gindl had given me, back in Switzerland. It helped that day, and it allowed me to sleep that night, but I couldn't take it again. It felt like giving in. Perhaps I was already slipping back to my former ways of thinking—observing Aviva on her futile quest, I no longer believed that pain was avoidable. I began to feel skeptical about the hopefulness I had allowed myself, began even to resent her for allowing me to think I could have a different kind of life, where music served a good purpose or none at all, beyond pleasure, and where friendship could grow into passion, in good time.

Al-Cerraz wrote to me from Spain: *Is she doing all right? Has she tired of Weill's silly opera?*

I ignored the question and wrote nothing about what I saw daily in the schools, feeling that the only advantage I had over him was information and proximity. I was determined to help and protect her and did not appreciate being second-guessed.

He wrote again. *Is she drinking heavily?*

I wrote back, rattled by my own inadequacies and resentful at his insinuation: *Not really. Not anymore.* And that was true, as far as I knew, though she looked worse than ever—thin and sallow—and though she did slip away from me occasionally at night, to attend nightclubs with other young musicians from the troupe. I hated those nights most of all, waiting for her to get back, listening to her cough herself to sleep after too many hours in a smoke-filled cabaret.

I know Al-Cerraz wrote to her directly as well, but those letters disappeared into a violin case or a coat pocket as soon as they arrived, and they were not shared with me later.

Before some of the performances, Aviva would set her bobbed hair in curlers, but by winter she was doing it haphazardly, missing large pieces in the back, which hung down limply. She stopped taking care of her fingernails, which was a particular embarrassment—even the schoolchildren stared at them when she played. But I did not have Al-Cerraz's eye for style or vanity, or his forthrightness, and I was thankful he was not there to rebuke us both. And Aviva, who had always seemed beautiful to me, remained so.

By midwinter I had memorized every line and note and cue of *Der Jasager*. But I did not risk missing a performance or school visit. I stayed close to Aviva at every moment, until that day when I went to fetch an extra E-string from her violin case, and came upon a letter she was evidently in the midst of writing to Al-Cerraz:

He's become terribly strange. He follows me everywhere. He is awake when I fall asleep and again when I wake, usually staring at me. He has no humor at all. Except for playing the cello in his hotel room, he doesn't have much to do. I'm not sure when he plans to return to Spain or why he hasn't left already.

The letter took my breath away. It was like a mirror thrust suddenly in front of my face—a mirror in a house of mirrors. Aviva was making me sound like the obsessed one, the addled insomniac. She could not pretend I drank, because I did not; she could not pretend I was the one losing weight. But what had she said just the other night? Her voice had been thick and slurred, her voice sadistic and bitter, dirty fingernails pressing into my leg as she tried to stand: "I think you like me being a little sick. If I weren't, I'd be in America."

She had let it slip, also, that she had been using the morphine tonic, which I had stowed in my cello case.

"How many doses have you taken?" I asked her. I went to retrieve the bottle. It was empty.

"There's worse things."

"Maybe so, but you took something that didn't belong to you. And you're abusing your health, and abusing the trust of your mentors."

"It isn't like smoking opium," she snarled.

"How would you know?"

"You're blind. But that's not the saddest part of it," she lashed out. "You're jealous. At least I know what I'm doing here. You don't believe in what I'm doing, but at least I'm doing something."

I kept arguing in one direction, she in another, on nonconverging courses. I don't remember what I said or how I ended things, only her parting shot as she left the room that day. "Who is to be pitied here: the crazy person, or the person who is following the crazy person in circles?"

We came to a truce the next weekend, one I questioned as soon as we made it. I refilled my morphine prescription and gave it to her; in exchange, she promised she wouldn't smoke opium—something she had done, she admitted, in Berlin and elsewhere, with her other "music friends."

But then one night, she did not come back to the hotel until dawn. I stayed up waiting for her, vowing to say something about the letter she'd written to Al-Cerraz, and about many other things besides.

The next afternoon, after yet another dreary performance at a small brick schoolhouse in Ingolstadt, I followed Aviva to a classroom full of young children, where a curly-haired blond boy of perhaps six or seven years old had been asked to play the piano for her. Afterward, the teacher asked me to help her wheel the piano back to a storage room. I was pushing the scarred instrument down the hallway when I heard a high, cheerful voice behind me, and turned to look. It was the cherubic boy, walking with Aviva down the hallway, in the opposite direction. She carried nothing with her—no violin, no coat. But just as they vanished around the corner she took his hand, and I knew immediately what she was planning to do.

I abandoned the piano and the teacher and ran. When I rounded the corner there was no sign of them. I ducked my head into each room that I passed. At the end of the hallway, a door had been propped open. It led to a schoolyard, and beyond that, to an empty street. Panting, I began to call her name, first outside, then back in the hallway, until faces came to all the doorways: the faces of a few students at first, and several teachers, and finally a white-haired man who questioned me sternly and walked me around a corner and into a larger room with a frosted window—his office.

When the headmaster shut his office door, I saw the long wooden bench along one side. Aviva was sitting there, with the boy next to her. She looked at me once, then hid her flushed face behind one hand. Around her neck she wore a small bronze medal I'd never seen before, on a thin blue ribbon. It was a thank-you gift from the school. The boy had walked her to the principal's office to receive it because Aviva did not know the way.

———

"I'm going to tell Weill," I told her after we argued that night in our hotel room.

"What will you tell him—that you are obsessed? That you are imagining things?"

"I will tell him," I said again. Four quick raps on the wall beside the bed made me jump—it was Frau Zemmler in the next room, letting us know our voices carried.

"Maybe I was wrong about that boy—"

"Of course you were wrong. He wasn't even the correct age! And what do you think I would do if I found the right boy—just walk away with him? Kidnap him?"

I didn't answer.

"There's only one more month—then we take a break for the summer. I'll be ready to leave Germany."

I whispered again, "I will tell him: first, that you are obsessed with these children. Second, that you have been taking morphine and opium, that you aren't to be trusted."

"But this year's tour is almost done. I'm almost finished—"

"You *will* be finished after I talk to Weill. You may not respect me, but he does."

I lifted my head, and with an energy coursing through me that I hadn't felt in months, I saw that finally Aviva looked afraid. She sat down on the bed. After a minute she went to the bathroom, and some-time later, she came out wrapped in a towel and sat on the bed again. She said, "What do you want from me?"

The rapping sound came again from the next room.

Aviva glared at the wall. Then she turned toward me, all light extinguished from her eyes. In a harsh whisper, she said, "I'll do anything you want."

CHAPTER

~ 20 ~

Returning to Spain after so long away was like waking from a dream and realizing one has overslept disastrously. I spent the next month with an imaginary alarm ringing in my ears, alerting me to all that had happened in my absence, on both musical and political fronts.

Several renowned conductors requested my appearance as a soloist in the upcoming year, performing the Dvořák Cello Concerto in B Minor, Elgar's Concerto in E Minor, and Glazunov's Concerto Ballata in C Major. Just as many civic organizations—several of them without any connection to the musical world—asked me to speak to their members. Having traveled across Europe and America, didn't I have a better view of how Spain stood in the world and how she should choose to stand in this era of rising nationalism?

Rita had decided to get married that year, and had resigned her position as my secretary. I could have found another, but I didn't want the help or the company, preferring instead to busy myself in the comforting piles of unanswered mail and telegrams that had accumulated while I was away. I needed to immerse myself in my old life—the letters and awards and royalty statements and requests, antidotes to the powerlessness and invisibility I'd felt in Germany. I needed time to sort out what had happened—that last week, that last night with Aviva.

In Salamanca, I had requests, too, from other cellists—younger musicians wanting master classes, letters of introduction to conductors, or my approval for recordings they had made. I took this role seriously, enjoying the chance to help others and to establish high standards, not only for music, but for behavior. I kept a close eye on the rising stars of the day, and did not lend my name lightly to others' pursuits. How good it felt to be in control again, to have my views sought, my advice heeded.

Of course, I continued to write to Aviva. I couldn't have abandoned her completely as she was that last night, but I couldn't have stayed. And yet, much as I tried to forget what had happened next, it kept coming back to me.

"I'll do anything you want," she had said, the towel loose around her chest, eyelids heavy. When I wrapped my arms around her, they found dead flesh. Sharp elbows collided with my chest; cold, damp hair flicked against my cheek. I opened my eyes in time to see her lean back into the bed, one tear running sideways, across the bridge of her nose, expression fixed halfway between submission and revulsion. Suddenly she sat upright, shouting. My palm stung, though I had no awareness of using it. But there was the proof, blooming across her reddening cheek, the sight of which only fueled my wrath.

They say that empathy and compassion are the first steps toward peace. But the empathy I felt in that moment brought no one peace. Because I did not come closer to understanding Aviva in that moment; I came closer to understanding Don Miguel Rivera. I felt the frustration he must have felt, the fury that comes when a person has not bent to your will, when a situation cannot be endured, when humiliation overwhelms your senses. I almost believed in that moment that I could make her obey me, and love me—then everything would be better. I did not do what Don Rivera did, or what Aviva's own teacher had done, or what Franco and his men in Morocco had done and would do again— but I came close enough to taste what they had tasted. Sand and sweat, salt and blood—the taste of passion, pain, and justification.

I had never been so angry in my life, or so afraid. I walked out of that hotel room without speaking. I took the next train out of Germany, feeling that I had escaped just in time. From that moment, my life changed again. I gave up, finally, on personal satisfaction. I became more wholly dedicated to practical concerns, to fighting an enemy I finally understood.

Al-Cerraz was in Málaga, on the southern coast, when I returned to Spain.

We'd planned to join him in Barcelona in April, with ample time to discuss programs, to have some new photographs taken to keep Biber happy, and to sort through the recording offers he had forwarded, as well as to rehearse before we commenced our summer tour.

I knew I would have to tell Al-Cerraz what had happened in Germany—at least enough to explain Aviva's changed appearance if she returned, or her absence if she did not. But there was no point in alarming him if there was still a chance that everything would soon be set right—or right enough. And so I delayed, hoping each day for a letter or a telegram from Aviva, something more than the short note she had sent me as soon as I'd arrived back in Spain, in which she had apologized for her behavior and forgiven me for mine. She had written:

> I know that wasn't the real you in that hotel room. It's easy for me to believe, since I know that wasn't the real me.

I had written back:

> I'm sorry, too. Let's not talk of it again. Just come and we will perform together, like old times.

But she sent no indication that she had decided one way or another.

If Al-Cerraz had any sense that our concert season faced disruptions, he would have been expecting public difficulties, not private ones.

Across Spain, the political climate had been tense for several months. The dictator Primo de Rivera had lost the support of the army and stepped down, to be replaced by another bland dictator who didn't last long enough to make an impression. Since then, the King had agreed to municipal elections. Posters, flyers and banners papered every lamppost. Early polls predicted an antimonarchical landslide, even with the rural vote controlled by the headstrong political bosses.

I met Al-Cerraz at his hotel on April 12, and we spent the day together going through the motions of preparing a tour. A photographer met us in the lobby to discuss his fees and schedule a session. Al-Cerraz showed the man what we already had: a horribly dated photo of him and me from ten years earlier and a beautiful shot of Aviva, problematic only because we weren't in it with her. She'd had it taken months earlier in Berlin—face forward, slim nose, darkly shaded eyes; the top of her head covered by a fashionable, nearly brimless cloche, with brown curls on each side of her face. She looked so well, I couldn't bear to tell him.

That following night we had dinner at an outside table on the Ramblas. Al-Cerraz said, "Funny that she hasn't telegraphed the hotel. Maybe they lost it. I suppose we should stop by the station tomorrow morning, in case she's on the 11:15 coming south."

A paperboy ran by, calling out the latest headlines.

I cleared my throat. "It might not be the best time for a tour."

Al-Cerraz let his gaze wander to the boy, galloping away from us with a fat sheaf of papers under one arm. "The election? No matter who wins, someone will dispute it. It will drag on for months. It will be the same old mess it always is. You can wake me when it's over."

"Yes—I mean, no." A waiter came to clear our dishes. "I meant the tour might not work without Aviva. I don't think she's coming."

"That's ridiculous. Have you heard from her?"

"Not recently..."

"There you have it. Of course she's coming. We'll go to the station tomorrow."

"And if she's not on the morning train?"

"Well, there are only two—the 11:15 or the 2:38. She knows we have a concert in one week. I wrote her a letter explaining everything we'd need to do first. She'll be here tomorrow at the latest."

"And if she isn't?"

He didn't respond.

I said, "You haven't heard from her in weeks either, have you?"

The waiter brought us coffees that cooled, untouched, on the table.

"It's my fault," Al-Cerraz said finally. "That argument I had with her, back in the fall, the last time I saw her"—he mulled it over, struggling with his memories—"I thought we'd patched it up. But maybe not."

"Well, she and I had arguments, too," I said quickly—cringing as I said it, because as true and innocent as the words were, the intentions behind them were not. It would be so easy to let Al-Cerraz think he was to blame. "One really bad argument at the end," I tried to say, more forcefully and honestly. "It wasn't pretty. I have to say—she wasn't well. Not at all..."

The catch in my voice caught me unaware. I tried to speak again and then gave up, and finally hailed the waiter angrily, to tell him that the coffees were cold.

Al-Cerraz studied me warily.

After a while, I said, "Maybe it's impossible to rescue a person."

"I don't know. I've been rescued two or three times in a day—and that was before dinner." He smiled and patted my shoulder. "I remember when I came to see you in Madrid. I had to throw you into a pond just to shake some sense into you. Some people would call that a rescue."

It wasn't a fair comparison. But all I said was, "What I did to her was worse."

"I trust that it wasn't." He looked at me more sternly. "You know, losing hope is what gets people in the most trouble."

"She's in a fantasy world. Her problem isn't losing hope, it's about seeing clearly—"

"I wasn't talking about Aviva," he interrupted. "I was talking about you."

The next day a telegram came at breakfast—not from Aviva but from Biber, explaining that our Madrid concert was being postponed, due to concern about the election and the mayhem that might ensue in the coming week if a new dictator arose.

"Well, let's just cancel then," Al-Cerraz said without looking up from the newspaper he had opened to the sport pages.

"Madrid?"

"All of it. The spring and summer tour."

He wasn't upset. "So we had another year together, because of her. We made one great record. I'm back on my feet; you're busier than ever."

"That's it?"

"When she's done with Weill and his projects, she'll come back." He closed his newspaper. "Find somewhere to spend your energies. Create something beautiful. Be the kind of person she'd want to come back to, if you're still thinking along those lines."

Later that day, in a cab bound for the train station, I asked him, "Where will you go?"

"Málaga."

"Whenever you're not touring—always Málaga."

"It's warm."

"The entire south of Spain is warm this time of year."

"No," he laughed. "I mean it's very warm."

"Well, I suppose—" I stopped. "You don't mean Doña de Larrocha?"

His mustache twitched. "She is recently widowed."

"I'm sorry."

"I'm not. Anyway, with liberalism running amok, the communists will be terrifying the *latifundistas*"—they were the owners of the immense southern farms. "She has Civil Guards to watch her fields, but at her manor house, Doña de Larrocha will want another man around, to look after things."

"What will you do—guard the front door with a pitchfork?"

"I think she has one of those old blunderbusses in a back closet. Word is that once they get the eight-hour workday passed, the workers will have more leisure than they know what to do with. They say the *braceros*' plan is to gather up all the wives and daughters, to create orgies of 'obligatory free love.' If I fail to stop that from happening, and the forces of free love break down our door, then I will enjoyably submit to the insurrection. If I manage to keep those scoundrels at bay, Doña de Larrocha will shower me with amorous gratitude. That is, more than she already has…"

I held up one hand. "Don't feel you need to share the details."

But he couldn't contain himself. "I'm not talking about physical relations, Feliu. I'm talking about money. She has paid all my debts, every last one. Every last cent to Thomas Brenan. My future compositions are mine alone."

He grew more serious. "I was still willing to tour, but the truth is I don't have to anymore. I am free."

I smiled. "Free from everyone except Doña de Larrocha."

But he wouldn't let me put a damper on his happiness. "Some of her wealthy neighbors are leaving for Sevilla or the south of France—or at least sending their money there. But she's a tough lady." He smiled, savoring the thought. "She's like one of those prize bulls in their special pastures, glowering at the mischievous boys who stroll past, daring them to annoy her."

Al-Cerraz got out at the train station. I stayed in the back of the cab, brooding, until the driver asked a second time, "Where to?"

"Anywhere."

He dropped me on the Ramblas. I paid for one overpriced drink at a wobbly table in the flow of pedestrian traffic, remembering how my mother had grieved over her lost grocery money on our first day in Barcelona. With the midday sun beating down on my head, I left a tip that was more than the cost of the drink, went to another café table under an awning, and ordered a coffee I barely touched. The waiter picked up my cup and saucer, wiped the table, and set it down again, eyeing the line of waiting patrons, but I refused to be rushed. The air was warm, the boulevard's graceful plane trees were green. Though I wasn't hungry, I ordered a cold cod salad, just to be left in peace. Everyone seemed to be out on the boulevard today, waiting for something. A popping sound at another café several doors down caused dozens of heads to turn, but it wasn't a pistol or explosive, just champagne.

Al-Cerraz had left me with the program materials we'd been assembling—worthless now. I thought about dropping the whole envelope into the nearest garbage bin, but then I remembered the publicity photos inside. I took out Aviva's again and stared at it. The longer I looked, the more this perfect image crowded out the last real images I'd seen of her, coming out of the bathroom, sitting on the bed, looking at me as if I were her captor, or worse.

I was still studying that photo when the news came. I heard it from the waiter who brought my salad. He kept dashing between my table and the café kitchen, where the staff had their ears pressed to a radio: King Alfonso was leaving the country, bound for exile, possibly in Italy. I listened intently, ready to hear who the next dictator might be, and in what manner these latest pro-Republican elections would be suppressed. But there was no mention of a dictator, or of any sort of conservative backlash.

When the next announcement came, the café erupted, its patrons spilling into the street. One and then two waiters ran out and pulled off their aprons. A little boy shinnied up a lamppost and began to sing indecipherable words at the top of his lungs. A man who had just bought flowers began to hand them out, and then ran back for more, but the flower seller distrusted the gleam in his eye and waddled to the front of her kiosk to pull the metal shutters closed with a long hooked pole. Her reaction goaded him; he reached around her for the flowers while she brandished her pole at him, prepared to strike. Other sellers, equally wary of anarchy, began to close up their kiosks and follow the crowd up the street, to any café with standing room. An older man sitting in the sun next to me pushed away his plate, stood, and said to his wife calmly but knowledgeably, "They'll let all the prisoners out—the innocent ones and the common criminals, too. Best to be getting home."

Merriment, disbelief, joyful tears—all of it flooded the Ramblas that hour, that day, and into the raucous evening. There it was, that word, on everyone's tongues: *República*. The Second Republic. The First Republic, in 1873, when my own parents were children, had lasted only eleven months—and yet they'd talked about it for years, a time when colors were brighter, food tasted better, and music was everywhere. Now people were saying that a general election was yet to be held, but procedural challenges aside, the unthinkable had happened already. The King had admitted defeat, and no one had rushed forward to usurp parliamentary leadership, no martial law had been imposed. Could this republic be permanent? Was democracy possible?

The dancing started. A group of older women set their handbags in the middle of a circle, joined hands, and began to perform the *sardana*, a Catalan dance that would one day symbolize political defiance, but on this day was simply a spontaneous expression of unity and joy. And from a fourth-floor window overlooking the street, a radio blared the triumphant strains of Beethoven's Ninth Symphony.

Al-Cerraz had missed the festivities by mere hours. But the advice he'd given me rang even more true, given the news: Find somewhere to spend your energies. Create something beautiful.

And wasn't this beautiful? Our Second Republic, born on that spring day, and like Aviva herself, best contemplated and most easily loved in idealized form, before complications could set in.

In the weeks that followed, I began to see that image everywhere: full-color posters of *"La Niña Bonita,"* the pretty girl. Instead of a cloche hat, she had a bejeweled helmet, and purple rays radiated from her light olive skin. That was simply how one poster artist had decided to portray our newly proclaimed republic. But to me, it was Aviva, and when later I heard the phrase *"La Niña Bonita,"* I applied it not just to the Second Republic, but to that entire period, the years 1931 to 1933. It made me think of the "pretty girl" I had known, before obsession and addiction had tarnished her features.

If I had been busy upon my return from Germany, I was twice as busy during the Republic's first years. I said yes to everything, sat through as many meetings as rehearsals, and accepted every title and honor the new Republic wanted to bestow upon me, as long as it would further peaceful causes.

I attended one dinner after another, one discussion after another: *Does art belong to the elite? Does art belong to the masses? Should intellectuals be involved in politics? How should one support and train poets and musicians if every untrained peasant or laborer is already a poet or musician at heart?* In contrast with my years with Al-Cerraz, who had performed tirelessly but refused to engage in serious political discussions, I now shared meals and cabs and train cars with artists who excelled at political talk but balked at creating or performing. There would always be a better time, later. "The future is my muse," one socialist thespian told me when I came to inform him that my colleagues in the Ministry of Education couldn't continue to subsidize a playwright who never finished any of his plays. "Perfect," I told him. "Then come to us for money in the *future*. As for now, you might need to get a job."

I traveled frequently between Salamanca, Madrid, Barcelona, Córdoba and Sevilla. I woke up thinking I smelled the sea, only to remember I'd gone to bed in an urban hotel on the central plains. I went to bed red-eyed and groggy, thinking I was staring out some guesthouse window at the twinkling lights of farmhouses, only to remember I was in a harbor town in the south, looking toward a line of boats.

What did I do? Whatever was asked of me. I had been a conductor long enough to appreciate the role of the percussionist who waits three hours to clap the cymbals once. I was that percussionist. I traveled, I attended, I advised; I lent my name and appearance and reputation to the cause. And what was the cause? Not just artistic matters, but a fundamental reorganization of society. It's easy to laugh now at the era's lofty chatter, the programs that ran out of steam. But in the meanwhile, we succeeded in making fundamental changes. We gave women the vote. We eliminated titles of nobility. We secured basic rights for laborers. We stripped the Catholic Church of its monolithic power. We stayed too busy for heartache or regrets.

Yes, I continued to write to Aviva. Yes, she continued to write to me. But how did she say it in German? *Es macht nichts.* It does not matter. Now we each had our own noble causes to pursue.

Despite the great hopes of April 14—*because* of the great hopes—discontent brewed from the Republic's start. A threat of rebellion from clerical rightists was followed by a vengeful spate of church burning. Azaña, acting as Minister of War, made the decision not to send out the Civil Guard to stop it. "All the convents in Madrid are not worth the life of a single Republican," he proclaimed. His comment would dog him for eternity. Alfonso sympathizers and Church conservatives repeated it as often as possible, to reinforce the image of the Republic as disordered and dangerous. In the streets, rightist thugs provoked fights. It was in their interest to make the Republic seem untenable and frightening to the middle class.

For those of us on the left and middle—a diverse group, to be sure—it was in our best interest to make the Republic appear vital. Crop prices were falling, the economy was out of our hands; but education and the arts were the areas we could attempt to control. We struggled to create a secular school system to replace the private Catholic schools—an impossible task, given the lack of money, buildings, and teachers. Perhaps President Alcalá-Zamora had expelled the Jesuits too soon; perhaps the anticlerical legislation was too strict.

I did my part by creating a national music curriculum, patterned after the Orff method from Germany, which emphasized simple percussion instruments. It never went very far. Spanish children, armed with castanets and guitars, proved to be less malleable and mechanistic than their German counterparts. And when we allowed them to sing— *How dare we print Castilian lyric sheets where Catalan was flourishing? And if we paid more to print the lyrics in Catalan, then what about Euskera?*—all hell broke loose. It might have been funny, if we hadn't needed some semblance of national unity so desperately.

Every political organization splintered into two or three factions; everywhere, people spoke as if in code: *CEDA, CNT, FNTT, PCE, POUM, UGT, PSOE, FJS, JSU*. If acronyms were chickens, we would have eaten well in those years!

Perhaps it says something about the liability of abbreviations that the group that had none—the Spanish fascist party—dominated the country in the end. It was called simply the Falange—an Englishman would say "Phalanx," from the ancient Greek word for a united body of soldiers, moving as one, protected by their joined shields and lances. The opposite of division; the opposite of alphabetical obfuscation. Not the only reason they won, not even the main reason. But a name has power and direction; it creates its own momentum, like the wind formed by a wall of flame, born by fire and birthing fire, carrying embers downwind.

And meanwhile, it was our job to pretend that things were still well. To admit that wealthy people were hoarding their hams and flour and olive oil, that southern farmworkers were forced to scour the countryside for rabbits and acorns, that anarchists were blowing up telephone exchanges, that it was unsafe on such-and-such dates to attempt a concert in Casa Viejas or Bajo Llobregat, was to play into enemy hands. If the nation was hungry or the streets were unsafe, then perhaps the new Republic wasn't working, perhaps democracy didn't have enough power to shake a chaotic society by its lapels, to make it behave. Regardless of how people had voted in 1931, the wealthy still controlled the land, and desperate people still reacted to hunger, evictions, and wage cuts with violence. They had expected the Second Republic to heal all, to provide everything, regardless of the worldwide economy, which was in ruins.

Idealism: That was the problem on all sides. On both left and right, everyone had some shining image in mind, the ideal society, toward which they ran at such full tilt as to guarantee a bruising collision. Quixote and his windmills. Never forget that Cervantes's hero, while the victim of undeniable public cruelty, did the worst damage to his own hide, while fighting phantoms.

The Catholic press applauded Germany's Nazis, with their emphasis on fatherland, authority, hierarchy. The word for that system was "fascism," and perhaps that was what we needed, they argued. Better than its alternative, communism. And what was communism? Now it was a label applied to anything the landowners did not like. For generations, townsfolk had been allowed to gather windfall crops, to scour the countryside for firewood, to water their beasts on the *latifundios*. But now those actions were considered threatening.

I stayed in touch with Al-Cerraz, a man who'd never used acronyms in his life and who'd never belonged to any official party. But his leanings and sympathies—or lack of sympathies—were clear. He wrote to me once, in 1932:

> *You have to understand. In Málaga, these people are kleptomaniacs. They'll steal anything that isn't nailed down—they think it belongs to them. And they don't look ahead. They'd eat all the seed in the storehouses if they could, and then there'd be no chance of planting next year, when things are better.*

On January 30, 1933, the Spanish newspapers paused in their coverage of local bombings in Barcelona and Sevilla long enough to report bad news from abroad. Hitler had been named German chancellor. Two months later, I received a letter from Aviva—short, confused, written in haste. Weill had been warned that the Nazis were coming to arrest him. He had left the country, bound for Paris. Brecht and hundreds of other intellectuals had left as well.

And none too soon, it would seem, considering that Hitler's Nazi police commissioner, Heinrich Himmler, had arrested so many political opponents that he couldn't find room to imprison them all. According to newspaper reports, the Nazis were busy solving that problem by opening their first camps—concentration camps, they called them—in Bavaria near Dachau, with three more camps to open soon near Berlin.

Try as I might to read the news about Weill soberly and sympathetically, my stomach also registered light flutters of anticipation. If Weill's productions were blacklisted, then Aviva would be leaving Germany, too, wouldn't she? She'd be an outcast there, perhaps even an enemy of the state, based on her race and her affiliations. I read on, expecting a request for help from me and Al-Cerraz. Perhaps we could record again, or go on a tour. Perhaps I could find her a position within the Spanish school-music program.

I read on, to find that Aviva wrote only of her need to find another local musical position.

I wrote back to her, trying to drill sense into her, and to dangle before her opportunities that she could not resist. Perhaps—did I dare turn my back on my own Republican colleagues?—perhaps we could even leave Europe for a while, if that was her desire. We could go to England, or the Orient. An orchestra in Japan had asked me to guest-conduct a symphony by Mahler, of all things.

She wrote back with more descriptions of the changes in Berlin:

Jews everywhere, even the artists and musicians and theater people of all kinds, are being fired from their jobs. It is official policy. There is a Staatskommissar *for the* Entjudung—*the De-Jewification—of cultural life.*

Again, I read on with hope. She was coming, then.
She was not.

Thank goodness I am in Berlin, where the people are clever enough to craft a response to the problem. So many Jews were dismissed en masse that they have started a new association, the Jüdischer Kulturbund. *It will operate a theater for Jews only, under the plan of Dr. Kurt Singer. So there will be jobs, after all. Always, there is a way to ride out these things.*

Furthermore, she wrote, the Nazi leadership supported the *Kulturbund*. It could serve the artistic needs of one group, the propagandistic needs of another. It would give Hinkel, Himmler, Goebbels, and all the rest a chance to prove to the outside world that they didn't necessarily mistreat Jewish people. "Jewish artists working for Jews," Hinkel had said with pride. Aviva thought that Hinkel seemed to fancy himself a paternalistic protector.

The only problem she foresaw was that the Jewish theater planned to specialize in music and drama with which she wasn't familiar. Jewish audiences preferred what all Germans preferred: the latest plays and operas, or classic favorites such as Shakespeare. But the *Kulturbund* leaders and Hinkel wanted more distinctly ethnic content. Folk music. Yiddish culture. Plays about Palestine. Jewish opera—if there was such a thing as Jewish opera. Aviva wrote:

> *What do any of us know about that?*
>
> *The last time I was in a synagogue I was a child, and it was a school field trip, for history class or some such thing. Most of these so-called Jews don't speak Yiddish and couldn't find Jerusalem on a map. We have a Wagner expert among us, a Beethoven expert, a Bruckner expert; but we're being asked to put on plays about golems and sing "Shalom Aleichem" to audiences that clamor for* A Midsummer Night's Dream. *We've had to recruit more culturally Jewish musicians from outside Germany to come and lead us. They are offering classes in Hebrew and Yiddish inflection so the German actors can play their parts more authentically. See why I tell you not to worry? You are reading in your newspapers about some Jews trying to leave Berlin, but what you are not reading is that Jews are moving from Denmark and Palestine and probably even Spain to Berlin, where* Yiddishkeit *and* Judenkultur *are booming.*

Competition in the *Kulturbund* was so fierce, and loyalties so fragile, that she couldn't risk leaving the job, even temporarily. It might not be waiting for her when she came back. German mail censorship had begun in February, the same month the Nazis burned down their own Reichstag and arrested all of the legislature's communist members.

Aviva might have sent other letters that month, but if so, they didn't arrive.

Have I mentioned that the Spanish posters had changed? The beautiful, lifelike images I'd first seen all over Barcelona in April 1931, "*La Niña Bonita*," had undergone a transformation. She had lost her pink cheeks and soft brown eyes, the hopeful rays emanating from her cloche hat. She had become monotone, verdigris, thicker-lipped, with a harder jaw, the hint of an Adam's apple at her neck, and thick forearms—drawn in the same style as the workers and soldiers on all the communist-style posters that shouted: PEASANT! THE REVOLUTION NEEDS YOUR EFFORT or TÚ!—WHAT HAVE YOU DONE FOR VICTORY? A girl for one month only, she had become a statue, empty-eyed, as if to say there was no time for humanity now, no time for individuality; only time for symbols and causes.

In 1933 the *Bienio Negro*—the Two Black Years—began. An electoral landslide by the right wing allowed the Republic's enemies to reverse many of the reforms of the last two years. Yet even that wasn't enough. Everywhere there was talk of disorder, and the need for strength; conspiracies, and the need for iron will. Young Spaniards eyed news photos from Italy and Germany with envy; they who did not remember 1921, or 1914, nonetheless spoke as if with personal knowledge of 1898, that end of the era in which Spain had known true power and pride. In driving sleet, they lined up in columns, twenty thousand strong, wanting to shout *Führer!* or *Duce!* but having no such comparable Spanish word yet, and no single charismatic leader. They settled for calling out *Jefe! Jefe! Jefe!*—Chief! Chief! Chief!—relying on the wind to carry their incantation to any man who might step forward to guide them.

PART VI

Bull Season

1936

CHAPTER

~ 21 ~

Picasso's Spain was the land of *matadors* and *picadors* and *banderilleros,* and so was Hemingway's; but not mine, not my Catalonia. But bull-rings did figure vividly twice in my life, framing a year that proved to be bloodier than a *corrida.*

My most striking memories from that year consist mostly of visual flashes: A naked baby held up toward a passing truck while a man pushes it away, mouthing *"lleno"*—full. Thin striped mattresses doubled up alongside the road, with feet sticking out from between the folds. And this: A woman dashing across a plaza at midday, in pumps and a party dress, pearls glowing at her earlobes, a spaniel nipping at her heels, when a sniper bullet catches her near the pelvis. She falls, clutching her purse against her hip, her face registering first embarrassment, as if she'd only slipped; then, only slowly, the terror of dawning realization. She could not believe what had just happened. I couldn't believe it either, watching from across the square, as the next two shots stilled her thrashing and sent her dog into frantic confused circles, lapping at the ground.

More like that—dozens and hundreds of images like that, numbly rendered. All of them, notably, without sound.

———

But I have let my story fall out of sequence, which I promised not to do. It is the influence of the Civil War itself, a series of events that resists objective, accurate retelling. I will begin again with the bulls, because it is with bulls that the war started for me, and with bulls that it nearly ended for me.

Al-Cerraz had invited me to attend Málaga's spring *feria*, which would climax in a series of bullfights, including one that would feature Doña de Larrocha's prize *toro bravo*. This was June 1936, and the pianist and I had seen each other only a few times since April 1931, when we happened to be in the same city together. Now that he had stopped performing, he rarely left the south. Most of my duties lately had been in the capital and in the north.

But in the intervening years, we had also corresponded regularly, even more so after 1933, when we'd last heard from Aviva. Just as her first appearance in our lives had knit us closer together, her absence now kept us so. Together, in our frequent letters and rare visits, we suppressed our anxieties about her welfare. Together, we indulged the naïve hope that the state of affairs in Europe would improve someday soon, allowing things to continue as they had before.

I was keeping an apartment in Mérida at the time, and Mérida to Málaga was a long way to travel to see a bullfight. But there was a subject I wanted to broach with Al-Cerraz, on behalf of the party officials with whom I'd allied myself during those fragile, final Republic days.

"There," said Al-Cerraz on the afternoon I arrived, leaning his bulk against a fence rail. "The Doña hasn't visited her children in years, but she comes to look at that animal once a day."

We both admired the bull standing under the shade of the great oak tree, twitching its narrow rump and flicking its long tail.

Al-Cerraz whistled. "The sacrifices she has made to keep that bull alive!" The bull glanced our direction, and Al-Cerraz winced. The Doña tried to limit the bull's exposure to people, lest it grow complacent about attacking a matador in the ring. But even with her guards, Al-Cerraz told me, she'd had a hard time keeping people away.

"They want to fight it?"

"Fight it?" He laughed. "They want to eat it. You might see a dangerous beast under that tree, but the peasants see five hundred kilos of beef. Some of them haven't eaten meat in the five years since that bull was born."

I nodded appreciatively. "Five years. So this was a bull born during our first Republican spring."

Al-Cerraz exhaled ruefully. "Is that how long it's been? He may die with the Republic, if what we hear in Málaga is true."

The most recent elections, in February, had transferred power yet again, from the right-wing parties that had held it during the two-year Bienio Negro back to the left, which finally and belatedly had managed to assemble a Popular Front. Even its superior resources, which funded an immense propaganda campaign—ten thousand campaign posters and fifty million leaflets—had not allowed the right to retain its grip. In my own party, however, we knew better than to celebrate a lopsided victory too freely. In the parlance of *el toreo*, we knew that a wounded bull is more savage than ever, and that a matador is most likely to be gored when his back is turned. That is why I had come to speak with Al-Cerraz.

I smoothed a hand through the thin hairs blowing up from my mostly bald pate, and launched into my speech. "Catching the eye and the ear of the people—that is the key to everything, these days. We need every artist, every writer, every musician who has ever spent time in the public eye—"

"But Feliu," he said, leaning his forearms on the fence, "the left is going to lose."

"We won in February," I said. As if he couldn't see through me; as if he didn't understand what I, what everyone, feared. Parliamentary democracy was in its last throes; talk of revolution and counterrevolution occupied all sides. Military zealots clamored for martial law. The fascist Falange was more powerful than ever.

"It's a dangerous game," Al-Cerraz started to say, and for a moment I thought he was talking politics. But he was staring at the bull again. "You see those caramel-colored horns? They're deadly sharp at the tip. Not filed. They say bulls use their horns like a cat uses its whiskers, to estimate the width of something, to know where they're aiming. If the bull thinks his horns end there, and the owner files them to here"—he narrowed the span of his upraised hands—"then the bull aims wrong. But that's cheating."

I mumbled an assent, then tried to steer the conversation around to politics again. "The Republicans aren't stupid. They sacked Franco as chief of staff and sent him off to the Canary Islands. And the other generals, too—Goded, Mola—they're scattered to the four corners. Their most devout army followers are in Morocco, too far away to do harm."

"Morocco," he sighed. "You know, when they have sandstorms in Africa, we wake up to yellow grit in our sheets. It's not that far, really."

I tilted my face toward the sun and closed my eyes. "Justo, please listen to what I'm saying. We'd like your help."

He watched the bull in silence for a while. Then he said, "I'm glad you came. And I'm glad you asked. Doña de Larrocha and I get along because she needs me. That is a condition I understand and cultivate.

"*Sin embargo,*" he paused dramatically, "I visited Barcelona last year. In the streets—well, I'm sure you've seen them—they were selling these sheets of Republican ballads. Sorry, not Republican—more anarchist, I suppose, glory of the worker and that sort of thing. I bought one to look at. I studied it for ten minutes, but I couldn't understand it. I went up to a shoeshine boy whose box was painted black and red. '*Qué quieres tú?*' he says, looking at my suit. '*Tú,*' he says, not

'*Usted.*' 'What's up?' he says to me, not '*Buenos días,*' even though he can tell from my clothes I could give him a tip bigger than what he earns all day—if tipping were still legal.

"And I know I'm asking the right boy. I show him the lyric sheet and I ask him how the tune goes, since there aren't any notes printed. 'Any way you like,' he says. I figure he is being sassy, but we talk for a while, and I realize he means it. He can sing the song a dozen ways. They sell these lyric sheets all over, different songs every block, so that all the leftists can lift their *botas* and belt it out together. The music doesn't matter, just the foolish, sentimental words.

"Feliu," he said. "We're living in a time of messages, not art."

"I suppose."

He continued, "I have tried, these last years, to stay out of the public eye. I am not a great communicator—sometimes my right hand doesn't talk to my left—"

"Coming from a pianist, that's ridiculous."

He continued, "That beast over there doesn't know what's coming. But we do. I recommend the middle road."

"But you're not middle—middle is moderate, loyalist, pro-democracy..."

"No. The other middle."

"Which is?"

"Survival."

Our plan for the next day was to watch the *encierro,* during which Doña de Larrocha's bull and five others destined for the ring would be set loose to run through streets at one end of Málaga, chasing any youths who chose to risk their lives on the wrong side of the barricades. We would convene again several hours later at the *plaza de toros,* where the six dazed and furious bulls would be waiting in dark pens for the main event. Doña de Larrocha's "Flor" would be second.

At the last minute, though, the *encierro* was called off. No one seemed to know why. Al-Cerraz and I circled the neighborhood where it was supposed to have been held. Walking down a narrow street between two high walls strung with clotheslines, we found ourselves surrounded by men in dark pants, collarless open-necked shirts, dark caps. Al-Cerraz, always a fastidious dresser, had become even more formal with age. A short man with curly red hair grabbed his tie and yanked it. Another man jabbed at his fine hands and polished nails. "My girlfriend doesn't have hands this pretty," the stranger simpered in falsetto.

It was like a scene from a schoolyard; I found myself stifling nervous laughter. I told myself these men were only confused, bored like us, frustrated by the cancellation of the *encierro*. But the way they studied Al-Cerraz and me—our clothes, our hands, our nails—told me differently. I noticed the bulge of a pistol tucked inside one man's waistline, and a bandanna held taut between another man's purpled fists.

"Work," the redhead said. "What kind of work do you do?"

Al-Cerraz didn't answer.

The *pistolero* grabbed at his waist and I saw, to my great relief, that it wasn't a pistol he was harboring after all, it was a hammer. But my relief ebbed when the stranger grabbed Al-Cerraz's wrist with one hand and brandished the hammer in the other, snarling, "Why do you need hands this pretty?"

Al-Cerraz didn't move, his hand still extended, like a sleepwalker, even when the man let go of his wrist and grabbed for mine.

"How about you?" the redhead demanded, yanking my right hand.

"Olives," I said.

He laughed. "With these hands?"

I yanked my right hand away and gave him my other, palm up. "I'm left-handed."

"Look at this," he said, admiring the calloused pads on my fingertips. "Granada?" he said.

"Campo Seco. Near Barcelona."

At the end of the street, another man whistled. The redhead dropped my hand and, without another word, the thugs moved on, leaving Al-Cerraz and me under the clothesline's sheets and bloomers, sweating.

"Are you thirsty?" Al-Cerraz asked.

"Terribly."

Continuing toward the bullring, we found refuge in a café, where we tried to make light of the confrontation, toasting ourselves for not having wet our pants in the face of danger. Still, the incident hung over us.

After the first round Al-Cerraz grew quieter still, and I thought he was brooding on the thugs again. But when he spoke he said, "Changing times have hurt la Doña, too. She still provides me with an allowance of sorts, but it isn't enough."

I nodded sympathetically. "Do you want me to buy the next round?"

"*Gracias. Muy amable.*"

We enjoyed a second. Without apology, he stuck me with the bill for a third. I refused his direct request for a fourth. At that point, Al-Cerraz rose unsteadily and told me to hold our table while he stepped outside. From my seat, I watched as he unfolded a piece of heavily marked paper from his pocket and waved it in front of passersby.

The crowd heading west, toward the *plaza de toros,* was growing heavier by the minute. Al-Cerraz darted from one pedestrian to the next, talking, gesturing, bowing, apologizing, tapping a shoulder here, pointing to a pocket there, pressing his lips together to hum. I tried to call him back to our table inside the café, but he gestured defiantly— *stay there.* I pointed to my watch. He squinted toward the end of the block and flapped his hands. *Just wait.*

My curiosity was unbearable. "*Está bien*—" I said finally, joining him on the sidewalk, where a young man in canvas trousers was inspecting the sheet. "What is this about?"

"I was closing a sale."

"What?"

"In order to buy the next round."

"You've had enough. And we're out of time."

"I insist on paying you back for the last two, then. I need some money in my pocket, in any case." He turned back to resume his pitch.

"Give me that," I said. "Whatever it is, I'll buy it."

The young man had been ready to walk away, but my sudden interest gave him pause. "Hum it again," he said.

Al-Cerraz held the paper in his left hand and conducted with his right, while he hummed the first few bars of an unfamiliar melody.

"I don't know," the young man said.

"Give it to your girl. Tell her it was written in her honor. There's no two like it."

"You don't have other copies?"

"Other melodies, yes. But no other copies of *this* melody. I write down something once, and then it lives its own life—"

I interrupted. "You're selling one of your compositions on the street? And you don't have another copy of it?"

"Trying to..." Al-Cerraz grumbled.

"Let me see another," the young man said.

Al-Cerraz fished another folded paper from his pocket. Facing me, he said, "Those lyric sheets in Barcelona gave me the idea. Why not?"

But without a familiar melody, and without lyrics, the young man wasn't interested. When he walked away, I said to Al-Cerraz, "You have a pocketful of these? That's quite a development."

He shrugged. "Yes, just a few years ago, I would have thought so, too. Once I stopped trying to write my masterpiece, my *obra maestra,* an endless number of *obras mínimas* spilled out. Like the little black notebooks I used to keep when we toured—full of overheard sounds and mental clutter." He waved his hand over them. "But they're worthless, of course—as are any unconnected fragments. Like your political parties on the left..."

I ignored the jab. "That's what you've been working on, then?"

"Yes."

"Since...?"

"After Burgos. After I threw away everything."

"You shouldn't give up. Brahms spent fourteen years writing his first symphony."

"I'm not Brahms."

I tried again. "Don't give up is all I meant."

"Don't worry about that," he said, forcing a note of cheer into his voice. "I don't give up any of my bad habits."

At the *plaza de toros,* we found our seats in the shade. Doña de Larrocha called out to Al-Cerraz from amidst a gaggle of her friends, pursing her dazzling red lips to blow him a kiss. I'd stayed in her home once, years ago, and performed for her friends, but she barely acknowledged me now. Al-Cerraz asked if she knew why the *encierro* had been canceled, and I strained to hear her answer. Evidently, there had been some threats that someone would try to sabotage the street event.

"*Escandaloso,*" murmured the woman behind her.

"*Qué lástima,*" from the one to her left.

"*Qué vergüenza!*" This from her right.

Across the ring from us, the sun seats were empty of all but a dozen spectators, and they filed out after the first matador had killed his bull. On our side of the ring, the crowd cheered wildly, tossing *botas* and flinging handkerchiefs.

I studied the empty seats opposite, ear tilted toward a growing rumble that originated from somewhere beyond the arena, accompanied by a heavy knocking sound far below our seats. I turned to question Al-Cerraz, but he and the rest of the party were cheering even louder as the matador circled the ring grandly, followed by his team, who with the aid of horses were dragging the dead bull. The two men who were reapplying the white powder line around the sullied ring heard what I was hearing, though. I saw them lift their heads in the direction of the noise—the rumble again, and the heavy knocking, as if the Doña's bull, due next to fight, was thrusting its unfiled horns into the wood of the paddock door.

Just as the matador finished his celebratory perambulation, the paddock door flew open. Doña de Larrocha's bull staggered forward a few steps, head low, and collapsed. There was a long silence as the bull's blood seeped into the sand. The matador had stopped and turned, weaponless hands flexing nervously, as if fearing that his own vanquished bull had risen from the dead. Then the crowd let out a collective gasp. Doña de Larrocha's bull was sliding backward, into the dark paddock, centimeter by centimeter. Someone on my left pointed at a rope cinched around one of its back legs. We watched until the rope slackened. Another pause. And then—finally—the surge. Men began to spill out of the shadows, from behind barriers and stalls. One of them ran to the bull's neck, and in a flash of silver slashed it—rather humanely, I couldn't help thinking.

Doña de Larrocha shrieked. I pressed my back as flat against my seat as I could while Al-Cerraz and two other men pushed past to get to her. My view thus blocked, I didn't see the next minute or so, as the forty-odd peasants below succeeded in pulling the bull back into its paddock and out a back door, to the growing cheers of hundreds more hungry *braceros* and workers in the streets outside. Near us, a white-haired man in the regalia of a retired general brandished a pistol and shot it wildly, managing only to graze one of the *picadores'* horses below.

By the time my view was clear, Doña de Larrocha had shifted from despair to anger, and was screaming at the top of her lungs, *"Cobardes!"*—Cowards!—to the matador's *cuadrillas* below, who, though armed with lances, had stepped aside once the peasants broke into the ring.

Al-Cerraz tried to comfort her, first with tenderness—"Yes, sweet-ness; a shame, unspeakable…" Finally he lost his grip and shouted, "The damn bull was going to die in ten minutes anyway!"

His flood of immediate apologies did nothing to assuage her, and as she attacked him with her fan, she shouted, "They have no respect for ritual!"

But she was wrong. The peasants who dragged the dead bull away were traditionalists, too. Even with the Civil Guard due to arrive at any moment, they took time to sever the bull's ears and toss them into the ring.

Al-Cerraz did not forgive the peasants for what they'd done, upsetting his lady friend, ruining the day, making a mess of one of the few plea-sures that remained in Málaga for a person of moderate means. He was not a political man. He drew his conclusions about world events based on personal experiences, personal affinities, the way others' needs in-tersected with his own—as we all do, though I wouldn't have admitted it at the time. I cut my visit to Málaga short. I knew I'd lost him to my cause: the Republic's cause.

For some people, the civil war had started more than a year earlier, when the Asturian miners' revolt was viciously suppressed by rightist military forces, under the leadership of then–Chief of Staff Franco, before he'd lost that post. I've said that the civil war started for me that day in the bullring. But it wasn't at the moment when Doña de Lar-rocha's bull was killed; it wasn't while she was screeching, weeping, shouting the beast's name. It was minutes later, as we prepared to leave the arena. She drew herself up, tall and suddenly stoic, and turned to the cluster around her—me, Justo, the lady who had been sitting be-hind her, the white-haired general with the bad aim. She said, "But it won't be a long wait, will it?"

They all shook their heads in unison: No, it won't. Not long.

"Let Flor be remembered," she said, "as the first who spilled his blood for a good cause. There will be others."

Cierto. Certainly. Yes, there will.

And maybe people were always saying these things—claiming special knowledge, forecasting doom or victory and the settling of scores, threatening revenge. In fact, that was just the problem in Spain—the long accumulation of such prophecies and grudges. I knew I had my own. In any decade it *could* have happened. But in July, a month after Doña de Larrocha's bull died ten minutes prematurely, it *did* happen. One spark leaped into a century's accumulated kindling.

What happened then surprised everyone. We expected a brief uprising, or *alzamiento*, leading to a swift change in power; instead we got a prolonged civil war. Franco was not the mastermind, nor a likely figurehead. He was not Spain's Hitler, but only a general who emerged, quickly and stealthily, into a position of power. At moments, he seemed to be unexceptional—"Miss Canary Islands 1936," the other anti-Republican generals had nicknamed him ironically just weeks earlier, expressing their bemused disdain for his timidity—his timidity!—while he stewed in the tropical Isla Tenerife heat, waiting for orders, ready to support any number of causes. But he wasn't timid at all—just opportunistic and cold-blooded.

Also, lucky. Destined, many would later claim. The Moors, and men like my brother, who served alongside Franco during the Africa campaigns, had called his invincibility *baraka*. It explained why he had survived numerous near-death experiences, why he could advance on a white steed through whirlwinds of sand and clouds of smoke, not only undamaged but strengthened, as if his success fed upon others' tragedies.

If the military commander for the island of Gran Canaria hadn't died on a shooting range on July 16, conveniently and mysteriously,

Franco wouldn't have received military clearance to attend the funeral, traveling unsuspected from nearby Tenerife the next day. That evening, Spanish garrisons in the Moroccan cities of Melilla, Tetuan, and Ceuta rose against the Republic. The next morning, July 18, Franco and another general, Orgaz, took over Las Palmas, on Gran Canaria.

As a sixteen-year-old boy, I had fled Barcelona's "Tragic Week" without understanding the most basic matters of who was fighting whom, and how, and why. I had not understood the twelve years of colonialist turmoil that had led up to the military disaster that claimed my brother's life at Anual. Now I resolved to understand the chaos that was unfolding around me, day after bloody day. I watched as the coup d'état was greeted with cheers in the Catholic strongholds—Burgos, Salamanca, Zamora, Segovia, Ávila. I read the gory details of the first leftist purges in those old central-plains towns. Within a week, all of northwest Spain, except for the northern coast near Bilboa, was a Nationalist zone, secured by General Mola.

On July 18 I took a train south from Salamanca, where I'd been meeting with the symphony, to Mérida, where I had a studio apartment. I recall transferring my return ticket from the right front pocket of my pants to the inside left pocket of my suit jacket for safekeeping. The return trip specified a date—July 22, I believe. But I was certain that in a week or two, when the government crisis was sorted out, whether it was suppressed, as I hoped, or solidified into a new rightist government, I would be allowed to use my rail ticket.

I never set foot in Salamanca again.

Franco's significance within the uprising grew every day. On July 20, Sanjurjo, one of the key plotters, died in a freak plane accident. Sanjurjo, it was later said, was one of the rightists who would have pushed for early negotiations, before a shaky coup degraded into all-out war. More fate, a companion force to Franco's *baraka*.

Franco had flown from Gran Canaria to Morocco, where an anti-Republican army had assembled from the ranks of *Regulares*—Spanish troops—and mercenary Moors. These troops stood ready to surge across the Strait of Gibraltar, hampered only by lack of transportation. Republican warships controlled the strait. Franco needed planes. Mussolini refused to help at first, then surrendered a dozen Savoia-81 bombers in exchange for cash.

Like Italy, Germany was not eager to get involved, and Franco's initial appeals elicited little support. But Hitler was at Bayreuth's annual Wagner festival that week in July, indulging his taste for mythology-inspired operas about good and evil, morality and desire. Opera had been his passion since adolescence, when he'd first stumbled out of *Rienzi* rubbing his red-rimmed eyes, overcome with emotion. The music of Wagner was his religion, he said.

I had visited Bayreuth once myself, in the 1920s; nearly every music lover who passes through Bavaria did, before Wagnerism became synonymous with Nazism. I had experienced the excellent acoustics of the *Festspielhaus,* so enchantingly designed by Wagner that operagoers were said to wander the village in a daze for hours after a performance, barely able to distinguish fantasy from reality.

On the evening of July 25, when Franco's emissaries arrived in Bayreuth to petition for military assistance, Hitler had just returned from a performance of *Siegfried,* performed under the baton of his favorite conductor, Wilhelm Furtwängler. Before the night was over, Hitler had crafted a bigger offensive than Franco had requested. He named it *Unternehmen Feuerzauber*—Operation Magic Fire, a name taken from one of Wagner's musical motifs. Another night, another place, a different set of musical motifs ringing in his ears—who knows, even a less skillful conductor—and perhaps things would have been different.

I heard that story, months after it occurred, from a fellow music-loving Republican (who nevertheless had a hard time giving up his Wagner records). Should I have been surprised? I was. Surprised and horrified. Music's potency was proven to me, yet again, just as music's impotency had been proven to me, an equal number of times. Where was the pattern? Did art succeed in furthering only bad causes, providing emotion and justification for the evil already nesting within men's hearts? Did it provide solace, but only to those who might have fared better in the harsh light of reality, unconsoled? Did artistic inspiration only reinforce what destiny had already decided?

If music had power, then I had power, more than I had responsibly applied so far. If other men had destinies, then so did I; the burden of that realization was as great as it had ever been. Greater. I had spent the last fifteen years building up my reputation to be ready for a day such as this. Now the day had come, but I still had no idea how playing a cello—or being known as someone who played the cello—could make a difference in the world.

Once I had believed art had no fatherland, that art was a thing upon which vice could not impose. Now I believed that art was political, had a purpose, could literally move men and send foreign bombers screaming toward southern Spain. That made it debased, but it also made it— and me—responsible, powerful, and potentially guilty.

There was so much to be done. Yet I was unable to find anything worthwhile to do, beyond attending meetings, writing letters, and attempting the occasional short speech prior to a concert—none of which convinced the British or American governments to assist us. Meanwhile, I played Bach daily, to remind myself that Germany and Hitler were not synonymous, and because I needed the sense of order and meaning implicit in Bach's musical structure.

Franco crossed the strait. Workers' militias fled from the slaughtering Moors they'd always feared. Sevilla and Córdoba fell. In Granada, Falangist squads rounded up thousands of leftists, brought them to the cemetery, and shot them. One of them was the poet Federico García Lorca.

Now there were Nationalists both north and south, planning to meet in the middle. Franco made an appointment with a foreign reporter to meet him at a certain table in a certain Madrid café; he was that sure he'd be taking the capital according to his own timetable.

I listened to the nightly radio "chats" of the rebel general Queipo de Llano, broadcast from the Sevilla region, detailing the advance of Nationalist troops through southern Spain. He singled out well-known Republicans by name, describing the treatment they'd receive when they were caught. It wasn't enough to say he'd kill you. If you were a soccer star, he threatened to cut off your feet. If you were a musician or artist, he threatened to cut off your hands. For me, hands weren't enough—he said he'd take my arms, "to the elbows."

One night, I was just about to turn off the radio after one of these inflammatory chats when he announced that the record to follow would feature a work for piano, performed by the man whom Franco had just named honorary president of a newly created National Spanish Culture Institute. I waited, wondering who it could be. Manuel de Falla? He was a conservative clericalist, but as a friend of García Lorca, could he have accepted the post?

The next sound was not a name, but the dry hiss of the needle navigating the groove of the record itself, followed finally by the sound of a cello, and then a violin. It was the 1929 recording of the Dvořák Piano Trios that we had made with Aviva, the year we had met her. It was Al-Cerraz who had been named president of the fascist institute, one step away from a future cabinet post.

Once the initial shock had passed, I felt no lingering surprise. They had offered him acceptance and an audience, two of the things he cherished most. My apolitical partner had eclipsed me, stepping boldly into the most political—and least forgivable—role of his life.

What had happened, I found out later, was this: While other southern cities fell, Málaga managed to hold out, until February 1937, when the Nationalists swept through and the tables were turned. Outside the gates of the *plaza de toros* stood sticks festooned with twisted bits of what looked like fruit peel or salt cod, drying in the sun: leftists' ears. Local aristocrats like Doña de Larrocha claimed it must have been the Moorish mercenaries who did it—heads on pikes were one of those things you heard so much about in African countries. But everyone knew, Al-Cerraz later told me, that it was local Falangists, fighting for the Nationalists and exacting retribution for the bullring episode of eight months earlier.

The ears were too much. Al-Cerraz left Málaga then, and the Doña. But he had not left her political sphere. He accepted the position with the Spanish Culture Institute in hopes of composing official music for what he assumed would become the new government.

Unable to return to Mérida since the civil war broke out, I had been staying in a hotel in Torrepaulo, in a loyal part of the southwest. In early 1937 the war arrived there, too. I woke one morning to the sound of planes bombing the city and all the outlying roads, which was followed by the sound of strafing maneuvers as the planes punished the fleeing crowds. Dragging my cello, I joined the exodus, walking toward the part of the horizon that seemed least obscured by smoke.

I had given away my shoes and socks to a feeble older man who had run out of his apartment in nothing but underwear and a beret. Now my feet registered the incredible heat of the narrow route, which had been bombed so repeatedly that the rocky dirt smoldered like volcanic rubble. Some young men alongside the road were wrapping torn shirts around their feet, and I did likewise. Then, remembering the large cotton cloth I kept in my cello case for wiping away rosin dust, I fashioned a *serape* by tearing a slit in the cloth's middle and putting my head through it. It covered my shoulders, at least. But even through the rags on my feet, I continued to feel the heat rising and I smelled—or thought I could smell—my skin cooking. Eventually I left my cello by the roadside so that I might walk faster—though not my bow, which hung in its tube around my neck. Music could do nothing for me at that moment, but how desperately I wished for a pair of shoes.

I arrived that evening at the neighboring city of San Ramón, where I hoped to find an acquaintance who had retired from the Salamanca Symphony. I had trouble recognizing his house. The top floor had been blasted off, leaving the beams exposed. But while there was no plumbing and no heat, the ground floor and basement still provided shelter. My colleague offered me some bread and cold garlic soup, and after dabbing iodine on a few cuts and wrapping my ailing feet in gauze, I fell into the deepest sleep of my life. Hours later—it seemed like just a few minutes—I woke to the feeling of something jabbing my feet. In my dreams, it was the sharp rubble of the hot street again, poking into my soles. In real life, it was an old-fashioned bayonet.

The Nationalists rounded us up: me, the friend who had sheltered me, and thousands of others. While the streets were still dark, they marched us to the *plaza de toros* at the edge of town—the other bull-ring in my story. They searched my pockets and found the return ticket to Salamanca—Nationalist territory for a while now—and a card printed with my name. I was stood in a separate line outside the ring while many others, mostly men and a few women, were marched inside. I heard the machine gun shots, a lazy spray, repeated at regular intervals that rattled on for an eternity, even as the sky lightened to an ugly pale yellow. I don't know how one could sleep in that situation, but at some point, I did. I fell asleep on my feet. And opened my eyes to his face: the soulful brown eyes, the pudgy cheeks, the weak chin.

"It's true," he said. "We are precisely the same height. Perhaps I am a little taller. Then again, you're not wearing any shoes. Where are your shoes?"

These were the first words Paquito Franco said to me. I was too stunned to answer him.

"I owe you nothing. My debt was paid sixteen years ago. The other day, I chose not to intercede even on my cousin's behalf. Do you know that? Say it."

My mind was a blank.

"Say it," he repeated.

"Say what?"

"Say I owe you nothing."

"You owe me nothing."

"It's true," he said, morosely. Then: "I was shot in the stomach, you know. Years ago. But I lived. Perhaps you have a little *baraka*, too. Two of your brothers dead now—isn't that true?"

"Three."

"And your father."

"Yes." I was too tired to be afraid.

From his pocket he withdrew a familiar object. A compass, my father's gift to Enrique, which I might have chosen all those years ago, if things had worked out differently. He popped open the lid dramatically, pretended to study it, and clasped the lid closed. "Madrid, our next destination— northeast. Good. It still works. You see? I will never be lost. A real man knows without a doubt where he is going, what he is doing, and why."

He pushed me away from the wall against which I'd been leaning. Intuitively, I headed toward the plaza door through which I'd seen so many others march—what a sleepwalking victim I was, at that pale hour! But then he nudged me away, in the opposite direction. I walked, expecting to feel at any moment the shot in my back, pushing me off balance, just as I'd seen the woman fall in the plaza, months earlier.

Unlike Franco, I did not know where I was going, but the survivor's impulse had rekindled within me, and I knew to keep moving. In an hour, I was on the city's outskirts. Sometime later that day I was on a train east, skirting the southern edge of Nationalist territory, heading to one of the few remaining Republican enclaves, in Barcelona.

———

The city had a strange inside-out look. Here and there, in the middle of busy commercial streets, militiamen had set up wicker armchairs and wooden rockers behind walls of sandbags. Everywhere, people pried up cobblestones to build barricades.

As the war progressed, factions would turn against each other—the anarchists against the Stalinists against the Trotskyites; the uniformed soldiers and assault guards against the informal militias. Then the city truly fell apart—and that was before the fascists overtook it. But I saw it when it was only mildly disheveled, and still hopeful. Few Barcelona residents had seen what I had: the strafing planes, the bullrings transformed into killing fields. Later, those scenes would arrive here, too.

From Barcelona, I made my departure plans. But before enacting them, I hired a car to take me south, to Campo Seco. While the driver waited in the street, grumbling about the cost of petrol and how little I'd paid him for this errand, I climbed the stairs of my family's home. In the main parlor, I shared embraces with my sister and her son Enric, who had sprung into a tall, quiet man I didn't recognize, and my mother, who had developed a pronounced stoop in her shoulders. To look me in the eye, she had to cock her head to one side and roll her own eyes sharply upward, which gave her a distracted air.

The four of us shared the latest news, as we'd heard it. I described the streets of Barcelona. They talked about food shortages and kept trying to peek behind my back, as if I might be hiding gifts. But I'd brought nothing except an invitation. I hoped the surviving members of my family would come with me to France. One might think it would be a conversation of the highest priority. But my nephew had something to attend to—he apologized and left the house. Luisa, patting smooth the first gray hairs in the part of her outdated bob, was concerned about the rice she'd left cooking in the kitchen. Mamá was intent on dragging a heavy armchair away from the balcony doors toward the dining table until I took over the task, arranging the chair alongside its mates for a dinner I wouldn't stay long enough to share.

She waited until we were finally seated together, alone, to rebuke me. "You didn't come to your Tía's funeral." My father's elder sister had finally passed away a year earlier.

"I couldn't. I was halfway across the country...."

But she wasn't interested in my excuse. She stood up and began to rearrange the chairs again, counting them with difficulty. Each time she'd get to the fourth and then stop and look around for another.

"Mamá, leave the chairs. I can take care of them. It won't take more than a minute. What I was saying about France—"

She began counting again, under her breath.

"You don't need more chairs," I said. "There are only four of us: You, me, Luisa, Enric. Only four. And anyway, I won't need one. You may not need any of them. Please, will you pay attention?"

She wandered away, toward the kitchen. I followed her, grabbed a fifth chair that was next to the counter, and pulled it into the main *sala*. "Now will you listen to me?" I called back toward the kitchen. "Luisa, will you come here?"

"The rice will boil over," she called back.

"Fine. Mamá, let's go in the kitchen. I need to talk to you both—at the same time."

She patted me on the arm. "But we did talk all together, when you first arrived. And we have the chair now, from the kitchen. Let's talk at dinner."

"It can't wait. I have a driver outside. I'm not staying for dinner."

Below us, through the balcony doors, I heard the driver step out of his car and shut the door. I heard the dull pop of a hip leaning against already-dented metal, and then the strike of a match. I smelled the rising cigarette smoke—the scent of restlessness. I had told him we would be out within a half hour, with our bags. All four of us, with any luck.

"Mamá, you must understand what will happen once the Nationalists come to Barcelona."

"Yes, well," she said. "Barcelona."

"What does that mean?"

When she didn't answer me, I said more loudly, "What does that mean—'Yes, well, Barcelona'?"

She patted my arm again. "It wouldn't be the worst thing. Don't worry." Then she changed the subject. "I do wish you had married, Feliu."

Our conversation continued in this contrapuntal vein. She discussed the funeral I had missed and the wedding I'd never have, while I struggled to discuss the ferry from Barcelona and the living conditions in Paris, until my head felt ready to explode.

"Do you know," she said finally, her voice sharpening, "that in this day and age, in Catalonia, it's illegal to have a church wedding? The Republicans have gone too far."

I agreed that it was a little extreme. But everything was extreme. Aberrations and abuses were to be expected. Didn't she remember the First Republic of her youth, the one she had always talked about?

"It was nothing like this," she said bitterly. "It was beautiful."

Luisa had heard the change in my mother's tone, from peaceful confusion to rising stress. She came to the kitchen doorway, a spoon still in her hand. "Feliu," she said, "we're not leaving."

I kissed Mamá on the forehead, begging her not to rise. On my way out, Luisa embraced me, then disappeared into the house and reappeared holding a dusty bottle. The very last of my father's liqueur, she said.

In the car, I opened it and passed it to the driver, explaining it was the only tip I could afford. He flashed a gap-toothed smile, took one hand off the wheel, and accepted a swig, the grass-colored liquid dribbling from the side of his mouth. Then he leaned out the window and spat furiously. We'd saved it for nothing, all these years. It had gone bad long ago.

I'd left a cello behind in San Ramón—it would be firewood by now; and another behind in Mérida. I still had my bow, but I didn't feel lucky at all.

CHAPTER

~ 22 ~

Later, the Nationalist forces would bomb the Barcelona harbor, making it difficult for boats to come ferry away escaping citizens. Later, refugees by the thousands would be forced to cross the Pyrenees on foot. But I left early, and my April 1937 passage was easy—a swift and uneventful boat ride from Barcelona to Marseilles.

I continued to Paris by train and walked into the Spanish Republican embassy, to ask what I could do. Within a day they had set me up in a modest apartment on the rue des Grands-Augustins and advanced me a small loan. My label, Reixos, had offices in Belgium and owed me some royalties, though future profits would shrivel, with the Spanish market in chaos and economies across Europe struggling. Nationalist authorities had frozen my bank accounts in Salamanca and Mérida.

A day later, a woman in a head scarf appeared at my door with a cello.

"You will forgive the crack at the bottom," she said, her eyes downcast. "It was my brother's. I'm afraid we stored it in a closet after he passed away."

I replied, "I'm sure I can rent or purchase one somewhere." But in truth I wasn't sure I could afford anything more than bread, cheese, and a second set of clothes.

"The winters are dry. We should have kept it in a more humid place. But it's a good cello, I've been assured."

"Really, I can't—"

"The embassy told me you would need it."

An hour later, I reported to the embassy to complain. I had asked how I might help, and so far they had only helped *me,* twice. On the fifth such visit, a man with slicked-back hair and round, black-rimmed eyeglasses exited his office, spotted me in the waiting area, threw his arms around me and kissed both my cheeks. He introduced himself as Max Aub, the embassy's cultural delegate; he'd recognized me immediately from the photograph on my recordings. "Of course we have work for you." His eyes shone with emotion. "Do you mean to say you've been in Paris all this time without an assignment? I do hope you've been keeping your fingers nimble…"

"Nimble enough."

"The apartment isn't too chilly?"

I thought of the tea left at the bottom of a cup that froze into a light brown lozenge within hours, and the way my hands cramped from the cold even though I had cut the fingers from my only pair of gloves in order to practice. "It's fine," I said.

Over lunch, Aub explained that he and the Catalan architect Josep Lluís Sert had been frantic with preparations for the Spanish Pavilion at the upcoming World's Fair, to open soon at the base of the Eiffel Tower. That was the only reason he hadn't paid me a personal visit after hearing I had arrived safely from Marseilles. "Our budget is nothing compared to the other countries, yet we're in more need of publicity than anyone. The planners set Germany and the Soviet Union opposite each other. On purpose, of course. The Soviet Union has a three-story tower with menacing steel sculptures of giant workers. Germany's building is even bigger, with an eagle sneering down from the cornice."

"And ours?"

"Well," he paused. "Low, flat, simple. Directly under the German building's shadow."

A waiter delivered our cutlets. Aub raised his eyebrows at the thin yellow sauce, poked at the meat with the tines of his fork, tasted it finally, and nodded with satisfaction. "Not as good as the old days, but certainly better than what they're eating in Bilbao."

"What's that?"

"Cats, mostly."

He didn't notice when, after several bites, I pushed away my plate.

Aub and Sert couldn't get half the building materials they needed. "I can't push for money when militias in Barcelona and Madrid don't have proper guns." Aub shrugged. "But what we'll put inside the pavilion should count for something."

The fair's theme was technology, and its purpose was entertainment. But nearly everything displayed in the Spanish Pavilion, from photomurals to films by Buñuel, would focus instead on the horrors of war in Republican Spain. It was the only way to get a message out to a world that had showed little concern so far.

Aub said that he and Sert had visited Picasso, knowing that the painter still considered himself fiercely Spanish, although he had lived in Paris for thirty years by now. They had asked him to paint a new mural in time for the opening of the fair in May, but he'd been hesitant about accepting a commission for an overtly political work. "His heart is with us," said Aub, "no doubt about that. He promised to keep thinking about it. And we know that he has ordered an immense canvas, fitting the proportions of the pavilion. So even at the last minute, he may come around."

Picasso's studio was on the same street as the apartment the embassy had found for me. Like the proximity of the German and Soviet Union pavilions, it seemed a convenient coincidence, especially when Aub remarked, "We hoped you'd pay him a visit."

How could I tell him how strange I found it, that anyone believed me to be persuasive? I had never proved myself able to convince anyone of anything through words alone. In fact, my words often seemed to raise a wall between myself and others. Only by playing music had I ever been able to break down that barrier.

"I don't know him," I said, in lieu of explaining.

"Probably better that way. It means you won't have crossed him in the past. Anyway, I'm sure he knows of you." He moved a toothpick from one side of his mouth to the other. "The cello? It suffices?"

"Very kind. I forgot to ask for the woman's address, to send a note."

Aub shook his head and waved the concern away. "You want to write letters, I have a list a kilometer long. You were invited to perform at the White House once, were you not?"

"Correct. For President Hoover—"

But his mind was racing ahead of my answer. "Let's see: Roosevelt first, members of Congress, philanthropists—anyone who believes in this myth of nonintervention, who might be convinced by a reasonable letter or two or ten thousand to consider facts. In England, it would be...well, come to my office next week and we will review the names together."

I begged Aub for something more to do, something more than the letters—perhaps a benefit concert abroad?—but I'd already learned from my efforts back in Spain that the idea was a tough sell. A London backer was willing to sponsor a typical concert, but not a pricey and controversial fund-raiser mentioning the Spanish Republican cause. Subtracting my travel expenses, the proceeds would be minimal. I could raise just as much by playing in the streets of Paris, with a hat overturned to catch the coins.

Aub checked his watch distractedly. "At the pavilion they're having trouble engineering the flow of liquid mercury through a modern sculpture we'll have there, a sort of fountain." He rose, kissed me on both cheeks again, and said, "Without Picasso, the Spanish Pavilion doesn't have a chance." He hastened to add, "It has little chance without you, as well, of course—but we've always known where you stand. Visit me as soon as you have any news."

And so it was that I walked down rue des Grands-Augustins one morning shortly thereafter, with a sense of import, and trepidation. The feeling in my heart—as if I carried some essential portfolio or secret message—was not matched by the emptiness in my hands. Halfway to Picasso's address, I stopped to purchase an inexpensive bottle of Beaujolais. The wine meant I wouldn't have any money for dinner, but my appetite had waned in recent weeks.

The artist opened his door and simply stood there, hands on his hips and a lumpy brown cardigan tied over his sailor-stripe shirt. A few white strands of hair stood up on his otherwise bare, tanned pate, as if he'd just rolled out of bed. I could hear another voice inside, a clatter of dishes, and a record player. I introduced myself. He prolonged the silence a moment more, then said, "Well, I can't turn away news from home, can I? Come in, come in," and took the bottle from my hands.

The studio was large, echoing, and only a little warmer than my apartment. Tilted against the wall was the canvas, three and a half meters tall and nearly eight meters long. A ladder leaned against one end. The canvas itself was perfectly blank, but everywhere around the room the painter had tacked studies, sketches, drawings, postcards, pictures ripped from magazines; and underneath various tables there were empty bottles, stacked framed pictures, masks, hats, volcanic glass, enormous round sponges, jars of colored pencils and tins stuffed with paintbrushes, some of them lashed to long sticks. To one side there was a sagging couch and standing mirror; to another, mismatched chairs, splattered with paint. It was such a clutter that my eyes could rest only by settling upon the canvas, but to stare at the blankness there seemed like an invasion of privacy, like staring at someone not yet dressed, or prying into someone's undecided mind.

He knew why I'd come.

I shared what I knew of the Nationalists' latest advances, and especially what I'd seen from loyal Barcelona, where Picasso's elderly mother still lived. All the while we talked, I heard the dishes clattering and cupboards closing from a room off to the side. I knew Picasso had a wife, Marie-Thérèse—or was it Dora Maar?—and assumed it was she, or perhaps some more recent substitute.

"I think that Señor Aub would sleep better if he knew..." I started to say. Suddenly I stopped, my eyes tracking to the kitchen doorway. There, where I expected to see some fashionable young waif or heartsick housewife, stood a familiar large figure, fists extended, fingers crooked around the stems of three glasses and the neck of a bottle different from the one I'd brought.

"So it *is* you!" Al-Cerraz exclaimed. "I figured it was just another Catalan official." He nodded at the bottle. "I came to toast the man who lent me his couch for three nights. Thank heaven you brought a bottle, too—this deserves more than one toast."

"I shouldn't intrude—" I stammered.

"Nonsense. I'm happy to see you're alive! I've talked one of Pau's ears off already," he said, using the Catalan version of the artist's name.

Politely but coolly, I inquired where Al-Cerraz was staying, for the longer term. "Here and there," he said. "An extra bed, a floor—I'm not choosy." I noticed only then how his jacket and shirt hung from his frame, and the crude woven belt hitching up his loose pants. He'd lost easily fifteen kilos since I'd seen him at the Málaga bullring.

"Have you asked for help at the embassy?"

"The embassy? Bother them when other people are still behind the lines, hiding from the bombs, with nothing to eat?"

He might not have meant it as a criticism, but I felt its sting all the same, and then the heat of my own anger spreading: Who was Al-Cerraz to judge anyone who sought the embassy's help, when he was in league with the fascists? He was more than a Nationalist sympathizer— he was a prominent artist collaborating at the topmost levels with Franco himself.

Picasso had walked to a corner table loaded with paint-smeared newspapers. Much as I refused to turn a blind eye to Al-Cerraz's activities, I wasn't trying to expose him, either. I whispered, "I heard Queipo de Llano on the radio, saying you were president of some organization—"

"The Spanish Culture Institute," Al-Cerraz boomed. "Yes, that." He smiled. "For one week, until I met the Caudillo himself. There's a story. Pau—you'll want to hear this one." Al-Cerraz glanced meaningfully across the room, then winked at me. "Pau is the new director of the Prado. He understands about these honorary positions."

"Director del Museo—my other hat," Picasso said, balancing atop his head an old-fashioned bowler he'd pulled from a costume box. Watching him clown around, I thought what a sham it was that the dying Republic was propping itself up by sweet-talking apolitical, apathetic exiles into such high-profile roles. I had no inkling then of the important work Picasso would undertake in that role, spiriting the museum's priceless artworks out of Madrid to Geneva for safekeeping.

"And here's one for you, Justo," Picasso said, presenting him with a *tricornio*, the patent-leather uniform hat of the ultraconservative Civil Guard.

Al-Cerraz laughed and waved it away. "Not for me—*no, gracias.* I am finished with all that." So Picasso knew something of Al-Cerraz's Nationalist associations. Yet he'd still allowed the pianist to sleep on his couch. I didn't know what to think.

"But the story—please, let me tell it," Al-Cerraz said, opening the bottle he'd brought—a Beaujolais cru, finer than the one I'd chosen— and winking as he filled the glasses.

Al-Cerraz had met Franco in September 1936, just after Al-Cerraz was named honorary president of the cultural institute, and before Franco had risen above his fellow generals to be declared chief of state.

The pianist had prepared a short, original piano work for the occasion. General Franco was late to arrive, and a young man in suit and tie introduced himself as the associate director of cultural services. Was the piano's tuning to the maestro's satisfaction? It was fine, Al-Cerraz told him. Anything else he could bring? Something to help the pianist loosen up?

"Just quiet," Al-Cerraz said. He had always been superstitious and finicky about being alone before a performance.

The associate director smiled obsequiously and put a finger to his lips. Yet as soon as Al-Cerraz launched into the prelude, he piped up again. Was that a *malagueño* rhythm?

"Something like that," Al-Cerraz said.

"Or maybe more of a Cuban *guajira*, was it not?" He clapped out the three-quarter rhythm.

Al-Cerraz started over from the beginning.

"Just to let you know," the associate director interrupted, "The *Jefe* is hoping for real Spanish music. *Muy puro.*"

"What is pure? Does that mean nothing gypsy?"

"Oh, no, the *Jefe* loves gypsy flamenco."

"Flamenco?" Franco had a reputation for being rather fussy and prim.

"Well," the associate director winked, "the tourists love flamenco. So he likes flamenco. Currency, you understand."

"It's a little early in the war effort to be thinking about tourism, isn't it?"

"Are you kidding? Tourism, marketing—it's essential. They're already naming a new sherry after one of the generals. Hats, tires, just about everything. And wait—look at this."

The young official retrieved a folder and extracted a stack of brochures that still smelled of wet ink. "Visit the Routes of War!" proclaimed the cover, over a montage of scenic routes along the northern occupied coast. Route 3 to Madrid, the map boasted, would be "open to traffic by 1 July 1938."

"Open by 1938," Al-Cerraz joked. "He'd better get going. What's he doing wasting time listening to a pianist?"

The associate director's smile faded. But as soon as Al-Cerraz resumed his warm-up, he was back at the pianist's shoulder. "That bit had a Basque flavor. You know that General Mola has had quite a time with the Basques, don't you? No, not the whole passage, just those few measures. Play them again. Yes, that's what I'm hearing."

"You're quite the musicologist," Al-Cerraz commented drily.

An hour later, Franco finally arrived, flanked by two officers. Introductions were bypassed. The general sat down without removing his sunglasses, and Al-Cerraz began to play.

The pianist settled his wide hands into the opening chords, lifted them dramatically, then placed them back in his lap. His left foot continued to tap out the time. His hands stayed in his lap for a tense minute.

Finally Franco stood up and turned to the officer on his left. "What is the story with this pianist?"

"He's famous. And eager to compose for us."

Franco turned to Al-Cerraz. "Is this what you have composed for us?"

"Hold on, another part is coming. A good part." Al-Cerraz played an isolated measure—one that hadn't been criticized by the associate director—and then lifted his hands away from the keyboard again.

"This man is mocking us," said the officer to Franco's right.

Franco pulled off his sunglasses. "What is this man's name?"

Al-Cerraz stopped tapping his foot and looked at the general. "Sir, I was under the impression you requested me directly. I've already been named president of the Institute."

"Get me this man's name," Franco seethed. "Not just his name—his file. I want to know who recommended him."

It was clear from the sweat pouring off the associate director's face that the file wasn't necessary.

Al-Cerraz folded his arms across his chest. "If you don't know my name, you should. I was famous before you were born. I expect to be famous long after you have passed away."

Franco, who was busy conferring with his fellow officers, didn't acknowledge the comment.

"Really," Al-Cerraz continued, "if you look at the average duration of a prime minister or a president—even a dictator or a monarch—it's not a long span. If you count the number of governments we've had since 1898—"

Franco cut him off. "Someone recommended this buffoon, and I want to know who it is. Immediately."

The associate director did an exaggerated double-take at Al-Cerraz's face and erupted in a high-pitched, hysterical giggle. "I recognize this man! He's the piano tuner. Who put him up to this? What a terrible prank they've played on us!" He began to tug at Al-Cerraz's jacket sleeves, trying to pull him away from the piano bench.

The officers on either side of Franco exchanged shrugs. Franco pushed the sunglasses back onto his face, exasperated. He'd spent most of his life in military academies and remote barracks, where he'd grown accustomed to tomfoolery.

"I'll get to the bottom of this," the associate director shouted, pushing Al-Cerraz out the stage door. And then, louder than necessary, "Get going! And if you see Maestro Justo Al-Cerraz out there, tell him we're still waiting and he's shamefully late!"

"Can you imagine?" Al-Cerraz laughed a final time, refilling his glass. "Me, a piano tuner? It's only a little more improbable than me as a fascist composer—what a lark that was."

Picasso applauded the story. Neither man seemed to notice my silence.

"And yet," Al-Cerraz added, growing suddenly serious. "Franco did me a great favor. Once I realized that some of my 'piano miniatures' might offend him, I recognized also that they had more value than I'd presumed. Isn't it true that all valuable art offends someone? I've had it backward all these years, thinking Spain needs large-scale compositions. Maybe it takes a demagogue to show us that even humble works have their subversive power."

He glanced at me again, plainly waiting for me to respond, but I was still too aggravated to speak.

"Your Franco story reminds me of something," Picasso said. From a pile by the wall, he retrieved a series of cartoonlike etchings—some simplistic, some grotesque—of a figure seated on an old horse, underneath the type of smiling sun a three-year-old might draw. It was Franco, abstracted into a strange Don Quixote–like character, wearing striped armor and brandishing a sword. His head was distorted, somehow phallic, pornographic, even though in one panel he wore a lady's lace mantilla as well as a crown. Picasso read us the poem he had written to accompany the etchings, a rambling, nonsensical piece of whimsy that failed to impress, full of nets of anchovies and shrouds stuffed with sausages and "the skyrocket of lilies." But the cartoon images stayed with me.

A panel of a bull attacking Franco-Quixote reminded Al-Cerraz of the last time we'd seen each other, and he launched into recounting the untimely demise of Doña de Larrocha's prize bull. But Picasso didn't seem to be listening. He set down his wineglass, picked up the pad he had left lying next to his chair, and began to sketch. I thought he might be hinting that it was time to leave him to his work, but Al-Cerraz wasn't one to leave a story unfinished or a glass undrained. And as he continued I saw that Picasso was sketching with increasing fervor. He wasn't irritated at all—only inspired. As he finished each sketch, he ripped it off the pad, laid it aside, and started on another. I saw the image of a bull, angry at first, haughty, then pained. The *picador*'s horse, wounded by the retired general, with a gaping hole in its side. A woman—I suppose it was Doña de Larrocha herself—with her face tilted toward the sky, screaming in distress.

And all the while he sketched, Al-Cerraz continued to regale him, with anecdotes from his long and lively career and his opinions on art, music and life. By the time Picasso set aside his sketchbook, Al-Cerraz was just finishing a story about meeting Monet at Giverny in 1923, when the old man was still painting his beloved water lilies.

"All those variations! That light! Well, it's exactly what I try to do with the piano—one keyboard, one viewpoint perhaps, but an infinity of colors." He scratched his beard and adopted a confessional tone. "Pau, I'm no fan of modern art, I have to admit that—just as I expressed it to Monet. I told him, 'I'd hate to be thought of as a reactionary.'"

Picasso looked up. "What did he say?"

"He turned to me and said, 'It isn't about styles. To observe the world honestly will always be revolutionary.'"

An hour later, Al-Cerraz accompanied me out the door and down the street, a battered carpetbag-style valise hanging from his thick fist.

I marveled at how easily he had interacted with the painter, despite their brief acquaintance, whereas I could find little to say to my partner of twenty-three years—or little that wouldn't end in recriminations. And he, apparently, had just as little to say to me.

Finally I muttered, "So you've made a new friend."

Al-Cerraz cocked his head. "I'm really just getting to know him. He's complicated. There was some tricky business the second day I was there, when his mistress came by and started fighting with his wife."

"And...?"

Al-Cerraz smiled ruefully, recalling the scene. "Pau up on a ladder, bamboo paintbrush in hand—the mistress with her big black camera, trying to get pictures of the genius at work—the wife dancing between them both, pulling her hair out, telling Picasso he'd better choose."

He laughed once, then grew serious. "I've broken a heart or two, but I've never set one woman against another. And while they were fighting with each other and pleading with him, sobbing all the while, he just kept humming and painting." He sighed. "Maybe I'm not hard-nosed enough to be a great artist. Not like you and Picasso."

"Me?"

"Able to forget people. Able to focus on the work."

We'd stopped at a corner and waited to cross. Was he baiting me? "You certainly were chummy with him today, though."

He pretended to study the traffic, shoulders slumping. "You know I talk when I'm nervous."

"Nervous?"

"Embarrassed."

"By Picasso?"

Al-Cerraz hesitated. "By you. By the way you had come there to in-fluence him—to tell him what to paint."

I was taken aback: Al-Cerraz had the nerve to judge *me*? "Not *what* to paint," I said.

"Come now. You know they don't want one of his fractured ladies or blue guitars. They want a political poster, ready-made—but they want to call it art."

He waited, and when I kept walking, he added, "It wasn't too dif-ferent from what that lackey of Franco's did to me—telling me what to put in and what to leave out. An artist can't take directions that way."

I felt my jaw tightening. "I suppose it depends on what's at stake."

By then we were nearly to my apartment. When Al-Cerraz asked if he might stay the night, I said the heating was broken. And then, en-couraged by that small departure from the truth, I told him that work-men had taken over the place and I wasn't sure I'd be able to sleep there

myself. He'd better amble onward toward some other acquaintances, of
which I was sure he had many.

Guernica was bombed that week. I walked to the embassy in a daze,
clutching my address book and some letters I had already written. But
the embassy was in chaos, with a line stretching out the door and reporters standing in the stairwells. Aub had no time to meet. I was hoping to get more details from him about the bombing. Some news
reports said the Nationalists had bombed the little northern Basque
town. Others said it was the Nazi Condor Legion, testing out a new
strategy of warfare, with the Spanish fascists' eager consent: a relentless air attack on civilians, conducted in the middle of a market day, for
maximum effect.

But we didn't know all the ways truth would be warped in the weeks
to come—only that something terrible and new had happened. Civilians had been targeted directly. Nearly all of Guernica had been razed,
and fleeing residents had been picked off by low-flying planes. It was
the first time in modern warfare that such an outrageous, unilateral
strike, with no clear military target, had taken place. Later, it would be
called the rehearsal for Dresden, London, Hiroshima. That day, it was
simply unthinkable.

I needed something to do, something much more than playing a
brittle cello with gloved hands. I walked to the embassy twice a day,
though usually there was no one available to talk to me. I wrote dozens
of letters at a time, until my right hand cramped. I received many re-
sponses, all of them unsatisfactory. I wrote to statesmen about arms
and aid and the need to pressure Italy and Germany. They wrote back
about Beethoven and Fauré, how they'd enjoyed some performance of
mine, how I was welcome to visit their country and play again. I
couldn't help turning each letter over, looking for some other message

on the back perhaps, to explain the disconnect between what I had written—what I had begged—and what they had written in response.

Spring's warmth had not penetrated the dark corners of my tenement lodgings. The kitchen pipes had burst from the cold, and I kept a block of ice in a large ceramic bowl, chipping off chunks to heat on the tiny two-burner stove when I needed water.

One day I was chipping ice while I listened to the news on a little radio I had bought, which was prone to tempestuous bursts of static. The newsman was echoing Franco's claim that it wasn't the Nazis who had bombed Guernica, it was the Basques themselves who had lit their own city on fire with gas cans, just to make fascist Spain and Nazi Germany look bad. I talked back at the newsman—What of the eyewitness reports? What of the bodies in the streets? What of the bomb craters? What of the shells?—until the static roared, like a door slammed in my face. It astonished me, the way everything could be turned upside down—innocents into enemies, guilt into blamelessness. It rattled my senses, even more so when I looked down and realized I had chipped through the ice to the bowl's bottom, and beyond. Shards of ceramic lay on the counter in front of me. Rivulets of water ran down my leg. A neighbor girl was knocking on the door: "Monsieur Delargo, are you all right in there?"

Inspired by the bombing of Guernica, Picasso finished his mural a month later. It was a marvel: horses, bulls, bare cellars and bare lightbulbs, women with dying children in their arms—an abstract portrait of horror that filled an entire wall with its terrible shades of gray.

I visited the mural at the World's Fair, and stared as long as I could, the shapes melting as my eyes filled. But not everyone was equally moved, or satisfied. A few viewers took exception to the painting's political content. Many more, including some of the Spanish Republican officials who had pushed for its completion, were disappointed that it wasn't more explicitly political. Where was the clear message, the assignation of blame? Was that bull in the corner Franco, or was it all of suffering Spain? Which figure was the aggressor, which the victim? What did the wounded horse mean? What should anyone do?

After the Spanish Pavilion closed, *Guernica* toured the United States, where it succeeded in raising only seven hundred dollars. Later, the painting would be recognized as Picasso's most lasting masterpiece. But not while the Spanish Civil War still raged; not when it mattered most.

Visual art, I realized then, was a dull blade with which to fight a war. But it could provoke. I observed that firsthand while doing my small part, performing solo on a side stage at the pavilion. By the time fair-goers arrived there, they had already taken in nearly everything: the mercury fountain, the photomurals, and certainly *Guernica*. They came and went as I played, chattering about what they'd seen.

I recall two Americans, an older woman and a younger, who dropped thankfully into the half-circle of seats that had been arranged next to my small stage, talking loudly about their sore feet, the size of the fair, the size of Picasso's horrid painting, "So *awful*." Did he have to paint it that way? Could things really be that bad?

"Yes—and worse," I wanted to say, but I was busy with the final repeat of a Bach sarabande.

"That's better," I heard the younger woman say, nodding in time to the melody.

"Now, that's really lovely," the older woman said. And when I had finished, "Are you the same Señor Delargo who played on the BBC two years ago? Would you sign this for us? It would make such a fabulous end to our day."

And I knew the women would forget what they had seen of *Guernica,* that I had helped them to forget it. A painting was a dull sword with which to fight a war, and a painter himself could be a hypocrite. But music was a numbing, soothing poison, which—dripped into the general water supply—contaminated everyone.

And so I came to my decision. It seemed the only thing left to do was to stop playing altogether. Now, I realize that to someone who has followed my life story, it may seem as if I'd made such a choice before. But that is only hindsight and compression at work. To me, the choice I made in 1937 was not the same choice I had made in 1921. After Anual, grief and horror had struck me dumb, as if my music were too pure to associate with evil. This time music itself struck me as evil. Not directly evil, perhaps, but passively so, like Roosevelt's neglecting to aid the Spanish Republic, like Chamberlain's appeasing Hitler, like all the Allies who refused to recognize what was happening to Jews and gypsies and Spaniards—yes, Spaniards, too—in the concentration camps. The power that brings no true peace and offers no solution—that only obscures—is itself a negative force. That is what I believed.

It did not help that each passing month showed we were right, and they had all been wrong. As we loyalists had claimed, the fall of the Spanish Republic paved the way for totalitarianism elsewhere. The forces that had stood against Spain, the forces that had lent fascists their guns and planes and men, now turned those well-practiced troops and fine-tuned weapons against the rest of democratic Europe. We had begged, pleaded, screamed, painted, played. What else was there to do?

And if I should not play, then no one should. Perhaps then, people would pay attention. If they had no music, no theater, no entertainment, then perhaps they could not continue to ignore fascism's march across the globe. Manuel Rocamura, a young cellist whom I had trained through master classes in 1934 and 1935, was scheduled to tour America. When a reporter asked what I thought of Rocamura, I said I thought he should be home fighting—or at least resisting, as were

many of Spain's finest—not entertaining the nations that were refusing to aid Spain. My name carried weight; my comments were widely
disseminated. Rocamura's indignant response, also widely reported, inflamed the controversy. And soon, I heard, Rocamura's recording label
had pulled out. His American tour was canceled. He was only twenty-
eight years old at the time. Even after World War II, I never saw his
name in the newspapers again, though I looked.

Perhaps my logic was wrong. Perhaps my emotions were over-
wrought. But consider what we would learn later, of the Jewish musicians who continued to play in Nazi-sanctioned organizations—
organizations they believed would save them. By continuing to perform, by refusing to flee, by entertaining their fellow Jews and distract-
ing them from the dangerous deterioration of their situation, the
musicians hastened their own demise, and perhaps even aided the Nazis
in their terrible task. One might argue that even until the last days in
the camps, the Jewish musicians were shoring up spirits, aiding survival. But the facts suggested differently. In the camps, the Jewish
musicians did not have stronger spirits, were not buoyed by their dedication to art. In fact, they committed suicide at higher rates than their
comrades did. They were tormented by guilt—the guilt of playing in
pathetic ensemble as the Nazis paraded victims to the gas showers.
There was no nobility in these final serenades; this was not the heroic
quartet clinging to their instruments as the *Titanic* sank. This was
doing the devil's own bidding.

I did make one last public effort. All summer, I kept to myself, but in
the fall, Aub came to my door and talked me into making a trip with
him to the south of France, where most of the Spanish refugees were
living in camps surrounded by barbed wire. We spent a week talking up
our trip and gathering donations—packets of powdered milk and

boxes packed with needles and gauze. We traveled by car, with a lady photographer who documented the lines of seated men who looked like children, eating their chunks of bread off the yellowing grass while officials walked between them to make sure no one stole or moved in hopes of being served twice. The real children had dirt-stained faces and bowl-shaped haircuts. The women wore shapeless dresses and hugged themselves against the autumn cold, studying us distrustfully as we carried our meager charity boxes across the compounds.

Some of the refugees slept in huts, but there weren't enough huts for all, and some of them slept like animals, in holes dug out of the sandy soil. The photographer made me stand next to these burrows with hands clasped in front and hands clasped in back and hands clasped in front again and then crouching farther down with my forearms on my thighs so that she could photograph the burrow hole more clearly and then in profile, with a look of concern—No, please, directly into the hole, not at me—until I finally let myself look, really look, and I saw two things at once while the photographer stayed hidden behind her camera. One: I saw a dark shadow resolve into a hank of dark hair and a lump, which proved to be a dark brown dress. An old woman was still in one of the burrows, though it was midday, and she seemed to be motionless. Two: I recognized why the whole scene was familiar—the gray watercolor sky, the stiff clumps of grass, the sandy holes. My chest tightened with the sudden, flooding memory of it, a memory that left me with no doubt at all, and little breath.

I had glimpsed the scene before, in a nightmare. It was the dream that had awakened me, when I was nearly six years old; the dream that had caused me to rise early and go with my mother to the train station. In her anxiety over the arrival of a coffin, she had asked me if I'd dreamed about a box. She had been reassured when I told her it was not a box, just sandy holes. These holes. And the sense of something terrible inside.

Some camp orderlies came and dragged the woman, blue-faced and stiff, from her burrow, murmuring regretfully that she'd had no relatives at the camp, and no one to notice when she hadn't shown up for morning call or last night's dinner. I told Aub I had to leave then—not tomorrow, not the next day—because I knew something had happened to my own mother. I could not cross back into Spain but I could return to Paris, where I was sure the news awaited me. And I was right. The telegram I found under my door told me my mother had died four days earlier, in Barcelona.

And so I realized, all these years later, that what my mother had thought was a dream of my father's death had really been a dream of my mother's. All along, I had felt unable to impress her, unable to fulfill whatever hopes she had for me, or to make her lack of hope more bearable. Now that she was dead, that potential was finally revoked. The person we are by the time our parents have died is the person we shall always be; any aspirations to further development are delusional. We have had our turn, and now we stand just one generational step away from our own deaths, every year passing more quickly than the last.

I proceeded to sleep away most of the next three years. In Paris, rationing tightened. Three days a week were so-called meatless days; three days a week, hard liquor couldn't be served in restaurants; three days, there were no pastries. It mattered little to me. I could subsist on beans, bread, water. I bought the occasional chunk of hard cheese and left it wrapped on the counter for days, untouched, like my little squares of childhood chocolate. I had always taken pride in my asceticism, my ability to do without.

Likewise, my cello sat, untouched and unplayed, in the far corner of my room. Once, Max Aub called on me. He had heard about my determination not to play. He assumed that meant public performance only, and he was taken aback to see my instrument in its corner, with a long coat thrown over it. I did not tell him that I had placed a bowl of water under that coat, and the coat itself was not a mark of dishonor, but a drape intended to maintain some humidity close to the instrument's brittle wood. I bore the cello no grudges. What I did not respect was this age, this world, this life.

Waking late each morning, grudgingly, slowly, I would swing my legs off my thin mattress, cough for several minutes, push myself to standing, and make my way across the room to dress. On the way, I never failed to glance at the cello, to peer at the bowl and refill it when necessary, as one refills a water bowl for a cat. The bow, I should add, stayed even closer to me; in its case, under my bed—protected from nocturnal thieves, I told myself.

Quitting something that one has done all one's life is like quitting any addiction. The first days may be easy, sometimes alarmingly so. But then there are the deep pangs, the cumulative sense of unwellness, the dangers of relapse. I missed the feeling of my body wrapped around those curves of wood. I missed the gliding bow strokes. I missed the feel of the strings against my calloused fingertips, the oscillations of the vibrato, the pressure and release and speed and surrender; my entire body had become attuned to the cello over all those years, and without its mediation nothing made sense anymore, not weight or gravity or the rhythm inherent in anything—my breath, my heartbeat. The water tap developed a drip, and that drip drove me to distraction. Deprived of music, my ear went searching crazily for sound, like a stray dog wandering the alleyways, and wherever it found it, seized and shook it, wouldn't let go. I wrapped a washcloth around the spigot, but there were other sounds—people's footsteps over me, squeaking beds, the wheezing rattle in my chest as I succumbed to winter bronchitis.

The only place where my body felt at peace, and where my mind could freely enjoy some remembered melody, was in sleep. I slept twelve hours at a stretch and still felt tired enough afternoons to nap two hours more. On hot days I sat in my worn trousers and damp undershirt. On cold days I kept my tattered blankets wrapped around me at all times, dragging them back and forth across the room, polishing one narrow path on an otherwise-dusty wooden floor.

Visitors knocked at the door. Sometimes I answered, and many more times I did not. Envelopes were pushed through the crack and piled up on the floor. Every few days, obligation would force me to open them, to search for some sign that my hundreds of earlier letters—to government officials, to major philanthropists abroad—had finally brought some significant and heartfelt response. But mostly they were letters of mild concern, from people who had appreciated my playing in the past and wanted to know I was all right, or small offerings of charity folded between pages of embossed stationery. When relapse threatened, and my hand trembled and longed to touch my bow again, I punished it by inflicting it with a marathon session of letter writing, indignant new attempts to reach out to the world that lasted four hours, or five, until exhaustion drove me back to bed again.

And I dreamed, how I dreamed. Not about the sandy holes—that image had been put to rest by my mother's passing. Not about the world's real nightmares: continued repression in Spain; Kristallnacht and the extermination of Jews in Germany; the advance of fascism and Nazism everywhere. Instead, I dreamed memories, starting with the recent past and moving back year by year, like a movie shown in reverse. I dreamed of Aviva prying notes from her violin, thin arms heaving and feet spread wide. I dreamed of the trains rocking and clanging and singing, and the rhythm of oars on the Retiro pond. I dreamed of the back of the Queen's head, nodding slightly, and the soft, wet heat of Isabel. I dreamed of the jostling of the Ramblas, and the light flashing down through the leaves of the plane trees, and the dazzling reflections of light in the Liceo's Hall of Mirrors. Back and back, night after night, filled with all the things that day deprived me. No wonder I couldn't wait to be under the covers again. And beneath it all, the sense that something was feeding the dreams, keeping them alive. Something as close, perhaps, as the tube under my bed, the bow that had chosen me or asked me to choose it or simply fallen into my hands as the result of that early waking. Something as close as my fear: of ceasing to matter, of returning to the place that had almost taken me at the moment of my complicated birth, the place of deepest silence that waits to take us all.

CHAPTER

~ 23 ~

By 1940 I was forty-eight years old, but I felt ancient, worn, frail—older then, in fact, than I do now as I tell this story, three and a half decades later. Who knows how much longer those dreams might have sustained my hibernation, if the knocking at my door had not suddenly grown insistent. Three times on one June day I ignored it and even pulled my window closed despite the sticky heat, to block out the shouts of an unfamiliar, self-important voice from the landing below my window. The shouting went away, but a fly stayed to torment me, beating and buzzing against the window. It so wore down my resistance that when the knocking started again, I rushed to the door and flung it open, only to find this time an altogether-different pest.

Al-Cerraz came in, swinging in each hand a glass gallon jug filled with cider-colored liquid. He didn't offer me either of them, but only set them down, tested the mattress with one balled fist, and made himself comfortable on my bed.

"You've missed me?"

"I haven't." I was puzzled to realize that in all my dreams, he'd never appeared. I stifled a laugh. "My mind seems to dwell on everyone and everything, except you."

He wiped his brow. "There's only one explanation. You're mooning over your undistinguished past. I'm in your future." He went to the window, looked out, and sat again. Then he explained all the knockings and callings I'd heard. Handbills were being posted throughout the city, and at least a few colleagues had tried to notify me, knowing I'd become a shut-in.

"Not a shut-in," I objected. "I go out to shop every few days, to take care of my own business..."

Al-Cerraz ignored me and pulled a paper from his back pocket, unfolding it so I could read the words: *Citoyens! Aux Armes!*

He translated: "Citizens! To arms!"

"Yes, I know," I said, exasperated. They were taken from the lyrics of *"La Marseillaise,"* the French anthem. But after a moment I had to ask, "What *does* it mean, exactly?"

"It means the Germans are maybe a week away. Maybe only a few days, depending on their appetite for Paris luxuries. The French army has failed. Officially, it means Parisian citizens are preparing to fight— *quartier* by *quartier,* they say."

He advised me to leave the city. When I said I wouldn't, that I didn't care, he said, "Come out for lunch, at least."

"I have lunch here."

"Do you?" He went toward the small cupboard behind the table that doubled as desk and dining table. He flung it open, nodded at the pitiful contents, then returned to the bed again, where he sat down heavily, testing the springs. I winced at the squeaking, the grinding of metal against metal, the knock of metal against wood...

"Stop—my bow!"

Al-Cerraz stood reluctantly and with one large hand gripped the white porcelain rail of the bed, lifted the whole thing as if it were nothing more than a suitcase, and moved it aside. Underneath was my bow tube, still sound, nestled like an egg atop a nest of thousands of papers and envelopes, stacked nearly as high as the bed frame itself.

"Dear, dear," he murmured. "Do you have a match?"

———

I agreed then to leave the apartment with him before he talked himself into building a bonfire and burning down the entire building with it. Outside, we walked, pausing to look into windows and to watch people. At the café where we stopped for lunch, it was as hard as ever to get a table. Ladies were dressed in their floral best, men in suits despite the heat, raising their glasses to toast with that season's most popular phrase: *Chantons quand même!* Let's sing nevertheless!

Along one of the boulevards, we watched gardeners digging out withered flowers from an embankment and replacing them with fresh geraniums offloaded from the back of a truck.

"Clearly they don't think the tanks are coming," I noted.

"No, but *they* do." Al-Cerraz pointed down the boulevard to a squat, stone-faced government building, along which more trucks were lined up. Men in crisp work shirts, sleeves rolled up, came out pushing one dolly after another, loading with fat, uneven stacks of paper barely secured with twine.

"See? They're doing what you won't—destroying the papers that the Germans shouldn't see."

"Or moving it."

"Yes. Probably." He laughed noncommittally. "Citizens to arms— guard our rears while we retreat."

"If *they* think it's too dangerous to stay, shouldn't everyone leave?"

"The train stations are jammed. I went there this morning, just to see. Ten people for every one seat. Children separated from their parents. It looked like a refugee camp. Already, people have been trampled."

"And yet..." I paused, glancing back at the gardeners.

"'*Chantons quand même!*'" he said. "In our land it was '*No pasarán*'— but it happened all the same. Let them pass, and make music anyway." He lifted his chin and said more loudly, "Make music. Make gardens. Make love. Admirable, in some ways. But I won't hang around to see how it ends—not past Monday."

We stood a while longer, watching the gardeners in one direction and the government office workers in another. Al-Cerraz added, "For anyone with initiative, it's still relatively easy to leave now. In a few days, it won't be."

"Why are you doing this?" I asked him.

"Doing what?"

"Why are you trying to help me?"

He adopted an incredulous expression. "Come now. We've always had our differences. But we've made music together. And I trust you. You've seen the worst of me—and here we are, still talking."

Looking back on that day now, I wish I could say he'd already seen the worst of *me*.

Later, he asked a favor: Would I keep his cider bottles for him until he left? His latest accommodation was in the home of a lover, a married woman whose husband was at the front. She let him sleep there, but she wouldn't let him store his belongings, for fear her mother-in-law would spot them during one of her frequent unannounced visits. It seemed a small thing to ask.

"Tonight I'll come by with a few more, if that's all right. And then a few more again in the morning, if I'm lucky."

"It's a bit late to be starting a cellar."

"No." He ran a hand through his thick hair distractedly. "It's not too late at all."

By morning, we all knew the handbills had been a political mistake. Even as they were being printed, even as some citizens boasted the Germans would never succeed in taking Paris, the government had already decided. No one planned to fight after all—not soldiers or citizens. Paris was declared an open city. Two of the city's five million residents had left or were preparing to leave; some quickly and some slowly; some bitter, some relieved, most fixated on this newest reality of getting out before Nazi flags were raised over every government office, every hotel, every historic landmark.

In Spain, I had seen great masses of mostly poor people fleeing cities. But here the poor and the rich fled together, and no one had it easy. Near my apartment, there was a veterinary office, and the next morning as I returned from a shopping trip I saw a long line of women and a few men outside the lobby, all holding their cats and Pomeranians and poodles, trying to keep them from leaping free and igniting their own Gallic wars. It might have been funny, except that after a couple of inquiries I discovered the reason these elegant people were queuing up in such numbers. They were putting their pets to sleep, knowing how difficult it would be to carry animals while fleeing the rapidly approaching German front.

That day, as planned, Al-Cerraz came with a fifth jug and a sixth. One last time, he tried to convince me to join him.

"They know your opinions about everything," he said, looking around my apartment at the stacks of unsent letters. "They'll arrest you."

"It doesn't worry me."

"You were lucky in Spain."

"Lucky?"

He threw his hands into the air. "I still need rope and a few small things. I'll come back in an hour. Then I'm leaving Paris, with my jugs. I can't force you to see reason."

After he left, I sat near the window, my coat-covered cello visible out of the corner of one eye. The day's heat was building. I opened the window to a day that seemed the more awful for its heartless sunshine. Outside, I heard a man calling, "Bicycle for sale!" I imagined the traffic that must be choking the city's gateways, as every kind of car and tractor and pushcart and bicycle joined the exodus. I heard an explosive pop—too light for a gun—and I thought of champagne, and that infernal toast: *Chantons quand même!*

I couldn't decide which scenario seemed worse: to be trampled by refugees or maddened by naïve collaborators, the kind who thought, "It's better this way" or "It's easier," or who proclaimed "a return to traditional values," meaning fascism of the kind I'd already experienced in Spain. There were plenty of Parisians who not only tolerated the Germans but welcomed them, admiring their goose-stepping efficiency, their espousal of fatherland and family, their good public manners. And in any crowd, loyal or disloyal, there would be men as foolish as Al-Cerraz, storing up his cider or Chablis or whatever it was, as if elegant refreshment mattered at a time like this.

But what could one do? The train stations were mayhem. Al-Cerraz seemed to have a different plan for traveling, but I hadn't asked what it was, hadn't even wanted to know. Wiping my face, I went to the sink and turned the tap. Nothing happened. It did not surprise me that someone had tampered with the pipes on this day of flight, and I acknowledged that perhaps Al-Cerraz hadn't been entirely silly to stockpile beverages. Shrugging, I lifted one of his jugs, felt the saliva dampening my mouth, and twisted the cap. I had the jug close to my lips when the fumes flooded my nose. I recoiled, barely stifling a sneeze. Then I drew close and sniffed again. Petrol.

Had I said he was foolish? He was a genius.

When Al-Cerraz returned, he burst through the door ready to argue his final case. "Forget what I said before. The truth is the Germans adore you, and that adoration will be worse than torture. The Nazis love classical music—didn't I once read that Hitler owns your recording of the Bach cello suites? They won't leave you alone a single day unless you perform for them."

"You're right."

"And you won't get away with saying you don't play anymore, that you've taken some kind of principled stand..." He paused, belatedly absorbing the fact that I had agreed with him.

"You're right. I'm ready." I gestured to the bed, where one small valise lay waiting, my bow tube across it. He hesitated. I said again, "I'm ready. Show me to your car."

Then the spell was broken. He laughed. "My car? I don't have a car."

And I realized that nothing in wartime could be easy, but I had followed his lead for years and I felt willing, against my better judgment, to follow him again.

Al-Cerraz's experience years earlier, crossing an arid land in a Stanley Steamer, had taught him that vehicles don't matter if you can't find fuel. We followed the long lines of traffic out of the city, hitchhiking easily at first when people recognized us by the cello Al-Cerraz had demanded I carry along, lashed to my back with rope, and walking when we couldn't get a ride, Al-Cerraz struggling under the weight of the tethered jugs. The exodus was chaotic and slow, with vehicles of every kind backed up by roadblocks. Some citizens, more optimistic or at least militaristic than France's own generals, had towed boulders and other obstructions into the center of roads, to slow down the advance of the German tanks. But in the east, where it mattered, the tanks had no trouble getting through; they'd simply gone around the roadblocks, across fields now greening with spring wheat. Within days, Paris was buzzing with German motorcades and Hitler was having his photo taken in front of the Eiffel Tower, and the boulders blocked only the exodus of refugees.

As drivers' tanks began to run dry, as hearts hardened and faces grew frantic, we bargained for rides with Al-Cerraz's petrol. It gained in value the farther we traveled from the capital. Occasionally we came across rural stations where we could refill a jug or two, but the stations were spaced widely, and demand far exceeded supply. Nearly every station was noisy with altercations, as station owners claimed their tanks had run dry and desperate drivers accused them of lying and price gouging.

Kilometer after kilometer, Al-Cerraz strategized. He refused to help drivers of cars broken down along the road, insisting that we couldn't hitch our destinies to lost causes—a few more gallons of petrol wouldn't get an empty car to Marseilles. Better, he explained, to wave down a moving car and contribute only as the needle dipped low, giving drivers the insurance they needed to make it to the next rural station. In this way we traveled south on fumes, on others' hopes, on Al-Cerraz's unwavering resolve.

We did not rest until we smelled the ocean again—not the untainted shore of my youth, but the briny, diesel-perfumed air of a major port: Marseilles. France's southeastern corner had become a mecca for fleeing artists and intellectuals. It was the part of France that everyone hoped might stay free—and it did, in principle, as part of Vichy France, once the Germans drew their occupation line in a zigzag south of Dijon and Tours, dipping low to the west, south of Bordeaux.

But Al-Cerraz and I had barely found a flophouse before the Nazis arrived in Marseilles, too, assisting the collaborationist Vichy to route out critics of Hitler and other enemies of the state. According to the armistice, the French agreed to surrender on demand any German nationals within Vichy France, including citizens of the many countries Germany had overrun. Considering Hitler's expanding reach across Europe, we knew that eventually no one would be beyond the Nazis' reach. Exit visas were restricted, locking within France's borders thousands of persons anxious to emigrate. Germans in dark green uniforms strolled the streets of Marseilles with an air of luxury and leisure, taking their time in arresting the wanted men and women they knew to be holed up in various houses and hotels, sweating out their last days of relative safety.

Two months had passed since our flight from Paris, and our cash reserves had dwindled to nearly nothing when we heard that an American was openly assisting refugees and clandestinely granting a chosen few help in leaving the country altogether. His name was Varian Fry—but we were told he winced at the feminine sound of his first name, and anyone who hoped to win his favor called him Mr. Fry. We heard about his arrival in Marseilles, with three thousand dollars taped to his leg. And we heard most of all about his list: the names of two hundred artists, musicians, and writers that he and his emergency-relief committee back in America believed were most in danger and most worth saving. My name was on that list. Al-Cerraz's was not.

Fry received visitors at his room at the Hôtel Splendide, but Al-Cerraz did not want to be seen there, lined up with the other petitioners, under the direct scrutiny of local gendarmes and Nazi informers. At present, Vichy was tolerating Fry's activities, under the guise of purely humanitarian efforts. Officially, he had permission to hear sob stories and offer minor financial support, not to forge documents or deal in foreign currencies, all of which he did. The game would end up lasting for thirteen months, until they sent him packing as an undesirable alien. I say thirteen months rather than rounding down to a year, because every month—every day—mattered. In that time, he helped some two thousand people flee to safety.

Some of the local artists were initially suspicious of the former journalist, astonished by his boldness and his youth and his apparent naïveté, to be operating so publicly when many of us, I suppose, thought aging politicos and spies should handle these things. My own first inclination was to steer clear, until Al-Cerraz asked me, "Then you're ready to pawn your bow? The Marseilles Mafia might want that sapphire, when they learn it belonged to a queen."

"You know I'd never sell it."

"Then the least you could do is play," he grumbled. Since our arrival, Al-Cerraz had performed privately here and there for well-heeled socialites, expecting the kind of instant patronage he'd found easily most of his life. But local largess was wearing thin. The night before, he'd left a party with a small white bag handed him by the hostess, a countess. He thought it held a discreet portion of cash. Instead it held scraps from dinner. The wealthy of Marseilles weren't living as well as they once had.

We knew that Fry dined with the likes of Hannah Arendt and Marc Chagall and other renowned Marseilles refugees; we knew he supported Jews and known homosexuals, so-called "degenerate" artists and other hard cases. Al-Cerraz persuaded me to wait until a September weekend when we knew Fry would be in the countryside, where he and his associates had rented a nineteenth-century villa and converted it into a hostel for select desperadoes.

We arrived at the gate of the Villa Air-Bel in September, were allowed in and guided past the fruit trees and unkempt garden and sprawling patio where one man sat with an easel and several others reclined in folding beach chairs, reading the newspapers. Later, we learned that when Fry was a boy, he had enjoyed regular visits to an orphanage run by his grandfather in Bath Beach, part of then-rural Brooklyn. This aging eighteen-bedroom chateau overlooking the Mediterranean was much like that seaside orphanage, full of just as much rambunctious mischief and bickering, though in this case there were no real orphans in residence, just creative artists who occasionally acted like children.

We nodded at the men on the patio and passed into the house. Fry's secretary showed us into a wood-paneled office and offered cigarettes and slices of pear. We accepted all of it, nervously puffing with sticky fingers as we waited to be seen. Finally Fry entered, shook our hands, and took his place behind a fussy, narrow desk. He looked like an accountant or perhaps a bookish schoolmaster, with his thick, round tortoiseshell glasses and close-buttoned pinstriped suit. We'd heard he was fluent in several languages, and a quick study when it came to maps and money and evaluating risk. He tended to look away as he spoke, and opened and closed shallow desk drawers as he listened to us, fingers searching restlessly for the stamp or envelope or franc notes that might solve a given problem. At first, I mistook these mannerisms for social nervousness. I might have even thought he was awed by me or by my partner or both. But Fry's jumpiness had nothing to do with us. It was simply excess energy made visible; sparks escaping from a mind occupied with lists of names, locations of hotels, exchange rates, appointments.

After we'd told him about our most pressing needs, he trapped his fingers in a thoughtful steeple and angled his head toward me. "I wish I could tell you I traffic in microfilm and secret capsules, but mostly I deal with old-fashioned paper. Visas. Because of your reputation in Spain, your prominence, and your letter-writing activities, you were identified early as someone best served by emigration. We have an emergency entrance visa for you. The exit visa from France is more difficult, but we can forge one; or perhaps better, since you dare not cross into Franco's Spain, simply smuggle you onto a boat from Marseilles."

"To...?" I asked.

"America, of course."

He paused and studied a piece of paper on the desk in front of him. "As for you"—he stumbled over the pronunciation of Al-Cerraz's name—"you are not on the list. Furthermore..." he stopped again. A young woman in an hourglass-shaped tweed suit entered without knocking and whispered in Fry's ear.

"We have no ice?" he responded. "Send someone to get some. For now, anything cool. I don't suppose we can waste a piece of steak..."

Al-Cerraz's eyes grew round at the mention of steak, and he winked at me and smiled, until the lady retorted, "That's funny, Mr. Fry. And the shipment of fresh butter, cream, and coffee is waiting around back."

After she left, Fry explained, "One of our residents punched one of our lady visitors in the eye. She was just leaving, but I can't see sending her back to Marseilles with a black eye. Her ill health has attracted enough attention already." He tapped his fingers on the desk and turned back to Al-Cerraz. "The problem is not your lack of artistic reputation, but the facts of your reputation."

We waited, and he continued with evident reluctance. "Our first priorities are prominent critics of fascism. Not collaborators."

"But I'm against Franco now," Al-Cerraz sputtered. "I fled Spain years ago—in '37. Even the Spanish Republican embassy in Paris offered me some assistance. Who are you to say—"

"Come on, Justo." I reached for his arm.

"I'm not leaving. I have nowhere to go."

We stayed in our seats, Al-Cerraz huffing, Fry fingering the edge of his desk. It was a stalemate.

Finally Fry said, "What about you, Mr. Delargo?"

"I came here hoping for shelter or a temporary loan. I'm not leaving France—I never intended to. List or no list, I don't think I'm in serious danger. Frankly, I'm tired of running from place to place."

Fry exhaled. "Of course you are. Half the artists you'll meet in Marseilles say the same thing, until they're arrested or threatened. The lucky ones get a second chance. But I'm not in the business of convincing anyone."

The lady assistant cracked the door again and stage-whispered, "I'm sending Yehoshua to town for the ice. André requests that we pick up more wine for tonight; Jacqueline says he has had more than enough. Do we need anything else?"

Fry rose and straightened his jacket, looking harassed. "I hope he wasn't the one who punched our Italian violinist."

"He wasn't."

Fry smiled in our direction. "We already have one artist missing an eye—that's Victor Brauner, the Rumanian surrealist, do you know him? You are welcome to stay for dinner and meet him and all the others."

While Fry and the assistant discussed the market list, Al-Cerraz and I exchanged glances.

"Mr. Fry," I interrupted, "please tell us the name of this lady violinist. We know many European musicians."

"Let's see." He scratched his head. "I'm usually good with details, but I can't recall her last name. Of course she told me, but there were six syllables at least. It seems to me that she doesn't use it publicly."

"Is she Jewish?" Al-Cerraz asked.

"Yes. And she is disliked for the company she has kept over the last few years, which brings out the worst in some of our other guests. You see the problem I have here? If they're not arguing about the quality of the morning pastries, they're arguing about politics."

"If she can stay until her eye heals, then I should be able to stay, too," said Al-Cerraz.

Fry exhaled again. "I can't help you leave the country, but I won't deprive you of a bed or camaraderie, at least until you've planned your next move. Some of the surrealists are planning an art showing tonight. Stay and enjoy, please—both of you."

"Don't say anything," I said to Al-Cerraz on the way out. "I just want to see her." He nodded curtly. I could feel that he was as excited and nervous as I was, both of us stifling the urge to run through the orchard, tear open doors, put our hands around the neck of the cretin who had struck her.

We found her in the kitchen, slouching on the kitchen counter while a young girl, the cook's helper, patted at her cheek with a damp towel. When Aviva spotted us, she drew back, startling the girl, who stepped away. Al-Cerraz moved forward first, and Aviva made a choking sound and threw her arms around his neck, then made room for me, looping one arm around my head so that we huddled awkwardly together. Pressed that way between us, she weighed almost nothing—a mere vibration of the past, with limp hair clinging to her damp face, and a bruise forming as we stared.

That night, the Villa Air-Bel was loud with games and frivolity. On the patio, torches glowed with fragrant light, dispersing the autumn chill. A dozen residents and Marseilles guests had gathered, and several of the painters had hung their latest works from the trees, creating a gallery in the open air.

Aviva and I kept to ourselves, withdrawn to a half-lit corner. Al-Cerraz, unable to accept exclusion, made an attempt to penetrate the society of this downtrodden estate, and he succeeded in part. Wine-glass in hand, he circulated, gathered intelligence, and managed to beg or borrow personal items from the wives of several of the artists and writers gathered. He brought these and the latest news back to us, along with a dusty bottle he'd taken from the cellar. "France will starve, but she won't go without drink," he said.

"They're gay beyond belief," I grunted back, watching a man dangle upside down from one of the trees.

"It's an act," Al-Cerraz said. "Three or four of them are making a run for the border tomorrow, with Fry. They'll take a train and then try to cross the mountains into Spain on foot." He pointed out an over-weight man and his well-dressed wife, her profile hidden behind a peaked green hat festooned with dark lace. "She's had a lot to drink, but her hands are still shaking. And look at him—he has a heart condition." He cleared his throat and tried to sound buoyant. "More important, she is jettisoning some of her personal effects. She gave me this." He opened a flat leather case to reveal a set of shining silver manicure tools and a small pair of pearl-handled scissors.

Aviva glanced at the kit with little interest.

"Someday," Al-Cerraz said, trying to engage her, "you will tell your children that your hands were once manicured with implements belonging to the ex-wife of Gustav Mahler."

But the mention of children had been a gaffe. Aviva turned away, toward the shadows beyond the patio's glowing center.

After a while, I said, "Please, tell us the rest."

Aviva grasped the neck of her dress, pulling the lapels closer to-gether, fighting a chill the rest of us couldn't feel. "Tell you what? Tell you why I'm not already dead—like that ignorant jackass wanted to know this morning before he slugged me? I suppose the fact that I am alive at all proves I'm guilty of something."

"Never mind," Al-Cerraz said. He reached for her free hand, stud-ied it, and spread the fingers across his broad knee. "No musician can feel human with dirty nails. Then we'll tackle your hair."

She shook her head gravely. Her lips strained to form a half-smile. "Just promise me you won't touch my elbows."

"Feliu—do you know what she's talking about?" Al-Cerraz said facetiously.

"Not a clue."

From off to one side, I watched them edge their chairs together, until their knees touched. I had found Al-Cerraz's insistence on groom-ing petty, but once again I soon saw the wisdom in his priorities. As he clipped and cleaned and buffed and massaged, Aviva's arms loosened, her shoulders fell. He murmured banalities as he worked, as if we'd all been in close contact, as if she hadn't been lost inside Germany for five years, as if there was nothing important to ask or to know. I heard her breathing deepen and saw her eyes close, the swollen one still leaking an occasional irritated tear.

"I shouldn't have asked Varian for anything," she said in a low voice.

"Fry," I corrected. "Mr. Fry."

"Oh, stop," she said. "I'm tired of men deciding my fate. I'll call them by their first names if I like—Benito, Adolf, Bertolt, Varian. Do you know he decides which artists are superior enough for his services? Do you know he asked me to play for him?"

"I'm glad to hear you have your violin," I said, guessing Fry had only been attempting to be polite. Aviva's politics were her problem, not her performance abilities.

She ignored me. "I'm tired of auditioning. And I'm tired of traveling. God—I've been on the road my whole life."

"It's the style these days," Al-Cerraz said. "Half of Paris is on the road, taking an extended holiday."

Aviva's shoulders had tensed again. He massaged her lower arms and gave her fingernails a final buffing, though they already shone.

Above the hum of voices and clinking glasses and occasional laughter, I could hear the night sounds of the country around us: the two-note songs of the frogs, the chirping of crickets, the thrum of beating wings. A man ran across the grounds with something in a jar, shouting that he'd caught a praying mantis, and everyone must come to take a look. Even this didn't open Aviva's eyes.

"Is it true you don't play the cello anymore?" she said after a while, in a drowsy voice.

"That's true."

"It makes perfect sense," she said.

Al-Cerraz muttered skeptically under his breath.

"No, I mean it," she said. "I admire Feliu tremendously. Ask any Jewish musician in the Third Reich—ask my colleagues in the *Jüdischer Kulturbund*. We were wrong to play…" But she couldn't go on. After she'd steadied herself, she said to me, "I'm sure you have no regrets."

"I have one."

At last she looked my way. Al-Cerraz focused more intently on her hands.

"Your son?" I asked finally. "Did you find any sign of him?"

She took a deep breath. "No sign, alive or dead."

Al-Cerraz said, "Well, that's better than knowing for sure that he's dead."

I glared at him. "Not necessarily."

Aviva pulled her arms free and opened her eyes. "I've missed you both." Then she walked away, to be alone in the orchard's unlit corners.

Later that night, after Aviva had gone up to the room she was sharing with André Breton's young daughter, Breton joined Al-Cerraz and me on the patio with the last of the liqueur he'd pried from the fingers of the cook's assistant. Breton wore his dark hair slicked straight back from his flat, lined forehead, like a movie gangster—if gangsters spent their evenings spouting poetry. He closed his heavy-lidded eyes, savoring the weight of the glass in his hand before relinquishing it to the tabletop and said, "Your friend—she reminds me of people I met in the last war."

"Writers?"

"Nutcases. I worked in a psychiatric ward. She has the same look. The worst part was the night shift, sitting up late and listening for any sign that they were trying to slit their own throats. But the resigned ones are really quiet about it."

He stood up. "Good night, gentlemen. Sleep well."

I went up next, leaving Al-Cerraz brooding, forearms on his thighs, an ear cocked toward the frog song of the estate's dark corners.

The next morning, Fry and several of his charges left for the train that would take them within walking distance of the Spanish border. I watched them go, apparently dressed for nothing more than a weekend holiday. Alma Werfel, Mahler's ex-wife and now the wife of novelist Franz Werfel, wore a fashionable summer suit, with a close-fitting skirt and high-heeled sandals. While the men struggled to load the suitcases into Fry's car, I drew alongside him, sharing some last-minute tips on Spanish phrases and ways to differentiate between various kinds of Spanish police and military uniforms.

I gestured toward the car and said in a low voice, "I hope I'm not out of line, but those are terrible clothes for hiking the Pyrenees. Her shoes in particular. And if she's going to wear a fancy hat, at least it might have a brim, to protect her from sunstroke."

Fry locked his hands behind his back and rolled on his heels, like a parson watching fondly as his congregants left the sanctuary of church for the hazards and temptations of the outside world. "I've been here only a month or so," he said in a gentle voice. "But what I've learned so far is you have to work with the materials you've got. I can't make an elegant woman dress down. She would look suspicious in jodhpurs and flat shoes. But that's just part of it." He paused, pressing his lips together. "The other part is, you can't take away people's idea of themselves. Not at the last minute, when they're facing a dangerous situation. It makes them less stable, less predictable. Everyone clings to some silly thing or other. Everyone seems to have that one thing they can't live without."

We both looked toward the car, where Mrs. Werfel was haranguing her husband for having failed to find room for all the bags she had insisted on taking.

I said, "Just *one* thing?"

Fry laughed, loudly and openly, the first and last time I'd have the pleasure of seeing his face free from worry.

After the car had pulled away, I went looking for breakfast. I asked Imogene, the cook's assistant who had treated Aviva's eye, to inform me when Aviva or Al-Cerraz came in for breakfast.

"They've already eaten," she said. "They finished early and went for a walk. Just down the road, I think."

I spent the morning waiting for them to return and thinking about Aviva, about whether an inland location might be better for her given that Marseilles was guarded so heavily. The port was a place the authorities expected desperate refugees to gather; every backcountry road in view of the Mediterranean was patrolled by both French Vichy and

German officials. I wondered how we might convince Fry to help her with French identification papers for internal transit, at least, so that she could take the train west with fewer chances of being arrested.

Little did I know how close and imminent the threat truly was.

Later, Al-Cerraz would explain to me that the walk had been his idea, to begin to put a blush back in Aviva's sallow cheeks. A motorcycle with a sidecar had approached them, sputtering. It died on the road, within view of where they were strolling, and the motorcyclist called out in French for assistance. He was young and thin, wearing a peaked cap and goggles, a dark uniform and black knee-high boots. At closer range they saw the armband with its familiar symbol.

Al-Cerraz spent half an hour with the man, bent low to the road, touching wires and poking at the hot exhaust, his sincere love of mechanics helping to mask his apprehension. Aviva sat off to the side on the embankment, her arms wrapped around her knees, trying to hide her face behind her hand with exaggerated yawns.

"You speak excellent French," the guard said after they'd fixed the bike. "But you're not French. Spanish?"

"Good ear." Al-Cerraz said.

"You look familiar to me, like someone I very much admire."

"A movie star?" Al-Cerraz joked.

"No, a pianist."

Al-Cerraz bowed his head slightly in acknowledgment.

"I didn't believe it at first," the German continued. "But then I watched your hands while we were working. I once had a photograph of your hands over my desk, if you can believe that. My daughter used to visit my office and lay her hands over the picture, trying to match her fingers to yours. I told her if she ate her vegetables and practiced her scales, her fingers might grow just as big someday."

Al-Cerraz couldn't help smiling. "Did they?"

"Nearly as long, but not as wide," he laughed. "She didn't succeed as a concert pianist. I didn't either—but that was a long time ago."

A hot breeze rustled the long blades of grass lining the ditches on either side of the road.

"All my mementos are back in Germany. Would you mind?" And the young guard went to the pannier hanging over his motorcycle's rear wheel and pulled out a small camera. He took Al-Cerraz's photo; first his face, then the fingers of both hands, splayed against the black leather seat of the motorcycle.

"I'm almost out of film. Would your girl like to be in the next one?"

"I'm sure she would," Al-Cerraz said, still smiling. "Come on honey, over here. She's a little shy; and with her fair skin"—he emphasized *fair*—"she can't stand this sun. That's why we take our walks early."

"Please come," the guard said.

And then more directly: "Come." Aviva's reticence had worn the solicitous edge from his voice. When she continued to bury her face in her hand, feigning exhaustion, he made five long, slow strides toward her, the sun glinting off his boots.

"Papers, please."

"I don't have them with me."

He lifted her chin with a finger, noted the bruise on her cheekbone. "Someone hit you?"

She didn't answer. Al-Cerraz spoke up, "A lovers' quarrel—you understand how it is."

"I don't believe it," the German said.

No one spoke for a moment, until he tilted his face back toward Al-Cerraz, eyes shielded beneath his cap. "I've read enough about you to know you'd never hit anything. You are obsessed when it comes to protecting your hands—isn't that true?"

Al-Cerraz forced a laugh. "Never try to outwit a fan. You're right about my hands. But you've misunderstood me."

"Oh?"

"I said it was a lover's quarrel. I didn't say *I* was the guilty lover."

"Oh. *Oh,*" the German said, the note of surprise extending into a pleased, gravelly chuckle that trailed off only slowly. Then he stepped close enough to touch her. He eyed the narrowness of her legs and arms. He set a hand flat against the side of her torso, feeling the ribs beneath the thin fabric.

"Not ticklish?" he said. If only she'd had the energy—or the temperament—to shy away girlishly, or to bridle, rather than letting her head and shoulders fall as she did. He took her hand in his and slowly rotated the slim wrist, looking up and down her arm for the sign of a tattoo. There was none.

"You're staying nearby?"

"Visiting friends for the weekend," Al-Cerraz interjected.

"Your papers are there?"

Al-Cerraz started to speak again, but Aviva interrupted. "In Marseilles. I left them at our hotel."

"I'm going to Marseilles now," he said. "I'll take you."

He walked her toward the sidecar, holding her wrist, and over his shoulder said to Al-Cerraz, "There's only room for one. My apologies. But I hope to see you in town—especially if you are performing. What I would give for that!"

Al-Cerraz tried to delay him. "What would you like to hear?"

The German dropped Aviva's arm. "That's a difficult question." He took his time considering, while Aviva stood by, hands hanging long at her sides, hair fallen in front of her face. "Should one choose something he has heard before, or something he has never heard? Everyone says you play Chopin better than anyone in Europe, but I've heard more than my share of Chopin. What I know and love best is your recording of the Dvořák trio."

"Number four, I am guessing. The Dumky," Al-Cerraz said.

The guard clicked his heels and bowed slightly. "Of course." He started to turn away.

"I can't take much credit for that recording," Al-Cerraz gushed. "It's all in the cello, isn't it? I will tell Señor Delargo how much you loved it."

"You are in contact with Maestro Delargo?"

"In contact? I'd call sharing a double bed too *much* contact."

The German advanced toward Al-Cerraz, forgetting Aviva altogether and gripping the camera tightly in his right hand. His eyes grew wide as he whispered, "Where?"

And so, my partner of all these years—my colleague, my shadow, my friend, my rival—lured the wolf directly to our door. They would have heard of me soon enough—I took few pains to conceal my presence. But there were other people in that villa: André and Jacqueline Breton, their daughter Aube, the Trotskyite writer Victor Serge, and several other artists and writers still lazing in their beds, sleeping off the effects of the previous night's excesses. Even the cook, Yehoshua, had been arrested once already in Marseilles for using forged ration cards to purchase more than his—our—share of limited foods. It could have been a disaster for any of them if the guard had wanted to make trouble, or impress his superiors. Fortunately, the Werfels and Heinrich Mann had already left. Unfortunately, Fry, the quickest-thinking among us, and the best at sweet-talking officials, had not yet returned. We were left to cope on our own.

"I don't play anymore," I explained to the Gestapo officer after he'd pumped my hand and begged me to play something for him.

We were on the patio, next to one of the ironwork tables, from which Imogene was hurrying to clear half-finished plates full of torn rolls and smears of jam, the late breakfasters having absented themselves at the first sound of boots on the herringboned paving.

"You don't play anymore?" the German repeated, working his fingers around the edge of his cap.

"Temporarily," Al-Cerraz explained quickly. "He has gout. A type of arthritis, isn't it? Inflamed joints."

"Of course! My grandmama has the same problem." He studied my face. "Do you eat much seafood?"

"When I . . . can," I said slowly.

"Red meat?"

"When it's available."

"That's the problem. Meat and seafood are terrible for gout. How long do these spells last?"

I looked to Al-Cerraz. He said, "A week, ten days. Comes and goes. In between, we can practice with him a little, but not very much."

"You still play together?"

"Why wouldn't we?"

"Good," the officer said under his breath. "I'm glad to hear it isn't permanent. My grandmama swore by various fruits and vegetables, but especially cherries. Fresh cherries."

"I'll take it under advisement," I said.

The German looked around. Al-Cerraz and I both followed the sweep of his eyes, out toward the grounds. Aviva had crept away during our introductions, and he seemed to have forgotten about her entirely. Relaxing, I let my eyes wander to the tops of the trees over-head—and spotted one of the surrealists' paintings, still hanging in the arboreal gallery of the night before. It showed a naked woman, pressed close to a man-creature with enormous, doelike eyes, crab claws, and a distinctly brushy mustache.

"Oh, God," I exhaled.

Al-Cerraz looked up, looked down just as quickly, and stepped toward me, taking my hands in his. "Is the pain that bad? I think our friend is right—it must be your diet. Have a look."

And with unnerving boldness, he held my hands to the German officer's face, caressing my knuckles, drawing attention to the lines and folds and bumps that were my normal hands, nothing more or less.

"They do look swollen," the officer clucked gently, clinically. "A shame. Well," he said, straightening, "it's been an interesting day. If there's just one favor I could ask..."

At Al-Cerraz's urging, Imogene jumped to attention, and ran to retrieve my bow tube from the bedroom I'd used. The German went to his motorcycle to retrieve his camera. I stood for a minute alone with Al-Cerraz, wanting to kill him—yes, kill him, a sentiment that everyone in the house would profess by that evening.

Then we were all together again, and the Gestapo officer was posing me with cello and bow.

"Can you hold it the other way—I know it's less natural, but I want the sapphire in the picture. That's what makes it recognizably yours, after all, isn't it?" He looked through the viewfinder, then pulled the camera away from his face again without snapping. "I consider myself a devotee but there are some greater fans." He shielded his face with the camera again. "This one will be for Herr Doktor Goebbels himself."

Then the final disappointment of the German's day: "But I'm out of film! Well, it's destiny again. Maestro, we will have to meet another time. As soon as possible. I don't get out this way very often, but I'm sure you come into town...."

And with more hand-clasping and tender words all around, he left, saving his final words for Al-Cerraz: "Take care of this man's health. I'll hold you personally responsible if he doesn't get better!"

The fading putter and bang of the officer's departing motorcycle was still audible from the patio when Al-Cerraz elected to make his exit. He walked quickly to his room, to pack his bags and tell Aviva to pack her own. It wasn't the German's immediate return he feared half as much as our wrath, simmering at the very moment in the far corners of the house. A distant door opened and slammed shut. A baritone voice rumbled through an open window over our heads. Imogene sat down on the ground to cry.

Al-Cerraz recounted to me then everything that had gone before, ending with a plea: "You must trust me about this. It was the best thing I could do."

"It's all right."

"Perhaps it was an opportunity. There are many more like him— did you hear how he referred to Goebbels?"

"Justo, haven't you learned anything?"

Yehoshua came around the corner. "Miss Aviva is waiting in the car, if you still want a ride to Marseilles."

I shook myself, flexed my fingers and started to follow Al-Cerraz around the corner of the house, toward the idling car, but he stopped me.

"You told her the other night you had one regret."

I acknowledged him with a curt nod.

"If you care about her, you'll make sure she gets out of this country soon."

"She may not want to go…"

"Of course she won't. She'd rather be in Germany now, still looking for that ghost boy of hers. Never mind the concentration camps; he might have died from dysentery or typhus or a thousand natural causes years ago. No wonder she can't find him." He exhaled sharply through his nose. "You *should* go. I *want* to go. But she *must* go."

I took another step toward the car.

"Don't say good-bye to her. She'll get the wrong impression. We'll be in touch soon."

The baskets of stemmed cherries arrived two days later, perfect and brilliant and red, though local cherry season was long past. We took it as a sign that our visitor had connections, to distant lands and to air delivery, to power.

"Turkey?" André mused, spitting out the pits.

"Who knows?" I said, feeling glum.

Then Fry arrived, tired but pleased with his success. All of his charges had safely made it into the Spanish mountains, at least as far as he'd been able to see them go. Next they would travel to Lisbon, where they would board a boat—legally—for New York. At the last minute, Alma Werfel had confessed that in one of her many bags she was carrying the original score of Bruckner's Third Symphony as well as a draft of one of her husband's novels.

"I tell you this," Fry said, over a celebratory dinner, "not to encourage you to attempt the same, but to discourage you. If you must try to smuggle out a manuscript of any kind, please let me know. I have couriers who can attempt to move some items. It is always safer to separate the banned material from the banned person. Please let me do my job."

No one wanted to upset Fry's tentatively happy mood by telling him what had occurred in his absence. But it couldn't be avoided, and the half dozen refugees still in residence spent a good hour airing their collective scorn and fear.

"It must be that Spanish temperament," a painter named Gustav said.

"What does that mean?" someone asked.

"What Al-Cerraz did. It was brash, stupid—hot-blooded."

Fry interrupted. "We have another Spaniard present who has none of those traits. Let's leave the ethnic stereotypes to our enemies, can't we?"

Someone tapped a glass with a fork. "Hear, hear."

A woman ventured, "No one has a cooler head—and a better heart—than Maestro Delargo. He's certainly made enough sacrifices."

More clinking.

But Fry stopped the toasts with his next question: "What was the German's name?"

No answer.

"Gestapo—are you sure? Not another branch of the SS?"

"They are not synonymous?" Jacqueline asked.

"Brown uniform or black? Insignia on his uniform—badges, special medals...Did anyone look? A personal card with the cherries? Did someone notice?"

Faces disappeared behind napkins. One person coughed.

"He did mention the propaganda man, Goebbels," I said. "Perhaps he knows him personally."

"Why does all this matter?" Jacqueline asked indignantly. "We are artists and philosophers at this table, not spies. You can't expect us to pay attention to these imbeciles."

Fry sighed. "They pay attention to all of you."

"We're flattered," Gustav muttered.

After a moment, as if regretting his terseness, Fry elaborated. "Some are friendlier than others; some are smarter or better connected."

"Just stay away from them all—that's my advice," André said.

"It's not possible," Fry said. "I'm having lunch with the inspector of police tomorrow, and he's likely to bring some Gestapo associates. How do you think I know who they're looking for in any given week?" He pushed up from his chair and wished us all the best for the week ahead; tomorrow, he was due back at the Hôtel Splendide.

Later that night, Fry knocked softly at my door. "I can't do much for your friends, you know," he told me. "I'll keep an eye on them in town, if they hang around. But as far as helping them get out..."

"I understand."

"In the meanwhile, I have a project for you."

Knowing I had no plans to leave France immediately, Fry suggested I begin to write an account of my life under Franco, the problems that I and other Spanish Civil War refugees faced now under the German occupation of France, the further threats that future months would bring if the Caudillo and the Führer joined forces. Hitler had bombed Guernica and assisted the Spanish fascists, but Franco hadn't returned the favor by joining the Axis powers. With France's fascist and collaborationist head of state Marshal Pétain under his wing, Hitler was close to controlling the continent. If he won Franco's assistance, he might take control of Gibraltar, and in so doing secure the advantage necessary to conquer Great Britain.

Spaniards—especially those with communist affiliations—were already among the European nationals suffering in the concentration camps. But the Nazis hadn't taken much interest in routing out all of Franco's enemies for him. That could change if Franco entered the war in earnest; if the two dictators declared warmer sympathies for each other. Lucky for us Spaniards—for everyone—Franco was bristly, stubborn, and proud, an isolationist at heart. As of September 1940, Hitler and Franco still hadn't met in person, although it was clear such a meeting had to be imminent.

"Tell us all that," Fry said, when I puzzled aloud over what Americans would most need to understand. "But remember that we are trying to move hearts as well as minds. Stories equal more dollars, more visas. I hate to be crass, but it's that simple. Be accurate, but make it personal."

"How personal?"

"That's up to you," he said, and then smiling, added, "But don't forget, I have only so much paper."

The energy that I had dissipated over recent years by writing letters I now redirected into writing my memoirs. I had not meant to go all the way back to the beginning, but it was easier. The recent past made no sense to me; my early adulthood involved more people, more places, more questions. My childhood was the clearest, the least corrupted. I told myself I was writing for myself alone, as a warm-up, in the way that I had played daily scales all those years, starting with the simplest keys. I told myself I would select later the elements fit for public consumption. Despite what I told myself, I quickly lost control, and memory itself took over.

While I was writing, Al-Cerraz was in Marseilles, telling his own tales. I don't know if he planned the whole scheme from the beginning and planted it in some official's head, or if someone approached him with the idea and he merely accepted and perhaps accelerated it. He knew that time was limited. That week the gendarmes had begun to register all the Jews in Marseilles, calling them to their offices in alphabetical order, then allowing them to travel home again—"Just paperwork," they assured teachers, pharmacists, accountants. Aviva did not fit easily into the pigeonholes. She was not French, not an enemy of the Italian regime, not a German national; but she was a notable Jew, and she had eluded Nazi roundups—they would realize that soon enough. They would scold themselves for having let her slip out of Berlin, unless her present liberty suited their purposes, which remained to be seen.

In October Al-Cerraz sent a note asking me to meet him at the Café le Croix in Marseilles "to discuss some ensemble work—our most creative collaboration to date."

Aviva came, too, looking better than she had at the Villa Air-Bel: rested, well-fed, wearing a bright red belted dress with yellow daisies as big as saucers. It had padded shoulders and it flared at the hips, hiding her gauntness.

"I see you've decided against blending in," I said warmly, reaching for her hand above the café table.

"Justo says we can do better by sticking out."

"Is that so?"

"The key is not to be invisible. It is to be indispensable." He patted the yellow carnation in his buttonhole. "We have nothing to fear. We are celebrities here—all of us." And he took my free hand, and Aviva's, so that we were sitting in a cozy triangle of clasped fingers.

"I realized the mistake I made on that day in the country. I let a stranger think Aviva was just some girl, when I should have explained that she is one of Europe's most famous violinists."

I leaned forward and whispered. "Even in France, they're banning Jewish music now. What does that tell you?"

Al-Cerraz lifted his voice and addressed the crowd around us. "But we heard Offenbach played just the other night. Isn't that so?"

I shook my head, confused.

"The cancan," he explained, laughing. "No one's thought to ban that. We heard it at the Moulin Gavotte—I think they played it a dozen times in one night. And there were German officers dancing to it, on their chairs."

"Are you crazy?" I whispered back. "That German from the Air-Bel could have been there."

"He was. He apologized to Aviva. He introduced us to his superiors. He bought us champagne."

I groaned under my breath. "Champagne..."

"Well you have to have champagne when you're closing a deal."

I let go of the hands I was clasping—first his, then, with greater reluctance, hers. Suddenly every sound around us seemed amplified: the scrape of a chair leg against sidewalk, the high, brittle click of a glass making contact with a tile-topped table.

"What deal?"

Al-Cerraz lowered his voice to match mine. "The deal that allows all three of us to travel legally all the way across France, to a nearly unguarded port on the open Atlantic, where there are many small boats. It happens also to be on a rail line where some important men will be meeting. I have tickets and safe-conduct visas in my pocket. We depart in three days."

I pushed out the words between clenched teeth: "To what end?"

"To the only end that ever mattered." He was speaking loudly again. "To the end of making music, of course."

"Even if it was a benefit for the Virgin Mary herself, I don't perform anymore."

"Oh, Mary won't be there." He studied his fingernails, then raised them to his teeth, and spoke into the anonymity of his cupped hands, whispering, "Only Hitler and Franco and a lot of newspapermen from both sides."

I didn't say anything. Aviva reached for my hand but I ignored her. She pushed a water glass across the table. When I ignored that, she dipped a napkin in the water and held it toward my brow.

"You can't say yes on my behalf," I said finally.

Al-Cerraz looked to Aviva, who looked away. Then he turned to me, wincing slightly. "I already did."

Al-Cerraz refused to take no for an answer. By the time I got back to the Villa Air-Bel, a messenger had already left a note for me. It said, "I'll never ask another favor. After this, you'll never see me again." I should be so lucky, I thought—but I did not believe him.

He must have met with Fry at the Hôtel Splendide, too, because Fry came to me later, and to my astonishment suggested that the plan was a good one. Bold, inventive, and sound, he said, except for one fact: "It certainly will destroy your reputation."

"I don't care about that."

"If that's true, then why aren't you willing?"

The question deprived me of sleep all the next night.

Fry came to me again the following day, to share what he'd learned from one of his best sources, a man who had worked for the British embassy.

Al-Cerraz had not been inventing stories or exaggerating the rank of our proposed audience. The concert would be the centerpiece of the welcoming festivities at the railroad station in Hendaye, France, just across the westernmost border of Spain, where Franco and Hitler planned to meet for the first time in both dictators' lives. Still, it didn't make sense to me. Given that Al-Cerraz and I were not Franco's favorites, why would Nazi authorities consider us the best musical accompaniment for a Spanish-German summit?

"Hitler and Franco will both be taking pains to annoy each other," Fry guessed. "Franco never managed to force you to perform for him or his government—I doubt he could have succeeded. But if the Nazis can, then it's Hitler's way of showing how much control of Spain he has already. It's all tied up with public image—cultural showmanship, philosophical innuendo. As a propaganda plan, it has Goebbels's finger-prints all over it."

"Wouldn't my appearance just make Franco angrier?"

"It might. But Hitler has tried friendship with Franco for years al-ready. I think he's ready to settle for intimidation."

The day before our officially ticketed departure, I had one last visitor. Aviva arrived at the villa on a black bicycle she had borrowed from the madame of a brothel. We sat outside, next to the pear trees. A few of the unharvested pears had fallen from the trees and been left to bake and decay into pulpy splotches between clumps of unmowed grass. I hadn't noticed them before, but on this unseasonably warm autumn day, the wasps buzzed insistently between us and the sticky ground. We sat as still as possible, trying not to aggravate them.

"There are two things I need to tell you," Aviva said. "First, I un-derstand why you won't play the concert." She swallowed hard. "Even when I wasn't well in Germany—wasn't in my right mind—I under-stood you. And I think, despite your concerns, that you understood me. I admire your principles, Feliu. I always have."

Little could she know that she was praising me for a firmness I did not feel. She continued, "If you tell them you won't be playing, it makes the whole thing suspect. So we want you to come with us on the train. They already believe that you have arthritis. Ride all the way to Hendaye and at the last minute say you can't perform—a medical ex-cuse. Then Al-Cerraz and I play, and we leave the concert, and then..."

I sat quietly, considering both what to say and what to do: not just later in Hendaye, but there, at that very moment, in the villa's garden, while she sat just across from me—her hand within reach, her cheek only a bit farther, if I stood now and leaned across the table.

"That way," she added, "there is no harm to your reputation."

There was that word again. But in that moment, I did not care about my reputation. I did not want to be revered, I wanted to be loved.

"Wait," I said.

She looked at me quizzically, smiling. I'd been watching a wasp circling her head lazily for the last several minutes.

"There—in your hair."

She shook her head impatiently. "The second thing is harder to say. I don't know how you'll take it."

The wasp had landed on a dark brown curl behind her ear, trapping itself there as she shook her head from side to side. She looked more annoyed than fearful; it was taking all of her energy to find her words, and she didn't want to be interrupted.

"Justo and I—" she clapped her hand hard against her neck.

I reached toward her. "You'll just get it—"

"—are getting married."

"—angry..."

Our words had crossed, and I was only beginning to absorb what she had said.

She stiffened, closing her eyes. "Too late."

For a full minute I sat, silent and stunned, until she rose to her feet. Ignoring the reddening spot at her throat, she said, "I have to go. The madame warned me that she imposes strict overtime penalties on all her customers."

I watched her struggle to bunch her skirt between her knees and extend one leg over the crossbar. "Just remember," she said. "No one can make you do something you don't want to do. You've always been your own man."

Had I? She seemed as sure of it as Al-Cerraz had seemed sure I'd follow his lead. But why should this matter when I'd just lost Aviva?

Why should I care what she or anyone thought of me—what the entire world thought of me?

Precisely because now it was the only thing I had left.

I had written perhaps half of my life story so far, if the thin pile of hand-scrawled sheets I'd filled could be called a life story, and now this trip to Hendaye imposed a deadline. Fry had promised to smuggle my manuscript to a clandestine courier at the end of the week, while I was away.

Pushing Aviva as far as I could from my grieving mind, I continued to wonder about the choices I had made in my life, or failed to make; the lines I had drawn, not only for myself but for others as well. I had been fortunate in many regards, endowed with opportunities and gifts. But I needed think only of the gemstone in my bow to recall how many of those gifts had weighed upon me, upsetting my balance in more than one sense. With the same kind of fervor I'd once displayed in Alberto's apartment, bowing until my tailbone ached, I kept writing, remembering, and searching.

That afternoon, Fry came to the Villa Air-Bel, and I told him I had used up all the paper he had given me. "Both sides?" His question embarrassed me. I hadn't meant to be wasteful. I thanked him and returned to writing, filling the backs of all the completed pages, writing faster than ever—a *scherzo* of pen strokes.

One by one the house lights went out, the pure dark country night pressed down upon the house, and I continued to write in an insomniac trance. One might assume it was the events at Hendaye that were costing me sleep, but the truth is I didn't spend more than a minute imagining them. I worried about only one thing: Had I explained myself? Whether or not I performed, I knew the Hendaye concert would change the way the world thought about me. There was a chance that something might happen to me. The manuscript I was writing provided answers, a defense, an explanation for everything I had ever done, or failed to do. But rereading the parts I'd already written, I knew I hadn't explained anything well. Was it true I had lost contact with Alberto, distancing myself from him even after my own experiences at the palace had showed me that any musician can be ensnared by a situation beyond his control? After I—and everyone else—turned against the monarchy, why had I been unable and unwilling to return the Queen's gift? Had I really ruined the chances of that young cellist, Rocamura—and how many other musicians besides? What had I ever done for my family? What had I ever done for art? For love?

I did not want to be remembered for the life I had so far lived. In the dark of the night, as I sat shivering and hungry with a cramped writing hand, I felt consumed by incompleteness. In the emotionalism that sweeps over a person rubbed raw by exhaustion, I suddenly became teary, thinking of the chorus from Mahler's Second Symphony, which I had conducted once in Salamanca: *Prepare thyself to live!*

I did not feel prepared to live, or to die.

I wiped my eyes and turned over a piece of paper, to use the other side—it was filled. All the pages were filled. But I had more to remember, more to say and explain. I paced the room and wandered the house and found myself suddenly outside Fry's door, and before I knew it I was banging on it, waking the poor overworked man.

"Paper," I said.

He rubbed his eyes. "Tomorrow."

"I leave tomorrow, very early. It's my last chance to finish what I'm writing."

"Go back to bed."

"I wasn't in bed. I need more paper."

"There is no more paper."

I shrieked inconsolably, "I need more paper!"

He turned slowly and disappeared into the darkness of his bedroom. I heard rustling, for two minutes, three. He shuffled back to the lighted doorway with a sheaf of manuscript pages in his hand. He thrust them toward me, eyes still squeezed into half-slits. "It's all I have. Keep them in order; you can write on the backs and someone can recopy them later. They're going with the same courier. Leave them with Imogene in the morning, before you leave."

He started to close the door, then reopened it a crack. "He called them 'everything I know.' Be careful with them."

Back in my room, I held the first page under the light of my gooseneck desk lamp. It was a music manuscript: short works for piano, by Justo Al-Cerraz. Some of the pages had dates ranging across many years. Unable to help Al-Cerraz leave France, Fry had apparently agreed to smuggle out page after page of his work.

I wiped at my burning eyes with a calloused fingertip and tried to focus on the first page. One brittle corner was marked with a wineglass stain so perfect and round and red it looked like a passport stamp. And a date: 1921. I held the blemished page to my nose, wondering if the smell of cheap Rioja would still be there, and with it perhaps other scents—rosemary from the Alhambra's red-soiled slopes, the iodine of Mediterranean shores—but the only thing I could smell was dampness. A purple constellation of mold stippled many of the papers' edges.

I read the first bars of the first page silently. The solo piano piece started with a percussive sequence: a sixteenth note followed by a dotted eighth. Again. Again. Again. *His heartbeat,* I thought. *I'm hearing his heartbeat...*

"*Olvídalo!*" I cried, and jumped at the sound of my voice echoing in that dark, empty wood-floored room. Forget it. And all my curiosity, all my concern, vanished in a fiery halo of indignation.

I caught my breath, tried to read more, to translate the inky markings into mental music. But my anger would not allow it.

Every measure bore his trace. The music refused to stand alone. It was always about him, and he was inescapable. How many times had I lain awake in a sleeper train climbing into the Pyrenees, listening to his snores and his flatulence? In Italy, ten minutes before the conductor raised his baton—and years before we met Aviva—I had been forced to witness him seducing a young violist, grunting into her neck like a pig unearthing truffles. Every day for months at a time, over three decades, I could have told you what he ate, whether he'd changed his shirt, how his intestines and feet were faring, if he'd suffered nightmares or enjoyed erotic dreams. His bodily rhythms demanded more than their fair share of attention.

And yes, perhaps age had mellowed him, or at least made him more fit for mixed company. But look at the company he sought! He was a political opportunist of the worst kind. And finally—finally—when he had seen the error of his ways and shed his political opportunism, he had grasped an opportunity of a different kind. He and Aviva were leaving together, to be married; to disappear together. Where would they go after New York—Los Angeles? Mexico? Brazil? His disappearance might be an improvement. But hers—unacceptable; an unjust prerequisite for her survival.

He had called this suite of piano pieces "everything I know." *He* was everything he knew. Of course the rhythm of the very first page was his heartbeat.

I turned the page over, told myself it was just paper, and tried to return to my own task. I continued to fill pages with scenes, memories, justifications. As dawn broke, I heard Yehoshua outside, warming up the car to take me to the train station, as we had arranged. I piled the papers together, and I knew I could not leave them behind. My story wasn't over, I hadn't told anything correctly or well, and I did not know whether I would manage to return after Hendaye. I had no choice but to take the entire manuscript with me, with the work of two men— the interpretation of two lives—in my shaking hands.

PART VII

Cuba
1977

Hendaye
1940

CHAPTER

~ 24 ~

"And then?" the journalist prompted after I'd refilled his glass. He'd asked for whiskey, but foreign brands were hard to procure in Cuba, at least for someone of my means. I'd given him rum instead.

I told him, "The train, the checkpoints, the heavily guarded station in Hendaye, our nerves, arriving to discover we'd brought inappropriate clothes, trying to find two tuxedos with the help of the Gestapo officer escorting us—terrifying a tailor in town when we all walked in, four of them and three of us, and the look on the face of the tailor's wife, poor woman! And then giving up—I was quite small, Al-Cerraz was quite large—having the suits we'd brought ironed for us—the Germans were always better pressed than the French.... Well, I had no time to write during all that. No time to write or think at all."

"You carried it with you, place to place."

"In the side pocket of my cello case. I didn't want Al-Cerraz to see it, to know I hadn't left it with Fry."

"If anyone looked—"

"It would look normal. We were musicians, on the highest state business. Carrying instruments and bows and sheet music. Now, if they'd wanted to read the backs of the pages...that was foolish. I'd written everything there, describing not only my feelings about Hitler, but our problems with the Gestapo so far, and even hinting at what

Al-Cerraz and Aviva hoped to do as soon as the concert ended. I wasn't thinking. I was a mess, but no one noticed that. Al-Cerraz was watching Aviva, worrying about her."

"She was afraid to perform?"

"She was having second thoughts about escaping."

"She was afraid of being caught."

"No. It was true she had some concerns about the swim out to the rowboat anchored in the harbor, or being seen as she and Al-Cerraz rowed past the estuary to the open Bay of Biscay, where a larger fishing boat would be waiting for them. But sneaking, swimming, illegal, legal—that wasn't the main problem. She felt terrible about leaving Europe; it was her second try, you'll remember. She'd made it as far as New York in 1929—but that was when she still believed that her son was being cared for. This was worse. If there was any chance that he was still alive in Germany, then she was abandoning him. She'd talked with people who had seen the camps, who had escaped them. She already knew the things we all would find out later, from the photos taken by the liberation troops.

"She had considered letting herself be arrested and transported on purpose, so she could look for him there—Birkenau, Auschwitz. Friends reminded her that a typical prisoner lasted six weeks in those camps, children less, but she imagined he had eluded such a fate. Talented musicians were recruited into camp symphonies that performed not only death marches, but gay music for the guards and administrators—entire musical productions. A child prodigy might be kept around for years in a camp, like a songbird in a cage, just to amuse some high official. And who was to say that her baby had not become a prodigy?

"On the train to Hendaye, she leaned her head on my shoulder and described how her son had huddled, wide-eyed, under the piano. 'He pushed aside his curly blond hair and pressed his cheek to the wood, to feel the vibrations as the doctor played over him.' She spoke with such confidence that it was with effort that I pulled away and looked into her eyes, saying as gently as I could, 'You never saw him do that. Aviva— you never saw him. Remember?'

"I was reminded of something she had once quoted Brecht as saying, about the suspicion with which Jewish refugees were treated— even by their relatives, even by their friends. She had the ambivalence of those who have left someone behind, and that made her unpredictable, a dangerous person with whom to link one's fate."

"Go on."

I took a breath and shuffled the pages in my hand, smoothing the edges. I hadn't read from them directly, but I had turned the pages as I'd spoken, following a line here or there with my finger. They had given me direction and support.

"Go on," Wilhelm said again.

"I didn't write any more—as I told you."

He'd been patient for hours—for years, really, considering how long I'd avoided him, led him on, disappointed him. I had become aware of him in 1957, when he started working on the Al-Cerraz biography; I had pieced together his full significance only when the book was published in 1962, under the title *Vanished Prodigy*. The biographical information under the photo on the flap of the jacket was brief, but it told enough: Wilhelm Erlicht had moved to New York with his adoptive parents when he was seven. He had been a pianist until the age of thirty, when he turned to writing, a shift propelled by his interest in the past, in genealogy and history. And also, the text implied, by what he'd learned of his origins at that age.

Now Wilhelm stood behind his chair, gripping the blue cloth of his jacket hanging over the chair's back, wrinkling the linen.

"Take your time," he said. "Don't worry about the order. Just remember, and tell me what happened at Hendaye."

"Everything went wrong," I said in the flattest voice possible. "Not like the petrol jugs or any of Al-Cerraz's other schemes. *Wrong.*"

He waited.

"Wilhelm, I did a terrible thing."

When I didn't resume speaking immediately, he turned his chair to the side and sat again, hunched over, with his elbows on his knees, cuffs of his trousers raised to reveal worn loafers that clashed with his black silk socks. He had the look of a creative person who has had to adopt the dress code of a more conventional life. He listened without facing me.

"I don't trust my memories," I said.

"I'm listening."

"I don't trust the words. Who can trust words when they can be so easily changed and misunderstood? My name," I said. "Just one example. My mother had wanted to name me Feliz. In Spanish, it means happy—"

"I know it means happy!" the journalist shouted, startling me. "Then the notary, your brother, your aunt—it was changed to Feliu— your sister in the cellar, your mother coming down the stairs. I already know that story!"

I leaned back in my chair and held the manuscript to my chest, shielding the back of the last page with my forearms. "I'm sorry, Wilhelm."

"If you were sensitive about names," he thundered, "you would stop calling me by the name I don't use. My driver's license says William. My friends call me Will."

"I'm sorry. I apologize."

"Your childhood, your early career—I've listened for hours. But this is more than a professional interest. If you blame yourself for what happened to her, then tell me exactly what happened. If you're trying to tell me you killed Al-Cerraz, or that you informed on him, then just say it. You've made it clear that you thought he had ruined your life."

"He *did* ruin my life. I helped him to do it."

He crossed the room and refilled both our glasses, and then walked back quickly, ignoring the trail of drips he left behind on the wooden floor. He pressed my glass into my hands without making eye contact.

I said, "This is how you get your stories? By shouting at people?"

"Of course not."

We sipped our drinks in silence for a moment before I spoke again.

"You're believing your own book. I understand you felt the need to present every remote possibility. But you know I wasn't involved in anything like that...."

"I never named you. I simply said that he'd made enemies among musicians and artists."

I ignored him. "He didn't die in Europe that month. He went on to finish his one-act *Don Quixote* the next year—"

"Discovered after the war; published and produced posthumously, to bad reviews," he corrected. "Proving that even a dead composer doesn't always get a break."

"Posthumous only if he was dead. I'm sure he wasn't."

"Maybe he had written it before October 1940," William said. "It was in your custody, and you sent it—or Varian Fry mailed it earlier."

"But can't you see what it was about?"

"It was a defense of fascism. Don Quixote as Franco, the misunderstood hero."

"Oh, William!" I let the disappointment creep into my voice. "Don Quixote as Franco? Al-Cerraz's Don Quixote was a woman."

"Franco dressed perversely as a woman. The image invented by Picasso."

"No, no. If it were merely metaphorical, the best guess would be Don Quixote as the Republic of Spain. But this Don Quixote was based on a real woman. The only woman Al-Cerraz was thinking about that year."

I leaned forward, trying to meet his gaze. "Aviva was the dreamer among us. She believed in the impossible: your survival."

He looked away and cleared his throat, masking his feelings with professionalism. "So the critics were wrong in panning it as unfashionably fascist."

"Absolutely wrong."

"And the long-suffering British patron?"

"He was crushed."

"I don't recall you correcting the critics' misinterpretations."

"I did not."

"Cigarette?" William said after a while.

"No, thanks."

"Bother you?"

"A little."

He lit up anyway.

"Let's start again in Hendaye. Easy things first. Tell me how it looked, when you first saw it."

Beautiful. Hopeful. Marseilles had been more industrial, more polluted. But Hendaye reminded me of Campo Seco: clean air, the smell of the sea.

Arriving by train, you see all the red roofs, the curved, overlapping ceramic shingles. Then the white walls of the connected houses. Narrow streets veering off at unexpected angles, but everything orderly. Wooden balconies and bright green wooden shutters. Potted red geraniums. Arches of gray stone embedded in the white walls above each tall, narrow window.

Farther out from town, there is a wide sandy beach, and hotels lined up along it, fronting the Bay of Biscay, with some sea stacks just offshore that look like squashed brown hats.

The center of town sits on the eastern bank of the Bidassoa River, just where it meets the Bay of Biscay. There is an old fort, some narrow rusted cannons cemented into an ancient Basque seawall made of gray stone, with tiny wild violets growing in the cracks. At its mouth, the little river widens, making a protected pocket of water—a natural harbor, blue and sparkling. That's where all the little boats anchor—

fishing boats and sailboats with their wooden dinghies rocking next to them.

The boundary between France and Spain runs directly down the middle of the river, through the boats; and another town, Hondarribia, is visible just across the harbor—nearly a mirror image of Hendaye. When the clock tower in Hondarribia chimes, it is audible in Hendaye, and when the Basque fishermen head out of Hendaye's harbor to fish off the wide beach, they rub shoulders with Hondarribia's Basque fishermen. At sunset the lighthouse on the French side winks at the lighthouse on the Spanish side. And the green hills rise up behind both towns, enfolding them.

Our duty that first afternoon, in addition to meeting the local Gestapo chief and attempting to dress ourselves more appropriately for the next day's concert, was to notice all these details and to understand where one nation ended and the other began, and how each guarded its border.

But there is a detail I haven't explained. I told you we had a Gestapo officer helping us to find better clothes in Hendaye—and not just that. He had been attached to us since our departure from Marseilles, an official escort. He was young—twenty-three or twenty-four. I will not tell you his name, because I know that, given your propensity to research things, you will look him up. I don't know if he is living or not, if he had any descendants, but if so, it would not be right to bother him or them about this. He crossed our paths this one week only, and it was to his misfortune, as well as ours. I will call him Kreisler—it's close enough.

The motorcycle-riding officer we had met briefly at the Villa Air-Bel had been the one to recommend Kreisler, who was an acquaintance of his daughter.

"Are you thinking of marrying her when this whole thing is over?" Al-Cerraz asked him.

The young guard's ears flushed red. He said, "The SS does not encourage us to marry. Only to procreate. To spread the Aryan race."

Al-Cerraz rolled his eyes. "You boys have all the fun."

Kreisler had blond hair, stubbly on top, shaved close around the ears. The back of his head and soft, lined neck looked like an infant's. I asked him if he'd played piano as a child. No, he told us, he had sung in a choir. He had been a regular police officer in Stuttgart, until his police branch was absorbed into the state police. He liked France. He had always wanted to visit Spain, and he ticked off the musicians he knew on his fingers: "Albéniz, Granados, Cassadó, Casals..."

Just after the train pulled out of Marseilles, he asked us for our autographs. Aviva thought it was a trick and refused. In Toulouse, he disembarked and bought flowers for her. That softened her up a little. At the next stop, he came back with sandwiches—ham for Al-Cerraz and me, beef for Aviva, though she hadn't mentioned any dietary preferences. It was clear to all of us: He knew who she was, or rather *what* she was. And still he maintained his deferential attitude, and several times left us unguarded, for a quarter of an hour at a time.

When Al-Cerraz chided him on his leniency, Kreisler grew suddenly officious. "I have two primary directives," he said. "First is to safeguard this man's health." He nodded toward me and opened a bulky leather valise to present another basket of cherries, of the type I had received at the Air-Bel a month earlier. "Second is to escort you for your own welfare, to beware of thieves and so on. My superior officer takes a great interest in musical objects, and in Maestro Delargo's bow in particular."

"Other than that, we're free to get into trouble," Al-Cerraz teased him.

"No, please. That would be a bad idea for all of us."

After we settled into the hotel rooms that Hendaye officials had provided for us, we asked Kreisler for permission to see the town, and he granted it. Al-Cerraz, Aviva, and I walked from the town center to the ancient seawall and harbor, and back to the train station. Then we walked a little farther, to see where the train tracks led. The tracks followed a slim bridge very high over the river, where the Bidassoa narrows. Just upriver, a second high bridge echoed the first—this one had a road over it. At the foot of the road, there was a French guardhouse on the Hendaye side, and on the bridge itself we could make out a small convention of dull green and brown uniforms, the glint of medals and belt buckles and the flash of rifles well-oiled for the dictators' impending meeting.

No one seemed to think it strange that the three of us were out walking, squinting toward the water and the bridges, although a shopkeeper called out to us, "You must be very famous to require all this protection."

The townspeople hadn't been told about the more famous men expected the next day. But they'd been told about the concert, and a select number had been invited, or ordered, to the train platform to hear us play. The members of a local civic orchestra had been told to report as well, with their instruments and every piece of sheet music they owned; they would perform some patriotic music to introduce us. But they didn't seem to know why there would be music on this day, why the train platform instead of the church or the grassy park by the seawall. Or they pretended not to know.

The two dictators were to meet the next afternoon in Hitler's private railcar. With one well-placed undercarriage bomb, French resistance could have deprived the world of two dictators, had anyone been aware of the plan. Meanwhile, afternoon gave way to evening, and the station's parking lot filled with motorcycles and official cars. The café across the street was crowded with gendarmes sipping double espressos, in preparation for a long vigil. Normal train traffic on the route had been interrupted, for security reasons. Officially, the tracks both south and north were "under repair."

Returning to the hotel, Al-Cerraz volunteered to Kreisler, "Maestro Delargo seems to be rubbing his hands. I hope the gout is not starting to bother him again."

That alarmed our Gestapo guard. He immediately called the front desk and inquired after local sources of cherries.

"Maybe it was the prawns he ate for lunch," Al-Cerraz volunteered between phone calls.

"He ate prawns?" Kreisler asked, looking queasy himself.

Al-Cerraz adopted a guilty expression. "We tried to stop him. He's the one you should be keeping a closer eye on."

The mischief I had known from our earliest train touring days had not been purged from Al-Cerraz's soul. I glared at him, incredulous, hoping that this tomfoolery had some purpose. In the meantime, Kreisler came and went, bringing me every type of produce he could procure at the last minute, including that item his superior officer's grandmama had vouched for. Over the course of an evening, I spooned the contents of three entire jars of preserved cherries into my mouth. Ever since, I haven't been able to look at a cherry without feeling sick.

Each jar bought us a half hour or so of freedom from Kreisler. We three gathered in Aviva's room; I looked out the window while Aviva and Al-Cerraz leaned their heads over a map sketched on a matchbook and took turns reading from a pocket-sized phrasebook:

"*Kaixo,*" Al-Cerraz said.

Aviva repeated: "*Kaikso.*"

"The *x* is like 'shhh.' *Kaixo.*" He pushed on. "*Zer moduz?*"

"*Zer moduz.*"

"*Nola esaten da hori euskaraz?*"

"Oh, Justo—I'm not going to remember that."

"But that way you can point to things and find out how to say them in Basque. It will help you with everything else."

"We'll be with them for a few days at the most, until the next boat from Portugal. I don't plan to talk," Aviva said. "Only to listen."

"All right. Then here's one you should learn to recognize: *Kontuz!*"

"What does that mean?"

"Caution."

—————

At one point when Kreisler returned to the room for the third or fourth time, cherry compote in hand, Al-Cerraz told him that he and Aviva were getting married. It astonished me how far he dared go.

"After the concert?" Kreisler asked.

"Just after."

"So this is an early honeymoon for you, so to speak."

Aviva's face lit up.

"Does that mean you'll let us go have a night on the town, just me and my girl?" Al-Cerraz asked.

Kreisler looked pained. "It's late. It's dark. Everything is closed. Better tomorrow, after the concert." He smiled. "After the concert, you have a nice dinner, you two alone. I will pay for the champagne."

That fit their—our—plans perfectly. Al-Cerraz's wizardry seemed to be working its spell again.

When Kreisler left again, Al-Cerraz went over the plan—what time we were expected at the station in the morning, to inspect the delivered piano and rehearse under Gestapo supervision, the point at which I would explain to Kreisler that my arthritis had flared up and I could not play, how they would execute a modified program. Then they would return to the hotel, leave again for their dinner—and wait by the seawall for that precise moment when the sky's peach blush faded to pink, then light purple, then blue, and the twin lighthouses winked on, alerting the fishing boat hiding beyond the sea stacks that they would be arriving. Then around the curve of the seawall and down the ancient steps to the quiet harbor, and to any of several anchored rowboats, floating there, waiting.

And I—I was not going with them. They had invited and urged me several times, but I hadn't the will. Instead, I accepted my land-based role in the charade. When Kreisler noted Al-Cerraz's and Aviva's absence, I would share his alarm that my friends had sneaked off for a romantic beach swim and not reappeared. Some gendarme would no doubt find the twisted, damp pile of discarded clothing—pants and shirt and lady's dress—on the seaweed-covered tidal rocks at the beach's farthest east margin, where the rocky hills sloped toward the shore. Two drownings. By that afternoon, Hitler would be well on his way east, and Franco south, and every local gendarme would be wiping his brow in relief at having survived the incursion of police and intelligence agents from two other nations. By comparison, the drownings of two visitors would stir little excitement. I would stay another day, frequenting cafés and restaurants and socializing with minor officials if it was required, and then return on the train on October 24, as my ticket stated.

And if Kreisler alerted other Gestapo officials insistent on questioning a convenient disappearance? Let them. My spirits had sunk beyond caring.

Al-Cerraz and I shared a room. Kreisler's was one door down; Aviva's a door beyond that. Sometime during the night, I heard a bed creak, the clink of glasses, the door opening and closing. Some hours later, it opened and closed again. Al-Cerraz's hand tugged at mine.

"She's having second thoughts," he whispered.

I told myself this was the last time he'd ever wake me in the night. I sat up, turned on the bedside lamp—

"No! Turn it off!"

"If it's about marrying you, I'm not surprised."

He sat at the corner of the bed, weighing it down.

"I said that so she'd leave, so that she could picture having a life."

"You don't want to marry her?"

"Of course I do. Someone should."

"*Someone* should?"

"Feliu, you could have done it long ago. She would have accepted.

Your refusal to have a joyful, normal life can't be a death sentence for her."

I stared into the dark, too full of anger to speak. I did not feel that I was losing Aviva; I considered her already lost. How dare he dangle this shred of hope in front of me?

"She's in her room, wide awake, not being rational," Al-Cerraz continued. "She's going to fall apart and destroy everything, in front of everyone."

"She's stronger than you think."

"We'll all be taken away. I need you to help me with this."

"You said this journey was the last favor you'd ever ask. I'm here at greater risk than either of you."

"Aviva…the Gestapo…"

I raised my voice. "What about Franco? I'm sure he'd be all too pleased to add me to his trophy case."

In a low voice, he said, "So even you have nerves." He continued, "She knows I'm a bit of a storyteller—"

"A liar."

"A wishful thinker," he corrected me. "Everyone trusts you. The moral purist. She'll have to hear it from you to believe it."

"To believe what?"

"To believe the thing that will allow her to let go, to start a new life. Help her close a door that should have been closed long ago. Some fantasies are destructive. And anyway, what you'll tell her is probably true."

The next morning, I was up before dawn, before Kreisler had come to get us. I stood outside his hotel door and heard his voice high and clear over the sound of running water. Sweet innocence, in unexpected places. He was singing while he shaved. In that moment, I decided to tell him.

"I'm not playing today."

He pulled me into his room and closed the door. "Your hands?"

"No," I said. His whole face relaxed. He excused himself to dress, pulling his black uniform over his underclothes, pulling a belt through the pants, strapping on a long knife in its black leather sheath.

"It's not the gout," I continued. "I've decided not to play on principle."

His face turned ashen.

I said, "Let me make this simple for you: Franco. Since he came to power, and I went into exile, I have refused to play the cello. This entire concert was a mistake. I can't perform for him. I won't."

The pause that followed was one of the longest in my life. I faced this young man, neck red from hurried shaving, stray white soap flecks in front of his large ears. He was at least a head taller than me, so I had to crane my neck to meet his conflicted stare. On the chair next to us: his peaked cap, with its death's-head emblem. Shadows danced at his jawline, at his temple, as he ground his teeth together.

Finally he said, "It is essential to trust a leader with all one's heart. Al-Cerraz—he is an opportunist. But I know you are a thoughtful person. For you to dislike the Caudillo that much…" He shook his head gravely. Then suddenly, he lifted his chin and opened his mouth. To my astonishment, he started to sing: "Oh believe!"

Flushing, he dropped his jaw and spoke—slowly and clearly, reciting the words that I recognized instantly:

> Thou wert not born in vain!
> Hast not lived in vain.
> Suffered in vain.
> What has come into being must perish.
> What has perished must rise again.

The final movement from Mahler's Second Symphony—lines penned by a Jewish composer, banned in German occupied territory. I joined him, reciting more quietly:

Cease from trembling.
Prepare thyself to live.

We stopped there, not speaking, not moving: the most complete silence, round and rich, with the sky just beginning to lighten behind filmy window shades.

Then suddenly: an immense roar, as if we were being bombed. The floors of the hotel trembled and the framed pictures danced on the walls.

It was a convoy arriving: armored cars, military trucks, more motorcycles, spilling down from the road to the northeast. This was the advance guard, arriving by coastal road from the east. Kreisler said under his breath, "Lockdown."

He didn't say anything more to acknowledge what I had told him. We joined Al-Cerraz and Aviva for a morose *petit déjeuner,* and waited. At precisely ten o'clock, we were allowed to leave the hotel and ride in a black Mercedes to the train station, where Al-Cerraz confirmed that the piano, transported the day before from a chateau east of town, was in tune. Everything we'd seen so far—a few guards here and there, gendarmes at the café—was nothing compared to this. The entire town was under siege. Most people—unless they had been "invited" to the concert—stayed inside, doors and shutters latched.

Back to the hotel again, where we waited in the lobby, under a painting of Louis XIV. Outside, a banner with a Nazi swastika had been raised; not speaking, we watched it flutter in the wind.

Franco was to arrive by rail from the south at two o'clock. At ten past one, we were shuttled to the train station. The platform was decorated with more banners, flags of Germany and Spain. A hundred folding chairs awaited the audience. An official-looking railcar was parked on the far tracks, but we saw no sign of any occupant. Kreisler escorted us to a small private waiting room in the station, and left us there. "There will be a guard posted outside," he said. "For your security."

When we three were alone in the room, Al-Cerraz whispered, "Did you tell him?"

"I told him."

"I didn't expect so many police," Aviva whispered, voice breaking. "They'll have people with guns posted along on the seawall."

"They'll be watching the border and the station," Al-Cerraz said, more firmly. "The train will stay parked, for the meeting. Every person will be trying to get a glimpse of *him*. They'll be entranced."

"But how will we get away, to dinner? They're moving us place to place. They wouldn't even let us back to our rooms."

"Kreisler said you could go to dinner," I reminded her.

"But that was before all this—perhaps he didn't know how heavily they'd close down the town."

A knock at the door. Another black-uniformed guard—older, with gray streaks in his brown hair. Kreisler stood behind him, not speaking. The older officer faced me. "You're having a medical problem?"

Al-Cerraz grabbed at the guard's arm. "It's his hands—arthritis. He can't play the cello."

"Fine," the older guard said. "I will get you a baton. When the Führer and the Generalísimo are ready, and standing on the platform, you will conduct the civic orchestra."

I struggled for words. "I don't know what they play. I don't know what you'll allow us to play. Dvořák? Mendelssohn?"

"That is not allowed."

"What is allowed? You wouldn't allow a Spaniard to conduct Wagner, would you?"

"No."

"You wanted us to play Spanish music. But this orchestra may not know Granados or Turina."

The guard furrowed his brow and clamped his jaws together. "Ravel! The *Bolero*. It is French, but it sounds Spanish."

"Dear God, not an amateur production of Ravel," Al-Cerraz whispered under his breath.

"That's not an easy work to perform, unrehearsed."

"It will fill the time. Mostly percussion, isn't it?" the guard asked. And left.

Kreisler stayed behind. After the door had closed, he said quietly, "He will go and talk to the orchestra. They will tell him they don't have the instrumentation or sheet music for *Bolero*."

The door opened again. A different man entered, smaller, with black hair and deep brown eyes, the hairline high and square. He was limping slightly. I didn't need the introduction—I had seen his picture in the newspapers: Goebbels.

Kreisler saluted and stood at attention, his back flat against the wall. Goebbels lowered himself into a chair that appeared from behind and addressed me. "We are disappointed that you have reason not to perform. If Goering were here, we might peek into his bag and try an injection of some kind, to relax the hands. But I'm not sure that would work."

He kept staring at me, smiling, the skin tight around his cheekbones and chin.

"Maestro Delargo," Goebbels said, "you have chosen to come out of retirement for a very special occasion. We will find some way to celebrate your presence here. The photographers are looking forward to seeing you, and so is the Führer."

He broke eye contact to glance around the room. "You understand that we were not as interested in a duet. And this lady"—he nodded toward Aviva—"I'm aware your trio employed a woman—a violinist who lived in Berlin for some time, correct? But that was many years ago, before the war…"

None of us spoke.

"Some of my men do make mistakes, it's true. They hear an Italian accent and they assume, 'Catholic.' But let's not spoil the day with accusations. We will have more to talk about after the festivities are over. I will expect to spend some time with all three of you."

Outside the room, in the echoing train station, the orchestra struck up the Nazi anthem, *"Horst Wessel Lied."* "There," Goebbels said. "They've begun. He tired of waiting. Someone has decided against *Bolero.* You will excuse me."

We waited, hostages in that small room. Kreisler returned twenty minutes later, while the orchestra was still playing. "Something is wrong," he said. "The Caudillo has not yet made his appearance, and we are told there might be a substantial delay."

"Late," Al-Cerraz muttered. "It figures."

"The Führer is on the platform—there are citizens, other officials." Kreisler was flushed, out of breath. "We are trying to maintain appearances. I was told to keep the music going until Generalísimo Franco is arrived and on the platform. You will be called to begin shortly."

He left again. Aviva began to pace. Her face was even-toned, normal; but red welts had shown up behind each of her ears, reaching down her neck. "This isn't working." Her voice had become high and strained. "They're not happy with us; they'll be watching more closely."

"Damn you, Feliu!" Al-Cerraz said suddenly. "Just come with us to the platform and play. Goebbels and all the rest will be so pleased they'll let us out of this box. They'll be so busy taking your picture and toasting you that they won't even notice when Aviva and I slip away."

"You'd leave now?" I asked him. "In daylight?"

"I don't think we'll have another chance," Aviva whispered.

They both looked to me. I had underestimated the potency of this moment, the knowledge of that man just beyond the door, standing stiffly in his dress uniform, a false smile below his brushy mustache as he awaited the Spaniard intent on deliberately insulting the efficiency-minded Germans. Fry had been right: Everything about this meeting had been engineered to allow each side to annoy the other.

I answered my partners. It was the same answer I'd given to Al-Cerraz in Marseilles, the first time he had asked. Aviva nodded swiftly as I made my position plain. Al-Cerraz stood and inhaled deeply and held his breath, chest inflated, glaring. But that didn't change anything. It was the only thing I had left to control, the only thing that hadn't yet been sacrificed, the only choice I could make, if "choice" can be used to describe a terrible mistake—the worst, or second-worst—of one's entire life.

Kreisler entered again. "Fourteen-forty. Your leader is very late now. Everything has changed."

"He isn't my leader," Al-Cerraz muttered.

"Everything has changed!" Kreisler shouted, and pounded his fist against the wall, just behind him. We all jumped.

Kreisler stood taller and tugged at the bottom of his uniform jacket. "To extend the festivities, Herr Doktor Goebbels makes this request. Maestro Al-Cerraz will come out first, and play the piano. Applause, pictures. Leave the platform slowly. Then Maestra Aviva with the violin. She bows, exits. Then finally Maestro Delargo, who will appear and shake hands—applause, pictures again. No hurrying. By this time, we are quite sure Generalísimo Franco will be present and the music can be finished and you will have your meeting with Herr Doktor Goebbels and everyone can go home."

"Home?" Aviva whispered, sounding dazed.

"To the hotel. Escorted. No one is to walk the streets for the duration."

The windowless room in which we were waiting was an administrative office: a desk, a typewriter, three chairs, and travel posters on the wall: vineyards of Bordeaux, the beach at San Sebastián, a Roman bridge in the Italian countryside, old white windmills of Castilla–La Mancha.

Aviva stared at the pictures. "I won't leave."

We were alone. Kreisler had given the three of us a final moment together. Then, at the sound of his name blared over a megaphone that rattled the walls, Al-Cerraz had gone to the platform. Even through the closed door, we could hear him playing: first, a romantic piece by Augustín Barrios Mangoré, transcribed from the guitar, full of broken, flowing chords alternating with single lightning-fast notes that recalled a repeatedly picked guitar string.

"I hope they appreciate what they're hearing," I said, ear cocked. "It's the best he's played in ages."

Aviva repeated in a whisper, "I can't."

The second piece was equally melodious and virtuosic. Distinctly southern, but for the first time in decades I couldn't identify the composer. Something in it made me recall a certain night on a balcony, and Spanish women with flowers in their flowing hair—the "perfumed hours" of our younger years.

I said, "He's giving them their money's worth."

"Oh, God." Suddenly Aviva clutched her stomach. "He forgot. It's back at the hotel room."

"What?"

"The money, for the boat captain. He's planning to go directly to the rowboat, but he doesn't have the money. The hotel is too far—all the guards."

Instinctively, I pushed my hands into my coat pockets, reaching for my billfold.

"No," she said. "He brought a lot. Eight hundred dollars, U.S."

"Where did he get that?"

"Fry. He sold him his compositions. Fry said it could be a loan, but Justo insisted it be a sale. He made Fry promise to have them published in America. He didn't care about the rights or the future royalties—he just wanted them published, no matter what happened."

I couldn't tell her what I'd done.

I told her then not to worry about payment—that I would give her something to take to the rowboat, more valuable than eight hundred dollars, and small enough to hide in the palm of one's hand. I no longer needed proof of Queen Ena's former favor. I would outlive this day. I would be favored again. Al-Cerraz had played for Hitler, but I had not, would not. Photographs might show me on a railroad platform next to him, but not with a cello, not with a baton—as a hostage, merely. I could still walk away from this, my reputation intact.

I pushed my thumbnail into the bow frog, hard, and the jewel popped out—blue, sparkling, so much smaller than I thought it would be. How could it have weighed anything?

"If they stop me, they'll search me," she said.

"They won't." I returned the bow to its tube.

"Should I swallow it?"

"It has hard edges. It might hurt you. Just put it somewhere. I'll turn around. Take it."

"I can't," she said.

"Tighter—you're going to drop it."

Her shoulders were heaving. "Feliu, I can't leave him behind!"

That's when I told her about her son. I had to be quick, I had to be blunt; I did not have Al-Cerraz's skill at fabrication.

"But how could you know?" She was crying, but there was a thin, hard edge behind the ragged breaths. "Was it Fry? He knew?"

We heard the megaphone announcing her name, and then Kreisler's knock at the door. I told him I'd like to follow her out, to watch her play. He said that was fine—Al-Cerraz had made the same request, to watch from the back of the room, behind the orchestra. He followed the two of us out, carrying my cello and bow tube.

On the platform, I saw no sign of Al-Cerraz. There was an open door behind the last row of folding chairs. The blue harbor was visible through it, and the masts of sailboats swinging gently side to side atop the waves, with metronome precision. There were no guards near it. They had moved closer to the music area, to form a cordon around the Führer, who was standing, watching, from the back of his railcar. Another line of guards was facing entirely away, down the tracks, willing Franco's train to appear.

Aviva walked to the cleared area between the track and the makeshift stage. She looked forlornly at the unattended piano. Then she made a quarter turn, planting her feet widely, her profile to the Führer. Her violin hung from her left hand, looking impossibly heavy. I could still remember how it had felt to play that instrument as a child, when I'd found it hard to hold it to my chin.

Every second that she did not lift the violin to play, my stomach clenched more tightly. Goebbels leaned toward a uniformed man and whispered in his ear. The sound of my own beating heart pounded in my ears, and my ears themselves became more acute, so that every sound outside the station—the bell-like tolling of boat cleats and clips and posts ringing against each other, the light slap of waves against the seawall—was amplified.

And then another noise—not my heart, though just as regular. It was a train coming from the southwest.

The guards posted at the south entrance of the station squinted into the sun and down the tracks. But not Hitler. And not Goebbels, next to and slightly behind him. Their eyes remained fixed on Aviva. A few guards and officials, noting their line of sight, emulated them, fixing their own stares, though they could not control the twitches and throat clearings that made it plain how badly everyone wanted to look the other way, toward Spain.

For a moment, I thought she was saved. Her panic, her failure to perform, would be forgotten as the train rushed into the station, washing us all in a dust-laden breeze, obscuring our view with steam. If she walked away quickly to the back of the room, and kept moving as the excitement of Franco's entrance swept the platform, she could get to the seawall, and down the stairs to the water's edge. What a strange and unexpected white knight Franco had become, at that moment.

But the train did not arrive in a rush. We heard the tee-*kah,* tee-*kah* of its motion down the tracks, the squeal of brakes. It was slowing well before the station, out of view.

A German voice rang out: "Begin!" All faces turned toward the sound. Hitler's dark eyes burned beneath his peaked cap. The prolonged wait had enraged him.

That shout, that command, melted the last of Aviva's resolve. I looked at her just in time to see her knees buckle, toppling her forward, shins smacking against the hard black platform. The violin flew from her wrist, spun once, and stopped, two meters away. A circle of uniformed men appeared around her. Between their legs and the butts of their guns I could make out her hair, one slim arm trying to push herself up—but not her face.

I do not pretend that my choice to stand up then—to approach her and part the circle of guards and lead her away to a chair at the back—was in any way heroic.

Hadn't Enrique always said I was like Paquito, my fellow matchstick-legged stray, eager to prove his worth, his stature, his meaning in this world? He had insisted on making his own delayed entrance, and so had I. He had insisted on controlling the flow of the day's events, as if to pretend he was not a pawn, not subservient to a stronger foe, and so had I. And to what end? Only to the end of raising the stakes yet further, worsening the consequences. Hitler's and Franco's negotiations that day would not go well. Nothing that day would go well.

My last words to her, as I leaned over to reach my cello strap, were: "When I begin, and no one is looking—go."

Until then, Al-Cerraz had always been our showman, our master of ceremony and surprise. But on this day, I surprised them all: Goebbels, whose large brown eyes grew even larger and wider, while his mouth remained a thin pencil-line of strategy and manipulation. The three photographers—one French, one German, and Hitler's personal portraitist, Heinrich Hoffmann. I surprised even Hitler, who gripped the black edge of the railway car's balcony, and then, to the sharp snap of extended arms, stepped down to the platform. He gestured to a chair, and it was drawn up for him. There was no chair for me. I looked for Kreisler's face and found it briefly, at the edge of the room, clouded with confusion and dismay. Then it was gone.

In place of a proper chair, I proceeded to the piano bench, pulled it just away from the piano, extracted my cello, and reached out to tune quickly.

The sound of the distant train started up again, pulling forward, but no one looked down the tracks this time. Not when Hitler was sitting in a chair, alone, in the center of everything, looking soberly entranced. I pulled out my bow, testing its new weight in my hand. Then I pulled it across the strings and began to play the first Bach cello suite.

I was playing to save a woman's life—perhaps too late. I can make that claim for the first measures, at least. And then I was playing only for myself: all six movements. It had been so long; not just the two and a half years since Guernica, but the nineteen years since Anual, the twenty-six years since Madrid, the thirty-one years since Barcelona. I did not see the man for whom I was playing, or even the train that finally pulled in behind us both, releasing three guards followed by Franco himself, who surely must have been astonished to arrive without fanfare, the Führer's back to him, as I continued to play. I was not there. I was living the words written by a Jew and spoken by a Nazi— *Cease from trembling, prepare thyself to live!* I was being resurrected on that railway platform—destroyed, too, but in that destruction, reborn.

For years, people would try to understand why I was willing to play for dictators on October 23, 1940, considering all the statements I had made, the careers I had ruined, my life history. I would have my accusers and my detractors; when I sought entrance to the United States, it would be denied. Cuba would offer me a home—no small irony, considering that a future dictator would reign there as well; but by that time, I had learned to stay out of the limelight completely. I did perform once more, a decade later, but I never recorded again. Far more people made excuses for me than I ever made for myself. The full truth could not be known.

But in that moment, it did not matter. I was that boy—the boy Al-Cerraz had seen once, in a dusty town, lost to playing; the boy Al-Cerraz had attempted to convince himself was not even real, whose unachievable purity had brought him to despair. He had brought me to this moment—the moment of my destruction and my rebirth. But hadn't he been present at every important moment in my life?

The applause echoed through that cavernous space. I set down the cello awkwardly; it rolled forward, cracking the bridge. The bow, without its sapphire, still hung from my right hand. I reached down and grabbed the case with its music manuscript inside, but not the cello. There were voices everywhere, buzzing in my ears. I dared to look— there was Franco, full lips set grimly, downturned eyes watery with self-pity, as Hitler extended a hand toward him belatedly and the camera strobes flashed.

I walked, and kept walking. Out the front station door, down the stairs. No one stopped me. At the street I looked left, and saw a tall uniformed German approaching with a long, purposeful stride. I looked right and saw a cluster of men clustered like bees around a hive, two of them walking backward. They were lifting something, half-dragging it. The officer to my left walked faster—it was Kreisler, his face stern, coming from the direction of the harbor.

The men on the right called out to Kreisler in German. He shouted an order back at them, came quickly to my side, and grabbed my left elbow. I felt a moment of relief until I looked into his eyes. "I thought you had integrity," he muttered in French. "I would have done anything to save you and your music. But you have shown me—music is just politics and opportunity. It is worthless." He gripped my arm painfully.

"There," he said. The cluster of men on my right dropped what they were carrying and parted slightly. Two of the men were wet and capless, their uniforms dripping. My mind refused to see, to admit. They had been walking from the wrong direction—not from the sea-wall, not from the harbor, but from the other way—from the bridge.

Her hair was wet and stringy; her skirt clung to her thighs. Seaweed had wrapped itself around her calves and one shoe; the other foot was bare.

"She jumped from the bridge," he explained. "They saw it and dragged her out."

One of the wet officers explained something in German to Kreisler. I moved toward Aviva, got down on my knees, searching for signs of life in her gray face.

"Stand back," Kreisler said. I moved quickly, thankfully; the vision of the flowers he'd bought at Toulouse filled my mind; the vision of Aviva smiling as she received them. Despite what he'd said to me, I expected him to save her.

One of the wet men leaned forward to put his mouth against hers.

"No!" Kreisler shouted. "Don't contaminate yourself. She is a filthy Jew."

He unbuckled a flap at the side of his leg. "They say she swallowed something just before she jumped. Jews are always doing this—stealing before they escape." He unsheathed his knife. "Gold teeth, diamonds. We find all sorts of things."

And like an angler crouching on a riverbank over his catch, he hummed softly to himself and opened her. A straight line from the esophagus down; pressure, the sound of a cracking sternum. I looked away.

I begged him to keep what he found, but he pressed the sticky sapphire into the palm of my trembling hand. "It would not be allowed," he said coldly. "On principle."

To the other guards he said, in French for my benefit, "Let him walk. He can't do anything now. He is a ghost."

CHAPTER

~ 25 ~

"The Nazis killed her," William said.

"We killed her. We took away her illusion and forced her to believe her son was dead—we had no proof either way—so that she would do what we felt was right. We cornered her into taking her own life."

The journalist said nothing.

I continued. "Fry had warned me. He had told me you shouldn't take a person's idea of herself away, especially when that person is preparing to embark on a dangerous journey."

"And Al-Cerraz?"

"For a moment after I played inside the train station, I felt real gratitude toward him—not respect exactly, but sympathy and gratitude. But then I saw Aviva, and I understood the damage we had done. I hated him again—no less than I hated myself. I vowed never to be in contact with him."

"She might not have escaped anyway."

"That is true. But *he* did manage to escape—I'm sure of it. I imagine he hid in the rowboat for hours, waiting. There were no shots; he couldn't have known that she had died, but I suppose he guessed something went astray, and finally rowed to the sea stacks after dark and talked the captain into taking him, even without the money. He could talk anyone into anything. And later he pieced it together, from the story that ran in the French newspaper; you've seen that one. It inspired him to write *Don Quixote* as he did—whether it was a message to me, an effort at reconciliation, or just a way to deal with what had happened, I don't know. We never spoke."

William said, "At least now I know why my mother killed herself."

We didn't speak for several minutes. Then I broke the silence. "She would have loved to have known that you became a concert pianist, in America."

He snorted. "I didn't."

"Well, you tried. It's a different musical world now. There is more competition; it's even more celebrity-driven than it was in our day— something I wouldn't have thought possible. Anyway, the world needs critics too, and music biographers—people who can explain our stories, mixed up as they are."

"Is that why you brought me here? To help you explain your story?"

"No."

I got up, refilled our glasses a final time, and gave him one.

I had been clutching the pages so long that I had left damp marks from my fingers on the edges. Where I had pressed the top page against my shirt, a spot of blue ink had transferred. I laughed at the ridiculousness of it—a thirty-three-year-old stain. I turned the pile over on my lap, so my manuscript was face down, and Al-Cerraz's piano compositions were faceup.

"William, I told you on the phone, when I asked you to fly here, that I had done a terrible thing."

He wiped his face roughly with his hands, pushing his hair back. "Yes."

"Not everything I did—or failed to do—involved your mother. There was also this."

I gestured for him to approach. He stood behind my chair, studying the first page, and then motioned for me to hurry and turn, so that he could read the second one. But I wasn't ready. I pointed at the first page. "That dotted rhythm. The first time I saw it, I felt sure it was his heartbeat. But it wasn't. It was the train."

"Which train?"

"Our train—all our trains. Our Spanish tours. Before. In every town, he was listening, piecing it together; I'm sure he didn't know the value of it for many years. He always felt pressured to compose one great symphonic or operatic work, but unity has never defined Spain. We are a country of many kingdoms. By the time Al-Cerraz and I were together in southern France, he had started to understand. He had said as much—that even small works could be subversive and that after meeting Franco, he had seen the power in even the simplest folk-inspired melodies. And he had let himself be inspired by Monet, by impressionism—by the idea of capturing the real Spain in these small, disconnected pieces, which is what Spain is: diverse, irreconcilable."

I continued. "Until recently, I didn't let myself look at the other pages. I was angry at first. Then, frustrated. And then: I simply underestimated him. I did not respect him or his work. Me—of all people."

"Anyone could overlook—"

"No," I interrupted. "Don't try to make me feel better. Who more than I should understand the power of a suite for solo instrument? I have always valued simplicity and humility—I have always been able to perceive larger musical meanings in what appears to be disconnected."

"It's easy to miss what's right in front of us." William gestured toward the piano. "May I?"

He reached for the manuscript, all of it. I squeezed it more tightly to my chest. I wet a finger, and slowly started peeling off the top forty pages or so; the pages that were Al-Cerraz's manuscript.

"Come on," William said, suddenly impatient. "What are you afraid of?"

I was afraid of what would happen next, what did happen. William started sight-reading, slowly at first, then warming to it, playing with confidence and with style.

I tried to talk through the first three compositions, to point out the elements as I recognized them—there was the sound of the train, yes; and there was an imitation of the strumming style of Andalucían guitarists. But there—another corner of the country again, a fluty Galician sound. A rhythmic reference to the banned *sardana* of my home country, Catalonia, followed by a blend of Arabic and Spanish elements that I'm sure represented our trip to the Alhambra; less romantic than Falla would have written it, less harmonious. There were sounds and images from the New World, too—Caribbean sounds, Central American rhythms, all the places the empire had touched.

At last William raised a hand to stop me. "You've done a lot of talking, Maestro," he said gently. "Listen now. Please."

I did, and soon enough, I could not make out the notes on the distant page, or the back of William's head. As I tried to blink away the tears, everything was a blur. This was my life in music, but more than my life. It was Spain's life, both interpreted and preserved.

I'm sure I would have recognized it as beautiful in 1940. I had heard one of the pieces at the Hendaye concert. But I couldn't have appreciated the entire suite then, because I wouldn't have realized then what music could ultimately accomplish, or what it could contain.

Franco had stayed in power an astonishing thirty-six years, from 1939 to 1975. In that time, Spanish culture had faded, succumbed, blended into a simplistic parody: "Sunny Spain." Tourism posters. One music. Simplified dance exhibited to tourists. Few literary works.

Cultural homogeneity. Even from my exile in Cuba, I'd come to understand how successfully Franco had wielded his power. Mussolini was killed by the partisans. Hitler killed himself. But Franco lived on, beating them all. And beating us. We had accepted his "pact of forgetting," as people began to call it. We had lost our soul. In defiance of him, I had requested that musicians stop playing, that artists stop painting—and that had only made his mission easier. Silence had been his ultimate weapon, not mine. And the one who would not be silent, Justo Al-Cerraz, had seen farther than us all, seen to what would truly last: art, and art alone.

Now Franco was finally dead. Why had I outlasted him? Perhaps only so that I could do this.

The directors of the new Spanish museum had been sending me letters all month, wondering when I would deliver my bow, as I had been promising since Franco's funeral. I had stalled for a year, but now at least one person understood why. If they wanted the bow, I would make them take the manuscript, too; and not only that, I would see to it that they treated every page—every note—with more respect than I ever had. They would let national experts verify its authenticity, evaluate it, perform it—and then, let history decide.

"You will help me, William?" I said when he had played the last of Al-Cerraz's Spanish Suites.

He walked over, gently removed the rest of the pages from my hands, and set them down. He put his arms around me, a little stiffly at first, our shoulders bumping awkwardly. I allowed my lips to brush his forehead, scarcely able to see his face through my tears.

"Will it make you happy?" he asked.

"Very happy."

EPILOGUE

On December 29, 1977, King Juan Carlos I and Queen Sofía of Spain presided over the opening of Madrid's new Museo de Música, where they accepted the gift of Maestro Feliu Delargo's bow, set with the sapphire that had once belonged to the King's grandmother, Queen Victoria Eugenia. On the same day, in the new museum's auditorium, they attended a concert featuring the recently rediscovered Spanish Piano Suites of Justo Al-Cerraz, who was posthumously awarded the ceremonial title of Duke of the Alhambra for his contributions to Spanish culture.

Six months later, William Erlicht, son of Italian violinist Aviva Henze-Pergolesi (1910–1940) published a revised edition of his biography, *Vanished Prodigy,* including a critical reappraisal of Al-Cerraz's *Don Quixote* (1941).

On August 5, 1978, Feliu Aníbal Delargo died in Cuba at the age of eighty-five, of congestive heart failure.

In February 1981, King Juan Carlos, grandson of King Alfonso XIII and the first monarch to lead Spain following Franco's death, survived a coup attempt. Contrary to historic precedent and popular expectation, he refused to impose a military government in response. Since that time, he has been heralded as a champion for democracy— and with his wife, Queen Sofía, as a supporter of the fine arts.

AUTHOR'S NOTE

In this novel the fictional pianist Justo Al-Cerraz is disappointed when he discovers that Manuel de Falla's "Nights in the Gardens of Spain" was originally inspired by a cheap book that the famous composer had purchased on the rue de Richelieu in Paris. (Al-Cerraz hears this from Falla himself. I read it in liner notes written by Phillip Huscher.) The Alhambra is a real place, and Falla would later live not far from it. But the Spanish composer started his score without having visited the Alhambra, and he succeeded in conveying the romance of that Moorish fortress rather than the fact of it.

Why should Al-Cerraz have minded? The pianist, I'm sorry to say, always had a hard time deciding whether he favored fact or fiction, romance or reality. (Even Al-Cerraz's claim to have been mothered by La Belle Otero may not be entirely reliable; the famous courtesan was sterile, evidently. But who can know for sure?)

We all enjoy hearing that a story is based on real people or inspired by real events. I know I do. But we also revel in fiction, a genre that allows us to find meaning and pattern in the otherwise confusing maelstrom of life. No matter how a work is labeled and no matter what we intend or desire—as readers, as authors, as people recounting our childhoods around a dinner table—what we most often end up with is a collage.

I love collages. (Is it any wonder I found room in this novel for Picasso?) I like the look of bits of newspaper and cloth stuck with paint, and violins shaped from torn paper, and familiar items rendered unfamiliar. This book is such a collage. While I would direct readers to pay more attention to the final fictional design, here are some notes on my materials for the benefit of readers who, like Al-Cerraz, may be on a quest for unadulterated truth.

I started this book planning to write a nonfiction account about the Spanish cellist Pablo Casals. This was in late 2001, about a decade into my career as a freelance journalist and travel writer. Most recently I'd been struggling to find a new way to write about marine environmental issues, but was bogging down in jargon, burdened by the knowledge of a limited audience that was resistant to hearing more about obscure or intractable environmental problems. Even I wasn't sure whether I wanted to hear any more about environmental problems. Then, like many Americans, I was jostled awake by the 9/11 terrorist attacks, which forced me to ask myself that clarifying doomsday question, *If I could do only one more thing with my life—if I could write about only one more thing—what would it be?*

What I longed for that autumn was a chance to immerse myself in something beautiful and hopeful; and, for me, the sound of hope and humanity has always been the cello. (Why the cello? I wrote this book in part to find out.)

The doomsday atmosphere of 2001 also infused me with the desire to find a heroic story to tell because that was the kind of story that I needed to hear. The search for a hero led me to Casals, a cellist known for his stance against fascism. In early 2002 I visited Puerto Rico, where the musician spent the last years of his life. There I studied archival footage of Casals, sifted through documents, and met people who had known the maestro or his students.

Almost from the start, there were aspects of Casals's life that didn't fit the story I wanted to tell; aspects of other musicians' lives that did; questions that could not be answered (problematic for a journalist, but alluring for a would-be novelist); and a rich overlap of incident and experience that showed me that Casals's life as a musician and public figure was not altogether unique. The lack of uniqueness did not mean I'd stumbled into a dead-end. It promised, instead, a doorway into other places and lives. Casals's story, itself more complex than I'd first imagined, pointed the way to stories of many other European musicians and composers and even visual artists. Most interesting to me were the similarities of these individuals' backgrounds, challenges, and moral dilemmas. I found I was interested in these composite stories and situations—a broader scope and larger canvas than my original vision had allowed, with room for quixotic digressions (and even for Don Quixote himself, another source of inspiration).

Where imagination promised to lead me in a fruitful direction, I followed it, becoming, to my complete surprise, a novelist in the process. In the end I chose to shelve all plans for a nonfiction book and instead write a novel about protagonists who ask themselves some of the same questions I had asked myself in 2001: *Is this what I should be doing with my life? In difficult times, is art an indulgence or a necessity? Must I sacrifice my own happiness to what is going on around me?* And, politics aside: *Who will remember me?*

While I ask readers to interpret the final work as fictional, music-oriented readers may still recognize purposeful similarities between Casals and my main character, Feliu Delargo. Casals and Feliu share a Catalan upbringing, royal patronage (by different queens), ownership of a gem-studded bow, and Republican political views. However, Casals was born in 1876, Feliu in 1892, putting them in contact with a different range of musicians, politicians and monarchs, and different artistic and political events. Casals never toured with anyone like the Al-Cerraz and Aviva characters of my book, had no relationship with Franco, and never performed for Franco or Hitler. While both Casals and Feliu refused to play (musicians and composers of the 1930s and 1940s commonly struggled with the question of performing in politicized situations), they did so at slightly different historic junctures, and with different consequences.

In a similar vein, Justo Al-Cerraz shares some superficial traits—including girth and a flair for mythologizing—with the Spanish pianist and composer Isaac Albéniz, but the two men are more different than alike. Albéniz lived from 1860 to 1909, so he was terminally indisposed before much of my story takes place. He had no political difficulties or involvement in the Spanish Civil War, obviously, and did not disappear at the end of his life. He never toured with a well-known cellist. His compositions, unlike Al-Cerraz's, were successful and accepted.

Having vouched for the fictional (or mostly fictional) natures of my main protagonists, I nonetheless admit to filling many smaller roles with characters drawn from real life—partly to enhance the appearance of reality, and partly for my own entertainment and for the entertainment or consternation of my protagonists. These less fictionalized minor characters include King Alfonso XIII and Queen Ena of Spain, Manuel de Falla, Sir Edward Elgar, Pablo Picasso, Varian Fry, Francisco Franco, Adolf Hitler, Bertolt Brecht, and Kurt Weill. Of course, I felt free to take liberties with all of them where it suited the needs of my story.

Travel, including visits to palaces, musicians' birthplaces, and other settings used in this book, was the most important component in my research. (I did choose to walk through the gardens of Spain, rather than rely on any book from the rue de Richelieu.) For period detail and thematic inspiration, the following books also proved essential: *The Spanish Civil War, 1936–39* and *Franco: A Biography*, both by Paul Preston; *Homage to Catalonia* by George Orwell; *The Week France Fell* by Noel Barber; *Picasso's War: The Destruction of Guernica, and the Masterpiece That Changed the World* by Russell Martin; *Kurt Weill on Stage* by Foster Hirsch; *Theatrical Performances During the Holocaust*, edited by Rebecca Rovit and Alvin Goldfarb; and *Ena, Spain's English Queen* by Gerard Noel. I learned much from *The Spanish Labyrinth* by Gerald Brenan and quoted from it directly in describing the "sin of liberalism" as taught to young Feliu by his catechism teacher. I also relied upon detail provided by a documentary, *Assignment Rescue: The Story of Varian Fry and the Emergency Rescue Committee,* directed by Richard Kaplan and written by Christina Lazaridi. For impressions of Isaac Albéniz, I am indebted to *Isaac Albéniz: Portrait of a Romantic* by Walter Aaron Clark. Interviews and museum visits provided primary source materials from the life of Pablo Casals; however, his voice comes across most clearly in *Joys and Sorrows: Reflections* by Pablo Casals as told to Albert E. Kahn.

During my 2002 research trip to Puerto Rico, I attended a performance of the San Juan symphony and fell under the spell of that orchestra's principal cellist, Jesús Morales. He agreed to give me private lessons while I was in Puerto Rico, putting up with my limited musicianship and indulging my curiosity about many aspects of cello playing, especially Hispanic cello playing. Mr. Morales also facilitated my visit to Pablo Casals's home in San Juan, where he performed from the Bach cello suites, a highlight of that research trip.

I am grateful to my editor, Rebecca Saletan, for trusting a first-time novelist to tackle the many collaborative drafts necessary to complete this project. Without the early confidence of my agent, Elizabeth Sheinkman, I wouldn't have made it past the first tentative pages. Thanks also to Stacia Decker, David Hough, Judith McQuown, Cathy Riggs, Liz Demeter, Jennifer Gilmore, Michelle Blankenship, Vaughn Andrews, Laurie Brown, Patty Berg, and the rest of the Harcourt team for their editing, design, promoting, and administrative talents, and to Ravi Mirchandani, Jason Arthur, and Jamie Byng in the U.K. for early enthusiastic support.

My husband, Brian, and children, Aryeh and Tziporah, have been my constant companions on this journey, willing to go anywhere and try anything in the name of music, literature, and Spanish chocolate. Thanks to fellow Alaska writers Bill Sherwonit, Lee Goodman, Ellen Bielawski, Nancy Deschu, Sonya Senkowsky, and Jill Fredston for their advice and support; to my sisters, Honorée and Eliza, and my mother,

C. Romano, for reading early drafts; to Amy Bower and Keith Jensen for long-distance encouragement; to cellists Linda Marsh-Ives and Linda Ottum for teaching me; and to Karen and Stewart Ferguson for more than a decade of friendship and many excellent book recommendations besides. For answering my e-mail queries about *Der Jasager*, I thank Dave Stein of the Kurt Weill Foundation; for interviews and assistance during my visit, I am grateful to the staff of the Museo de Pablo Casals in Puerto Rico and the Centro Cultural Manuel de Falla in Granada, Spain.

This project benefited from the generosity of the Rasmuson Foundation and the Alaska Council on the Arts, organizations that provided moral and financial boosts at critical moments.

Finally, a standing ovation to the amazing cellists, living and dead— including Pablo Casals, Han-na Chang, Hamilton Cheifetz, Lynn Harrell, Emil Klein, Yo-Yo Ma, Jacqueline du Pré, Nathaniel Rosen, János Starker, and Julian Lloyd Webber—whose recordings played in my headphones for thousands of hours while I was writing this book. I hope this novel encourages readers to seek out music that is far beyond the power of words to describe.